BLIND SIDED

Blindsided

Copyright © 2026 by Violet Page

All rights reserved.

No part of this book may be reproduced in any form or by any electronic or mechanical means, including information storage and retrieval systems, without written permission from the author, except for the use of brief quotations in a book review, or as permitted by U.S. copyright law.

No generative artificial intelligence (AI) was used in the production of this work. The author expressly prohibits the use of this publication as training data for AI technologies or large language models (LLMs) for generative purposes. The author reserves all rights to license uses of this work for generative AI and the development of LLMs.

This is a work of fiction. Names, characters, places, & incidents are either products of the author's imagination or used fictitiously. Any resemblance to actual persons, living or dead, business establishments, events, or locales is entirely coincidental.

Editing by Alexa of The Fiction Fix

Cover Design & Interior Formatting by Alex of Novel & Navy

Author Photo by Lavender Sage Photo

BLIND SIDED

LEGENDS OF LONDON BOOK ONE

VIOLET PAGE

AUTHOR'S NOTE

Hello, reader!
Writing about hot British rugby players was as fun as it sounds, and it's certainly even more fun to read. This being said, please be aware that Blindsided contains both American and British English spelling depending on the POV. While I did my best to be thorough, there may be instances I missed. If you happen to see one, no you didn't. Happy reading!

*For those who carry everything on their
shoulders, while longing for a safe place to land—
I hope you find one within the pages of this book.*

1

JADE

THERE'S a high probability the man next to me is dead.

I've been sitting on this rickety barstool at a pub near my new flat in Chelsea, and he hasn't moved once, not even when the bar collectively sang along to 'Sweet Caroline', and the *bah, bah, bah* made the walls shake. I briefly consider poking him to see if he'll reanimate, but I think better of it before turning away to sip my cocktail. Not my problem. I have enough of those without inserting myself into a potential crime scene.

My flight landed in London less than four hours ago with just enough time to drop off my *six* overweight bags at the flat I rented, sight unseen. That was my first mistake. I took one look around the place and high-tailed it out of there, straight into the arms of The King's Swan, established in 1806, if the placard outside is to be believed.

I may have been a little hasty in my search for a place to live, but in my overwhelming defense, I was catfished by the landlord. The pictures on the listing made the place look charming and bright. What I got was dirty walls, mold in the bathroom, and cockroach flatmates.

I took one survey around the room, sucked the tear threatening to fall at the sight of the mess back up into its duct, and decided to drown my sorrows in a watered down martini.

Now, there's a probable dead guy next to me, and all it'll take is one gust of wind coming through the door for him to fall over on me, effectively staining my cream cashmere sweater.

I take a long pull from my second drink of the night, grimacing as the acrid flavor floods my mouth. To be honest, I probably shouldn't have ordered a martini in a pub that caters to partying university students, but I needed something strong after the last week, month, *year* I've had.

My phone buzzes on the bar top in front of me, a text notification sweeping across the screen from my manager, the most vocal critic of my move to the UK.

MAXINE

Don't forget you have a meeting at 5:30pm PST. Time zone differences aside, your presence is mandatory. You don't want to lose investors' trust anymore than you already have.

The reminder rankles, leaving the bitter taste of gin clogging up my throat, and I shove my phone in my purse, desperate to steal a moment of peace. I've *never* forgotten a meeting in the years since creating Jaded, but after a decade under my employ, Maxine liked to overstep boundaries and forget that I'm her boss.

Reminder aside, and barring the fact that it'll be after one in the morning here, and I just spent twelve hours traveling across the world, I would be there fresh faced and looking every bit the leader that I am. I had to be—the work never stops when you're the CEO and face of your own label. It didn't make it any less exhausting though.

"You're a pretty little bird, aren't you?" My previously presumed dead bar neighbor reanimates, popping off the bar like a drunken jack-in-the-box.

His accent is thick as his mouth purses, forcing out vowels and sending the stench of beer wafting over to suffocate my air space. From the corner of my eye, I notice his glazed eyes leering over me like I'm the last fried doughnut at the county fair, and I shift away to try and create any semblance of space.

"Thank you," I say curtly, trying to discourage further conversation. All I came here for was to think and drink. On the extremely rare occasion I do go out, my resting bitch face usually does a good job deterring people from approaching me, but maybe men in England don't care. At the very least, this one doesn't.

Lucky me.

"American, eh?" His voice is loud, and the beginnings of a migraine start to form at the base of my skull. It's been awhile since my last visit, but I thought it was impolite to talk to strangers here, or was that just limited to tube etiquette?

I respond by giving a terse nod as I pull my phone out of my bag. The screen coupled with the dim lighting in the bar does nothing to help the throb advancing in my head. Even so, if I look busy, maybe this guy will get my point and leave me alone.

I quickly open my email and notice a minimum of fifteen demanding immediate attention, most of them pertaining to work back in LA, but a few have to do with why I'm here. A churning starts in my stomach when I think about the fact that I already spent the entire plane ride abusing the in-flight wifi, working and answering emails, only for them to have already piled up again.

Ignore them, a voice edging on desperation whispers in my head. It's the same voice that started to creep in with every ping of my email on the flight, getting stronger and stronger the further I flew from the West Coast. I ignored it then out of guilt and responsibility, but now, I heed its advice, putting my phone face down on the table. It's ten o'clock at night, and I'm trying to develop boundaries, I remind myself. Trying being the key word, because a second later, I grab my phone again to respond to a couple more urgent messages out of habit.

Never stop the grind; it's the American dream, right?

When I started working at the age of fifteen, posting silly videos online as a hobby—as a way to make friends—I never realized it could ever turn into what it did. I started small, talking about things I liked or books I was reading, but as I grew, so did my content. Suddenly, people were looking to me for beauty and styling tips, and it became less about me and more about the trends around me. I fell into a niche I cultivated a little too well, because I ended up with a brand empire. Product placement turned into small brand deals, which turned into *massive* brand deals, which turned into a permanent move to the West Coast. My once small corner of the internet amassed ten million followers by the time I hit my twenty-first birthday. I collaborated with major brands, created my own products, developed my own label, Jaded, by twenty-three, and invested a hell of a lot of money *really* well. Now, I'm here, in London, on what could possibly be a fool's errand.

"Can I buy you a drink?" he slurs, leaning back into my space, beer foam settling into the corners of his mouth. I think I'd prefer drinking with the cockroaches in my flat to this.

"No. I already have one." I put a little more bite into my tone.

"No need to be a bitch, I'm just payin' you a compliment. You should feel flattered."

God, I am so sick of men telling me what to do.

I level him with a death glare. "I'm floored by your generosity." Sarcasm oozes from every syllable.

He leans into me, and I lean back, breaking my spine to get out of the way while trying to not fall out of my seat.

"Thas' good, pet. So, drink then?"

I'm done. Beyond done. I'm tired, this cocktail *sucks*, and my feet hurt from the heels I've had on all day. I can't be responsible for what I do or say as incandescent feminine rage slithers over my body like a shield.

I drizzle my tone with honey. "Pet? How...cute. I could walk you down the street by my belt, and you would *thank* me for the honor. If anyone here is a bitch, it's you. Learn that no means *fuck off* and apologize to your wife when you get home for being an absolute pig. I suggest you sober up, drink some water, and go sleep off this embarrassment." He pales at the mention of his wife, trying to hide the ring I clocked on his finger by stuffing it in his jacket pocket.

He shoots up from his barstool, face red and puffy with anger, and takes a step toward me. I start to move off my stool, but before I can, a tattooed arm from my left comes out of nowhere, stopping the drunk in his tracks. The mystery man steps in front of me, fully blocking the other from seeing or reaching me. It also affords me a delicious view of his back—broad and tall, very tall. I'm not short by any stretch of the imagination, and he still towers over me at my five-foot-seven.

"She said to piss off, mate." His voice is deep, threaded with the promise of physical violence. Something in me purrs to life, making me desperate to match a face to the seductive sound. It's apparently effective in more ways than the one, too, because the drunk actually leaves, just like that.

A scoff crawls up my throat. "Of course he'll listen to a fucking man." I plop back down onto my barstool and signal the bartender for another martini.

When he turns around, I blink once. Twice. A third time, because…*holy shit*. I lived in LA for nearly a decade, encountered some of the most beautiful people you could imagine, but none of them hold a candle to *him*. He has the most striking blue eyes that glow like bioluminescence, a jawline men in LA pay thousands for at prestigious medspas, and a gorgeous head of deep brown hair set against sun tanned skin.

How is one that tan in a country that rarely sees the sun?

"I'm really sorry about him. We're not all like that here, I promise. I hope you don't let it ruin your visit." I don't correct his assumption that I don't live here.

"Thanks for stepping in," I reply with gratitude.

The smile he gives me is so disarming, I can feel my pulse start to speed up. "I shouldn't have had to," he says genuinely. "You had it handled. I was trying not to piss myself laughing at the look on his face when you laid him out."

This incites a rumble of laughter, and I realize belatedly the noise is coming from *me*. Jesus, has it been so long since I've laughed that I didn't even recognize my own? I take a rather large gulp of my cocktail to avoid thinking about that sad fact.

He must take my silence as disinterest in the conversation he was trying to strike up and says, "Right, well, I'll leave you to enjoy your evening."

He taps his hand against the counter, making to leave, when I blurt out, "Would you like to join me?"

The words startle me, and clearly, I've startled him, because he's quiet for a moment before smiling broadly and pulling out the stool next to mine to take a seat. He orders a whisky from a passing bartender after getting settled and turns to face me.

"What brings you to town?" he asks.

"Work."

"And what do you do for work?"

I hate this question, because people rarely take me seriously when I try to explain it to them. They check out the second I mention the social media aspect of the job, completely disregarding the part where I tell them I'm the CEO of my own brand and have a master's degree in business.

I settle for vague, not wanting this stranger to judge me for some odd reason. "I own a few businesses. You?"

A pause. "Finance…mainly." He looks away from me while taking a sip of the drink the server set down for him a moment before.

I cock my head to the side, studying him and dragging my gaze slowly down his body. He doesn't strike me as the finance type, but who knows? I'm learning loads about British culture tonight. Maybe extremely muscular, tall, tattooed men run spreadsheets all day here.

He can spread my sheets.

My obvious perusal doesn't go unnoticed, because his chuckle snaps me out of it, and my cheeks flame. He, however, looks like a cat who caught the mouse, smiling ear to ear, and Christ—he has *dimples*.

"I didn't catch your name," he states.

"I didn't give it."

"You're a bit of an enigma, aren't you?" He's surveying me with a look that says he very much wants to figure me out but isn't sure if I'll let him. And judging by the expression on his face, I think he likes the challenge. His gaze darts to the far corner of the pub, eyes lighting up with an idea. "Tell you what, love... How about we play a game?"

"I'm listening..." My fingers dance along the stem of my glass, a foreign lightness filling my chest.

"Back there is a dart board." He points to the game set up along the back wall. For each game won, the winner gets to ask the loser a question."

I glance behind me, trying to recall the last time I felt this loose, shoving the voice telling me I should go home and get some work done down to the bottom of my glass. "You're on."

"When I suggested the game, I didn't realize you were going to fleece me." He drags a palm down his face in mock anguish.

We've been playing for over an hour, and I've won every game except one, the first one...that I *let* him win to lull him into a sense of false security.

"Never underestimate your opponent. Answer the question."

"This is not fair," he whines. "If I knew I was going to lose so much, I would've made my one question so much better."

"But aren't you so happy to know my favorite breakfast food is an egg white omelet?" I tease him.

"You're not going easy on me, love." He gives me an adorable pout, but I just stare at him blankly, unimpressed.

"Men have it easy enough."

That earns me a hearty guffaw in agreement, and I *almost* smile back.

He narrows his eyes, a glimmer sparking in them. "What's really your favorite breakfast food?"

"What makes you so sure I'm lying?"

"Call it a hunch." How is he able to read me that easily? I deflect and raise a brow at his brazen assessment, waiting for him to answer my question. His left dimple pops. "Fine. My favorite musician is Harry Styles."

Now, I *do* smile. It's an unexpected answer, but I guess not all that surprising. Other than when he stepped in to help with the guy earlier, he's been the poster boy for golden retriever men everywhere: quick to laugh, takes everything in stride. It's been refreshing.

"Solid choice." I hold his stare. "I like blueberry lemon pancakes." Something softens in his gaze, and my heart starts to inexplicably race. I turn abruptly, walking to the dart board to retrieve the needles. "One more game?" It's nearly midnight, but the pub hasn't slowed in traffic at all. Around us, glasses are clinking, people are laughing, televisions above the bar displaying everything from rugby match reruns to *Love Island* episodes. Everyone in the room appears unencumbered and happy, like nothing can touch them here, and I'm starting to feel that same magic weave its way beneath my skin.

"One more game—" he agrees, but quickly adds—"but I want to tell you what my question will be now if I win."

"Why?"

He ambles over to me, stopping only when his shoes touch the tips of mine. "Because I want you to choose to let me win or lose." His stare is piercing, filled with an intensity I'm not used to and am not sure what to do with.

"What will your question be?" Butterflies wake in my stomach, wings beginning to flutter.

Slowly, he threads his fingers through mine, grabbing hold of a dart needle, but doesn't let go immediately. Instead, his thumb rubs against the side of my wrist where my pulse hammers. "If I win, I'm going to ask to kiss you."

The butterflies have fully taken flight, bouncing wildly against my ribcage. It's a fight to keep my composure. "Start the game, then," I challenge.

We throw back and forth, evenly matched. I don't know if he can tell I'm going easy on him, but I don't particularly care when all I can think about is the way his lips looked when he said he wanted to kiss me. When the turn to determine who wins or loses comes, I look my handsome stranger in the face and throw the dart wide until it imbeds itself into the wall with a deafening thunk.

Slowly, too slowly, as if to give me a chance to run, he prowls towards me. With each step he takes, I take one step back until I hit the wall, left with nowhere to go. When he reaches me, a smirk quirks up the corner of his mouth, and I roll my eyes.

His fingers are featherlight as they trail up my arm until his hand cups my neck, palm warm against my thundering pulse. "Cheeky thing."

I try so hard not to drift into his touch, to think about how *good* it feels to be touched.

He leans in, breath fanning against my ear, making me suppress a shiver. "I like your brand of bold." He pulls back to look me in my eyes before asking, "Can I kiss you?"

"Yes."

"So enthusiastic," he jokes to rile me up, and it certainly works.

"For fuck's sake, just ki—"

He silences me by pulling on my neck, bringing me forward into his chest. "I want," he places a kiss by my ear, "to take," another along my jaw, "my time." I hold my breath when he reaches the corner of my mouth, trying to chase it as he pulls back, feeling desperate and worked up just from a few pecks. "Look at you," he says, and I honest-to-God feel his phantom caress on every inch of my body.

Then, he leans in, *finally* pressing his mouth against mine, and all my good sense obliterates like a hand grenade was just tossed into the room.

The kiss starts off soft, just two pairs of lips tentatively testing and tasting. When I open to him, needing more, he wastes zero time slipping his tongue inside, and the way it moves against mine is so hedonistic, I absently think he might be winning *this* particular game. Before I know it, he's devouring me slowly, his movements erotic and sensual. This…I've never been kissed like *this*, so thoroughly and completely that my head starts to spin. My hands reach out to touch him, anything to ground myself as he matches me stroke for stroke, his hands gripping my hips firmly over the material of my skirt, pinning me to the wall. I slip my fingers into the top of his jeans and pull him closer to me, feeling something rigid connect with my stomach, and he grunts into my mouth like I'm causing him pain.

"Devil woman," he mumbles into my lips as he pulls away, trailing a path of kisses up my jaw until he takes my earlobe between his teeth.

I gasp, the sensation welcoming a rush of warmth to pool at my core.

I'm feeling so reckless. This whole situation is so unlike me, and yet there's something buried deep begging to burst free that *craves* this carefree alternate universe I'll never have again. Tomorrow, I can go back to being Jade McKallen, but for tonight, I want to be this nameless version who takes what she wants because she wants it, not for any other reason.

He works against my neck, driving me half feral as I

grind against him, feeling his own arousal against me. All thoughts leave my mind when the next words fly out of my mouth, breathy and uncontrolled, "Have you ever had sex in a pub bathroom?"

He stops his assault against my neck, and I hate myself for asking the question. He's silent long enough that I start to pull away, but he quickly tightens his hold on my hips, stalling my retreat.

"Are you drunk?" he asks.

"Not even a little. You?"

"Sober as a judge." His thumb strokes concentric circles on my hip, driving me crazy.

I don't say a word as I start to pull him toward the single stall restroom a few feet away, flicking on a half-working light as we enter and locking the door. I waste no time, pressing him against the door, reaching up onto my toes and kissing him again. He sighs into my mouth as I work my hands down his muscled chest and start unzipping his pants.

My fingers skirt below the waistband of his briefs when he grabs hold of my wrist. "Oh no, that's not how this is going to work." Before I have a moment to object, he's grabbing me by the waist, lifting me, and setting me on the edge of the sink counter. I let out a small squeal of surprise.

"Women first." He drops to his knees in front of me like he's ready to pray—to worship. I'm already so worked up that the sight has the power to send me headlong into orgasm, but I hold off, desperate to see how this will play out. "May I?" His hand gestures at my short skirt, and I nod my approval.

He wastes zero time pushing up the material until it settles around my hips, eyeing my center appreciatively. My body flushes unbearably hot while he stares at me like no one ever has. He looks *starved*.

"I *am* starved, love." *Fuck, I said that out loud?* "Can I?"

"Yes." The needy reply comes out breathy, nearly inaudible, but he hears it all the same.

He reaches his fingers up, pressing them against the lace of my underwear, and I'm already so hard up that even that infinitesimal touch has me banging my head against the mirror behind me. The sensations double when he stops being coy and slowly pulls my panties down my legs, completely exposing me to him. My mouth dries.

I don't know who I've become in the wake of meeting this man, but I'm equally nervous and excited.

"Suddenly feeling shy?" he teases.

"Shut up and put your mouth to good use," I pant.

His laugh sends hot air grazing against my center, causing me to squirm on the hard surface. "Yes, ma'am." His head drops, placing a kiss to the inside of my thigh. The gentleness of the gesture takes me by surprise, but it doesn't last long, because a moment later, the gentleness disappears when he swipes a hot stripe up my center before suctioning his lips over my clit.

"Oh, fuck!" I shout, a deluge of sensations roiling over my skin, threatening to topple me right off this countertop. But he doesn't relent or give me a moment of reprieve from the blissful torture he's waging on my senses. He continues to lick and suck around my clit, occasionally lightening pressure to bring me back from the brink right before I'm about to topple over. He does it again and again until I'm sopping wet and desperate whimpers escape my throat. The tension in my core builds to a boiling point, almost unbearable, and I'm desperate for relief when he presses two fingers inside me, causing my back to bow. I try to pull away, the pleasure becoming too much, but he yanks me back toward him, locking me in place as he works me in a perfect rhythm. I clap my hands around my mouth, attempting to muffle my moans, but it's no use: he's declared war on my body, and I'm helpless to defend.

I pull my hands away from my mouth and run them into his hair. My nails scratch against his scalp, making him growl into me, and the sound rumbling out of his throat and vibrating against my core, only heightens my pleasure.

I tug his perfect mouth away, and he stares up at me with a mix of confusion and elation.

"I want to feel you inside me. Now." I can't believe the words out of my mouth, but I've never had it this good, and if I'm going to steal this one night for myself, I'm doing it right.

His eyes burn like an inferno, and he stands slowly, bending forward to kiss me so I can taste myself on his lips. He's hard against my core, and my hips roll involuntarily, grinding against him, begging him to move faster.

He seems to be in no rush, and the frustration mounts in my body, desperate for connection—for release. Leaning forward while he's still kissing me, I reach into his already open pants, grabbing his erection and giving him a firm testing stroke. He hisses out a harsh breath as I pull my hand along his shaft again, using the precum gathered at his tip to drive him into the same dizzying state he had me in moments before. He wrenches his mouth away from mine, burying his head into my shoulder as if concentrating on anything else is impossible. I lean into him and pull his earlobe into my mouth, making his cock pulse harder in my hand.

He abruptly steps back but grabs my hips, spinning me around to face the mirror.

"I want you to see how pretty you're going to look when I make you come on my cock." He bends me forward to press my hands against the counter, arching my back and pushing my ass out towards him. "Fuck," he says, staring down at my exposed skin. Lifting my left leg onto the counter for leverage, he bends down to lick a path up my center with the flat of his tongue, making my legs quake.

I hear him reach into his wallet and pull out a condom, and I thank the stars for his forethought. He makes quick work slipping it on and lining himself up, rubbing his shaft back and forth against my soaked core. The head bumps against my clit before dipping into my entrance half an inch before he pulls back out and repeats the motion.

His resounding chuckle when I push back onto him makes me want to rip my hair out—or his, for torturing me like this.

"You sure you want this, love?"

"Please." I whine desperately.

"No need to beg," he says, arrogance ringing through loud and clear.

"Oh, shut u—"

He buries himself inside me. We both gasp at the sensation of his length filling me, of my walls stretching wide to grip him tight. It's maddening and bliss in equal measure. He gives me a second to adjust, but before long, I'm starting to squirm against him, pleading with my body to start to move.

He chuckles, running his hand up my back and into my hair before wrapping it around his fist and pulling my head back to kiss me. The angle pushes him even deeper inside me, and we both groan into each other's mouth as he starts to move, setting pace with me arching back into him.

"Fuck, you feel like glory," he grunts, pistoning his hips in and out of me in a punishing rhythm. We've barely just begun, and I already feel right at the edge of tipping.

I'm a music box in his hands, and I clench around him as his words wind me tighter and tighter, until my body is begging for the release of harmonies even while my head and my heart want to drag this out as long as possible.

"I—I'm already so close," I gasp, unable to form a thought more coherent than that.

He doesn't say anything, but I can feel he's right there too, right on the edge of oblivion with me. His cock is thick, dragging against my walls, and his movements don't halt when he reaches forward, settles his hand on my clit, and starts rubbing in steady circles while he pounds in and out of me. I'm no longer controlling how I sound, fairly certain everyone in the bar is able to hear what's going on in here, but I can't find it in me to care when I feel like I'm being transported to another realm.

My eyes close, and he tugs at my hair, pulling my head back so our eyes lock in the mirror's reflection. Cheeks flushed, faces sweaty and lips swollen as my hips dig into the counter. It's the hottest thing I've ever seen in my life. My eyes have never been so wild, the singular spot of blue in my right iris flaring brighter around the amber encircling it. My mouth parts as he hits deep, causing me to release a guttural cry.

"Are you gonna come on it?" he asks, and the words make me clench around him. "Yeah, I think you are." His movements start to go erratic, losing their rhythm when he adds more pressure to my clit, sending me right over the edge.

I detonate, muscles contracting around him so tightly, it sets off his own climax as he groans, biting down on my neck to muffle the sound. We watch every moment of our unraveling, and I silently thank him for putting us in this position, facing the mirror.

We're both panting heavily, chests heaving while we come down from the rush, as he languorously laves at the pulse point hammering on my neck.

A loud clatter sounds outside, and reality crashes back in, reminding me where we are—of who I am. I'm the first to stand upright, prompting him to pull out of me, and we begin righting our clothes so we look somewhat presentable before stepping back out into the pub.

"Can I get my underwear?" I glance down at the red lace poking out of his pants pocket.

"Afraid I'll have to say no to that," he states with a smile, running a hand through his hair.

"That's a bit serial killer-y of you, but whatever. Keep them, I guess," I say, straightening my sweater and finger combing my hair.

"Can I get your number? Maybe we can hang out again before you leave." He seems so earnest, and something in my chest pangs with regret. He wouldn't want the real me; no one ever really has.

"I don't think that's a great idea, but thank you for tonight. I really needed it." I stretch up to give him a final kiss goodbye. When I go to pull away, he grabs my hips and brings his mouth back to mine to extend the moment. It's honestly nice, like some form of fucked up aftercare.

When we pull away, I kiss him on the cheek before exiting the small room.

Either we got lucky and no one was around to hear us, or they all scattered when they realized what we were doing, because the back room is nearly empty.

I settle my tab, checking the time on my phone only to see a new wave of emails and a calendar reminder for the meeting starting in twenty minutes. Escapism could only last so long, I suppose.

As I make my way back onto the cobblestone streets of London, the early summer air crisp and inviting, I feel grateful for a stranger in a pub who made my first night in London a little less lonely.

2

TIERAN

CAMERAS FLASH like sparklers crackling in front of my eyes, uncomfortable and disorienting.

"Tieran! How do you feel coming back for a new season on the heels of last year's embarrassing loss?"

"Do you feel like you failed in leading your team on the field?"

"Mr. Stone! Think your ex sleeping with Oliver Hughes from Newcastle had anything to do with your lackluster performance last season?"

Questions fire off from every direction like bullets, each one hitting me with a blow to the chest. I take the insults as they come; no fighting back, or they'll just twist it and slap me across another headline. Months of having my name splashed through every paper, magazine, and gossip website —of being forced to look at the evidence of my mistakes in every food shop—I just wanted some peace.

I tear off my sunglasses and plaster a smile on my face. "Gentlemen, please. It's nine in the morning. Let a man wake up before you twist his balls."

My carefree attitude works, as all the sports reporters before me chuckle, easing their holds on their cameras.

I tighten my grip around the handle of my sports bag, knuckles going white as I try to ignore the strain in my chest. Avoiding the press during the off season was relatively easy, and I thought—I hoped—by now, the issues from last year would be old news, but that was a fool's wish. The media feeds on this sort of thing; thinking I could get into the stadium unscathed was idiotic. They're all sharks, and I'm chum in the water as they circle me.

"Last year was disappointing, but we're back and going to give it our all on the pitch." Some of them pipe up to ask more questions, but I interrupt them with a hand up. "Now, if you'll excuse me, there's a team meeting starting in a few minutes, and Coach will hang me up by my jewels if I'm late."

I can hear the clicks of the cameras as I walk away into Knightsbridge Stadium. The false smile falls the second I'm behind the solid metal doors to the private tunnels meant only for players and staff, but tension in my shoulders remains.

Reveling in the public's attention used to be easy. Press and media would lap up whatever I was willing to give them, and there wasn't much off the table in that respect. I was built for the public eye—loved it, even. Interviews, press junkets, brand deals—being the face of our team was an honor I shrouded myself in like a robe.

Until it all came crumbling down.

Now, every camera in my face, every reporter asking questions feels like I'm drowning under a frozen lake, banging on a three inch slab of ice I can't crack. The only way to cope is to hide behind sunglasses and fake bravado, and I've become so good at it, no one has even noticed me slipping further under the surface.

I trace my hand along the maroon-and-white-painted stripes lining our brightly lit hallways, making my way toward the men's locker room and staff offices. It's the first day back, which means Coach Ballard will want a solid thirty minutes to scold us into submission for the season ahead after introducing us to the new owner of the club. A real hard ass, from what limited information I've gleaned. All details have been kept under strict lock and key by administration, and it's done nothing to ease my anxieties.

A new owner—especially one who holds the majority share of the team—has the power to do just about anything they want, going as far as to overrule the other shareholders if they choose. And with my piss poor performance last season, I wouldn't be surprised if this new bloke wanted to sack me on the spot.

As captain, I was primed to lead our team to victory for the Premiership Rugby Cup, according to every sportscaster across ITV1, SkySports, and the BBC. The rugby world's eyes were on me and I failed. Failed my team and coach, the fans and my family—myself too, I suppose, though I don't feel I'm entitled to a self-imposed pity party.

Everything was going well until halfway through the season, when an aggressive case of the yips struck, and suddenly, things that used to come second nature to me felt as foreign as intercontinental trade affairs. I couldn't make a tactical decision to save my life, and every play I did make on the pitch ended up being the wrong one. With every failed attack based on my call, every collapsed defence strategy I orchestrated, I sank further into self-doubt. I started overthinking everything, and living in my head was like weeding through a bog. It cost us *every* match. I went to bed every night wondering if I was even capable of being their fly-half, let alone their captain, when I kept failing them.

The press ate it up, touting headlines that haunt me to this day. Things like, '*Rugby's Golden Star Falls from Grace*' and '*Say Goodbye to the Olympic Team*'. It's the truth behind the words that torments me most about those clickbait articles. What chance did I really have to catch the National Team's attention now?

I reach the door into the wing that houses the locker room as well as the offices for Coach and the owners, pausing before stepping over the threshold, and attempting to school my face from one of pathetic despondency to self-assurance.

Breathing deeply, I burst through the double doors.

"Hello fellas! I know you all missed me while on holiday, but I fear the time for suntanning your cheeks in Ibiza—" I point to our resident grump, "I'm looking at you, Cav—is over. Time to get back to work."

Cavan Darcey, our team's inside center and one of my best friends, grunts while pulling his headphones back over his ears as a few of my teammates greet me with slaps on the back.

Most of them are already here, scattered throughout the large room next to their personalized cabinets, changing into their gear for practice. I pass Harry, our equipment manager, and pull him in for a quick hug, though he remains stiff as a board, before I head toward my locker.

Myles Shepard, the Legends outside center and my other best friend, is sitting on the bench at his locker next to mine. He's lacing up his boots by the time I reach him, dark blond head dipped low.

"How's your mum doing?" I ask, sitting next to him and pulling my gear out of my bag.

He cocks his head slightly to the side, and I can see a weariness etched into every line on his face. "All tests so far have been inconclusive. The doctors have no idea what's going on."

"Everything will be alright." *At least I hope it will be.* I clap him on the shoulder hoping to bring him comfort, even knowing nothing will make him feel better outside of Louise being okay.

I get changed into my training uniform, pulling on a kit and shorts. I'm lacing up my boots when Coach Ballard comes in, his signature scowl marring his face.

"Conference room. Ten minutes. If you're late, you're running laps until you spew on the pitch." He turns and walks out.

"Is it just me, or has Ballard become meaner since last season? Bet it's because he's been wanking himself since the divorce." Connor Davies joined the Legends last year as our left lock. Wickedly good on the pitch, but he's young and brash and doesn't know when to shut the hell up.

I'm about to reprimand him as his captain, but Cavan beats me to it. "You'd do well to show some fucking respect." His deep voice is low, laced with warning, as he stands and heads out the door.

"Jesus, even my gran has more of a personality than him, and she's not been able to speak for a decade." He looks around, seeing a couple of guys smirking. It's enough to keep him from heeding any advice.

"Cav's right, Connor. Have some manners." He's about to argue, but I hold up a hand. "Get to the conference room before Coach makes good on his promise."

"Oh, *now* he wants to lead." He slinks off toward the meeting, but his words land their intended blow.

The churning in my gut intensifies as I turn and stare into my locker.

"Don't let it get to you. He's just being reactive. You know he's a prat who thrives off attention," Myles says from my side.

I plaster on my best charming smile. "Part of the territory. Let's go." Grabbing his shoulder, I steer us toward the conference room to see what fate awaits the team, wondering if I'll leave here without a job.

The conference room is filled with noise as voices buzz loudly while everyone tries to guess what's in store for the club. We know nothing about the new owner or what kind of changes they might implement. The previous administration didn't seem to care all too much about our well-being, only doing the bare minimum to meet regulations. In my experience, the people that high up in power don't usually care about the people making them money, just about how they can spend as little as possible for the most lucrative outcome for themselves. I'm a little surprised Lawrence Chapman, one of the two other shareholders, didn't try to buy out the rest of the shares for himself. He's always been a greedy little twat, and I can't help but feel slightly relieved he doesn't have more power over us.

"Everyone shut the fuck up. McKallen is almost here." Coach levels a glare at the rowdier units of our team before continuing. "I know it might be hard to not show your whole arse today, but I'm warning you to be on your best behaviour, or—"

"We'll have to run laps till we spew?" Connor scoffs. "Might want to brush up on your threats, Coach. I mean, what's this new guy going to do? Fire us before the season even starts?"

"*She* might."

My head whips to the side at the sound of a *too* familiar voice. Raspy and bold and unbelievably sexy when gasping out a moan.

It can't be. No fucking way.

She pushes through a sea of men congregating by the door, blocking her path as if they can barricade her from stepping into this role. My head is having a hard time grasping what it's seeing as I take her in, once, then twice. I blink to make sure it's really her standing here in front of me—us. She strides into the conference room, her razor sharp heels clacking against the floor until she comes to stop at the center of the room. She stands tall in front of us, a white chiffon blouse tucked into a pencil skirt that hugs her hips, and her nearly black hair slicked into a low ponytail at the base of her skull.

Formidable is the first word that comes to mind. Devastatingly beautiful is the second.

She looks around as a low hum runs through the room. Her unique eyes—a golden brown with one large spot of blue in her right iris—run around the conference room, weighing us all. The eyes that lit with fire as she put that drunk in his place, the same eyes that teased me while we played darts, the eyes that stared back at me in the mirror as she shattered around me in a pub bathroom not even a week ago.

They settle on me now, and I hold my breath, waiting for the match to strike. But they move past me as quickly as they came, no recognition, no shocking inhale of breath to see me here, nothing.

Surely she hasn't forgotten?

Insecurity roars through me. The night with her at The King's Swan was the best night I had in a long time. Talking to her, laughing at her sharp sarcasm, flirting with her the whole night until we tumbled into the loo, pawing at each other's clothes—it was the singular hottest experience of my life, and she doesn't remember it? How could she not remember it?

"Gentleman, this is—" Coach starts before he's interrupted by her outstretched hand.

She looks at him without a stitch of warmth on her face. It's hard to connect her to the person I spent my night with. "May I?" she asks.

Coach takes it in stride as he steps back and crosses his arms, yielding the floor to the hurricane standing before us.

"My name is Jade McKallen. The only things you need to know about me are that I own the sixty percent majority of this team, and that I'll do anything in my power to make it successful. If you have any questions or concerns regarding the team, my door is open. Does anyone have questions they'd like to ask now?"

Yeah, I do. How do you not remember me?

Connor pipes up, and I groan. "Do you even know anything about rugby, or is this a gift from your rich daddy?" I want to smack the condescending smirk off his face.

"What the fuck is wrong with you?" I grit out.

"What? It's a fair question. She's a woman and she's *American*." He shrugs, leaning back in his chair.

"It's fine," she addresses me, and I think surely, this is

when a flare of realisation will occur, but she doesn't even look at me as she angles her body towards Connor, crossing lithe arms over her chest. "Misogyny aside, your concerns are valid. However, it would be an unwise investment on my end to spend *millions* on a sport I don't understand, and a team I don't see potential in." Her eyes flick over the room again. "I don't take this position lightly and my plans to support the team and staff are vast. *Everyone* in this room is here because they love rugby, and together, we'll make sure the league knows we're to be feared."

Formidable. Strong. Badass.

She looks to Ballard, and he steps forward again. "Alright, that's that. Time to get out on the pitch."

Everyone stands at once, and I can't stop looking at Jade, willing her to look back at me to let me know I'm not crazy, that our night together wasn't a dream I conjured. But she doesn't spare me a second glance as she heads out of the conference room.

"Tieran." I tear my gaze away from Jade's retreating form. "Hang back. I need a word."

Cavan and Myles skirt around me towards the door, both giving me looks that read, *good luck* and *dead man walking*. I flip them both off as they abandon me in my hour of need.

"Yes, Coach?"

"Last year went a bit tits up." He stares at me, unyielding.

Shame makes my face flame. "Yes, sir."

"Are you over it, or do I need to prepare myself for another rough season?"

I feel like now is the appropriate time to enact a fake it till you make it mentality, because something tells me Coach won't accept the real answer. I don't know if I'm over the issues I had last year. In my head, it doesn't feel like they've gone away. It feels like they've made camp on my shoulders with no intention to leave. I'll only know for sure once I'm out on the pitch.

"Totally over it, sir." The lie rolls off my tongue.

"Good, because if you want a chance at the National Team and the Olympics, you need to be in peak form this season. Top of your game, focused, no scandals. Keep us at the head of the leaderboard and your name out of the press—unlike last year, you hear? The scouts are a conservative type who don't value drama." His meaning is more than clear—stay away from anything that will put my name on a headline.

"I won't let you down, sir." I smile wide, hoping he can't read the apprehension I feel coursing through my body on my face.

"Alright, out on the pitch, or I'll—" He cuts himself off. "Maybe Connor's right. I need new threats." He scrubs at the scruff on his face. "Let's not tell him that, though. Bit of a shite, that one."

Deep breath in and out, in and out.

When I step out into the hallway, I look around for any sign of Jade and fight the twinge of disappointment to find it empty. I guess it won't complicate anything if she doesn't remember me, but just the thought of her not recalling the best night I've had in ages, the possibility of her not feeling the same, leaves me sick to my stomach.

Focus.

This year won't be like the last. I'll clear my mind of any distractions and focus on the game. I owe everyone that; then, the only thing the sportscasters will be reporting on is our wins.

I shake my head free of stilettos echoing down the hall, and of burning topaz eyes with a spot of blue. As I burst through the doors leading outside, running out onto the pitch with false confidence, my heart pounds and the fear of failure chases my every step.

3

JADE

PAPER IS EVERYWHERE, and my office is pure chaos.

Why can't I find the one goddamn thing I need to find right now? If I had every organizational item from my office range, I would've found the roster already. But instead, I'm tearing through every file I brought in with me when I arrived at the stadium at seven this morning, and throwing the room into upheaval.

I plop down at my desk, resisting the urge to violently bang my head against it. My new office at Knightsbridge is large, with windows facing out onto the pitch, a sturdy mahogany desk, and several empty bookshelves lining the side wall. In the very center sits two cream couches with a white marble coffee table in between. It's a cozy space, albeit a bit too big. Who needs this much space?

Me. I do. I push up out of my seat and start pacing the length of the cavernous room. This is a fucking disaster. Just over two hours into my position here, and I've already fucked up. Majorly.

How did I not know? How did I not recognize him that night?

Where is that fucking team roster?

Walking into the conference room to introduce myself was a test to my nervous system. I stood outside, listening to their

26

rowdy voices rising to a fever pitch before I entered. Looks of shock quickly melted to skepticism when I stepped into the room. Then, seeing *him* sitting there among the players, with his searing blue eyes and rich brown hair...I could feel my heart start to thunder so hard, I feared cardiac arrest was imminent. I have never worked so hard to school my expression into one of severe neutrality more than I did in that moment.

When my gaze first settled on him, I thought my subconscious had conjured him up as some sort of fucked up mirage of comfort, something safe in this unfamiliar world I've thrust myself into. But then, his mouth quirked slightly, that dimple started to pop, and I realized he was *very* real, and I was *very* screwed.

I stride back over to my desk to tear through my extensive collection of files for a third time when I finally find it.

He's not there.

Flipping the roster backward and forward, I check the date and, yes—this is definitely the most recent version.

Bringing the page within an inch of my face, I go one by one, analyzing each player and recommitting their names and faces to my memory. My gaze snags on the team's fly-half, and I bring the page even closer, scrutinizing every detail, flipping the paper to the side, upside down, right-side up, pulling it a foot away from my face and...is *that* him?

Tieran Stone, it reads under his picture.

I grab for my laptop, waking it up and typing the name into the search engine. My finger hovers over the enter button, not ready for whatever answers the Google gods are going to give me.

Jesus Christ, Jade. You have faced down boardrooms filled with the world's most influential people. You can do this. Woman up.

My finger smashes the button, heart racing as I wait for the results to load.

Why is it taking so long? My foot starts to tap anxiously

against the floor. First order of business as the new owner of this team: upgrade the shoddy Wi-Fi.

Pictures start to load, and I sit up in my seat, my heart sinking at the confirmation.

Tieran Stone, fly-half and *captain* of the London Legends, is the same man I shamelessly asked to fuck me in a pub bathroom not even a week ago. The groan crawling up my throat can't even be contained, and I finally give in, dropping my head onto my desk and banging it heavily against the horrendously colored wood.

One. Two. Three.

That's all the time I allow myself to have a mini freakout before I pull myself together, reaching up and making sure not a hair is out of place.

Placing the printed team roster against the Google search, I allow myself a small infinitesimal bit of forgiveness, because it's no wonder I didn't recognize him. He's virtually unrecognizable.

His team photo is a far cry from the man I met at The King's Swan. *This* version has long hair down to his chin and an overgrown, unruly beard. The version I met in the warmly dim bar has hair cropped short, faded on the sides and longer on top, with a five o'clock shadow at most—short enough to see his dimples.

Stop thinking about his dimples.

Shoving the document back into its folder and cramming it into a bottom drawer of the desk, I decide that strongly disassociating is the only logical course of action. That's always been my coping style when anything in my life goes awry. This was just one of the tiny messes in life I have become an expert on dealing with. The situation with Tieran wasn't any different than a business deal—complicated but easy to compartmentalize. I would simply file him, and that night at the pub, in the very back of mind and move on with my life. I doubt I'll even see him that much, outside of team meetings or the individual ones I plan on having with each player tomorrow.

After that, I can avoid him and his dimples at all costs.

A curt knock sounds on the door to my office before a man of average height, a receding hairline, and a sportscoat lets himself in, barreling into my office like it's his own house.

"Lawrence Chapman," he introduces himself, and I bristle as he plops himself down in one of the chairs across from me, back ramrod straight and distaste written clear across his face.

"One of the additional shareholders," I acknowledge him and his position within the organization alongside a nod of my head. "Will Ron also be joining this impromptu meeting?"

He bypasses my question completely. "I'm going to shoot straight to the point and not mince my words, Jade." The informality with which he uses my first name, despite not knowing me, is highly intentional, a pointed attempt to assert dominance because he's insecure about having less power than me.

I lean forward and fold my hands on the top of my desk. "You may call me Miss McKallen."

Chapman keeps his composure, but I can see a subtle lick of anger flare behind his eyes.

"You swooped in out of nowhere and offered Landry over his asking price. He was going to sell to me." His jaw grinds as the words squeeze out between thin lips. "They should have been my shares."

I relax back in my seat. "And yet, they're mine. Money talks, Mr. Chapman, and I have a lot of it." Very rarely do I feel the need to flaunt my wealth, but in times like this, when a man like Lawrence Chapman feels like he's entitled to something I acquired fair and square, well, it makes me a little combative.

"What's it going to take to get you to hand 'em over?" His tone is cocky, accent thick.

"They aren't for sale."

Spit spews from his mouth. "I had a verbal agreement in place."

"A cleared check holds more weight than a handshake, Mr. Chapman." His face continues to burn with every sentence out of my mouth. "I won't apologize for going after what I want, if you have a problem with this business deal, you can speak to Landry, but it won't change the fact that this is *my* team now. It's probably best if you make peace with it."

He seethes before abruptly shoving himself out of the chair. He places his hands on the edge of my desk, staring me down as if the height difference will intimidate me into submission.

"Do you even know anything about the sport?" he sneers down at me.

Apparently, the joys of men underestimating women is a global epidemic, not limited to back home.

Despite what everyone here seems hellbent on believing, I know rugby quite well. Since I grew up in coastal Maine to divorced parents, my mom had me on the weekdays, and I spent weekends with dad. They were always my favorite. For as long as I've had memories, Dad would always wake me up early with a steaming hot cuppa and a slice of strawberry jam toast, and we'd watch whatever match was happening here in the UK, a piece of Dad's homeland that he brought to the States and shared with only me. It was magic—screaming at the tv whenever a bad call was made or when our team lost possession of the ball. That kind of behavior wasn't allowed at my mom's house.

Going to Dad's was a haven from the intensity of staying with her throughout the week. He became my best friend, and our time spent watching matches, learning about the sport, and seeing how much he loved it…it was the best. He always let me be me. He was the one who encouraged me to start making videos online after seeing me watch a hundred on his decades-old computer. I think he was worried I was too disconnected from the world at such a young age. He was probably right.

"I know there's a ball involved; running too, I think." My stare is flat, unamused.

Chapman scoffs. "One day, you're going to prove you're unfit for this responsibility, and I'll be waiting to swoop in."

"Right—well, until then, please leave *my* office with this fantastic view." I motion toward the floor to ceiling windows and the players beyond warming up. "I've got some work to do." I turn away from him, a slight he won't soon forget. I can hear him stand, and the spiteful demon inside me decides it wants to poke the bear a little further. "Oh, Lawrence!" I call out to him before he can leave. "You wouldn't happen to know where I could get a new desk, would you? This one's not quite to my taste."

He slams the door on his way out.

Trudging up the narrow staircase to my second floor flat feels impossible after the day I had. Each step feels as if I have cement cinder blocks attached to my feet, and I'm dying to wash my face, take off my bra, and crawl into bed.

After being blindsided by Tieran's presence, my *friendly* chat with Chapman, and a day's worth of meetings between the team and my personal brands back in LA, I need to cleanse this day from my psyche and find time to eat before my call with the head of production for Jaded the Label, the clothing sector of my brand.

I've just made it to the landing outside my new home when the door opposite my flat flies off its hinges, and a beautiful young woman with brown skin, rich mahogany eyes, and dark curly hair that fades into a deep caramel steps out. She pays me no mind as she reaches back into her home and drags a man over the threshold by the chain around his neck, giving him a push towards the stairs.

"You and your furry fetish have got to go. I *do* kink

shame, and I will not tell you for a third time that I'm not putting on an animal mask. I'm *claustrophobic*."

The man turns to her, an idea igniting in his eyes. "What if you just wear the tail and mittens, no mask?"

My neighbor's eye twitches involuntarily. "Goodbye!"

I search for my keys so I can scurry into my place and away from whatever is happening out here, but I don't find them in time.

"Men, am I right?" She huffs out a laugh.

I nod, giving her a disinterested smile. I am trying to get in bed, not make idle chit chat with someone I don't know. Or anyone, really.

"I'm Aanya. You must be my new neighbor. I've gotta say, you already look leagues better than the last guy. I was starting to think I might need to call the letting agent, because I thought he could have died." My body reacts with mild horror at the prospect of living in the abandoned flat of a deceased person. "But next thing I knew, he was moving out, and my problems were solved." Her voice is too chipper for this conversation.

"Jade. Relieved to know I won't have to worry about the spectral ghost of tenants past. And that the smell stuck to the carpet isn't one of decay. If you'll excuse me…" I move to go inside my place, ready to leave this conversation and the rest of the day behind me.

"You look like you could use a glass of wine. Let me go get a bottle!"

"Oh, no, really, that's okay. I wouldn't want to impose." If I think she'll take the hint for what it is—rejection—then she doesn't let on and is totally undeterred.

"It's no problem. I'll be right back." I can't even argue before she's left and returned with a bottle in hand. "Alright, let's go. There's girl talk to be had."

The energy to fight an overly chatty neighbor who's unable to read between the lines is nonexistent. And admittedly, a glass of wine does sound nice after the day

I've endured. Surely, I can hold on to my sanity for another fifteen minutes.

Unlocking my door and stepping inside, I usher her over the threshold and flick on the light.

"Fucking hell." My body jolts at the sudden exclamation, and I look over at Aanya, who is taking in the state of my flat with horror on her face. "What the hell happened in here?"

Her cinnamon eyes bounce between the water damage that's growing mold, peeling wallpaper, decades old carpet, and the errant roach skittering about.

I shift into the kitchen to scour for a bottle opener. "I rented the place sight unseen, and the landlord neglected to tell me the pictures on the listing were not entirely accurate."

"Who rents a place sight unseen?" Her tone is jovial, but my hackles rise at the reproach.

I am not the type of person who jumps into things lightly. I think through my decisions, weigh lists of pros and cons, and run it past a team of advisors. My residence being a disaster is *not* something I am coping with well, and the reminder I've also fucked this up grates.

"Someone whose assistant was handling the leasing and neglected to inform her when the original flat fell through before said assistant was found in bed with someone's boyfriend."

"Oh, fuck." Aanya's mouth drops open at my admission.

"Yeah." I huff out a derisive breath. "I lost my assistant and got saddled with an expensive flat that needs to be fumigated. I'm having a great time."

Aanya steps into the kitchen, grabbing the bottle opener from my hands. "Grab some glasses."

Doing as she says, we pour two generous helpings of wine and move into the living room to sit on the makeshift couch made up of a few throw pillows and blankets.

"I'm assuming you sacked your assistant?"

"Most definitely. I can't have someone I don't trust around me that much."

"And the boyfriend?" she asks, taking a sip of her drink.

"Haven't spared him a second thought." Detachment peppers my tone.

"Not together long?"

"Three years, actually." I fidget.

"You don't seem too out of sorts about it, or him," she observes. She also seems to not care that this is probably too personal a conversation for the first time we've ever met.

I take a long pull of my drink. "To be honest, I don't think I ever felt much for him. I was always too busy with work, and he was just…convenient."

"Harsh," she remarks lightly, but something pangs in my chest as a memory resurfaces.

"All you care about is work, Jade. Does it even matter to you that I would cheat?"

"I don't value disloyalty."

Brendan scoffs. "This is what I mean. It's like I'm talking to a robot, you're so unfeeling."

"What do you do?" Aanya asks, bringing me back to the present.

I suppress a flinch. This career has given me a lot, but it's also cost me *everything.* Life, friendships, relationships, time with my dad I'll never get back. Making friends and keeping them has been impossible when everyone proves to be a snake in the grass.

"The answer to that particular question is a bit loaded." I readjust my body so my feet are tucked beneath me on the pillow couch.

"Well, I sent the beast fucker packing, so it's safe to say my evening's opened up." She says it so candidly, I snort out a laugh into my wine glass.

"I wear a lot of hats. CEO of several large lifestyle brands, but most recently, I became the majority shareholder of The Legends." My neighbor's mouth drops at the first job title, but on the last, her jaw practically unhinges.

"The rugby team?" Her voice holds both shock and admiration.

"The one and only."

"Holy shit. And you said *several* brands, as in more than one?"

I nod my head in confirmation, and she cocks her head to the side, studying me.

"Well damn. Color me impressed. My new best friend is a badass."

I flush at the familiarity, at the ease with which she befriends me, and I resent that it makes me instantly skeptical of her. When I lived in Los Angeles, friends were hard to come by. I made some in my early years, typically other creators I met through collaborations or brand events, but I quickly realized those friendships were usually serving one side of the relationship, and it was never to my benefit. I wanted companionship with the only people I thought could understand me, but they wanted the advantage of my following. I eventually stopped trying to make friends altogether, preferring people believe I was stuck up, than to trust the wrong person and be let down again.

The irony of my brand being named *Jaded* is not lost on me.

"Like I said, I'm busy. Too busy to figure out the mess of this flat or to ream the landlord for pulling a bait and switch. I've only managed to get a couple things booked for a home reno." The taste of my beverage goes sour on my tongue.

"I can help you with that!" Aanya is beaming ear to ear, full, rose petal lips stretched wide. Confusion must be written clear across my face, because she clarifies, "I've got a really bizarre work schedule, and I'm bored *a lot* during the day. I can be your interim assistant, get your flat sorted while you're out conquering the world."

"Why would you do that? You hardly know me."

The stare she gives me is gentle, and it makes me uncomfortable. I readjust my legs, pick at invisible lint on my pants—anything but look at her while she's looking at me like I'm some wounded kitten. "I've got a feeling about you." I look up then, and a sly smirk quirks the corner of her mouth. "Plus, you're going to pay me, of course."

A surprised laugh bubbles out of my mouth, slipping past my defenses. A refusal is on the tip of my tongue, a desperate need to do everything on my own rising to the forefront of my mind. But suddenly, a roach skitters across the stained carpet in front of me, and the vehement need for a clean apartment, or maybe even for a friend, has me agreeing at a speed that shocks me.

"Name your rates."

4

TIERAN

To: tieranstone@gmail.co.uk
From: jademckallen@jaded.com
Subject: Meeting

Jade McKallen has invited you for a one-on-one meeting to be
held in her office at Knightsbridge Stadium on Tuesday at 9:30am.

I HOP out of my cherry red vintage Porsche, bouncing on
my feet in anticipation for the meeting I'm embarrassingly
early to.

When the email invite came in late last night, my heart
started to beat out of my chest. At first I thought she was
reaching out to clear the air, but then I saw it was just a
calendar invite. All the possibilities about what the meeting
could be for kept me up well into the next day with
excitement, and trepidation. Maybe she wants to sack me
without the team around? Or maybe she wants to speak
privately, and that's why she was so aloof the day before?
Either that, or our night together wasn't as memorable to
her as it was to me.

Not knowing was driving me mad.

The speed with which I accepted the meeting invite
should probably be a mark against my character. Re: a too
zealous wanker whose pride can't take another hit. And it

would take a hit if Jade was able to let our night together slip from her memory, because it wasn't just the sex—groundbreaking as it was. I *thought* we had a connection that went deeper than physical attraction.

Maybe in hindsight, that idealism was idiotic, since we never even exchanged names—a convenient fact that could have saved us in our current predicament—but at that point in time, the anonymity felt exhilarating. It had been thrilling to have fun with someone, and there be zero strings attached. I wasn't the country's top fly-half turned laughing stock, or the jilted party in a *very* public breakup. No one was overanalyzing my words, looking for something they could stake to my chest like a scarlet letter.

I was just me.

It felt like freedom from judgement and expectation, and I can't remember the last time I felt that. The confidence I felt in Jade's company that night didn't feel forced or artificial because she didn't know who I was and I didn't know who she was. We were simply two people in a pub.

After an embarrassingly thorough Google search that led to an extensive deep dive through her socials, I could now say I definitely know more about her than is probably advisable.

A millionaire by her nineteenth birthday, hordes of loyal followers hanging on her every well-manicured word, several companies under her belt, and a savviness for business and investing—it was no wonder she had the means to buy out a whole damned sports team.

The question was why.

One would be a fool to believe she wouldn't succeed at whatever she put her mind to, based on her steely gaze alone, but what could have possibly compelled her to do *this*? It's the polar opposite of everything else she's done so far in her career.

I'm five minutes early by the time I walk up to the door leading into her office. Right before I can knock, the door flies open, revealing the team's left flanker, Thomas Wainsworth.

"Big man!" Tommy's thick northern accent calls out as he pulls me into a bear hug.

"What are you doing here?"

"Same as you, I'd reckon. Had a meeting with Ms. McKallen this morning." Oh. *Oh.* It's dawning on me now that my assumptions around this meeting are clearly in error.

My cheeks heat with embarrassment, and I duck my head, hoping he doesn't notice. "That's sound. Well, I better get in there then. Don't want to get on her bad side." I indicate toward the open office door.

"See you on the pitch, Cap."

I take a deep breath, trying to temper my embarrassment before I step forward and rap my knuckles against the door.

Jade is sitting at her desk, head tilted down with her phone tucked between her shoulder and ear, looking over some forms on her desk as she talks assertively to whoever is on the other line. Her midnight hair is pulled back in a ponytail at the nape of her neck, tendrils falling around her high cheekbones. From her seated position, I can see she's wearing a champagne satin blouse that gathers at her side, accentuating her figure. Somehow, she's managed to look severe and angelic at the same time.

She knocks me out of my open admiration when she finally addresses me, still not looking up from her work. "Please come in, Mr. Stone." Her voice is rich, with a slight rasp around the edges that makes a bolt of heat zing up my spine.

Only when I sit in the chair across from her does she finally look at me. I don't know what I expected to be met with, but it wasn't cool indifference. Not a single flare of recognition lights her honeyed eyes as I remain silent, waiting for her cue as she assesses me, that bright spot of blue beckoning my attention.

"I sent out individual meeting invites to each player on the team so I can gauge everyone's strengths and weaknesses, as well as ask them if they've felt supported in the past. If they haven't, I want to know how we as an administration can better lend aid and help everyone achieve their goals for this season and beyond."

"Where would you like to start?" I ask, forgetting about everything else in the wake of her professionalism.

"You didn't have the best season last year." Apparently, we're going straight for the throat, no preamble.

"I'm aware I failed my team," I bite out.

"I didn't say that, Mr. Stone." She levels me with a withering look. "Your ability to lead your team isn't contingent on the amount of trys the team scores or how well *you* play individually."

"Tell that to the rabid hoard of fans and reporters." I glance out the window, anywhere but at that intense spot of blue.

"I'm less concerned about what *they* think and am more concerned about what *you* think, Mr. Stone."

I hate that we're leaning too close to her baldly perceiving all my weaknesses—hate that she'll see me differently now than she did the night we met. "Call me Tieran." I plaster on a cheeky smile, feeling the need to distract her.

I shouldn't be surprised when it doesn't work, and she raises a single eyebrow at me.

"What happened last season, *Mr. Stone*?"

I suck in a fortifying breath. "I got a severe case of the yips halfway through the year and couldn't pull myself out in time to lead the team properly." My eyes ping pong all over the office, anywhere but at her.

"Are the yips still present?"

The desire to lie, to save face in front of her, is strong, but I resist. "I hope not."

"As the Legends captain, what can leadership do to support you, the team, and your own individual goals?"

"Honestly?"

"I wouldn't have asked if I wanted lies. If something is lacking, I need to know so I can course correct it. Players who feel valued are important to me, a pivotal aspect of building morale amongst everyone." Every word out of her mouth sounds clinical, but somehow, it still rings genuine. She *cares* about this, at least more than our previous leaders did.

Who is *this* Jade? Because she's a far cry from the one I met at the pub.

"Our equipment is older than the sovereign himself and needs updating. Previous owners only ever invested in the appearance of the stadium, wanting to maintain looks so they could justify price gouging tickets and leaving nothing in the budget for us. It may not seem important, because a ball is a ball, but the players notice the things the higher ups deem worthy, and it's not usually the puppets that make them money." How's that for honesty?

"What else?"

"Revamped uniforms would be nice, better hotels during away games, better meal stipends for when we're away."

"How much have they been giving you for meals?" Her tone is skeptical and inquiring.

"Twenty quid a day."

She smarts. "You're each at least two hundred pounds, more for the forwards. Twenty quid would only cover a breakfast with the amount of food professional athletes eat."

"Spot on." I lean back in my chair.

"Is there anything else I should know?"

I take a minute to think about the needs of the team. "Our equipment manager, Harry, could use some support. He takes on a lot by himself. He may need an assistant, or, at the very least, some updated machines for the washing."

Jade nods her head in acknowledgment. "And your goals for your time on the team? Beyond?"

This is not a conversation I want to have, but the resolute structure of her shoulders tells me I won't get out of it. "I wanted to qualify for the men's National Team…go to the Olympics." Maybe if I did, I would finally make Dad proud, get him to notice me—to care.

"Wanted?"

I huff out a laugh. "Well, I don't think they'll want anything to do with me now." My shoulders rise nonchalantly, and I shrug it off like I do everything else these days.

"I've seen you play, Mr. Stone." I grimace internally, thinking about this woman—*my boss*—seeing me off my game.

"Hopefully not a match from last season." Plastering a false smile across my face and opting for an unbothered approach has been serving me well over the last year, but I have to admit, it's starting to wear on me, acting like one person when I'm someone else entirely on the inside.

"I've seen you play," she continues, unfettered. "You are a *force* on the pitch. Your ability to determine the other team's strategies and adjust your own on the fly is… impressive. We'll get you on the Olympic team, but you still have to want it."

She's so sure, so confident in my ability, it almost makes me believe too. Almost, but not quite.

"That's all I have for you and my next meeting is in five minutes. Thank you for your time." She gestures toward the door so I can see myself out.

I stand to leave and make it halfway before my shoulders swivel around of their own accord. She's staring at her laptop screen when I break the weird bubble of plausible deniability we've been holding on to like a life raft.

"Do you really not remember me?" All the air has been sucked out of the room.

She doesn't look up from her screen. "Of course I do."

The breath I've been holding since she stepped into the

conference room yesterday expels out of my lungs like a deflating balloon.

"You weren't going to say anything?"

"There's nothing to say. We didn't know each other, and it was *clearly* a mistake. It's never going to happen again, so we might as well forget about it." Her words rush out of her, too quickly for someone who wants to appear unbothered.

Color me delusional, but that sounds like the justified ramblings of a woman who has been thinking about our predicament all night too. Her eyes flit back and forth across her computer screen, refusing to meet mine. I'm starting to think Jade is more affected by this development than she's letting on, and it makes me want to see how much I can prod at her until her perfect composure crumbles.

I take a few steps forward so I'm a foot away from where she sits at her desk, looming over her. "Do you really think you can forget what happened?"

She stares up at me, steel lining her warm toffee gaze. "Yes."

"You wound me."

"Something tells me you'll get over it." A challenge, a glimpse of the Jade I met that night.

"Oh, I highly doubt that." I pitch my voice lower. "Since I've thought of nothing else but you since that night."

My brazenness stuns her silent for only a minute. "Goodbye, Mr. Stone."

Her tone of annoyance makes me smile from ear to ear. A real smile this time. "Later, boss."

As I walk out to the center of the field where some of my teammates are gathered, the telltale signs of anxiety start to creep in and sit heavy on my shoulders.

Yesterday was easier to cope with. On our first day back, we spent half the day doing a team workout to build endurance and see where everyone is at post break. It's the best way for Ballard to see who maintained their fitness regimes during downtime. Anyone who hadn't was forced into punishing drills that resulted in more than a couple men getting sick on the grass.

The second half of the day was spent in meetings, talking about the upcoming season and setting expectations for playing as well as behaviour on and off the pitch.

Now that all the formality was out of the way, we'll be practicing—running plays and strategizing. The thing I'm meant to be able to do seamlessly, instinctively. The skill I'm paid a lot of money to perform and haven't been able to for the better part of a year.

Coach calls out for our attention, snapping me back into the present. "Listen up. Yesterday, I was being nice by giving you a warm up to ease back into the season—"

"That was his warm up?" Amari Ashford, the team's right prop, whispers as some of the other men groan their agreement.

"If you'd been diligent with your training, you wouldn't have spewed your breakfast all over the pitch yesterday after a few practice drills," Cavan chides, face immovable.

"Ach! Some of us like to have fun in our free time, old man." Cav rolls his eyes as he drops into a forward lunge, warming up his muscles.

"And you're paying for it now. Listen," I command, trying to focus their attention back on Ballard.

"Last year didn't go as we had hoped." It feels like dozens of eyes home in on me, watching…*waiting* for a reaction. A familiar surge of anxiety laps at my ankles. "However, that doesn't mean we can't come back from it. Show them why we're called Legends." Ballard nods at me to take over. "Captain."

He yields the pitch, and now I *know* every eye is on me. Shaking the stiffness out of my shoulders, I hold my head high and look at each and every one of my guys—starting with the two closest to me, my best mates. Myles smiles, and Cavan gives me a barely perceptible nod of encouragement, a grim set to his mouth. I haven't spoken to either of them about how muddled my head feels, not wanting to put my cross on their backs, but I suspect Cav knows. There's something about the special powers a dad has that gives him the ability to sense I've been faking all my perceived confidence. But I've been extra careful to give Myles nothing to worry about while he's been dealing with whatever is happening with his mum. He has a particular talent for trying to problem solve on behalf of the people he loves, and I'd be damned if I added one more thing to his already full plate. I could get my shite together—I have to.

"Alright, boys," I give a hearty clap, plastering a megawatt smile on my face. "Last season was a bit of a blunder, but it's a new year. We'll train harder than before, focus on our weaknesses, turn them into strengths, and absolutely bludgeon our opponents. If there's anything affecting you out on the pitch, or even at home, you can come to me, and we'll find a solution together. Now get out on the grass and tear it up!" The words feel like a false promise as they leave my mouth.

The resounding chorus of exuberant hollering reverberates around me as we all start to bounce on our feet, a thrill racing through the air around us.

We run through sequence after sequence of warm up drills, focusing on getting our limbs and ligaments loosened up to mitigate any potential strains or injuries.

We're finishing off the first hour of training with hip rocks when I feel another set of eyes on me, searing honey with a pocket of staggering blue.

I sit back on my heels, sweat dripping down my face, forcing me to lift my shirt to wipe it out of my eyes. When I drop my hand, my eyes immediately connect with Jade's.

Focused. Severe. Calculating. *Magnetic.*

"She looks like she's got a stick up her arse," one of the younger guys on the team says.

"Bet I could loosen her up. I'd start by unzipping that tight skirt and then—"

I stand and grab Connor by the neck of his kit, anger lighting up my spine. "Shut it, Davies, and have some respect for her position."

"Oh, I do. Believe me." His words are cocky and filled with innuendo. "I respect her position to be *under* me." He looks around him to see how many guys are laughing with him, and the fact that it's more than a couple makes me sick to my stomach.

I release Connor's shirt with an aggressive push. "Listen up!"

Coach Ballard looks on curiously but doesn't say anything as the guys huddle around me. "I'm only going to say this once, so listen closely. Legends do *not* disrespect women. We are not those kinds of men, and we do not enable those kinds of men. If I hear one more comment that doesn't treat Ms. McKallen with the regard someone in her position deserves, you will answer to me. And trust me when I say, it will be far more unpleasant than the drills coach has us run or Darcey's ugly mug. I shouldn't have to even say this. Do you understand me?"

The team shouts their agreement and scatters, getting into position to run plays for the next several hours.

Sensing eyes on my back, I turn to find Jade, arms crossed over her chest, looking severely irritated.

I shoot her a wink, not knowing if she'll even see it from this distance, but her shoulders stiffen, and then she's strutting out of the stadium.

5

JADE

"IF YOU DON'T STOP PESTERING me and let me watch the match, I'll call the local authorities." I walk into my dad's house in Blackheath to find him batting his lovely home health attendant away from his sacred television chair.

"It's the same game you've watched a dozen times, you old codger. C'mon, Mr. McKallen. The fresh air will do you good." Her deep voice is smooth like honey, trying and failing to coax my stubborn father out of his spot.

Dad scoffs. "The air outside is riddled with pollution. It'll probably kill me faster." He inclines a brow in her direction. "Is that what you're hoping for, Myrah? Because if I'm dead, then you're out of a job."

"Yes, because you're the only sick man in all of England." She rolls her eyes, a soft smile curling her full mouth.

"I think you should listen to her, Dad." I kick off my shoes by the front door and step into the sitting room to the left of the entry.

"Hello, Pumpkin." Dad reaches his arms out to me, wanting a hug but refusing to get out of his beloved chair.

I wrap my arms around his shoulders, breathing in the familiar scent of his aftershave, and instantly feel at ease.

"I'm serious. Doctor Hasana said staying active is the best way to keep you mobile for as long as possible."

"Can't I be *mobile* after the match?"

"Why don't you use the recording feature I had installed for you? That's why we upgraded your tv."

"Too many bloody buttons. Can't trust technology these days. Thought I was recording the Tottenham vs. Norwich match and ended up watching an episode of I'm a Celebrity…Get Me Out of Here!"

"Oh, I quite like that show," Myrah chimes in.

"I've never seen it," I reply.

"You have to watch it. It's an absolute tip, but so fun. Watch it with my boys every week."

"Maybe you two should go on a walk together and leave me to watch the match alone," Dad grumbles.

"No way. Off you pop." I tug on his arm, forcing him out of his seat and lightly pushing him into the hall while he mumbles expletives the whole way, only pausing to put on his trainers.

I grab a jacket for him out of the small entryway closet, handing it over, and his ire morphs into a sheepish look as he gives the tv behind me a final, longing look. "Can you still record it for me?

Rolling my eyes, I pop back into the sitting room to program the tv, recording the rerun match my dad has already seen a dozen times, before meeting him back by the door.

We slowly stroll our way north throughout his neighborhood toward the lush green lawn of Greenwich Park, my arm looped through his, helping to keep him steady.

With the sun hiding behind thick clouds, there's a lack of sunshine aiding the slight chill in the air, despite it being summertime. The weather is unpredictable in London, but it's safe to say that, with the grey skies and the small gusts of wind, rain is likely on the horizon. However, the overcast day hasn't deterred anyone from going outside, and the park is packed with parents pushing their babies around in prams, dogs frolicking at the end of a lead, and groups of friends hunting for the best spot to set down their blankets for a picnic at the top of the hill—likely planning on staying until the sun sets over the city in the distance.

"How are you feeling?" With how hectic everything has been in my first week at work, I haven't been able to get out to visit since I moved here.

"Don't fuss over me." He taps the top of my hand clenched around his arm.

"You don't take this seriously enough. Parkinson's isn't a joke, Dad." It's the biggest reason I moved here. After his diagnosis was confirmed, I immediately started making plans to move to England *thank you, dual citizenship*. We had visited a couple times while growing up and had been back for business, but I was never here longer than a week and always had no time to explore.

But with Dad's health, everything in LA starting to feel suffocating, and with the team going up for sale, the decision to move here was shockingly easy.

"I choke down the slop you force me eat, don't I?" he grumbles.

"Fresh fruit and veg is hardly slop. You're so dramatic," I huff out a laugh.

"You're not dramatic enough. You gotta live a little, lovey. You're too focused on work and never have any fun. You're young; you should be stealing every morsel of joy out of life you can."

What is he talking about? I've traveled the world, gone to events—I've been to Coachella *four* miserable times. I *have* experienced things.

"I'm exactly where I want to be."

He hums contemplatively. "And how are the lads?" Ever since I bought the team, he's taken to calling the guys on the team *the lads*, as if they're all his close personal friends by association.

The camera was turned the wrong way when Dad

answered my FaceTime call to tell him the news. After five minutes, and a lot of swearing while trying to explain to him how to get it to flip around, I gave up and told him I bought the team and was officially moving. I hadn't seen him move that quickly in a long time as he launched himself out of the chair and started cheering, *'I've got season tickets!'*

"*The lads* are fine." I steer us toward a bench so he can rest, because he'll never ask for it on his own. He never has.

"What about that Stone fella?"

Something in my stomach pitches at him bringing Tieran up. "What about him?"

"He didn't play the best last year. Do you think this year will be any different? I want to hedge my bets properly."

"Dad! You can't bet against our own team!" My voice raises before I remember there are people around me, and I clench my lips closed, afraid of nosey ears. I learned long ago that anyone would sell you out for a quick buck or fifteen minutes of the spotlight.

"I can if they'll make me some money," he chuckles.

"You know I can take care of you."

He's shaking his head before I can finish my sentence. "I never took money from you before, and I won't now. It's already bad enough that I let you pay for that nurse."

"Oh, come on." I bump my shoulder against his. "You like Myrah, I can tell."

"She's alright." He looks away from me, saying hello to a Dachshund trotting by and evading my observation, but I swear, there's a slight pinkening to his already ruddy cheeks.

We sit for another half hour, letting him rest and catch up on the week apart. He peppers me with more questions about the team, thankfully not bringing up Tieran again, and I ask about his friends from the local pub as we watch the sun slowly start to set, casting London in a warm golden glow.

My first week here has been far from smooth, but it's all been worth it to have moments like these again.

"Dad," I call out from the open refrigerator door. "Why is there no food in here?"

He grunts out something unintelligible in response as I make my way toward the front of the house, grabbing my bag and slipping my shoes back on.

"Where are you going?"

"M&S to get stuff for dinner. I'll be back soon."

"Why don't we just order take away?"

"How many times have you ordered in this week?" My hands ball and rest on my hips in reprimand.

"That's an inconsequential detail. Doesn't a chippy sound nice?"

To be honest, it does. Nothing makes me feel more at home than fresh fish and chips, but someone has to make sure he stays fit to stave off the worst of his symptoms. He's already a little off balance, and seeing tremors in his hands as he stirred his tea this afternoon made me want to cry. It was a fight holding back tears to avoid drawing attention to it, but Archie McKallen is, and always will be a prideful man. Needing assistance to do menial tasks made him feel weak, and I didn't want to pour salt in a festering wound by crying about it in front of him. In the moment it was a relief, but it made me feel like a coward, being willing to follow his lead just so I could avoid the reality of his mortality a little longer. It's still early stages, but watching your favorite person—someone who has always been larger than life—get older and slow down is excruciating.

"I'll see you in an hour with something green," I say as I step out the front door.

"No brussels sprouts, please!" His request trails out to me just before the door shuts.

Twenty minutes and three phone calls to Jaded's manufacturer later, I'm walking through the automatic doors of the local M&S Food with a hope and a dream but absolutely no plan. My stomach starts to grumble the second I smell the premade hot food lining the far wall. Doing a food shop while hungry was a fatal mistake, considering how everything is now tempting me.

Grabbing a cart, I make my way over to produce first, grabbing a couple zucchinis, a head of garlic, and a few lemons before somehow finding myself veering into the snack aisle.

Maybe just something small to tide me over until dinner—

I stop dead in my tracks when I see who's at the end of the aisle. Oh. Oh no.

What deity did I piss off?

Why, in a city of roughly nine million people, can I not stop running into Tieran Stone? How on Earth is he somehow in this same food shop, on the outskirts of central London, looking irritatingly good in jeans and a slightly cropped graphic tee that shows off the tattoos on his arms, giving the tiniest peek of his toned abdomen as he reaches up for th—

Stop.

How is the one person I am actively trying to avoid, the one person the universe keeps hilariously dropping into my path like an atom bomb? At this point, the only thing that will keep us out of each other's paths is a meteor crashing down and obliterating the planet.

I'm about to leave before he sees me when a small woman with pastel pink hair comes bounding over to him with arms full of candy, and a huge grin splashed across her cute face. She's wearing a gingham mini dress, oversized denim vest, and platform thigh high boots. She is effortlessly cool, with a smattering of dainty tattoos delicately painting her arms and legs, and I envy the air of freedom that emanates off her. She is the opposite of everything I am.

Is she his girlfriend? They certainly seem to be very familiar with each other, based on the way they're laughing together as they look over the shelves.

Something in my gut churns at the sight. It's so carefree, simple.

I've got to get out of here.

Taking tentative steps that won't draw their eyes, I quickly ease backwards to duck out of the aisle with my cart. I've only gone two steps when my back hits something hard and flimsy, scraping against the linoleum floor, and wobbling precariously. I turn to grab it, to stop the structure before it topples over, but it slips through my grip, hitting the ground with a deafening crash. I scrunch my eyes shut, praying when I open them, this whole thing will have been a dream, because the chances that he didn't hear are as non-existent as my dignity. When I peek an eye open, the evidence of my failure is scattered on the ground around me in the form of thirty packages of potato chips.

I can't believe snack food has betrayed me like this. This is what I get for deviating from my routine.

Standing up the cardboard holder, I start picking up the graveyard of chips, staunchly avoiding looking up and praying to any deity who will listen that he somehow didn't notice me.

But why would I ever be that lucky, I think, as booted feet step into view from where I'm crouched on the floor.

Slowly, I drag my gaze up past strong thighs, a trim torso, and settle on a tanned face with striking blue eyes. His smile grows wider by the second. A devil's smile—arrogant, tantalizing, teasing. It infuriates me.

"You know, if you wanted to talk to me, you didn't have to make such a scene." He crouches and starts grabbing bags, helping me place them back on the stand.

I ungraciously swat his hand away. "Leave it. I'll handle it."

"You don't have to handle everything on your own. Let me help you." He unknowingly strikes a nerve, and I bristle. Doing things on my own is all I've ever known. It's what works for me, and I don't need him waltzing in here and trying to be some valiant knight.

"Shouldn't you be getting back to your girlfriend?

He stutters. "My what?"

I'm ripping up the remaining chips now, aggressively tossing them back onto the shelves of the cardboard stand. I lower my voice to a sharp whisper. "You shouldn't have slept with me if you had a girlfriend." My gaze darts over his shoulder, settling on the alternative fairy princess at the far end of the aisle.

He follows my line of sight, tongue pushing into his cheek, suppressing a smile. "Ah."

I practically hiss. "Ah? That's all you have to say?"

"Oh, so now you want to talk about that night? Because to do that, you'd have to acknowledge it actually happened." That smug smile pulls at each end of his mouth, dimple popping in his right cheek.

"No. Stop smiling."

His stupid dimples pop deeper. "Whatever you say, boss."

I ignore him, and he keeps helping me pick up the mess despite my telling him not to.

"Do you live around here?" he asks.

"No. I live in Chelsea." Once the last bag is re-homed, I stand, and he catches my elbow helping me up. The small bit of contact has a current running up my arm, and I quickly pull out of his grasp.

"What are you doing out here then?" Why is he still smiling? Surely, it wasn't natural for someone to be this happy? I want to smack that smile off his face.

"Are you always this nosey?" I fold my arms across my chest, and his gaze darts down and quickly back up at the movement.

"When I need to be."

"Well, you don't—need to be nosey," I clarify. "It's unnecessary for you to know anything personal about me—"

"I'd say we know a fair deal of personal things about each other." I squeeze my eyes closed, trying to ward off the images that statement conjures in my mind. Dimly lit pubs, tiny, enclosed bathrooms, crystal blue eyes searing into mine through the reflection of a dust-speckled mirror.

I white knuckle the handle of my cart, words getting caught in my mouth, building up until I'm choking on them.

"Mr. Stone—" That stupid fucking smile grows bigger.

Tieran looks behind him to find the aisle empty. "I should probably go find my *sister* before she buys too much vodka and cheese with my money. She likes the expensive stuff when she's not paying for it." He starts to jog backward, pulling away from me. "But I'll see you soon, boss."

He's out of view when I audibly groan, grabbing a bag of cheese and onion chips off the stand I knocked over, ripping them open and snacking while I finish grabbing ingredients for dinner.

6
JADE

TWO WEEKS HAVE PASSED since I started my life in London. Two weeks of wondering if I was going to bump into the consequence of my reckless actions. Days on end dealing with the haunting memory of Tieran tugging on my hair, thrusting deep and hard like he had something to prove, and then failing miserably as I tried to burn the memory from my brain out of pure necessity. Countless mornings of contractors coming and going from my flat with Aanya at the helm, bossing them around. Early morning alarms waking me up only hours after I fell asleep all for the sake of filming content to send to my editor. Weekends spent stealing time with Dad in between zoom meetings with associates back in the States. Full days working at the stadium sun up to sun down before coming home only to work another several hours taking care of the various branches under Jaded: new collections for the clothing line, a range of homeware goods for my Anthro exclusive, and mountains of paperwork and legalese were just the tip of the iceberg.

It's a lot—more work than I've ever had at one time—but I'm managing.

Sort of. I'm not getting much sleep between all the virtual meetings in different time zones, but that's what eye patches imported from Switzerland are for.

I nearly forgot to take them off before running out the door, late to the morning meeting *I* set with the other shareholders. This is not how I wanted to start my day, but I slept through my alarm, missed the Pilates class I had booked, and had less than an hour to get ready and out the door. Now, I'm feeling off-kilter, and I have to square up to the room full of men who would do anything to see me removed from the premises.

My black stilettos click against concrete tile floors, carrying me through the staff-only hallways of the stadium toward the conference room. I'm no stranger to board meetings where I face men in suits who lob their money around and metaphorically whip out their dicks to measure whose is biggest, but something about this particular meeting has me intimidated.

Maybe it was the direct way Chapman made it known I wasn't welcome, that he likely has everyone behind the doors I'm walking up to already against me, but my gut reaction is telling me I'm about to be thrust back into high school. Ever the social pariah.

That's fine; I'm not here to make friends. My goal is to be close to my dad, to try something new, challenging—exciting. Doing variations of the same thing for the last decade was starting to feel soul crushing. I *needed* this change—even if no one understood it.

As I approach the door to the conference room, voices from inside float out to greet me.

"I don't care. I'll get her to leave." The voice no doubt belongs to Chapman.

"At least she's nice to look at." This from a voice I don't recognize, perhaps Ron, who I still have yet to meet, since he's conveniently ignored all my attempts at a phone conversation.

"That's all she's got to offer. She won't know the first thing about running the club; she's young and inexperienced, a stupid girl playing dress up who'll realize she's in over her head soon enough. And if she doesn't,

I'll find a way to force her out. This club belongs to me—"

"Come again?"

"To us," he corrects himself, but I hear the lie for what it is. Lawrence wants this team for his own, and he has no intention of sharing.

Taking the lull in conversation as my cue to enter, I open the door and watch both men—and who I assume to be their assistants—straighten in their seats.

"Nice of you to finally join us," Lawrence snickers derisively.

"Nice of you to keep my seat warm." I nod toward where he's rooted in the chair reserved for the head of the business. *My chair.*

His face reddens the closer I get until I'm standing next to him, looking down.

"Surely one of the other chairs would suffice," he says with false cordiality.

"I like *this* one," I state, placing my hand on the back of the chair.

I am definitely punching the bear in the face at this point. I have delivered blow after blow to his pride, and the slight of doing it in front of his male peers, people he clearly deems lesser than him, will not be easily forgotten.

"The head of the table is typically reserved for the leader of the organization, no? Does that differ here as opposed to in America?" I cock my head at the group of men in front of me. The assistants look scared, Chapman looks homicidal, and Ron looks ambivalent.

"No, miss. It's the same here," Ron says in a soft, lilting voice.

"That right? What do you say, Lawrence? Fancy showing me those British manners I've heard so much about?" I curl my head to face him, raising an eyebrow and delighting in the subtle twitch of his left eye.

He stands, chair legs scraping against the floor.

Adjusting his blazer, he glares daggers at me as he walks a couple places down and takes a new seat.

I stay standing at the head of the table, waiting for everyone to settle before sitting.

"As you all may be aware, over the last couple of weeks, I've met with each individual team member and player to ask what areas of the organization could be improved upon. I'm curious to hear what you all think as well."

I sit back in my chair and wait for one of them to speak up.

"No one has anything to contribute?" The disbelief is clear on my face. Reaching into my bag, I pull out my laptop, powering it on and pulling up my cross-referenced notes from each meeting. "That's interesting, because I have transcripts from at least forty meetings that would state otherwise."

I spear them all with a look over my laptop before closing it and folding my hands on top.

Chapman finally speaks up. "I don't know that coming in here and telling us everything we're doing wrong is the right approach, Miss McKallen."

"I'm not pointing fingers, Mr. Chapman. I'm simply looking for areas of opportunity within the club." I try to soften my tone, be less combative while still asserting authority. It's pandering bullshit, and a man would never have to jump through these kinds of mental hoops, but I do care what they think, since, whether they believe it or not, they're a part of this team too.

There's a cough to my right, and I look over to find Ron sheepishly raising a hand.

"Yes?"

"Did the players have a lot to say?" He looks almost scared to speak up, and it's immediately clear why when Lawrence scoffs. I glance over to see his jaw grinding, the subtle movement causing Ron to shrink in his seat under Chapman's unrelenting glare.

It's curious how both Ron and Lawrence hold the same

percentage of shares, but there's a clear hierarchy in the room. That will have to change, but that matter is much more delicate than a simple upgrade to equipment or uniforms.

"They did. First and foremost, I've been diving into our financial accounts and see there seems to be a surplus of charges on dining—"

"Are we not meant to pick up the bill when we take out associates?" Chapman interrupts.

"Of course." He looks all too pleased. "Within reason. With that said, a monthly spending limit will be put into effect, and those excess funds will be reallocated to the team's daily per diem while on away games." The smug look previously taking residence on his face drops.

"But—"

I hold up my hand in a show on authority. "It's non-negotiable."

"Who do you think you are?"

The need to defend my place here, again, grates like nails on a chalkboard. "The team needs to know they matter to us, that we want the best for them. Rugby builds community within our city. Inside every pub that plays a match, people gather to drink a pint and cheer on the guys together. Behind television screens across the UK and the world, people watch and rally behind their favorite team. We should want to foster those connections. The fans have to love our players to show us loyalty, and for that to happen, our players need to be happy. We aren't just here to make money; we're here to build a legacy." I pause and look them each in the eye. "Atleast, that's why *I'm* here. Why are you?"

The rest of the meeting passes swiftly, with slightly less hostility from the opposite side of the table. There is a reluctance for change that will be a hard wall to break down, but I've never been one to back away from a challenge. If I had a dollar for every person who's doubted me over the course of my career, I could have bought the rugby team with the amount amassed. At one point or another, that doubt would have crippled me. Now it *fuels* me.

Packing my laptop into my tote bag and slipping my stilettos back onto my feet, I stand to leave for the day. Lawrence, Ron, and their assistants left earlier in the afternoon, going on about grabbing lunch and making it a point not to invite me. Not that I particularly wanted to join, but if it would help bridge this vicious gap, I'd fall on my sword and make it work.

Tracing a path through the hallways, I casually make my way toward the field. To assess the progress of the team, I tell myself. I am simply performing duties that fall within my leadership role, nothing else.

Stopping at the mouth of the vestibule that leads out onto the pitch, I stop and stare, allowing the shade of the overhang to shelter me from being seen. Before me is so many thighs encased in *very* short shorts, all bulging with muscle. Even I have to admit, it's a sight to behold—professionally speaking.

Coach Ballard and his assistant coach consult over a clipboard while the players are scattered around the field, running through a series of cool down exercises. Stretching, they're stretching. Hip flexors, bridges, and forward lunges make up the field as the guys chat about their evening plans. A low laugh rings out over the noise, drawing my eyes to a tall figure.

Tieran stands over Myles with a smile spread across his face, a single ray of sun peeking out from behind the clouds for the first time all day, illuminating him in golden light. My eyes trace a greedy, illicit path down his form. Sweat glistens down his neck, soaking the jersey clinging to his sculpted abdomen, and his shorts are rucked up higher than necessary over his thick quads, showing off countless tattoos.

I can't make out what most of them are from this distance, but a fierce dragon or snake curls around his right kneecap, slithering further up his thigh. I noticed a few tattoos when we met at the pub, but with his current state of undress, I'm realizing there is a lot more than I could see that night. It makes me wonder how many others there could be. He's got most of one leg covered, several scattered over his arms, and my brain helpfully recollects one particularly tantalizing piece just below his ear, beckoning my mouth the night we met.

Heat settles low, and I chastise myself for indulging in these thoughts. That night *didn't* happen, and it would do me no good to delude myself of a fantasy that would never come to pass.

I turn to leave before anyone notices I'm here and jump when I see someone hovering behind me.

"Oh! Harry, hello. I didn't hear you walking up."

"Didn't mean to startle you, miss. I was just bringing out more towels for the players," the team's soft spoken equipment manager says.

"No worries. Thank you for your hard work." I move to step past him, hoping he didn't see me staring at a certain player for longer than appropriate.

Thirty minutes later, I'm stepping through the door of my flat and kicking my heels off.

I groan loudly at the sweet relief of not walking on toothpicks anymore and shuffle into the kitchen to pour myself a glass of sauvignon blanc.

Looking around my home, I make a mental note to buy a very nice gift for Aanya, because the progress the last couple weeks is nothing short of astounding. After a few glasses of wine the night we met, she told me she was a musician. She'd spent the last several years playing at pubs and in the underground scene, but that was why she had so much free time to help me. She's currently taking every gig she could to break into more mainstream avenues, hoping she'll be in the right place at the right time to meet someone who could take her career to new heights. It was on the tip of my tongue that I could probably help her, but fear kept me quiet about my own place in the public eye, afraid if she knew, she'd start looking at me as a meal ticket to a large platform of exposure.

It's a feeling I have become accustomed to over the last decade, but I don't think I could stomach the disappointment I would feel if the one…friend I have in London turned out to be the same as everyone else.

But by the next morning, she was outside my door with a surly exterminator and a large coffee for me, shoving her way in and putting the man to work. That, plus the cleaning crew she brought in, the interior painter who was here a few days later, and the mood boards she created for each room, *just for fun*, has her creeping dangerously close to sainthood in my mind.

The couch I ordered still won't arrive for a few weeks, so I settle onto the makeshift one I made of spare blankets, placing my laptop on top of a pillow before hopping on my first Zoom meeting of the night.

It isn't until halfway through my second meeting and my third glass of wine that I start to feel woozy and order dinner for delivery.

When there's a knock on my door, I hop up, head spinning as I rush over, ready to rip the bag out of the driver's hands and scarf down the carbonara I've been dreaming about for the past twenty-five minutes. Instead, I'm met with the beaming face of my neighbor.

"Try not to look so pleased to see me, or I might get the wrong idea." Aanya waggles her eyebrows at me.

I shove my head out the door, hoping beyond hope the delivery man will be just behind her. He's not, and my stomach growls as I shut the door behind me.

"What brings you by?" I ask.

"I wanted to invite you out to one of my shows

tonight." She's all frenetic energy, bouncing on the balls of her feet, baggy jeans slung low on her hips, a black bandeau top wrapped snug around her chest. She's accented her outfit with a cuff around her bicep, her always present nose ring, and smokey black liner. She's effortlessly cool in a way that looks like she put no effort into trying.

"I can't. I have to work."

Her face falls, and the springing halts. "But it's half eight."

"I know, but I have product development and review meetings in thirty minutes and about ten different reports I have to sort through."

"Weren't you at the stadium all day? That's not good work-life balance," she chuckles.

"Ah—that doesn't exist in my life," I try to joke, but her laugh vanishes, replaced with concern.

"Are you sure you can't come?"

The hope in her warm eyes is actually killing me. I want to go support her, repay her even a smidge for all she's done to help a person she barely even knew. But all my associates are already upset I've upended things by moving across the world; bailing on meetings last minute is not going to make the situation any easier.

"Maybe next time?" I say, not knowing if she'll bother to invite me again. I'm surprised to find the thought makes me sad.

The knock at the door saves her from having to respond as I walk over and wrench it open, seeing a pock-marked teenager texting and holding out the bag for me to take.

Aanya exits the door after he's left. "I'll catch you later, Jade."

"See ya."

Guilt eats at me, and for the first time, I regret what I do for work and the pressure I'm under to always be perfect.

To: wholesale@hampsteadhops.com
From: jademckallen@jaded.com
Subject: Home Brew for London Legends

Hello, I'm Jade McKallen, the majority shareholder of the London Legends. I'd like to set up a meeting with your CEO and head of production about a home brew for our team. I have a thirty minute break on Thursday, would this work for you?

Best,
Jade McKallen

7

TIERAN

MY NERVES ARE like a live wire jumping around in a rain puddle, sending sparks flying and singeing my skin. If I was a lucky man, one would land on my highly flammable game shorts and set me on fire, giving me an excuse to not play this game tonight.

Match days used to be my favourite day of the week, feeding me adrenaline and excitement to get out and play. My whole body would buzz from the moment I woke up until the second my boot touched the pitch, and I would relax, because muscle memory would take over. From the wild energy in the locker room, to the rush of the game—it made me feel alive. Now, all I feel is dread.

The past few weeks of practice have gone…okay. There have definitely been some mishaps, a few too many meetings with Ballard, but overall, it's gone as well as I can hope for. What I'm worried about now is how that will translate once I'm on the pitch. Will the cheers of the crowd that used to invigorate me feel suffocating under the pressure of expectation?

"You good?" Cavan's gravelly timbre floats over to me from a couple lockers down as he slips the team's burgundy coloured jersey over his broad tawny shoulders.

The team's two locks, Finn and Ekon, both glance over

at us before giving each other a look I don't want to decipher and pointedly choose to ignore.

I pull off my shirt so I can slip on my home match uniform, imbuing my voice with as much enthusiasm as I can muster. "Just thinking about what I'm going to have for dinner." I smile, selling the lie before we head out onto the field that will make or break me before the night's end.

We take the winding player tunnels that lead onto the field, passing large, framed photos of past teams, action shots, and moments of victory. We're a few paces back from the mouth of the passageway, and before the announcer starts calling for us to join the fray, the team huddles around me.

"Alright, lads, we've worked harder than Darcey's scowl whenever anyone tries to talk to him. Last season brought some blunders—" There are some murmurs coming from the team, and Cavan's aforementioned scowl makes an appearance, effectively shutting them up. Shame roils in my gut, but I press it down until it's flat enough to fold it up and put it in my pocket to deal with later. "But we've been running the pitch week in and week out. I know we have it in us to go out there and show them why they call us Legends," I rally, confidence I don't feel ringing clear in my tone.

A riot of gruff cheering echoes around me, banging against my skull as the guys start bouncing on the balls of their feet in anticipation. I stay firmly planted on my feet, fearing any excess movement too early when my nerves are as jumbled as they are may cause the sandwich I had for lunch to come back up uninvited.

Within moments, the team is being announced, and I'm leading them through a fog of smoke out onto the pitch.

The sound of the crowd is deafening, so loud that I feel the vibration surging from the stands and pulsing along the grass as it crawls up my legs, wrapping around my throat.

Don't look up. Don't look up. Don't look up.

But the impulse is too strong, and my eyes stray to the

packed stadium seats. Everyone is faceless, just a mass of people with no distinguishable features, my mind conjuring them up of its own volition. Each person casts a judgemental look in my direction, skepticism set into every groove of their face while anger lines their brows and beer sloshes out of the cup they're white knuckling. Contorted faces scream without the need for words, but I hear their voiceless cries; *you don't belong here anymore.*

The pressure in my head increases tenfold.

Our starters head out onto the pitch and get in their positions. I walk toward the center line to meet the referee and the opposing team's captain for the coin toss that will decide who gets possession of the ball first.

Stepping up to the center line, I shake the referee's hand as the opposing team's captain, Bron Stamwell of the Norwich Lions, steps up and does the same before toeing up to me.

"Plan on choking? Would really help me out if you did," he says haughtily.

"Funny, that. Said the same thing to your mum last night."

He takes a step forward before the ref interjects with a hand to Bron's chest. "Save it for the match, gentlemen." He looks at me, pulling a coin from his pocket. "Home stadium calls the side. What'll it be, Stone?"

Logically, I know there's a fifty-fifty chance of this going my way, but I still feel an immense pressure to choose correctly, almost as if this toss will set the tone for the whole season.

"Heads."

He flicks the coin into the air, and it flips end over end in time with my stomach before it falls to the ground…tails side up.

"Tails—" he indicates toward Bron with an open palm — "ball is in favor of the Lions. Stamwell, choose your move."

Smugness is smeared all over Brom's face, and as I turn

to walk toward my position on the field, I can't help feeling like the coin toss won't be the last loss of the night.

We're down by seventeen points, and there's only ten minutes left of the second half. Translation—we're fucked.

I'm running down the pitch towards the defence's goal post, boots pressing into the springy grass and propelling me forward. Cavan currently has possession of the ball but is being double teamed by several of the Lion's players.

"Darcey!" I shout, grabbing his attention, but the second the defence realises my intention for him to pass me the ball, I suddenly have an additional two players on my tail. Fuck, I shouldn't have called out to him. He would've got me the ball, but instead, I opened my mouth and cost us the advantage. As we get closer to the goal post, we've got one shot to score this try and bring the game at least a little closer in score.

I make a last minute decision to fall back and loop behind Cavan, dropping out of the hold of two players from Norwich trying to cover me. It leaves me slightly more open than I was previously, and Cav throws me the ball just before he's tackled around the calves.

Taking off like a light, I sprint for the try line, sensing a player coming at me from the right. I dodge swiftly, not anticipating the man coming up on my blindside to the left just as he tackles me. Pain radiates through my body as my knees hit the ground, grass and dirt scraping against my skin, pulling my shorts up.

But the ball is still in my hand, and I'm only three metres or so from the line now. If I can get out from under the behemoth on top of me, there's still a chance to score and bring this match just a little closer to even footing. No sooner do I have the thought does another player from the Lions join the fray, and a maul forms with me at the center. Bodies pile on top of me as hands reach from around and in between limbs to grapple for possession of the ball.

A familiar pair of arms coated in dark blond hair appear through the fray, and I take the opportunity to relinquish my vice grip to slip the ball to Myles. Before he can grab it, Norwich's scrum half throws himself into the melee, stealing it and running in the opposite direction.

I curse loudly, jumping to my feet as half the team gives chase, sprinting into action. I'm close on his heels, about to tackle him at the waist, when he drop kicks the ball to a teammate on the opposite side of the field.

Possession of the ball is tossed around from team to team, a push and pull of defence and offence, pinging back and forth like a pinball machine.

I'm bouncing on the balls of my feet, waiting to make a move, when a voice calls out to me. "I thought you would have improved after the break, Stone. You know, once all the media coverage calmed down, that was *well* embarrassing. I'm surprised they're keeping you around, with all the bad moves you've been making."

"Shut it, Toller," Cavan quickly defends from a few paces away.

"Can't even fight your own battles? Gotta sic your oversized mutt on me?"

Cavan tuts. "Scared of my size? I'm flattered."

They bicker back and forth, but all I hear are my own fears perceived by someone else. Does that make them more true? Clearly, I'm not the only one thinking them, and if Toller is, everyone else must be too.

The world goes in and out of focus as panic and self-consciousness war for my attention. My mind whirls and my stomach dips. I can hear voices shouting, the crowd, my teammates—I don't know. But the sound grows in volume, as does the rushing in my head.

"Stone!"

My ears feel stuffed with cotton wool.

"Tieran!" I snap back into reality, the pitch coming into

laser focus as a dozen men in varying jerseys barrel towards me.

My place on the field puts me in the closest proximity to the try line, and I look over to see Ekon readying to lob the ball in my direction. I catch it in time and rush forward, desperate to get this goal for the team, to prove to everyone I'm not out just yet. I can save this—I have to. The country is watching. Dad is watching. *She's* watching.

Bron is hot on my heels, shouting anything he can think of to tear me down.

Miracle you haven't been subbed by now.

You'll be out of a job by the end of the season.

And then, he goes in for the kill. *No wonder Olivia slagged you off for that bloke on Newcastle.*

The reminder of my ex's infidelity, that I wasn't enough to keep her happy and the entire world knows it, almost makes me trip, but I push harder, knowing my men are doing what they can to keep Newcastle from getting to me.

I'm within two metres of the try line, and I can practically taste the grass on the other side of that white zone marker. If I can get us this goal, maybe I can prove I'm worth giving another shot.

One metre away, and I dive for the line, extending my arm and the hand holding the ball as far as it will go—right as Stamwell clamps onto my calves, dragging me back. We hit the ground with a resounding thud that echoes throughout my body, sending pain splintering up my torso, the ball never leaving my hand.

But when I look up, it's to find it two inches away from the in-goal, and no time left on the clock.

I failed.

Stamwell lifts himself off me, jogging backward as he salutes. Sitting up, I rest my arms on my knees for a moment before Cav helps me up and claps his hand on my shoulder in solidarity.

"It's alright; it's just the first match." He's always so

level headed; nothing fazes him, and I envy his ability to self-regulate his nervous system.

I walk off the pitch, toward the tunnel and all the post-game interviews I'm about to endure, and the people who were once faceless now burst into crystal clear view. A mix of anger and disappointment lines each and every one of their faces as they watch me walk past, shame making it unbearable to look any of them in the eyes.

An hour later, after soul crushing press *interrogations* and a debrief from Ballard, I'm standing in the showers, letting scalding hot water beat down my back and give me second degree burns. Absent-mindedly, I note that the pressure coming out of the pipes has significantly improved—Jade's doing, if I had to guess. She's left no stone unturned.

"You coming to the pub, Cap?"

I glance back to see a couple of the younger guys gathered, all dressed for a night out. Envy roils through me, hotter than the water pelting down on me at their ability to shake off the night's loss so easily.

"Nah, I gotta get home." They almost look disappointed, though I can't imagine why after our defeat. I quickly add, "Next time, though." I wouldn't next time either. I'm not good company after a loss, last year proved that.

After I finish washing up and change into fresh clothes, I head out of the locker room and toward the staff car park. But I never make it there. Of their own accord, my legs carry me until I find myself back on the center of the pitch. The stadium lights are blindingly bright, a stark contrast against the empty, quiet stands. Despite the lack of noise around me, all I can hear is the collective disappointment that ran through the crowd sitting in these seats when the final whistle was blown.

My heart races, my head spins, my knees bend until I plop down in the middle of the field as the night grows darker by the minute, trying and failing to calm my racing mind. I drop my head between my legs.

Deep breath in. Deep breath out. Deep breath in. Deep breath out.

"You know you won't get overtime pay for moping on the pitch after hours." I nearly jump out of my skin, having not heard her walk up.

"It's alarming, how quiet you are," I grumble.

"My father taught me to never let them see you coming."

I huff, plucking blades of grass out of the turf, thinking she's succeeded, because I've never once seen her coming. Well—*no, not going there.*

Subtly looking her over, I take in her game day outfit of beige plaid dress trousers accented with a sleek belt and a white button down. She has simple gold hoops looped through her ears and black stilettos dangling from her hands. That shocking realisation causes me to look down at her bare feet, painted a delicate robin's egg blue. It's oddly endearing, that little spot of colour when she only ever wears neutrals, as if that's the only spot on her body where she allows herself to let loose—somewhere no one will see.

The juxtaposition of that fact makes something in my chest tighten.

"What are you doing out here, Tieran?" she asks, not gently—never gently with her.

"I don't know, to be honest. Just sort of wound up here." It's not a lie but it's not the full truth either.

"Do you want to tell me what's wrong?"

"Other than the global warming crisis?" Jade levels me with a glare, and a frown marring her full lovely mouth. I paste on a smile, glancing up at where she's standing above me.

"I can't help if you won't be honest with me. How can I make this team a success—*you*, a success—if I don't know the issue?"

"Are you always this serious? I'm concerned for your blood pressure, boss." My smile grows wider, and I lean back on the palms of my hands. Her gaze flits down to my mouth briefly, brow furrowing, before it shifts and settles on a spot off to the side of it.

She looks me square in the eyes, that spot of blue surrounded by deep topaz holding me in its snare. "The loss wasn't your fault. It was the first game back; it could have been anyone's match. We'll review the footage and adjust our strategies accordingly."

Maybe she's right, but my brain can't catch up to what she's saying, and I don't like that she's reading me so easily. All I do is nod in response.

"You really won't talk to me?"

"I'll talk to you about what *I* want to talk to you about," I say, wanting the topic to be off me and my failures.

"And what's that?" She crosses her arms over her chest, and I try my best to keep my gaze from wandering to the open neckline of her blouse.

I lift a brow and suck my lower lip between my teeth in answer.

"No."

Back to one word answers, I see.

"Because we can't talk about what never happened, right?" I hold her stare in challenge.

"Right."

I sit upright, and my hand falls so my finger grazes her foot. She jolts at the infinitesimal touch as if on fire, before she steps back. "Well, if you decide to pull your head out of your ass long enough to talk to me about what's bothering you, I have an open door." She turns to walk away.

"That sounded like an HR violation," I call after her.

"Then call them and complain." She shoots over her shoulder. I don't think I'm imagining the slight curve at the corners of her mouth.

As she walks away, I allow myself to look my fill, imagining the extra sway in her hips is for my benefit. And for the first time since I stepped into Knightsbridge today, the small smile on my face isn't forced.

8

JADE

THE LAST FEW days have passed by in a blur of waking up early to shoot, mornings at Knightsbridge, lunches spent with a realtor looking at storefronts because Jaded's investors want a brick and mortar where I'm based, and evenings spent at the stadium making calls to local vendors and contractors. But the work still isn't done, because once I'm home, all that awaits me is more work and more responsibilities. I'm practically glued to my phone, a thrall to the almighty Zoom.

Maxine had several choice words for me on our last debrief, not hesitating to inform me how much I've slacked off in the few weeks since I moved here.

I was loath to admit it, but she wasn't wrong. It's been a lot harder to juggle than I thought it would be. Being present one hundred percent in every aspect of my life is no easy feat. There's nowhere I can let the ball drop, and wearing multiple hats between two continents is already starting to wear me down. And the constant pressure to keep up with my social media felt frivolous in the face of everything else I handle on a daily basis. The one place I've allowed myself to lag is online. I didn't think it would be noticeable, that is until Maxine happily informed me that my analytics were dropping. I know I have to post consistently—create approachable, fresh media for people to consume just to stay relevant enough for them to care about me and my *influence*—I'm starting to detest that word—enough to want to shop my brands. But I'm not sure I'm entirely likable.

Successful? Yes. Smart? Yes. But likable?

It's a hard thing to believe when everyone who's ever been moderately close to you would say otherwise. Brendan always said I was cold—*hard to love*, I believe he said during a particularly rough patch.

"All you care about is work, Jade!"

"What else is there to care about?" I volley. Brendan's head rears back as if I've struck him. "I didn't mean it like that," I try to correct myself. It's not all I care about, but it is my whole world, I don't know how to make room for anything else.

"Yes, you did." He shakes his head, dipping it low. "I used to try to convince myself it didn't matter. Our relationship started off unconventional, but we made the best of it. Our sex life was good, so I thought I shouldn't complain. But lately, I feel like I'm talking to a robot. You're not an easy person to love, Jade. Take away your beauty and your success, and what are you left with?"

No, I don't think I'm likable. How could others like me when I'm not even sure I do?

They like the fabricated *idea* of me, covet the lifestyle I exude, but what else do I offer the world outside of an aesthetic? Outside of a *lie*. And it *is* all a lie, because at the end of the day, I come home, and the one thing I know will be waiting for me when I step through the door is my career and mountains of paperwork.

Sometimes, I wish I could ignore it all, just shut off my brain and not think about it ever again. Even a day would be a relief. But I don't know my life without a two ton workload.

Could I even relinquish control for that long? The reason I'm so swamped all the time is because I refuse to not have my hand in every single pot. Type A, perfectionist, workaholic—call it whatever you want, but I won't put my name on something I'm not proud of, that I didn't understand every facet of in some way.

Which meant long days of statistical analysis, financial reporting, creative directing, design, on top of being the face of every branch of the brand. I alone drove fifty percent of the businesses' sales. All of that was already a massive workload, so incorporating the responsibilities I had for The Legends into the fold was borderline insane enough to earn me a shopping trip for a straightjacket. Maxine would probably try to get it sponsored.

But I didn't regret moving here. I relish the challenge the team brings me, the stretch to my cognitive abilities doing something so different allowed, the change of scenery London brings, and being close to my dad. I wouldn't trade any of it for a lighter workload.

I wouldn't even change it for a flat that came in pristine condition, because the former disaster of a home I was walking into was now near spotless. The cockroaches have been evicted, the walls have been washed and repainted, and as of today, the old musty carpet is gone and replaced with wood floors. Thankfully, I convinced the landlord to let me upgrade the space at my own cost.

"Darling, thank goodness you're home. This nefarious gentleman was trying to get me to abscond with him to the countryside and steal all your best silverware." Aanya puts on a theatrical accent and throws her arm around me. "But I told him, I shan't leave my lady love—*that's you*—so turn that frown upside down." She pokes her fingers into the corner of my mouth and pushes up.

I glance over at the man installing the last bit of pop-and-lock floorboards.

"She's been at this all day, creatin' these fake scenarios in 'er head. I can't keep up anymore," he says, voice somewhere between confusion and charmed.

"She's quite creative," I reply.

"You'll be thankful for these memories one day when

my name's in lights, Colin!" Aanya floats into the kitchen as Colin packs up his supplies.

"You'll mail me the final invoice?"

"Aanya already took care of it, miss." I whip my head around to find her pouring two generous glasses of wine as Colin slips out of the flat.

She looks at me guiltily. "Don't give me that look. You gave me your bank details for a reason. Very foolish, though; I could have been a con-artist and swindled you for everything you've got."

I laugh. "I'm going to miss having you as my assistant."

"Lucky for you, I live just across the hall, and you won't be getting rid of me easily. You buy the good wine, not the cheap shite I buy."

I take in my flat, now mostly furnished, clean and smelling softly of vanilla and bergamot. The personal touches would come slowly as I found things I truly loved to decorate the space—to make it feel like home—but for now, the simplicity would do. Even without it, it feels more like home than my place in LA ever did. The space here is small, but that's what I love about it. It's cozy, warm, and intimate, with charming crown molding and just enough space for me but not so much space that I feel the emptiness closing in around me.

Shifting into the kitchen and pulling a glass out of Aanya's hand, I down it in one large gulp. When I look up, she is staring at me, mouth agape.

"You alright? Did something happen while you were out filming today?"

Last week, during one of her forced girls' nights, I finally told her about my less conventional job while only slightly inebriated. To my utter dismay, she didn't care. I had been so worried she would judge me for it, like so many others had in the past. But she shrugged, said *"wicked"* and continued slurping up the pasta she was eating. It felt like a hundred pound weight lifted off my shoulders, and I had to excuse myself to the bathroom so she wouldn't notice me getting emotional over it.

I stifle a burp, pressing a hand against my mouth. "Fine," I say, pushing my glass toward her for a refill.

She pours me another, and I take a more modest sip. "Really, I'm okay. Just a little concerned for one of our players."

"Did he get injured?"

"No, nothing like that. It's… I don't know, I think he's having an identity crisis of sorts." I move around the kitchen, gathering a few things to make us a simple dinner.

"Sounds like something the coach should handle. Don't you have bigger things to deal with?"

Yes. I do. But I can't shake the image of Tieran sitting alone on the pitch after everyone left, or that moment during the game when it looked like he was somewhere else entirely.

"Probably. It was odd. At the match earlier this week, it's like I could see this shift in his demeanor happen mid-play. The Legends were down, but they were hustling to get another try, and there was a moment where he just…froze."

"Maybe he was just having an off day?" Aanya offers.

"I think it's more than that. It's like a switch flipped, and he wasn't on the field anymore, but somewhere else." I put a pot on the stove to boil pasta and start seasoning shrimp.

"You must have been looking very closely to notice all that." The tone of her voice is curious, questioning, and it almost seems like she's suggesting something.

"It's my job to pay attention." Heat creeps up and settles on my cheeks.

Aanya prowls over to me and clasps my face in her hands, looking me over. "Why are you blushing?"

I wrestle away from her hold. "Too much wine."

"Jade." I look away—plausible deniability. "Do you have a *crush* on this player?"

"No." Sparkling white teeth framed by dimples flash through my mind's eye, entirely unwelcome.

"I mean, it would make sense. You're hot as fuck—even with the whole intense thing you've got going on—and there's obviously a certain appeal to rugby players. I mean, the thighs alone…"

You have no idea.

"And you're around them all the time, so it's only natural to develop a crush."

"I don't get crushes…" I leave the statement hanging in the air.

"But?"

I deliberate. On one hand, it would be nice to tell someone about this, but on the other hand, even speaking it aloud instead of internalizing it might invite unwelcome thoughts. I heave out a loud sigh; I guess I'm committing to this. "But I might have, accidentally, hooked up with one of them before I knew who he was."

She starts choking on her wine, spluttering red liquid out onto the counter. "Come again?"

"Please don't make me repeat myself," I groan, dropping my head into my hands.

Aanya grabs the pinot, taking a swig directly from the bottle before passing it to me. "Tell me every sordid detail."

Bringing the bottle's neck to my mouth, I tip it back and take a deep pull. The drink coats my tongue and imbues me with courage to finally say this out loud. I start from the beginning, when I first saw the disaster flat and how it had me seeking out the pub, then on to the creep at the bar, before I finish with blue eyes searing into mine through a mirror in a single stall bathroom, leaving out the depraved details currently running through my mind like a river.

"Wow. Only in London for a couple hours, and you got laid. Well done." She claps, and I roll my eyes.

"I wasted no time. Had to sample the local fare," I deadpan.

Aanya snorts. "Did you just make a joke?"

"Apparently, there's something in the English air that's making me do all sorts of unusual things." I return to the hob and take the boiling noodles off the eye, draining the water into the sink.

"Mmmm," she muses. "I think it's good for you."

"Ah, yes, breaking workplace ethics within hours of me being here is sure to get me *Employer of the Year*."

Grabbing a sauté pan out of the cabinet, I set it on the stove and throw the seasoned shrimp in to cook.

"Which player was it?"

I ignore her, not turning around as I push the crustaceans around in the pan. "Hmmm?"

"Jade, who was it?"

I choke out his name in a hybrid mumble cough.

"What was that?"

I repeat my answer in the same fashion.

"I'm going to swat you with a spatula if you don't fess up in a way I can understand," she laughs.

"Tieran Stone."

She blinks slowly before the squealing begins. "Fuck off! You bagged the captain of the Legends in a pub loo? I'm impressed, though not surprised, since you're basically temptation on long legs. But he is—" She whistles, and I start banging my head against the cabinets on the wall.

"How was it?"

"I'm not answering that." I spear her with a reprimanding look.

"That good, huh?" She chuckles. "At least tell me how big it was." She grabs hold of the near empty wine bottle, holding it up. "Tell me when to stop." As she runs her hand along the glass horizontally, her eyes get wider the longer I remain silent. "Seriously? Jesus, girl, how are you still walking?"

"Aanya," I lob a dish towel at her.

She ducks out of the way, adopting a pout. "Fine. Don't let a girl live vicariously."

"From what I've seen, you don't seem to have issues in

that department," I point out, reminding her that I live across the hall and have seen the men and women coming and going from her flat.

"Yeah, but they aren't rugby players. From what I've seen, he's got quite the reputation." I've seen those same articles, but I'm having a hard time reconciling the man I met in the pub—the man who looked so vulnerable sitting on the grass of an empty pitch—with who the tabloids say he is. "Are you still seeing him?"

I shake my head but can't meet her eyes. "It was a one off. I didn't recognize him from his roster photo because he had long hair and a beard. It won't be happening again." I plate up our dinner, careful to keep the presentation pristine and snapping some shots to post to my stories before handing her the Tuscan shrimp pasta I threw together.

"That feels like a crime. You said you had a connection that night at the pub, that even while you were talking the chemistry was electric. Can you really just let that go?"

"It's non-negotiable. I'm his boss, and it's inappropriate." I take a bite of my pasta, nearly groaning as the flavor bursts across my tongue.

"Doesn't that just make it hotter?"

I point my fork at her threateningly. "I'm going to kick you out and change the locks if you don't stop pointing out the obvious flaws in my logic."

"Fine. I'll drop it *for now*." She holds up a noodle-wrapped fork in surrender.

I guess it's all I can really ask for. I haven't known Aanya long, but in the short amount of time I've come to know her, I've realized she's someone who's fiercely loyal and who will bend over backward to make sure the people she cares for are taken care of. If she's pushing me in one direction— even if that direction is one I can't go—it's only because she cares about me. And after a lifetime of not really knowing the feeling of friendship with another woman that wasn't rooted in some fucked up sort of competition, it feels nice.

The nights she burst into my apartment using the key

she had made for *'emergencies'* are what I always dreamt of when I would long for the feeling of girlhood. Aanya is the closest I've ever come to having a best friend, and even still, there's a lingering fear that her friendship came too easy, that there couldn't possibly be no strings attached, and any day now, the red bottom is bound to drop.

The fear is hard to shake, but I didn't want these nights to ever end. It's the only socialization I get, after all, stolen moments with a neighbor during the thirty minutes I take to eat. It's this and visiting Dad… At twenty-seven, that fact rings a little sad.

Aanya is scarfing down the last of her pasta when she jumps up. "Alright, get dressed. We're going out!"

"I can't. I still have so much work to do," I say with regret.

"Too bad. It's Friday, you need to have a fun night out, and I'm playing a gig. Maybe you'll meet a footballer this time, shag him in the loo too, make it a ritual."

I choke on a laugh. "I'm sorry. I really have a million things to do."

She settles her hands on her hips. "Alright, I'm doing it. I'm pulling the *'I saved your arse and you owe me'* card. Now, go get changed; something sexy, because I'm not taking no for an answer, and I really want you there."

The genuine pleading look in her rich brown eyes does me in. "Fine. But only if you dedicate a song to me."

The smile that brightens her face warms me more than the full bottle of wine we demolished, and I think to myself that seeing her happy, this person who forced me under her wing, was worth the late night of work I'll have to do once I'm back home.

9

TIERAN

"DON'T LOOK, but the most beautiful woman I've ever seen just walked in," Myles says with hearts popping out of his eyes. "Actually, maybe hide under the table or something. I don't want her to notice you instead of me." He starts pressing on my shoulders, trying to shove me under the high top we're sitting at.

"You're an idiot," I laugh.

"I'm just making sure the odds are in my favor here. Your supernatural blue eyes tend to steal focus. I don't need my future wife seeing you before me."

It's a ridiculous sentiment, because Myles, like many professional athletes, is a walking Men's Health magazine— tall and built like the rugby player, lightly golden skin, with dark blonde hair and moss green eyes that make women trip over themselves.

Plus, he's worried for nothing, because my mind is still stuck on the woman I met the last time I was in this pub, still stuck on baby blue toenails, honey eyes and her razor sharp mouth.

"Don't worry, mate. I have no intention of dating at the moment." Not unless a certain brunette decides to admit to a particular tryst in this very pub. Otherwise, I'm good.

"I thought you were over Olivia?" He sips on his pint,

but his eyes don't stray from the woman who walked in for long.

"Oh, trust me, I am."

When I found out my girlfriend of a year was cheating on me via the world's stage—also known as The Daily Mail —I didn't believe it. The infamous gossip rag was notorious for publishing utter bollocks and couldn't be trusted. Olivia and I were solid; we had a holiday booked to Ibiza set for after the end of the season, and I was thinking about introducing her to my parents, despite her reluctance to meet them. There was no indication she was unhappy, that I wasn't giving her what she needed.

In my mind, it was all a lie and not something I needed to be worried about. The fact that I couldn't catch her on her mobile that day was merely a coincidence. Then, I was on the pitch with possession of the ball when Oliver Hughes, the man supposedly having an affair with my girlfriend, tackled me to the ground and said, *"I'm going to take this game, just like I took your girl—hard and easy."*

My stomach dropped, but my heart still couldn't believe it. How could it, when just two days before, she had been in my arms in bed, smiling up at me as she told me she loved me? But I had no choice when, at the end of the match— after we lost, because I couldn't focus—Olivia ran out onto the pitch in Newcastle colours and jumped straight into Oliver's arms.

By the next day, The Daily Mail had a new headline: 'Legends Fly-Half Hung Out to Dry', accompanied by a photo of me pissed out of my mind and slumped against the back wall of a pub. Every day of the week, there was a different news story.

Tieran Stone: A Cautionary Tale on Shooting for the Moon and Falling on Your Face.

Stone's Over Olivia! Legends Captain Seen with a Different Woman Every Night.

Scrum on the Streets: Tieran Stone Starts a Brawl After Another Match Lost.

It was a really bad time in my life. I felt like shite from drinking too much, I was underperforming at work, and I was heartbroken. I thought we had been building something. It wasn't perfect, but on paper, we worked—until she torched it. I grappled with trying to understand why. What did I do? The internet had its theories, and while it felt like my life was disintegrating around me, the world weighed in, and I didn't cope well. Rigorous practices during the day bled into drinking heavily at night, making choices I'd regret the next morning. It wasn't until Coach Ballard threatened to kick me off the team that I pulled my head out of my ass. Still, the blow to my confidence left me feeling like I couldn't trust my own instincts long after I got my act together, and it bled into every aspect of my life.

Suddenly, I was unsure about everything. If I couldn't even see signs Olivia was unfulfilled, what else was I missing? Was I a bad captain too? Did I support my parents enough? Did my friends really like me, or were we just mates because we were on the team together? How much would the fans hate me if I wasn't playing at the top of my game every match and bringing home wins? Overnight, everything felt like it was slipping through my fingers, creating a vat of quicksand at my feet that I was starting to drown in.

I *am* over the bullshit with Olivia. There's no part of me that misses, or longs for her. If anything, the distance gave me perspective. I just wish it hadn't played out so publicly, because even though I've moved on, the media is still hellbent on never letting me forget.

"I just need to stay focused on the game, you know? Get us back on track without any distractions," I add on.

"Fuck me, she's stunning. I'm going to talk to her before the night is over," Myles says, oblivious to the fact that I'm still talking.

My eyes scan the crowd as I sip my beer, trailing over to the bar so I can finally see who his future wife is.

"There she is." He points over to the end of the bar

closest to the door, where a woman stands, wearing a fitted black dress with a plunging neckline, strappy black stilettos, and eyes that make my whole body tighten.

"Jade?"

"Who?"

I point. "Miss McKallen. That's who you're talking about?"

His face clouds with confusion before his whole countenance shifts to something gleeful. "Oh, this is perfect. Jade!" he yells out.

"What are you doing?" I hiss.

"I just found an in, my friend. See the absolute goddess standing to the right of our boss?" I shift my eyes over and notice for the first time that another woman is even there. Next to Jade is a beautiful woman with deep tanned skin, sultry eyes, and dark hair that fades into a warm ginger. She's lovely, to be sure, but my eyes quickly find their way back to ones of burning topaz with a flame of blue.

Myles calls out Jade's name again, and this time, she hears him over the sounds of the pub and looks toward where we're sitting—only steps from where we first met. It's curious that she would come back here, of all places, when she's been so determined to act like our night together never happened.

Her eyes widen in recognition that melts into horror as her friend's eyes jump back and forth between us all, lingering on Myles a little longer than necessary. An argument of sorts seems to be happening between the two women before her friend grabs her bare arm and yanks her toward us.

My greedy eyes rove all over her body; she looks like sin incarnate in that dress, with her dark hair unbound, falling loosely in waves around her face and down her back. Her kohl rimmed eyes zero in on me, and a scowl mars her face at my obvious perusal.

Bringing the pint glass up to my mouth, I smirk into the

rim and see her back straighten a little more before they stop before our table.

Tension builds as the silence grows, no one making a move to say anything. My stare never leaves Jade's face, and, judging by the way she's ignoring my gaze, I'd guess she's trying very hard to not think about the last time we were in this pub together.

"Hey, boss. *Come* here often?" I suppress a smile at her answering glare.

Jade's eyes narrow as the tantalizing spot of blue burns like fire, promising hell for daring to remind her. "Once. Didn't enjoy it much, though."

The insult doesn't sting the way she intends. *This* is the Jade I met all those weeks ago, giving as good as she gets—confident, brilliant, absolutely stunning. Her stare is severe, but there's an undercurrent between us that softens it around the edges, making it playful.

When I first laid eyes on her that night across the pub, I thought she was a mirage pulled straight out of my deepest fantasies. Piercing eyes, soft, full mouth wrapped around the rim of her martini, and a body that made every part of me ache. Then, she started laying into the drunk next to her, and I was a goner. I needed to talk to her, know her.

"We'll have to change that then," I say back.

Her friend's eyes zip between the two of us as we hold each other's stare; Myles never looks away from her, completely taken despite her not having said a word.

Reaching my hand out but keeping my focus on Jade, I introduce myself to her friend. "Hi, I'm Tieran. This is Myles." I finally look at her and then nod my head in his direction.

Her friend turns to greet mine, grasping his palm in hers, her breath catching. "Hi," she stutters out.

"Hey…" His voice trails off in question.

"Aanya," she supplies.

"Beautiful," he whispers, and she flushes scarlet.

They're still holding hands, and now it's our eyes

pinging back and forth between our two friends. If love at first sight exists, I'd say I'm witnessing it right now.

"I'm going to go get a drink. Aanya, do you want to come?" Jade says, trying to break the trance they seem to be in.

"Nope. But I'll take a Negroni." She sits in the empty seat next to Myles, leaning against the table.

Jade snorts and turns on her heels to walk back toward the bar. I watch as her hips sway in the tiny dress clinging to the curve of her arse, hypnotizing me into standing and trailing after her.

When she gets to the bar, she wheedles her way through a crowd of people, fighting for a spot at the front. At least five different men are leering at her, some of them working to press in closer, before I walk up, shoving them away with a push of my hand and settling in behind her, too close to be casual.

I lean into her ear. "You're about to incite a brawl, Hellfire." Gooseflesh dances across the skin around her neck.

"Alert the media," she drawls sarcastically. "Men always do stupid things when they think with their dicks instead of their brains."

I laugh, and my breath coasts across her skin, making her fidget in place.

The barkeep is frantically flying back and forth, oscillating between taking orders, making drinks, and cashing people out. It's going to be impossible to get their attention with all these people around.

Or so I thought, because not a minute later, she leans forward just as the man handling the bar is walking by, gives him a friendly smile that strikes me a little dumb from a side view, and he stops dead in his tracks, walking over to her.

"What do ya need, gorgeous?" He throws the towel he uses to wipe down the bar over his shoulder.

"Can I please get a Negroni and a Mojito," she orders

before glancing back at me. "Did you or Myles want another?"

The man tending the bar doesn't pull his eyes off her, resolutely ignoring everyone trying to get his attention. I can't even blame him; she's all I can look at too. But right now, she's looking at me, and I feel like a lucky bastard for it.

"Another Fuller's and an Old Fashioned." I set forty quid down on the bar top. "Thanks, mate."

He's still looking at Jade, and I have to resist the urge to wrap my arm around her waist and pull her into me, a move that would surely earn me a jab to my solar plexus. Tonight is the closest she's even come to acknowledging our tryst; no way in hell she'd react well to me touching her. I wouldn't do that without some sort of sign from her that it's what she wants, no matter how much my fingers are itching to reach out and stroke her silk-covered hip.

He shifts away to make our drinks, and Jade turns in place to face me, leaning lightly against the bar, the movement making the scent of warm vanilla with a hint of bourbon drift over, and my head goes light and my cock stirs from the memory of the last time she was this close.

The King's Swan is getting progressively busier as the night wears on and the hour creeps closer to the live entertainment starting. The crowd is bustling, pushing at my back as I hold my place to make sure Jade has room.

"You following me then?"

She raises a perfectly arched brow at me. "Excuse me?"

I list off on my fingers. "First the pub, then the team, then the market, and now back to the pub. That's a lot of coincidences."

"One could argue *you're* following *me*."

"I would follow you," my voice pitches lower. "On hands and knees if you told me to." I stare down at her, knowing I've said too much but unable to take it back now that the words are out there.

"Don't."

Her eyes blaze—in anger or arousal, I don't know, but the skin on her neck flushes pink, begging for my mouth.

The group behind me is getting raucous, and someone's body collides with mine, pushing me toward Jade, forcing me to catch my arms on the ledge of the bar and caging her in with my body flush against hers.

I look down to where her hands have landed on my waist over my black jumper, helping to keep me steady. Her gaze flicks up under inky dark lashes, and it's got me imagining a whole lot of scenarios one shouldn't imagine in relation to their boss.

I'm about to say something, break the tension or add to it, when the barkeep pops up with our drinks. Jade turns, grabbing two and passing them to me to carry before grabbing the other two.

"This might be forward of me, but could I get your number?" the bartender asks.

She gives him a shy smile while I glower at him over her head. "That's really kind of you, but I don't have much time in my schedule for dating right now."

"We could keep it casual," he suggests, and I'm about to snap the glasses in my hands.

"She said—" I go to interrupt, but she stomps on my foot with her stiletto, and I bend slightly at the waist in pain.

"Thank you, but no." She turns away from him and pushes me in the direction of our table. When she sees I'm hunched slightly, her brow furrows. "What's wrong with you? Go."

"How rude of me and my foot injury to keep you from a hasty getaway."

"Do I need to have a whistle and clipboard in hand, shouting expletives, to get you to move?" She rolls her eyes, nudging me again.

"It wouldn't hurt," I grumble and start to walk back toward the table.

A throaty chuckle floats over to me, the sound light and

a little raspy around the edges. A shiver slithers up my back; it makes no sense, but I feel like I've won something with that laugh.

* * * *

Twenty minutes later, Aanya hops off her stool at our high top table and announces it's time for her set. Apparently, *she* is tonight's live entertainment.

My lovestruck best friend quickly stands after her. "I'm going to go watch."

"Me too—" Jade starts to say before Aanya stops her.

"No, no, you stay here. There's not a lot of room over there anyway." She points to the area by the modest stage, where every table is already filled with people. From the way her eyes jump from Jade to me, though, it's almost like she's trying to meddle.

"But—" Jade starts when Aanya spears her with a look before turning and walking away. "Fine," she mumbles. "It's not like she guilted me into coming out to specifically watch her play, but whatever."

"How did you guys meet?" I ask.

"She's my neighbor." She brings the straw of her mojito to her lips, and it's actually sick how the slight movement draws all my focus. "She also saved my ass, so I kinda owed her, which is the only reason I came out tonight."

"Why did you owe her?"

"My flat was a wreck when I moved into it, and she helped get it sorted out. Didn't know a thing about me, just helped because I needed it." It's clear from her tone, and the small smile on her face as she watches her friend take the stage that she holds a lot of affection for her.

"That's good to hear, since my best friend is a bit smitten," I say, nodding at where Myles stands behind the occupied tables in front of the small riser Aanya is standing on. He's as close to her as he can possibly get with the building crowd.

"Did you two meet on the Legends?"

I nod my head, taking a sip of my drink. "I was pretty terrified when I was recruited, and Myles…he just has this openness about him. He and Cav instantly put me at ease. Cavan's the steady, serious one in our group. We all balance each other."

The sound of a guitar lightly strumming flows through the pub, winding around tables and chairs, lifting the mood and setting the tone for the evening.

She looks contemplative. "And who are you of the group?"

"Isn't it obvious?" At least ten different answers to that question float across her face before I put her out of her misery. "I'm the devilishly handsome one."

She snorts. "Or the insufferable one."

"The comedic relief, one might say," I quip.

"No one's saying that."

"The one you go to for a good time."

"I doubt that," she says dryly.

"You have firsthand experience, love. I don't recall any complaints." I watch as a gorgeous flush crawls up her neck and settles on the tops of her cheekbones.

Coughing into her hand, she adjusts in her seat, as if she's trying to shake off my words. "And where is the third in your band of brothers?"

"With his daughter, Ophelia. It's his weekend." My chest fills with warmth when I think of my other best friend and his little girl. Ophelia is only three, and she's a spitfire who has stolen even the most grisly of hearts with a single sassy hip pop.

"That's nice." Fondness laces her tone, making me curious.

"Are you close to your parents?" It's risky, asking such a personal question, but something about this night mirroring the first time we met each other—before we knew who the other was and there were no expectations or restrictions to what we could or could not say—has me feeling reckless.

She hesitates long enough that I think I must have over stepped, but then she answers quietly, "To my dad, yes. He's probably my best friend and a big reason I moved here." There's an aura of love pulsing from her, and it softens all her sharp edges. But within a second, she seems to realise what she admitted—*who* she admitted it to—and straightens in her seat, clearing her throat and spearing me with a look.

Where anyone else would have looked away after being unintentionally vulnerable, she stares down the barrel of the gun and takes a step closer. And though she'd never back down, never ask for a reprieve, I give her one anyway.

I throw back the last of my Old Fashioned, savoring the burn as it slides down my throat. "So, what do you do for fun?"

"Pardon?"

"Fun. The thing humans do for personal enjoyment.

She rolls her eyes. "I work."

"That's not fun," I argue.

"Do you not find your job fun, *Mr. Stone*?" And we're back to formalities.

"I certainly do, *Miss McKallen*, but it is still work. It still comes with responsibilities and a lot of pressure. So while yes, I find rugby fun, it's not what helps me recharge. Maybe once upon a time, it did…" I trail off.

"I don't have time to unwind. I have multiple businesses, a rugby club to run, and a sic—" She halts what she was about to say. "I don't have time."

"We'll have to sort that out."

Jade rolls her eyes. "Do you have a habit of interjecting yourself where you aren't welcome?"

"Just with you, apparently."

It didn't sit well with me that all she ever did was work. The google search I did weeks ago told me she was only twenty-seven, just a year younger than me. It seemed a damn shame someone as young as her didn't have some sort of outlet. How did she express her emotions if she never had time to process them?

"I work hard, and I'm successful." As if that's all that matters, all she needs. Maybe she feels that way.

"But are you happy?"

She sips on the last of her mojito, staring me down with an expression I can't read before hopping off her stool.

"Where are you going?" I ask.

"Off to watch my friend perform. I've heard live music is *fun*."

The sound of her heels clicking against the floor is a drumbeat that accompanies Aanya's guitar and ethereal voice.

I pried too much, pushed too hard.

And every step she takes away from me feels like another nail in the coffin, sealing away whatever tentative friendship I thought we had been forming.

I can't figure out why that bothers me so much.

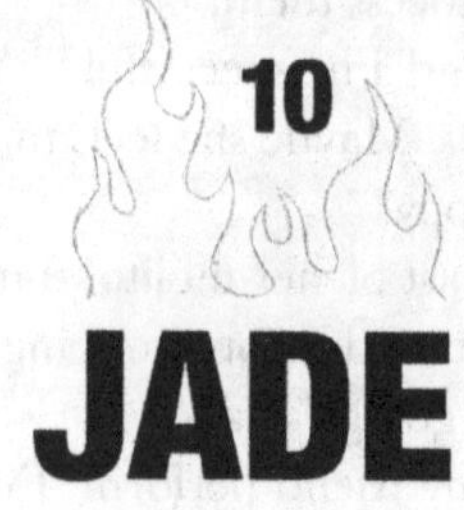

10

JADE

"YOU COULD PROBABLY TEACH your own class," my Pilates instructor, Poppy, says.

"I hope my equipment didn't get in the way or bother any of the other students." My breath comes out in short pants as sweat drips down every crevice of my body.

When Flex Appeal, a woman-owned Pilates studio a ten minute walk from my flat, reached out and asked if I wanted to partner with them on a video, it seemed like a no brainer. Pilates is my favorite method of working out, and I'd been wanting to find a local studio to become my go-to spot for early morning classes. Anything to help me shut off my racing brain for roughly forty minutes a few times a week.

"The opposite, actually! I think everyone was excited to have *Jade McKallen* in their class. We all grew up with you, you know? It's almost a bit surreal that you're here." Her face flushes the same shade of red as her hair. "God, was that super fangirly of me? I'm so embarrassed." Poppy drags a hand down her freckled face, cringing.

"Don't be ridiculous. I'm so happy you reached out. This is exactly the type of studio I wanted to find after moving here, and you saved me the stress of finding a studio I love. I hope you'll let me continue coming, but I don't want to cause any disruptions either." Today was pretty relaxed outside of a few girls asking me for pictures, but once people know I came here, it's likely to sky rocket in popularity. That's the name of the game in the age of influence—one person 'discovers' a product or a place, and suddenly, it's a feeding frenzy. Sometimes I hated that I contributed so heavily to the regress in society saying we weren't good enough if we didn't do, or have, what everyone else did.

It's all bullshit, and I built an empire off it.

I'm suddenly feeling sick to my stomach.

Maybe that's why I was so hellbent on buying a fucking sports team against the advice of every one of my financial advisors. Outside of loving rugby and reminders of early mornings with Dad, I craved something that felt more purposeful at this stage of my life, that challenged me in a way I hadn't encountered.

And fuck, if I didn't get my wish.

Poppy speaking breaks me out of my internal spiraling. "We'd love to have you. Hell, I'll even comp your membership. It seems only fair, since the exposure you'll provide the studio will be crackers."

I smile, even as my stomach sinks a little at her words. "That's so lovely of you, but I'd prefer to pay."

Confusion clouds her face. "Are you sure? I'd feel like I'm getting more out of this partnership than you."

"I'll tell you what." I towel off the last bit of sweat coating my face. "Why don't you run a giveaway with it instead? Give it to someone who might be interested in joining but doesn't have the space in their budget. I can sponsor it anonymously if it's too much for you to eat financially."

She looks at me contemplatively. "You know how sometimes you meet public figures in person, and they turn out to be total arseholes?" I hold my breath, hoping the next words out of her mouth are positive. "I'm chuffed that's not the case here. You're a class act, Jade McKallen."

I let out a relieved chuckle. "Let's get me signed up. I've got some work to get to soon."

"Surely not. It's Saturday!" She leads me toward the reception desk, handing me a tablet to fill out all my new member information while she goes over the terms and conditions.

Once I'm done, I stick my hand out in thanks, but Poppy swats it away, coming out from behind the counter to wrap me in a very sweaty hug. I don't mind it, though; it's actually kind of…nice.

I pull back, feeling a little awkward at the display of affection, adjust my matching active set, and set out in pursuit of coffee. A few years ago, when I really started leaning into a proper fitness routine, I created a sector of Jaded dedicated to activewear. The all black with white piping ensemble I have on today is one of my favorites.

As I step outside, I inhale deeply, absorbing the scent of the dampened pavement from a short summer rain, mixed with flowers from a shop next to the studio. It makes me feel calm, like the day is fresh and full of possibilities. I want to bottle it.

Maybe I could expand Jaded, add a fragrance sec—

No. I've got enough on my plate right now. But the brief flutter of excitement that ignited in my stomach when fresh inspiration hit me is a stark reminder of the days I loved my job. The thrill of a new idea, the planning and execution, seeing the final result—all of it invigorated me. When did I lose that feeling?

A cool breeze curls around my bare skin as I pass rows of colorful shops, charming Georgian buildings, and a local market hawking everything from jewelry to fresh produce. I'm tempted to stop and meander, see what else could inspire me, but I don't have a lot of time before the meet and greet my management arranged at a small boutique that carries Jaded in Central London. I'd have to go on another day, when I had more free time—*if* I ever have more free time. For now, I'll settle for a coffee before running home to get ready.

Flick the Bean, a cafe that specializes in locally roasted coffee and fresh pastries, is another women-owned business in the area. The bright teal shopfront boasts a large front window with their logo embossed in multi-colored lettering circled around a vertical coffee bean. It definitely looks like—never mind. I just hope their espresso is as strong as their branding.

I step inside, get in the queue that's already formed and pull out my phone, checking my emails to make sure I haven't missed anything urgent in the last hour that needs my attention.

The display board above the counter illustrates drinks named after iconic women in history, and it solidifies my choice to come here. 'The Dolly' is described as a *full-bodied* roast paired with a made-in-house apple pie syrup and topped with whipped cream. It's a coma in a cup, and I can't wait to indulge a little.

After ordering, I'm standing off to the side with everyone else waiting for their drinks when my phone rings. I don't recognize the number, so I screen the call, opting to enjoy my solitude a little longer. It won't hurt anyone if I steal another few moments to myself.

But my phone rings again. And again.

On the fourth ring, I step outside and answer.

"Hello?" I say into the mouthpiece.

"Is this Jade?" The voice on the other line sounds frantic, and it instantly sets me on edge, making my heart rate kick up like I was back in Pilates.

"Yes? Who is this?"

"Jade, this is Louis, your father's neighbor. Myrah gave me your number just in case anything happened while she was gone. Uhhh…" His voice trails off, like he's not sure what to say, and my panic is a full on stampede surging through my body.

"Is he okay, Louis? What happened?" I'm trying my

best not to yell into the phone at this nice man, but he is not speaking quickly enough.

"I was doing yard work, and I heard a loud clatter coming from your pa's. He wasn't answering the door, so I let myself in and found him on the kitchen floor. He's okay but seems to be in some discomfort and is refusing medical aid."

"Fuck." I grab my head and pace back and forth when I feel a presence walk up behind me. I choose to ignore it. Dad could be painfully stubborn when he wants to be. "Can you—I'm sorry, I know I don't know you, and this is a lot to ask, but could you stay with him for a few hours until I can get there?"

"I'm sorry, but I've got my niece's birthday party in an hour. I can stay till then, but I'll have to leave after that."

Shit. What am I going to do? I'm set to be on Oxford Street in just over an hour, meeting the very people who make my life possible. I can't cancel on them this last minute without pissing off my management. And just thinking about all the effort everyone went through to even host this event, it doesn't sit well with me. But I also can't leave my dad alone after an accident like that either. Myrah has the weekend off, and Dad insisted he would be fine alone for the weekend. Stupidly, I relented, figuring I would work from his home tomorrow, that surely, he'd be fine alone *one* day.

"Thank you, Louis. I'll figure something out within the hour."

I groan into my palm before I start smacking it against my head, hoping the jostling would shake loose a solution in my brain. Aanya is recording for her EP, so she's a no go, and I don't know anyone else. I have no one else.

A hand reaches out, grabbing my wrist and halting my assault. "Stop that. Your face is too lovely to bruise it."

The gravelly timbre of that voice makes my back straighten. I know who it is without looking up.

Tieran Stone is standing in front of me, tanned hand

lightly grasping my wrist. "I told you," I say, slightly in a daze.

"Told me what?" His azure gaze is piercing—intense and intoxicating. How does he possibly have this effect on me? It's annoying, inconvenient, and disturbing.

"*You're* following *me*."

He throws his head back on a laugh, and it stretches his neck, displaying the script tattoo he has starting under his ear and stretching down the side of his throat, too faint for me to make out this far away.

"I reckon it looks that way, doesn't it? I live not far from here. I was coming back from physiotherapy." His grip on my wrist tightens slightly, like his hand inadvertently twitched. but it makes me realize he's still holding me. I pull out of his grasp.

"Everything alright?" he asks, nodding to my phone and the phone call he no doubt overheard.

And I must have completely lost my mind, because I just blurt everything out. "My dad has Parkinson's, and he had an accident this morning. That was his neighbor calling to tell me he took a fall and is in some pain. He can't stay with him, and I can't get there for another few hours unless I disappoint *a lot* of people, and I—"

"I'll go sit with him," he offers, like it's a normal thing to watch after someone you don't know.

"No that—I wasn't fishing to get you to offer... No, that's kind of you, but I'll figure something out." I start searching the internet for someone who can get there and take care of him.

"Jade." His tone is so firm, my attention snaps up to find a serious look tightening his face. He pulls the phone out of my hand, clearing the tab with last minute health attendants. "Let me help."

"I can't derail your Saturday. You probably have plans." I wave my hands around in the air. "Pubs to visit, women to make swoon or something stupid," I mutter.

"Jealous, boss?" I can hear the smile in his tone without looking.

"Don't be ridiculous," I say, tone resolute.

"Where does he live, Jade?"

I look up into his eyes and find nothing but a genuine desire to help laying there. "Blackheath."

He smiles. "That's perfect. That's where my parents live, and I was already heading out that way to visit them today."

"I can't ask you to do this, and it's not appropriate." I shake my head, second guessing the fact that I'm actually considering this. I've well and truly lost my mind.

"I'd wager we've done far more inappropriate things. I don't think me checking in on your father ranks." His words are humorous but there's an undercurrent of something seductive—*honest*, in his tone.

My entire body flushes with heat at his words, trying to shove the memories of that night into the back of my mind where they belong.

My head wages a war against itself, one side saying letting him help isn't a big deal and I don't have much of a choice, the other saying that it would open up a can of worms that is best left closed.

In the end, my desire to take care of Dad wins out. "Fine."

Tieran smiles wide, that damn dimple popping brilliantly against his straight, white teeth.

"Text me the address, and I'll head over now, spend some time with him. I'll let you know how he's doing, so you don't worry."

"Are you sure?"

It dawns on me that outside of Aanya, Tieran is the person I know best in this entire city. If I have to impulsively trust someone with my dad's care, I suppose he isn't the worst I could do.

"Stop trying to talk yourself out of it. Parents love me."

He had no idea how much my dad already loves him,

which is its own problem that I can't entertain right now. He needs to go, and I need to get ready for my event.

I unlock my phone, handing it over to him so he can put in his number, and then text him Dad's address when he hands it back.

"Thank you," I say genuinely.

He leans in close, too close, and my heart starts hammering for an entirely different reason. "My pleasure, boss," he murmurs and walks away, hands in his pockets. It feels like no coincidence when the sun peeks out for the first time all day, shining down on him and locking me in a trance.

Stop staring at his ass.

Not a minute later, a text comes through, and I choke on spit when I see the name Tieran saved himself as.

> GOD OF SEX
>
> Stop staring at my arse.

As someone's coming out of the coffee shop, I hear, "Jade! Your Dolly is ready." It snaps me out of my shock enough to go grab my drink. As I head home to get ready, I can't help but think I just opened a door I'll never be able to close.

True to his word, Tieran texted me within an hour of getting to my dad's in the small village outside Central London.

What I was expecting was a brief text with an update on his condition. What I got was a selfie of Tieran with his arm looped around my dad's neck, both of them grinning from ear to ear. It's disgusting how much it charmed me.

> UNKNOWN NUMBER
>
> I told you, parents love me.

Deleting the name he saved himself as might have been petty, but I did it in the name of self-preservation.

ME

How is he?

UNKNOWN NUMBER

He's moving slow, but he's alright, in good spirits.

Thank you. If he seems okay, you can head out. I don't want to disrupt more of your day.

Lines that needed to remain in high resolution focus are blurring, but I can't help my gratitude. Regret will come later, I'm almost positive, but for now, I'm thankful I don't have to cancel my event and disappoint hundreds of people. Dad being chuffed as chips because he gets to meet a rugby player he admired is just a bonus.

A few hours after Tieran left me outside of the coffee shop, an Uber drops me off on Dad's doorstep in Blackheath, but nothing could have prepared me for what I'd find inside.

"You wouldn't know your arse from your elbow, boy. That was offside!" My dad is arguing with someone as I walk through the front door, and my heart stops at the voice that answers him.

"I'm literally a rugby player, and you're arguing with me?" Tieran says.

Why is he still here? I told him he could leave hours ago.

"Don't get smart, lad. I've been watching rugby longer than you've been wiping your own arse." Dad aggressively stabs his finger towards the telly from his chair.

"And when was the last time you hobbled to the optometrist to have your eyes checked, you old geezer?"

I'm standing just outside the sitting room, holding my breath, waiting to see how Dad will respond to such a brazen insult.

Dad pauses before throwing his head back laughing, until that laugh turns into a cough, and he tells Tieran to go make him a fresh cup of tea. Tieran, to his credit, hops off the two seater couch to head into the kitchen, doing as he's told.

But he can't get to the kitchen without passing me, and in my scramble to act like I wasn't listening in on them, we end up colliding in the tiny foyer of my dad's home. Tieran reaches out, steadying himself with his hands on my waist, fingers twitching and involuntarily tightening where they lay. Shivers dance up my spine from the touch.

I immediately pull out of his hold, stepping a healthy distance away from him before I start toward the kitchen, indicating for him to follow.

When we reach the linoleum-lined floors of the kitchen, he moves past me and starts filling the kettle with fresh water, setting it to boil before pulling a mug out of the cabinet and grabbing a sachet of PJ Tips from Dad's teabag jar on the counter.

"You certainly seem to know your way around my dad's kitchen." Seeing him in my father's home was making me distinctly uncomfortable. It was far too familiar, felt too natural.

"This isn't the first cup I've made him," he chuckles, dropping the teabag in the mug. As he waits for the water to boil, he moves to the fridge and grabs the milk in preparation.

"Why are you still here?"

"Why not?"

"Don't be cute." I roll my eyes.

"But then I wouldn't get to see the delightful little furrow happening here," he reaches forward and presses his thumb to my skin, "right between your striking eyes."

I swat his hand away. "Stop. Why haven't you left?"

He shrugs, leaning against the counter. "I like Archie. We're having a good time, and I had nowhere else to be."

I narrow my eyes at him. "I thought you were going to

your parents'?" He hesitates, turning to grab the kettle when it signals it's done, pouring the scalding water into the cup on the counter. "Tieran," I say sternly.

"Gotta go, boss. Your old man gets cranky if he has to wait too long for his tea." He skirts past me, making his way back into the sitting room, where he hands Dad the cup and claps him on the shoulder, the way one would a friend.

His eyes light up, making my chest squeeze painfully.

"Thanks for keeping me company today, Arch, but I better get going," Tieran says, and I watch Dad's face fall slightly.

"Already? But the match isn't even over yet."

"I know, it's sacrilege, and I should be strung up by my boot laces. But my dog's been up too long, and I didn't ask her walker to come by today. It's in my best interest to get her out before she retaliates by using my couch as a toilet."

I can't help but think he's making light of it all because he can see the disappointment in Dad's face and wants to make him feel better. I hate him a little for making it so hard to remember why I need to push him away.

"Well, next time, bring the pup with you." His hands shake as he brings the cup to his mouth and takes a small sip, testing if it's too hot before taking a longer pull. "Fine cup of tea."

"Will do, mate." He turns to me, giving me a magnanimous nod before he leaves, his hulking frame dipping out the small front door.

His departure allows me to breathe again for the first time since arriving, but the room around me feels colder—duller, somehow, now that he's gone.

"He's a good lad," Dad says. "You ought to be looking for a man like that, not like those prissy twats you dated back in Los Angeles."

"You never met any of the guys I dated in L.A.," I point out.

"Didn't need to. If they were good enough for you, you

would've introduced us. You've only been in England for a few weeks, and I've already met this one."

"Tieran and I aren't—it's not like that, Dad. He happened to be there and wanted to help." I'm trying to keep my blush at bay, desperate for him to not read into the situation.

"Like I said," there's a glint to his eye, "good lad." Dad sips on his tea, settling further into his chair as the match comes back on, and for the rest of the evening, I feel uneasy.

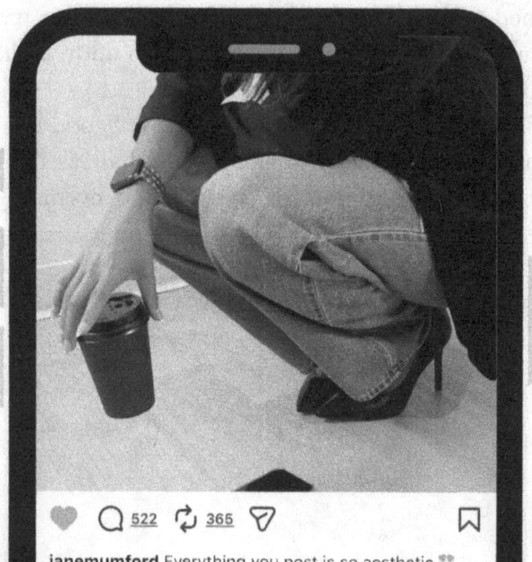

❤ 💬 522 ⇄ 365 ➤   🔖

janemumford Everything you post is so aesthetic 🐶
2 likes   Reply

dawn_p0rtman I'm dyiiiing to see the new collection!
When's the drop?
34 likes   Reply

kateishere I feel like she's been posting less. Do you
think it's because of the breakup?
11 likes   Reply
⎯⎯ View replies (13)

emilyinnyc Where are your heels from? I'm obsessed!!! 👠
45 likes   Reply

es38493873 Another rich girl fake from head to toe
trying to sell us shite. Your not pretty, your special. No
one cares what u do. Boring and unoriginal!
239 likes   Reply

    sweetmelody2 @es38493873 you're*
    carliescloset @es38493873 go away troll
    johnspeit @es38493873 they're all mad cos'
    your right mate 😂
    ⎯⎯ View 73 more replies

soltabeauty stunning! Check your dm's hun xx

11

TIERAN

I HIT SEND BEFORE I can second guess myself.

Fuck, can I unsend it? I shouldn't have sent that. It's none of my business if she doesn't do anything for fun. If she wants to work sunrise to sunset every day for the rest of her life, then that's her prerogative, and it is none of my business.

And yet, here I was, making a right arse of myself by making it my business.

She's going to tell me to fuck off any second now, and it's probably going to give me a semi.

My phone pings from my hand, making my blue staffy's head lift off my lap. Her soft grey eyes are inquisitive as her head tilts back and forth from where she sits next to me on the bed. My heart rate kicks up like I'm in grade school and my crush is calling when I see the notification from her.

A smile stretches across my face.

TIERAN

I believe I remember saving my name in your phone yesterday.

JADE

Your name? Are you confident in that lie?

My God-given name, yes.

You deleted it, didn't you?

Obviously.

How's Archie doing?

There's a long lapse in conversation, and I don't think she's going to answer. My stomach dips at first, but then three jumping dots appear, and I'm grinning at my phone like an idiot. This is ridiculous; she's made it clear she wants to pretend like nothing happened between us. So why am I putting myself through this?

JADE

He's doing okay today, thanks for asking.

TIERAN

If you need someone to stop by, I'll be at my parents' for our weekly Sunday roast tonight.

At your parents' two nights in a row?

...yeah. Want to come?

No.

Can Archie come?

Do you have a crush on my dad, Tieran? Are you trying to be my step-daddy?

Not really my kink, but I can adapt.

Too much, that was definitely too much, and I need to learn how to keep my thoughts to myself. There's just this impulse inside me whenever I talk to Jade. I *need* to get a rise out of her. I *want* to feel her fire and stoke it higher and higher until it burns me a little. Like if her boldness singes me, maybe I'll be imbued with a fraction of her confidence.

The reverberating silence on the other end of the conversation is loud, and it makes me itch to fill the void, to say anything to get her talking to me again.

TIERAN

London is a big city, you know.

JADE

Very astute observation. Is that big brain of yours what scored you the position of fly-half?

We do have to be very strategic and analytical. So yeah, it probably helped my case.

Apparently, humbleness isn't a requirement.

No, they actually encourage us to be insufferable.

Mission accomplished.

My many wonderful qualities aside...I'm concerned by your lack of leisure.

Stop thinking about it then.

You're 27. That's far too young to not be out experiencing life.

How do you know my age? Have you been stalking me?

Would you believe me if I said it was a lucky guess?

Not even a little.

Then yes, I did a light google search the day of the team meeting.

Creep.

Can you blame me? That particular revelation was a bit of a shock…

I guess I can't fault your curiosity.

That curiosity, and my impulsiveness, rears its head right now.

TIERAN

Is it safe to assume you may have also done your own internet search that day?

Those dreaded three dots jump on the corner of the screen, disappear, come back, and disappear again. When a response hasn't come in the last couple minutes, I jump up and get dressed for the gym, my dog nipping at my heels.

My phone dings while I'm changing my shirt, and in my haste to finish getting dressed and get to my phone, I end up shoving my head through the sleeve hole, temporarily suffocating myself.

Finally free from the constraints of man-made cotton, I reach for my phone, feeling like an idiot when I see the text isn't from Jade, but my sister, Charlotte.

CHARLES

Mum wants you to get here early.

TIERAN

Why?

Says you haven't been round in ages and her heart is breaking more by the day because she only ever gets to see you on the telly nowadays.

I was there last Sunday…

I'm just relaying the message, not trying to make sense of it. Don't be a prat and get here early. And bring Pebble. I miss my niece.

Fine, but I'm going to the gym first.

God forbid you go a day without aggressively dropping a 90-kilo bar on the ground.

*125kg

See you later, loser.

I finish getting ready for the gym, taking Pebble out on a quick walk before I leave, when my phone dings again.

JADE

Only to figure out why I didn't recognize you before.

To be a fly on the wall when she left the conference room that day. Jade is bold—assertive—and doesn't strike me as someone who enjoys not having control of a situation. Based on the way she held herself during the team conference, and the fact that she set up meetings with every player to determine needs and improvements, something tells me she's a hands-on type of leader, not someone prone to error. Seeing me that day must have been a shock to the system. Now, all she sees is a mess she needs to clean up. A headache.

TIERAN

I'm sorry if this…situation…created a mess for you. My only intention that night was to provide back up when that wanker wouldn't leave you alone.

JADE

I know.

Do you regret it?

Insecurity prickles at my neck. I don't know why I asked, why I feel this compulsive need to know if what I felt that night—what I can still feel writhing under my skin—is one-sided.

But Jade never answers the question, leaving me on read the rest of the night to wonder.

Pebble barrels through the door like a tiny bull, straight onto my dad's lap, tail wagging furiously and mouth spread wide in a smile with her tongue lolling out of her mouth.

My dad starts in on aggressively petting her, telling her she's the best girl and planting kisses all over her face. It's the only time I ever see him openly affectionate with anything or anyone—his family included.

"You spoil her," I rebuke.

The only response I get is a grunt as he continues to stroke her neck. Pebble soaks up the attention, flipping onto her back and wiggling so much in excitement, she nearly slides off the chair.

Lottie, Charlotte formally, Charles only to me because our parents thought they were having another boy, pops her pastel pink head around the corner. "My favourite family member is here," she exclaims, barreling past me and over to my dog to lavish her in love.

"No need to say hello to me," I say to the room at large. I may as well not even be here.

"Did you hear something, Pebble?" Lottie says within an inch of my dog's face while Dad's gone back to watching a rugby match between two Northern teams.

"Did you catch our match?" I ask him, feeling like a little boy seeking his father's approval.

Dad coughs. "I was on the road. Harold said you lost, though." He doesn't look at me, doesn't console me. I don't know why, after so many years, I still hope for a shred of kinship. It's not who he is.

Lottie's looking up at me with a regretful expression. "It was so close, though. I'm sure you'll ease back in soon enough."

My sister, ever the people pleaser, always trying to keep the peace.

"Tieran!" my mum calls out. "Come make batter for the yorkies. You make it the best."

I step past Lottie, messing up her baby pink hair, before following my mum's voice into the kitchen, where I find her lining a tray with duck fat to make the roast potatoes. Harriet Stone stands at the counter, dark brown hair streaked with silver pulled back and secured at her nape with a hair clip. Her blue eyes, the ones she gave me and my sister, shine bright in the fluorescent lighting of the kitchen.

"Hello, sweetheart," she coos. I quickly place a kiss on her cheek before pulling out a bowl and all the ingredients I need to make the Yorkshire puddings for dinner.

Together, we work on finishing up the sides as the roast cooks in the oven while Dad and Lottie entertain Pebble. Every now and then I can hear her speaking, asking about his week, and only getting short answers in return.

Sunday night dinners have been a Stone family staple for as long as I can remember. Mum started them when I was five or six, just after Lottie was born. She said it felt like it was the only way for us to spend quality time together on a regular basis, since Dad's job kept him away a lot. She's yet to admit that, despite the weekly occurrence, it hadn't bonded any of us to him more than what he allowed. Charles Stone is a good man who provides for his family in the ways that outwardly matter, but he's quiet and doesn't see a need for affection.

Even still, the tradition keeps me grounded amidst the chaos of my life. I can close my eyes and paint a picture of one of these nights from memory alone. The four of us around the table, Mum rolling her eyes at Dad as he tries to lean back in his chair and see the screen rather than have a conversation, Lottie sneaking a potato away for Pebble, whose head is resting on her knee, and me drowning my plate in a vat of gravy.

I was eight years old when I told the family around this table I wanted to play rugby. It's the first time I remember seeing my dad smile. Then, Mum started rejoicing, saying it would help me work off all my expendable energy. They signed me up for a local league the next day. After my first practice, I slumped through the front door caked in mud and sweat, and collapsed onto the sofa from exhaustion. When I woke up, I told them I loved it so much, I couldn't wait for next week. Dad clapped me on the shoulder, and I finally felt like I won something. I kept playing as a teen, eventually progressing to a university before getting called up to train for the Legends.

It was the only time I could get dad to have a conversation with me, and it set a precedent; rugby was equal to dad's attention. I was used to it now—had mostly accepted it, and in turn he was used to me being a professional player. The novelty wore off for the both of us, I guess.

"Alright you two," Mum yells out at the remaining family members currently petting an all too pleased pup, "dinner's ready, so get in here and serve yourself."

Everyone's sat down, tucking into their food and lulled into a false sense of security, when the questions start.

"How are things with the Legends? Do you like the new owner?" Dad asks, expression inscrutable.

I have yet to actually tell my family *who* the new owner is, and I certainly won't be divulging just *how much* I like her.

"Uh, yeah, it's good. The guys are training really hard, and McKallen seems to genuinely care about the club." I stuff my mouth full of roasted carrots.

"And how are you doing after the last match loss?" Mum asks gently.

"I'm managing. Don't worry, Mum," I try to reassure her, but she tuts, giving me those typical Mum eyes that are soft but that also say she's trying very hard not to pry out of worry.

"Have any National scouts come to the games yet?" Dad asks around the roast he just bit into, not meeting my eyes, distracted by the match playing in the adjoining room.

"I think it's too early for that." I take a sip of my water to wash down the food that's turned to ash on my tongue. "They'll probably start coming in a few weeks to see if anyone catches their eye, but I haven't been playing my best, so that's not likely to be me."

Mum sniffs. "I blame that tart Olivia."

"Mum," I chide.

Harriet remains unfettered and soldiers on. "It's true. I never did like her. I could sense there was something off about her, probably all the peroxide seeping into her scalp, making her stupid. To cheat on you was already horrible, but then to publicly humiliate you like that? She's why you struggled last season." Mum is getting visibly heated, death-gripping her fork while she stabs at her roast, sawing into it with her knife.

I put my hand on top of hers to get her to stop. "Mum, it's fine," she starts to argue, but I stop her. "Olivia and I wouldn't have worked out anyway. Her cheating just sped up the inevitable. Now please, the cow is already dead—stop trying to kill it further." I release her hand reluctantly.

"Alright," she takes a deep breath. "But I heard a rumor she's auditioning for the next season of *Love Island*, and I swear on Princess Di, if she makes it through and isn't universally hated by everyone in the UK, I will riot."

I don't know if that's actually true. The last I heard, she was still with Hughes. She'd have to be single to go on *Love Island*, and that made me feel conflicted. On one hand, I'd be chuffed if they split, but I also don't want her to ruin a perfectly good season of my favourite show.

"Sure thing, Mum." She was likely to post furiously about it to her Facebook and nothing more. "Enough about me. Why don't we grill Charlie now?" I look at her across the table and smile.

"Oh, I don't have anything going on quite as interesting as you do, dear brother." The smile on her face is so devious, Disney should consider casting her as a villain in their next live action.

"Surely that's not true. A fourth year at uni must have loads of stories and updates. How are classes? Dating anyone *special?*

She kicks my leg under the dinner table, and it takes everything in me not to grunt at the assault. I deserved it. I was treading dangerously close to sibling secret territory, because Charlie *was* dating someone special, at least to her, but it was definitely an off limits conversation. The guy is a professor at her school, and neither of our parents would approve of that. Hell, I don't think I'm too keen on it either, but as long as she's being safe, who am I to judge?

"I'm not. But aren't you?" It's a genius way to get the heat off her, because my mother's ears perk up at the small kernel of information. I don't know why she thinks I'm dating anyone, not unless she was reading tabloids at Tesco again. She knows better than to believe any of that rubbish. According to those rags, I'm dating anyone from the barista who took my order to the food truck guy who sits parked outside my gym. Spoiler, I'm not looking longingly at Frank —I'm eye fucking the kebab he overloads with garlic sauce.

"Darling, are you seeing someone new?" The excitement in Mum's voice almost makes me want to lie and say yes just to make her happy.

"He was chatting up some smoke show at the grocery shop a few weeks back. It looked quite cozy and familiar."

Fuck, she's talking about Jade?

"That's not—" I scrub a hand down my face. "She's my boss, not my girlfriend." Though I certainly wouldn't mind the latter option. "Her dad lives around here, and we ran into her that day, that's all. There was nothing more to it."

"That's not what it looked like from where I stood," Charlie unhelpfully chimes in.

"Well, get your eyes checked, dear sister, because that's all it was." Now, it's my turn to kick her under the table, but all I get is air. The menace has her legs crossed on the chair and not sitting on the floor. She smiles and winks at me.

I'll kill you, I mouth in her direction.

You can try, she mouths back.

"That probably for the best; workplace rendezvous can be messy, and you want to stay focused on the coming matches," Dad chimes in finally. "Might not be a good look to National scouts if the captain is shagging the owner of the club."

"Oh dear." Mum chokes on her bite of parsnip.

I would love nothing more than to start banging my head on the table until I pass out, or die from an inoperable brain injury. Anything to get us to move on from this topic.

"Can you pass the gravy?" is all I ask instead.

12
JADE

IT'S BARELY past eight in the morning when I get my twentieth phone notification of the day. Only this one is very different from all the others pulling me in different directions like I'm strapped to a medieval torture rack.

A single link from the man whose blue eyes and tattooed thighs have been running laps through my mind that would make Coach Ballard proud.

T

BOOKED! Crochet Workshop @ Get Knotty
for 7:30pm

JADE

Is that where you go to pick up little old
ladies? I know how much you like the elderly.

I never kiss and tell.

Thank God for that.

I immediately blush, wishing I could take it back. That one tiny slip was as good as an admission to the night we met, and I don't need any reminders when my subconscious mind already has no qualms conjuring up different scenarios while I'm sleeping and vulnerable.

T

You don't have to go, but my sister said it's
fun. It's booked under your name if you
decide you want to get out of your house.

As much as I'm annoyed at him inserting himself into my life, and I *am* annoyed, I'm also bizarrely touched. But I can't go. Can I? Do I want to? No. Maybe.

JADE

Will you be there?

T

Would that be a problem for you? Is there a
reason you might be trying to avoid me?

Yes. He means it as a joke, but he's right all the same.

When I don't respond right away, another text comes through.

T

If you feel like you can't handle being in the
same room as me, I won't go.

I pause at that, scoffing out loud. It's like he knows that by challenging me, it'll make me want to rise to the occasion. Absolutely ridiculous that it's working.

JADE

Good luck on the match tonight.

T

Will you be there?

I do own the team, so it's in my best interest
to go.

I realize then I've been standing at my kitchen counter, coffee forgotten this whole time because I was so wrapped up in talking to him. That alone is a problem.

A notification pops up a second later. My heart jumping in my chest is an even bigger problem. I have to get a fucking grip.

> You should wear team colours. You know…in support.

I needed to murder the butterflies in my stomach. A blowtorch should do the trick.

> Shouldn't you be heading into practice?

> Yes, boss.

I down my coffee and shuffle into my bedroom, heading to my closet, where I rifle through every hanger and drawer, but come up empty. My habit of wearing only neutrals means I don't own anything in my *own* team's colors. Displeasure shifts through me before I shake it off.

It's probably for the best. I don't want to impress anyone anyway. At least that's what I tell myself for the rest of the day.

* * *

It's twenty minutes into the first half of the game when the walking embodiment of an alternative forest sprite shoves her way into my row and plops into the seat next to me.

Tieran's sister is wearing a pair of chartreuse, wide leg pants with a fitted maroon crop top that stops just under her chest, showing off a tattoo peeking out at her sternum. Half her hair is pulled up into small space buns, the rest falling just past her shoulders in waves, allowing me to see multiple piercings adorning her ears. With the smattering of tattoos on her arms, no less than fourteen layered necklaces, and stacks of rings on her hands, she's infuriatingly cool.

"God, the things I'd do for a stale mince pie and a crisp pint," the pastel woodland creature says.

"Depraved things?" I ask.

"Morally questionable, for sure." She grins wickedly.

"Murder?" I raise an eyebrow in her direction.

"At the very least, a little maiming."

We both sit in silence before she snorts with laughter, and I crack a smile.

"Lottie." She extends her hand, and I grasp it firmly in mine.

"Jade," I introduce myself.

She nods solemnly looking out at the players running across the pitch. "The drunk from M&S who knocked over the tower of crisps, I remember."

I whip my head to face her so quickly, my vision spots. "I wasn't—I didn't mean to…" The words taper off when I see the devious smile gracing her coquettish face. "You and your brother are so similar," I mutter, refocusing on the game.

"Freakishly attractive? Disarmingly charming?"

"Mind bogglingly humble is what I was thinking."

She laughs as we both settle in, watching the players fly around on the pitch.

From the beginning of the match, there's been a weird frisson buzzing through the stadium. It's like everyone's on the edge of their seats, waiting for the smell of blood to permeate the air around us. I've gathered Newcastle must be one of our larger rivals, but this feels like more than typical feuding teams. Maybe it's because we're on home territory, and it's making the fans more riled up than usual?

On the pitch, a scrum forms with each team's forward players locking into position. Our scrum half, Alfie, tosses the ball between the two teams as they start pushing against each other, feet grappling for dominance in an effort to get it to the halfback, who's now moved to the foot of the formation.

Once Alfie has the ball in hand, he starts running toward Newcastle's try line. He doesn't make it far before he has multiple players on him, and he's offloading the ball to Tieran, who takes off like a light.

Possession switches hands and teams so many times, it's hard to keep up before it's back in Tieran's arms, and he's gunning for the line again. His thick, tattooed legs pump furiously to carry him out of the reach of the opponent who has been on top of him this entire game like there's a score to settle. A player named Hughes catches Tieran around the calves, tackling him to the ground, but he manages to toss the ball off to Myles, who sneaks it to our left winger just in time to cross the try line and touch the ball to the grass, scoring us a try.

The crowd all around us, including me, jumps to our feet, shaking the stands with our stomping and cheering while the guys celebrate their collective effort on the pitch.

London Legends 7- Newcastle Wolves 10

The score is so close; as long as we keep up this momentum, we can win this match. The guys just have to stay focused.

"I'd imagine this is a hard game for Stone," a man behind us says.

"Oi, I'd say. To have to keep his temper in check around the man who fucked his girl? Couldn't do it myself. It would send me into a blind rage. My hands would be flying."

I straighten at their conversation and Lottie goes still as a steel beam.

"No one's scared of your hands, mate," his counterpart chuckles.

"The slag's probably even here in the stands, waiting to rub it in."

"She's certainly rubbing something, bouncing around from player to player like that."

"Bit harsh, the way he found out though."

"Fuckin' embarrassin' being made to look like a tit in front of the whole of England."

Lottie snaps, whipping around in a ball of pastel fury.

"Are we watching a match or having tea with our gran? Shall I go get you ladies a scone?"

I glance back, and they both look properly chastised.

"Jesus," I mutter.

"So," she starts, chipper as a bird, "how are you liking London?" I flinch with the crowd when Cavan Darcey takes down one of Newcastle's players in an aggressive tackle. I look over at Lottie, and her eyes are alight with joy. "Ugh, it's so hot seeing men tackle each other."

I fear I'm dangerously close to liking this woman. "My dad's from here. It's been nice being close to him again." The statement is simple—detached. It gives information without divulging much.

Lottie, just like her brother, seems to want to ask more.

But there's a flurry of movement on the pitch that drags my attention back to the open play once more. Alfie tosses the ball to Cavan, who charges forward a few meters before he tosses it back to Alfie. Defense is gaining on him from the left and right before Tieran appears out of nowhere like a wraith in a maroon polyester blend as the halfback slips him the ball. It was a beautiful play, smooth and effortless in its execution, but it isn't over yet.

On the pitch, Tieran is a god.

Fast as a lightning strike, his muscled thighs carry him down the pitch, dodging and twisting out of Newcastle's grip with every step. He's so close to the try line, the audience can taste the score in the air. My hands grip my pants tightly, twisting and bunching the material as nerves wreck my body. If I was a young girl, watching this match from the comfort of my fathers house, this is the part where I'd be pacing behind his brown twill couch.

Three meters.

He dodges out of the grip of a right winger.

Two meters.

He's leaping over a player who dives for his ankles, skirting close to the sideline as he evades another player coming at him. Tieran is alive and electric—a *force*. It's hard to even fathom that he feels even a grain of sand's worth of self-consciousness about his talent on the pitch when he can move like *that*.

One meter.

Oliver fucking Hughes comes out of nowhere like a rabid boar hiding in the brush waiting to stab his prey with its tusks, but the bastard doesn't just take him down—he rams into his side, sweeping him over the side line and directly into a group of people on the wings. They go down like pins at the end of a bowling lane, plowed down by two massive players.

I jump up out of my seat, on the verge of yelling at the referee to stop dicking around and card the asshole for the gross penalty, but then I remember who I am. I have to keep my composure, because Lawrence Chapman is sitting only a few chairs away, probably cataloging anything he would deem inappropriate of a shareholder.

God, I hate that guy. I, genuinely and sincerely, from the bottom of my heart, hope the sock in his right shoe persistently slips down and bunches under his heel for the rest of time.

"Urm, hello!" Lottie stands on her seat, making her pink head rise over the row in front of us. "Are you going to make a call, or are you getting handies from Olli-pop to not do your job!"

The official heads toward where the two players are rising to their feet, reaches into his pocket, and pulls out a yellow card. A yellow card? That was definitely cause for a red, and I'm certain steam is coming out of my ears. Dad always found it amusing when I got overly heated as we watched a match together. I would pace the room, hands on my head, and try my best not to scream at the screen because then he would make me put money in a jar.

Let's just say my allowance always found a way back into Dad's wallet.

"Oh, fuck," Lottie huffs, her tone worried.

It snaps me out of my reverie, and I look to where she stares.

Across the field, Tieran is helping a small ball boy to his feet, the kid no older than eight. He kneels, clasping his shoulders, searching him over head to toe for injuries. I can't hear his voice, but I can imagine the worry that must be etched onto his face as he ensures the kid is okay before checking on the other people who got bulldozed.

Then, he stands, muscles flexing and contracting beneath his sweat-soaked jersey as he rolls his shoulders, slowly turning to face Hughes.

And then, all hell breaks loose.

13

TIERAN

ALL I SEE IS RED.

With the nature of the game we play, I can't fault Hughes for seeing an opportunity to take me down. I will, however, fault him for tackling me into a group of people, including the young boy who was now trying to put on a brave face for a crowd of people.

"Are you alright? What's your name?" I ask him before looking behind me. "Grab him a chair!" I call out before someone springs into action.

The boy nods. "Nathaniel." His voice shakes, but it's the tears lining his chocolate brown eyes and the sight of Hughes *walking away* without checking on anyone he just plowed to the ground that makes my rage snap like an elastic band pulled too taut.

"Nathaniel, can you sit down for me? I want the medic to look you over to make sure you're alright." He nods, a tear escaping his eye, and I reach forward and wipe it away. "It's okay to cry, mate. I do it all the time."

"Really?"

"For sure! I've gotta go have a chat with Hughes, but I'll check on you later, I promise." He nods, and I turn away, chasing after Oliver fucking Hughes.

When I catch up to him, I grab his shoulder and swing him around to face me. "What the fuck is wrong with you?"

The smug, satisfied smirk on his face makes me borderline homicidal.

"Just playing the game, mate." He shrugs.

I step further into his space, using every bit of my six-foot-four frame to intimidate him. "The game doesn't include knocking down bystanders, you pillock. Pull your head out of your arse, you sodding narcissist."

He snorts, not cowed in the least by the three inches I have on him. "That's a lot of talk for someone who hasn't won a game this season. What exactly are you fighting so hard for, Stone? You do realise your team blames you after every loss, right? You're supposed to be leading them to victory, and all you're doing is making them the punchline of rugby. Give up, or I'll just keep taking from you. I already have your girl warming my bed every night, and soon enough—once you've mucked it up beyond saving—I'll swoop in and take your spot on the Legends too."

I take an involuntary step toward him, wanting nothing more than to lay him out. But Coach's words from the start of the season sound an alarm in my head. *Stay focused. No scandals. Keep us at the top of the leaderboard and your name out of the press.*

Putting Oliver Hughes several inches into the turf would certainly kick up news stories, but he's not worth it. I take a step back.

But Hughes follows my retreat, stepping into my space with a puffed out chest.

Around us, I can hear the fans cheering—taunting, hungry for blood. They probably don't care whose gets spilled, they just want a good show.

"Go back to your side of the pitch, Hughes." I turn, giving him my back against every instinct warning me against it.

"Yeah, I think I will," he says too casually. "It's much closer to that delightful ray of sunshine sitting over in the Legends VIP box next to your sister." My step falters, but I keep going, giving nothing away. "That's your new team owner, right? Fuck, she's fit. Though she seems a little angry, by the looks of it. Maybe she just needs me to fuck that frown right off her pretty face. I bet her cunt will feel like heaven, even if her attitude is hell, and I do like it when they put up a fight."

The elastic band on my control snaps.

He's laughing, walking over to a teammate when I spin on my heel, rage overriding all sense, and tackle him around the waist in a way only a rugby player could.

Surprise works to my advantage, because Hughes is too shocked initially to shake me off before I straddle his waist, pull my fist back, and land a punch squarely across his cheek.

The stands are full of riotous excitement, and it holds me suspended in my anger. My soul has left my body, and it hovers above us, watching me grip his jersey in my left hand, lifting him off the ground slightly before slamming him back down and landing another blow to his face.

My rage is nuclear, hearing him talk about Jade like that—about any woman like that, I reason with myself.

Pain coalesces across my knuckles as they split on the third punch to his face. Blood shines across Oliver's teeth, pooling in the crevices as he smiles up at me like a lunatic. I'm about to land a fourth hit before I'm pulled off him, Cavan's thick arms wrapping around my shaking body, trapping my own arms down by my side.

He's talking quietly in my ear, but there's a buzzing that prohibits me from hearing him. All I can hear is Hughes' smug voice as he says, *I do like it when they put up a fight.*

Bile crawls up my throat, threatening to spill as my breathing comes in heaving gasps.

"Settle down," Cavan's deep voice says calmly. "Settle the fuck down. Take a breath in." I follow his instruction, inhaling sharply. "Good. Now, out."

I repeat his order a few more times, absentmindedly thinking he'd make a better captain as I inhale and exhale.

Cavan always kept calm, always delivered on the pitch. His presence is a balm to my anxiety riddled mind, and the team could probably use that more than me.

"Are you with me?" His gravelly voice is barely audible, but I nod, and his arms loosen their grip around me slightly. Three taps to his sun kissed forearm lets him know I'm not going to go on a rampage, rip off Oliver's left arm, and feed it to him—no matter how much I may want to.

My friend drops his hold, and I hazard a glance over to the VIP section, where Jade's sitting, but…she's not there anymore. Only Lottie remains, yelling expletives at me too colourful to repeat, and I swear, I think I hear Cavan chuckle. I must have hit my head during the scuffle and I'm imagining things, because Cavan Darcey *never* laughs.

"You saw him tackle me—card him," Hughes berates the referee when I rejoin the fray.

The ref pulls a red card out of his shirt pocket, holding it up in the air for fans and announcers to see. "Red card, Stone."

I accept my fate with as much grace as I can, turning to walk off the pitch and prepare myself for the reeming I'm about to receive from Ballard for being kicked out of the game.

"Red card, Hughes." The crowd goes insane with a chorus of cheering and dissent.

"You're taking the piss! For what?" he's shouting.

"Your illegal tackle and," he pauses, searching for the words, "ungentlemanly conduct."

I don't stick around to hear the rest, fighting a smile the entire walk to the sidelines. But it falls off my face when I see it's not Ballard waiting for me.

Jade stands at the mouth of the tunnel, arms crossed over her chest, a severe scowl lining her impossibly beautiful face. She looks like she's contemplating taking off her stiletto and giving me a lobotomy with it.

"My office. *Now.*"

Her tone leaves no room for argument, so I follow her, passing Harry, who hands me a towel and a bottle of water to cool down as I go, praying the whole way I don't finally get the sacking I've deserved for the better part of a year.

The silence blanketing the office is actually starting to frighten me, but not quite as much as Jade's singular focus as her right eye starts to twitch.

To an outsider, one might think she's calm, but I can tell that underneath the mask of neutrality, she's a viper ready to strike—something under my skin is humming for her to sink her fangs into me.

"Do you want to explain to me why my captain, England's best fly-half, just got red carded out of a game?"

"That middle bit's debatable, don't you think?"

"No, I don't." Her tone is sharp as a knife, quick to defend me even as she looks angry enough to chop off my balls and wear them as earrings.

"Careful, boss. That sounds suspiciously like you like me." The urge to flirt can't be stymied anymore. At least not tonight, while adrenaline from the game is still coursing through my body. I should probably feel some sort of remorse for my behaviour—for getting thrown out of a game for the first time in my career—and I probably will tomorrow, once the sense of failure starts to creep in. But for right now, all I feel is a strange sense of calm.

"I tolerate you at best," she hisses.

We're in a face off like two gun slingers in an old-time western film, and I won't be the first to draw.

She lets out a beleaguered sigh. "You have to be above reproach, Tieran."

My name falling off her lips is the first shot fired. *Fuck.* Has she ever said my name before? The two syllables have never sounded so appealing, like smoke barrel bourbon with a bite of vanilla. Bold, smooth, and subtly gentle.

"I know you have…personal issues with Hughes, but the team looks to you for guidance. Scouts for the National Team are randomly attending games, and they're going to hear about this. You don't want to lose your chance because the asshole who stole your girlfriend got under your skin. You shouldn't even give him the satisfaction of seeing you angry. I empathize with your situation, and I'm sure it must be hard to see them—"

"It's not about Olivia," I interrupt her.

She blinks. "Are you telling me…they're called Oliver and Olivia?" I purse my lips to keep from smiling. "Does that feel…incestuous to you somehow?"

A raucous laugh bursts from my mouth, surprising even me, as I bend at the waist trying to catch my breath. When I straighten, I can see a glimmer in her eye, even as her face remains neutral.

"A bit, yeah," I chuckle.

"If it's not about them, then why the visceral reaction?"

I sober, shaking my head, refusing to answer. To have her brilliance, and drive and strength and beauty, whittled down to what her body can offer isn't worth repeating. She doesn't need to be subjected to that.

"Was it worth it, at least?"

"Yes." No hesitation.

She reads my eyes—weighs the speed with which I answer her question. "Okay."

"That's it?"

"I trust my team. If you say he deserved it, then I'll handle the fallout around it." She nods to the chair opposite her desk. "Sit."

I do as she says, grateful to be off my feet after running, dodging, and jumping around for roughly three quarters of an hour.

Jade rounds the worktop, rummaging through a low drawer before she pulls out a first aid kit and walks back over to me, slightly perching on the lip of her desk.

"Do you expect to get into enough trouble to warrant a medical kit in your desk?"

Jade pops open the sage coloured lid to show every item perfectly lined up and organized, all labels facing the same way.

"I figured it was only a matter of time before a hulking brute came traipsing through my door, needing assistance. Hand."

I reach out my hand, and she grabs it none too gently. I welcome the bite of pain even as a frizzle of excitement shoots up my arm from the contact.

Her face sets into a mask of concentration, her brow furrowing slightly as she hunches over to clean and disinfect the cuts scattered over my knuckles.

"Will there be a lot?" I ask.

"Hmm?"

"Will there be a lot of fallout for you to deal with because of what I did?" It's probably the only thing that could make me regret my actions tonight.

"I'm sure there will be," she shrugs.

"I'm sorry. I'll talk to the press—"

"It's not them I'm worried about." The sting of the antiseptic has me sucking in a breath. "Don't be a baby. You can handle a two hundred pound man knocking you to the ground, but disinfected cuts are where you draw the line?"

"If it's not them, then who?"

"The press will be easy. I can wrap a PR story like nobody's business after this long in the game. It's the other shareholders I'm concerned about. They aren't too pleased about my presence here and are actively waiting for me to fail so they can have a reason to kick me out."

A fifty pound stone drops in my stomach, settling low in my gut and making me feel ill.

"That's absurd. You've done more for this club in a few measly weeks than they've done in years."

The soft curve of her mouth makes my heart start to

knock against my ribcage. It's the closest I've come to getting a smile from her since the night we met.

"Don't worry about it."

"But—"

"You have your secrets, and I have mine, Tieran." She looks at me pointedly, referring back to ten minutes ago when I wouldn't tell her why I went after Hughes. Fair enough.

She's holding my hand as she continues to clean cuts that no longer need cleaning. I tighten my hand around hers, my callouses scraping against her soft skin.

Her eyes drift up to mine from beneath lowered inky lashes. Our gazes hold, and I know she's thinking about it, that night.

"He said something about you." My voice is a low, choked out whisper.

My heart starts pounding out of my chest, and I can't get a single read on what she's thinking.

She abruptly drops my hand, reaching for ointment and bandages and shoving them at me as I stand, crowding her space a little, taking a sick sort of pleasure in watching her attempt to stay calm.

"Put that on, wrap it up, and try to behave."

"Yes, boss." I take a step forward, and she retreats, bumping into her desk.

"You're not wearing maroon." I allow my eyes to drop to her navy trousers and cropped grey cardigan.

"I've never let a man dictate how I dress, and I don't plan to start just because a cocky rugby player suggested it." She squares her shoulders.

"Maybe all this drama wouldn't have happened if you were wearing it."

She cocks her head curiously at me, eyes narrowing in a way that says she smells nonsense, the same look that always gets me half hard. "You don't strike me as the superstitious type."

"I'm a professional athlete. We all have our good luck charms."

"What's yours then?"

My gaze drifts from her eyes down to her pillowy mouth as it pulls in an infinitesimal gasp before settling on the spot of blue in her right eye.

"I'll let you know when I have it."

LEGENDS OR LOSERS?

Fans left frustrated after the loss of yet another match.

The country was shocked last season after a devastating Premiership loss took the rugby world by surprise. With the new change in ownership, fans and rugby enthusiasts alike have been on the edge of their seats waiting for the tide to turn in favour of the once great powerhouse team, but after yesterday it's left everyone wondering if they'll ever regain their former glory.

Everything seemed to go tits up in the second half of last season after captain and fly-half, Tieran Stone, suffered a lapse in performance leaving his teammates scrambling to pick up the slack match after match, leaving fans frustrated and confused. Stone has always been well liked by peers and reporters, but it's safe to say the Golden God of rugby is losing favour, and quick. With the uncertainty of new ownership, it begs the question on how long he may have left with the Legends if he doesn't get his head and heart back in the game.

14

JADE

"PUT YOUR TITS AWAY. I'm coming in."

Aanya barges in, as she always does whenever she feels the urge to come over, and finds me standing in my walk-in closet in only a bra and underwear.

She stops dead in her tracks, feigning a gunshot wound and slumping against the doorway. "I changed my mind. Don't put 'em away." Aanya walks towards me, hands outstretched and eyes glued to my chest. "Fucking hell, girl."

"You're just as bad as a man." I swat her hands away.

"Worse, to be sure." Aanya backs up a couple steps and plops down on the floor, legs crossed.

"How was your gig last night?" I ask.

"Oh! Hold that thought." My friend abruptly stands, leaves the room, and comes back ten seconds later with a bottle of wine, glasses, and…a jumbo pack of Maltesers I didn't buy.

"Where did those come from?" My eyes narrow as she pops one in her mouth and resumes her spot on the floor.

"I stashed them here a week ago so I'd have a sweet snack when I come over." She digs her hand in the pack, pulling out a few before tipping her head back and dropping them all in her mouth. "It's *seriously* concerning you don't like chocolates. That's basically a crime against womanhood."

"They're too rich and stick to my mouth." I turn, riffling through my clothes for the twentieth time in the past hour.

"Fuck me, and your bum? God really does have favorites, doesn't She?"

I shoot her a wolfish grin. "Stop staring at my ass, pervert."

"Then put on some clothes. And get that thing insured," she says, pointing at my backside before whispering what I'm pretty sure is, *I need to start going to Pilates.*

There's a black silk robe hanging on the back of the door. I grab it, slipping my arms through and tying it off around the waist.

A loud pop—the cork bursting from the bottle—sounds behind me, and a second later, Aanya is handing me a long stemmed glass with a large bowl full of pinot.

"So, the gig?" I prompt her again, crouching to sit in front of her in my closet.

A couple weeks ago, a manager expressed interest in her music, and, being as brazen as she is, Aanya didn't hesitate to invite him to her next show. That was last night, and I've been dying to know how it went. The fact that I was stuck in meetings instead of being there for her grated on me, but knowing Myles attended eased my guilt a little. The two have been inseparable since they met at the pub a couple weeks ago, spending every spare second of their time together. She liked to come over after their dates and debrief me, *in detail,* before I told her she had to stop because he was technically my employee.

Aanya takes a long pull from her wine, and a lump forms in my throat at whatever she's about to say that would require her to down half her glass in one go.

"Did the manager show?"

She nods her head slowly but doesn't make eye contact. "He did."

"And?" Long, painful silence is followed by more drinking. "Aanya Bhandari! Tell me what happened right now, or I'm changing the locks."

Her hand full of chocolate covered malt balls halts its route to her mouth. "You wouldn't dare."

"Then talk." I invoke my best business deal look and level it at her.

"All that look is doing is turning me on." She finally pops the sweet in her mouth, smiling wide and crinkling the skin around her brown eyes.

I grab one of them now and throw it, pelting her squarely in the forehead. "I'll tell Myles your affections have changed and we're running away together."

"Don't forget to tell Tieran too," she teases.

My stomach flips a little at the mention of him, remembering in too-vivid detail his sweat-soaked skin as he ran across the pitch, the shift in his demeanor when Hughes said the thing that finally made him snap, his fist crunching against bone, intensity in his gaze as he stared at me while I cleaned his knuckles in my office. None of it should affect me, but it was a scene that played on repeat for days. I couldn't seem to escape it—or him.

There was something about Tieran that made me feel out of control, but somehow grounded at the same time. Maybe I could chalk it up to the first time we met and how he was able to make me feel calm on a night where all I felt was uncertainty. Maybe it's his easy smile that irritates me to no end, or the way he's respected my flimsy boundaries, or his willingness to go help my dad, and ask for nothing in return.

The man is a walking green flag, and he is absurdly sexy in a way that's concerning to my own health. No one should be that hot and that nice; something needs to be wrong with him. Maybe he has a secret third nipple, or he's really into crypto or something equally horrifying—

taxidermy, maybe? I'll take anything at this point because I don't trust myself around him anymore. I can feel the professional barriers I erected the second I saw him in that conference room slipping away with every dimpled smile and easy conversation.

"The talent manager showed up," Aanya says, blessedly breaking me out of my train of thought.

I sit up straight, grateful for the distraction. "Tell me more."

"I have a meeting with him on Monday to sign a contract."

All composure leaves the room, and I launch myself off the floor, throwing her down and squealing like a girl whose crush just asked her to prom.

"You bitch! You had me going for a while there. I'm so proud of you," I say excitedly into her ear as she chuckles. I pull back slightly. "Don't sign anything until my lawyer reads over that contract."

She groans. "You just went boss bitch while you're on top of me in a silk robe. I'm only so strong, and I have a penchant for kissing my friends after too much wine."

"Think of Myles," I chuckle, sitting up.

"He knows I'm an equal opportunity kind of gal. He'd understand." She looks wistful. "He's actually kind of perfect, really."

"Are you in love with the big blond rugby player?" I tease.

Her cheeks redden, and she quickly changes the subject. "So why are we in your wardrobe?"

I hesitate. "I was looking for an outfit for something, but I think I'm going to cancel."

"What was it for?"

"Ummm." I sip my wine, trying to come up with anything else to say. "Someone booked me a crochet workshop, but I don't think I'm going to go."

Aanya's eyes narrow on me, all seeing. "You don't have any other friends."

"Rude." I look anywhere but at her.

"*Who* booked the class Jade?"

I roll my eyes as if it's not a big deal when I am, in fact, actively shitting myself. "You know who."

Now *she's* the one squealing. "Christ, why's that so hot?"

"Don't enable this!"

"I can't help it. Much like me, I think he's good for you. And you're going to that workshop even if I have to drop you off and make sure you go inside."

"It's… I—I can't go, Aanya. It'll send the wrong message."

"What, that you want to shag him? You already have, and I know you want to do it again." She raises her brow, daring me to disagree.

"Go with me. You can be the buffer."

"I'm no one's third," her words trail off as she thinks, "except for that one couple from Shoreditch, but that got messy quite quickly."

"So that's a no?"

"No can do, mate. I've got a date with Myles tonight, and I'm horny enough for him without you and Tieran's forbidden pheromones intermingling."

"He might not even come. The booking was just for me," I point out as Aanya stands.

"He'll be there." She starts perusing the rows of clothes, all neutral tones. "Now—what outfit says I'm here because I want you to tie *me* up in knots?"

A second later, she's chuckling as she dodges the shoe I send flying through the air.

✶ ◇ · ✶ ✶ ✶ · ✦
· ✶ · ✶ ✩ ◊ ·
✩ ✶

The cobbled streets of Camden are packed as I dodge tourists and locals alike in search of my destination. It takes passing rows of vibrant buildings with giant 3D objects protruding from them, grunge tattoo shops, and at least a dozen souvenir shops hocking Stay Calm and Carry On merch or masks with Prince William's face on it before Get Knotty comes into focus. It was almost easy to miss, with its demure sandwich board sign sitting on the sidewalk, showcasing a ball of yarn speared with two crochet needles crossed like swords, and an arrow pointing to the small set of stairs showing visitors to the basement level shop.

Every step is one step closer to an irreversible decision. With every thud down, my rational mind screams at me. *Thud*, turn around now. *Thud*, you're being an idiot. *Thud*, it's your funeral.

I push the hot pink door open, and a bell rings as the scent of patchouli and regret drifts out to meet me. The urge to cut and run before anyone notices me is strong, but before I can even consider leaving, a British Shorthair cat darts out of the crack I left in the entry.

"Fuck," I say trying my best *pspspspssps* to call the feline back while it looks at me from the top step of the stairs, tail swishing patronizingly.

"Yarnold! For fuck's sake, get back inside!"

I turn back around to find Lottie shaking a bag of treats. *Yarnold* trots gently back down the stairs, brushes against my legs, and slips back inside as if he didn't just make my heart stop.

"Hey, what are you doing here?" I ask, somewhat surprised to see her, even though she looks right at home in this neighborhood, in her lime green checkered pants and cropped band tee.

"Tieran didn't tell you?" I shake my head. Did he cancel on me and send his sister in his stead? Admittedly, that would be the best outcome, but I can't help but feel a kernel of disappointment. I shove it away quickly. That's exactly what I want to happen. The more distance between us, the easier it will be to not get swept up in this off-limits attraction. "I'm the instructor of the class! Let's head in; we're about to start."

Lottie ushers me into the small, single room store, where a large reclaimed wood table sits dead center, able to hold up to ten people. The ceilings are low, the lighting warm and inviting. Nailed into the right wall are rounded baskets housing bundles of yarn in every shade imaginable, and at the back of the room is a drink station holding no less than twenty different flavors of tea and a kettle that looks like it's seen better days. The whole place is utterly delightful

And standing next to it all is Tieran Stone, small cup of tea in his massive hand, talking to a sweet older woman who's looking at him like he hangs the moon.

He suddenly stands a little straighter, and the air feels like it's slowly being leeched from the room when he turns his head and spots me still standing near the door.

A smile breaks across his face, and his eyes flare like a lightning flash. It's a problem that I can so easily tell the difference between his smiles. This one is sincere, a little relieved, and it makes my stomach flip.

"Come pick your pattern," Lottie says from behind me, making me jump slightly.

She guides me to a small section of the shop just off the reception desk, a magazine organizer screwed into the wall holding laminated sheets of different stitching patterns to choose from. I quickly scan through them, opting for the coaster. It's just a square; it can't be that hard. Right?

After selecting colors from the baskets on the wall, I carry the bundles of yarn and choose where to sit. The long table in the middle of the room only has a couple people already at it, each place setting marked with a crochet hook and scissors. In my peripherals, I can see Tieran standing toward the other end of the table, chatting with his sister and the same older woman from before.

The head of the table closest to the entrance looks like a great spot, nice and *far* away from a certain six foot something rugby player who looks like a giant in this small shop. It also provides me with an unobstructed escape should I need it.

"Alright, you lot. Take your seats, and we'll get started," Lottie instructs.

I fiddle with my spools of yarn, pointedly *not* paying attention to the movements of any one person, zoning out so spectacularly as I stare at the vibrant green and pink I don't notice when the seat on each side of me fills.

"Hello, dear," a soft voice to my left says, warbled yet melodic.

Angling my head to put a face to the voice, I'm met with sharp brown eyes framed by the deep groove of wrinkles earned only by a life well lived.

"Hi," I reply.

"I'm Mrs. Cline. I've not seen you 'round here before." Placing her accent is difficult. Welsh, maybe?

"Jade. First time here," I say politely.

Mrs. Cline pulls her glasses out of the breast pocket on her quilted vest, places them on the bridge of her nose, and then gives me a slow once over. "Have you crocheted before then?"

Her tone feels slightly accusatory for some reason, but surely, I'm just paranoid because I'm in a new environment completely out of my wheelhouse.

"I don't believe she has, Dorris." The gravelly tone that rings out *much too close* to my right ear makes my spine straighten. "Jade's not one for hobbies. Are you, Jade?"

When I look over at Tieran, I find him with his arm resting against the back of my chair and his body leaning slightly toward mine. The smell of fresh laundry and warm skin reaches out to greet me, and I breathe it in involuntarily. By all accounts, I would have pegged Tieran as a flashier man, one who has a trove of grooming products scattered about his bathroom, including no less than ten different colognes. But every day, I'm more and more surprised by him. His personality is bold, but I think behind the commanding frontman is someone much softer.

"Is this your girlfriend then?" Mrs. Cline asks with obvious derision.

"No!" I shout.

"No need to answer so fast, love." He directs his attention to Dorris. "She wants me, but I keep shooting her down."

Before I can irrefutably deny his claims, Lottie pulls our attention to start the beginning of our workshop. She takes us through a series of terms and maneuvers—mostly to benefit those of us new to crochet—before showing us how to do a slip knot and connect it into another stitch.

Twenty minutes goes by, and I'm getting more pissed off by the second at my inability to get the hang of this. My fury only quadruples when I look over and see Tieran expertly hooking, knotting, and stitching—his project already taking form while mine looks like a heap of twisted yarn.

I've stayed quiet the whole time, trying to concentrate and drown out the sound of a certain overstepping rugby player's voice every time he speaks. Which is often, asking me mundane questions on a relentless loop. My refusal to answer never discourages him from continuing his one sided conversation, though.

The only time I acknowledge him next to me is when Dorris is being critical of my technique and Tieran steps in, soothing her crankiness with a couple sweet words and a cheeky smile.

I can't stop the words from vomiting out. "I knew you had a thing for old people."

His resounding laugh is so loud, it almost draws a smile out of me, but I look over and see Dorris scowling my way, so I school my face quickly.

The evening passes by in a mild conversation between everyone at the table, intermixed with Lottie going around and giving people direction. She, embarrassingly enough, has to stop by and help me a lot. The fact I can't get the hand of a simple knot and repetitive pattern is really irritating me—especially when Tieran is basically done with his.

"What are you even making?" I ask. "Is that underwear?"

"It's a bandana for my dog." He holds it up where I can see the strings he's working on that will tie it together. "Who in the bloody hell wears crochet knickers?"

"I don't know what you're into…other than people over seventy. Tell me, did the Queen really get your heart racing?"

"What can I say? I've always liked powerful women."

It's a fight to keep the corner of my mouth from curving.

"Here." He stands, coming up behind me.

"What are you doing?" He's towering above me from where I sit, and I feel very small despite my above average height.

Tieran puts an arm on each side of me. "You're getting confused because you're holding your hands wrong. When you watch Charlie, you're seeing the inverse. This is how you need to be holding the hook and looping the yarn."

He cups each of his hands around mine, placing my fingers in the correct positions, showing me how to best loop the thick thread.

I'm trying my best to concentrate, but the warmth of his chest is soaking through my blouse, making it hard to focus.

"Now try it on your own."

It takes me a couple more tries with his gentle instruction before I finally get one down on my own.

"Good. Give me another one." His voice is low in my ear, and it makes shivers skate up and down my spine.

I complete another few sequences of stitches, and before I know it, I have a whole row.

A self-congratulatory smile crosses my face. "I did it." I look up at him towering over me, a humorous expression on his face. 'Why was that so hard? I've been less angry in a conference room full of men who tried to explain *my* field to me."

"Now do another fifteen rows, and you'll have finished your piece," he says.

I look from him, down to my single row of knots, and then trail my eyes back up, glancing over his torso until I meet his eyes. "Do I have to?" I whisper.

He tosses his head back, neck elongating and showing off the tattoo just below his ear, and barks out a laugh. "No, we can go. Class is about over anyway."

Tieran runs over to say goodbye to his sister, and I try not to get stuck on the *we* so casually thrown around.

A few minutes later, we're walking down the street toward the tube station in silence. When we make it to the entrance, I turn to say goodbye.

"Let me drive you home," Tieran blurts out.

"That's not necessary." I try my best to keep my voice stable—strong. I can't let him see that my resolve is weakening with each quippy retort and knee-weakening smile.

"The tube really isn't safe at night. You should let me drive you."

"I spent a couple years in New York City. I'm pretty sure if I can handle a man called The L Train Lunatic chasing down extra terrestrials at the 8th Ave station, I can handle a university student named James who's a little drunk." I turn, ready to take the steps two at a time to get away.

Tieran's hand shoots out and grabs mine, stopping my attempt to flee. "Please," he hesitates, still holding onto my hand, "I know you can handle yourself but—please. Let me see you home safely."

The earnest look in his cerulean eyes has me folding like a lawn chair embarrassingly fast. I vow to build a stronger backbone…starting tomorrow.

"Fine."

Twenty minutes into the drive home, I finally break the bizarre silence.

"What kind of dog do you have?"

He seems surprised by the question but recovers quickly. "Blue Staffy. She's my own tiny happy hippo."

I want to throat punch him for becoming even more charming.

"What's her name?"

"Pebble."

"Pebble?"

"Yes." He keeps his eyes on the road, following the instructions coming from the GPS on his phone and pulling up to park outside my building.

Facing him, I ask the question on the tip of my tongue, the one that threatens to undo me because it's too goddamn endearing. "Your dog's name is…Pebble Stone?"

"That's right."

I've never seen his face so serious, and I can't help myself when laughter bubbles up my throat until I taste it on the tip of my tongue and it's suddenly spilling out, loud and uncontrolled. The fractured sound fills the small space and grates on my ears like rocks tumbling around in a polisher. I've never liked my laugh, and that thought is what sobers me enough to get myself composed again.

When I hazard a glance over at Tieran, he has a soft smile on his face.

"What?"

"Do that again," he says.

"Do what?"

He leans a little closer, and the air is sucked out of the car—the universe, and my head goes a little light. "Laugh—smile. London just lit up for a few seconds in the wake of that smile."

My breath catches a little as he inches a little closer. My eyes dart down to his mouth, full and forbidden, and I panic, because I don't know how to stop this. It feels like a meteor coming at me full tilt, spinning and spinning, ready to rain down destruction on everything I am.

Our mouths are inches away now, and I can smell the spearmint tea on his breath.

Stop this, Jade, the angel on my shoulder demands. I lean forward just barely, enough to give a signal.

His hand sneaks up under my chin, knuckles tilting my face up to meet his and—

A riot of laughter sounds outside the car, scaring me out of my skin and making me jump away and out of his hold.

"I, uh…I have to go. Thank you for the ride."

I hop out of the car without letting him reply, run upstairs to my flat, and walk straight into my kitchen, where I pour myself a glass of water I drink in one long gulp.

Too close—that was too close to compromising everything. And the scariest part was, I couldn't find it in me to care.

15
JADE

"WHOSE HOUSE ARE WE GOING TO?"

Aanya has managed to successfully peel me away from my laptop and piles of paperwork in favor of going out. She came busting through my door an hour ago, ignored me where I was working on the couch, and beelined straight to my closet, emerging five minutes later with the black beaded mini dress and strappy heels I'm now wearing as we get off the tube at Liverpool Street.

Aanya takes the steps out of the station at a pace I can't keep up with in my heels, and I'm pretty sure she's doing it to evade my question. Above ground, glass skyscrapers rise around us like lumbering giants. Towering business centers like The Gherkin are intermixed amongst the Victorian-style buildings that London is famous for.

"Is it a music friend?" We cut a path down a side street, getting into an area of the neighborhood where the vibe becomes more industrial grunge, and the scenery changes to trendy restaurants and clubs.

"I guess you could say they work in entertainment…" Her voice trails off as we come up on a row of three story Georgian homes just off the high street. Music pulses a few doors down, growing louder as we close in. Aanya leads the way up to the main door into the building, stops at the first flat on the left, and lets us inside.

We're walking down the narrow entryway, unable to see anyone, but the sound of chatter intermingled with the thumping bass of the hip hop song that's playing over the speaker is unmistakable. Apprehension settles low in my gut as I pick out one voice over all the rest, its familiar resonance itching something in my brain, begging to be scratched with no chance for relief.

No. It can't be. Not after I've successfully avoided him for the last week after the near kiss we had.

Going into the open room off the hallway, I realize I wasn't imagining anything but instead I've been duped by a very guilty looking *friend*.

"Aanya Bhandari, what did you do?" I hiss.

"Don't kill me." She holds out her hands in a supplicate gesture.

"Oh, I'm definitely considering it. The Thames isn't far from here; you're small, it would probably be pretty easy to dump your body."

"I love it when you're secretly funny, even if it's in threat to my life."

"Explain to me why I'm at a party with my entire rugby team right now?"

She knows I've been trying to avoid something like this happening—that I am trying to keep everything above board. One could argue a crochet class would be a breach of my own rules, but that's *different*, I rationalize. I wasn't inside one of the player's homes, wearing a very inappropriate dress with skimpy straps, a low back, and a slit playing high on my thigh.

"Because I wanted you to come, and you wouldn't have if I told you where it was," she pouts. I cross my arms, looking toward the door. "I know you *want* to be here, and you should be allowed to live your life. You're young and sexy, and you deserve to have an entire rugby team worshiping at your feet," she pauses. "Well, all except one."

"I'm leaving before anyone sees me." I turn to walk back down the hall.

"Bossman!" Ekon calls out, stopping me and drawing the attention of every person in the room.

I can feel a particular set of cobalt blue eyes searing into the side of my face as I turn toward the crowd of hulking players mixed with people I don't know.

The flat is a modest size, modern but warm, with mid-century style furniture; big enough that people aren't on top of each other but small enough that it still feels homey.

"Hi," I grimace, giving a meek wave.

"Ach! Don't worry, bossman. You can come in. We won't bite," Ekon says as he swings an arm over my shoulder, ushering me further into the flat.

"Not unless you ask us to," Davies shouts from the kitchen.

A moment later, Myles comes barreling around the corner and wraps Aanya in a hug, dipping her low and planting a kiss square on her red lips to the sound of the whole team cheering. When she comes back up for air, she looks dazed and happy, and I can't find it in me to piss on her evening by leaving.

"I need a drink," I mutter under my breath.

Am I in hell?

Connor Davies is on his third magic trick of the evening, each one worse than the last. The misplaced confidence of men is a truly staggering phenomenon to behold.

During the second mind numbing trick, Lottie arrived, dressed in floral printed denim pants with a fitted green crop top, hair unbound and wild around her face. When she spotted me, her blue eyes brightened, and she beelined in my direction. I noticed several eyes following her every step, but she's either unaware or unaffected, because she kissed my cheeks before plopping down on the couch, where we're now slowly being tortured by parlor tricks.

"I'm surprised to see you here," she says before taking a sip of her drink.

"I was conned." I point to where Aanya stands, snuggled into Myles' side.

Next to them, Tieran is telling a story I can't hear from where I'm sitting, but it's making everyone around him laugh, and I wish for a fleeting moment I could be over there instead of keeping my distance on the other side of the room. Not just to be near him, but to be a part of a group—to have a place where you know you belong.

But I can't, and the delusions my brain keeps cooking up need to stop.

There's a connection between us, that much is obvious. I wouldn't have hooked up with him in a pub bathroom otherwise, but it was purely a physical thing. It was a natural conclusion that my body reacts every time I see him, because I know what it's like to have him—and it's good. *So* good. It has absolutely nothing to do with how funny and caring he is.

Stop it, Jade.

"For my next trick," Connor starts.

"Man alive, he loves to hear the sound of his own voice, doesn't he?" Lottie murmurs beside me, making me snort.

"Maybe for his next trick he can make himself disappear," I whisper.

Lottie chokes on her drink, and the motion catches Temu David Blaine's eye.

"Lovely of you to volunteer, babe. Come stand by me." He grabs her hand, tugging her off the couch, and she gives me a brief look of panic before mouthing *help me* in my direction.

"I wanna see how this shakes out." I shrug.

"Traitor," she hisses, making me laugh into my drink.

Ekon and Finn, two of our biggest players, sandwich me on the couch after Lottie joins Connor in the center of the room.

"This can't be good," Finn says over my head to his friend.

"Certainly not for Cap's sister. Are you having a good time, Bossman?" he asks me.

"It's been…revolutionary." I try to scoot away, to get some distance, but I'm only met with a secondary wall in Finn.

Yes, I'm definitely enjoying my night of slow torture. On one end, I'm being forced to entertain party tricks by the team's misogynist, and on the other end, I can't stop covertly tracking where Tieran is in the room. Both things are irritating me. I need to get out of here.

"The new uniforms are class," Ekon says from my left. "Did you design them?"

I gulp down a sip of my now room temperature hard seltzer. "No, I uh—" the music's gotten louder since arriving, forcing me to lean slightly into him to answer the question. "I had the social media coordinator post a submission form for fans to send in their ideas. I brought the winner in, gave them a tour of the stadium before we collaborated on the final design. They got paid for their input and season tickets." Both the men look at me with shock written across their handsome faces.

"You did all that in just a few weeks?" I nod.

"That's mental." Wonder laces Finn's tone.

Embarrassment floods through me, but I'm saved from having to respond, from having to accept their praise, when the magic show of horrors pulls our focus.

Lottie stands next to Connor in the middle of the room, a look of severe apprehension on her lovely face as more people gather around them. A moment later, Connor snakes his arm around her waist, and she squirms, attempting to ease out of his hold. His hand only tightens as he draws her further into his side, an arrogant smile stretching across his face.

"Let go." Lottie pushes against him, but he just grins fiendishly down at her as he crowds her space.

"On with it, Davies." I scold.

His jaw ticks in response, but the smug smile never leaves. Finally releasing his hold on Lottie, Connor backs up just a little and starts looking at her profile. "What's that?"

She touches her pale pink hair. "What?"

"That." He reaches out, grabbing something behind her ear, and when he pulls his hand away, there's something silver and shiny between his fingers. At first, I think it's a coin, but as he starts to wave it in the air I realize it's the foil packet of a condom.

"What do you say we make some magic of our own?" He steps toward her, and she recoils, stepping back until she bumps into Cavan Darcey. He stands still as a statue, hands in his pockets, towering over Connor with a deep scowl lining his face. The contrast of Lottie in front of him, looking dainty and ethereal, casts his features in an even more dramatic sense of foreboding.

Lottie looks up at him, but he doesn't spare her a glance as he shoots daggers at Connor. "Piss off."

"Relax, mate. It's just a little banter."

Cavan remains stoic and silent, staring him down until he relents and walks away, muttering expletives. Lottie turns to say something, but Cavan's already walking away without a word.

Undeterred, Lottie shrugs and makes her way back over to me. "That was weird. Come with me to get another drink?"

I squeeze myself out from between the two large players, standing unsteadily in my heels. "Do you guys want another?" I ask Ekon and Finn.

Finn tips his cup to me. "No can do. Cap's got a one drink rule this close to a match."

When I look around, I notice that half the players are holding bottles of water. "The guys are okay with that?"

"Some of the younger lads get a little annoyed, but they

know it's for the best, and they respect Tieran enough to listen."

Something in my chest lifts. I wonder if he realizes how much these men care about him—trust him.

Lottie grabs my hand, pulling me through the throngs of people to get to the kitchen, but the bar area is crowded with bodies, and we're not having any success getting through.

"Maybe we should just wait until it empties over here?" I suggest.

She pouts. "Dammit all to hell, I really wanted a—" Her words are cut off as a corded, deeply tanned forearm snakes in between our bodies, holding a drink out to her. "…Vodka soda." We look over and see Cavan at the other end of the drink, his arm flexing slightly as Lottie takes it. Before she can say anything, he's walking away again.

She takes a sip of the beverage and looks over to where Cavan has retreated over to Myles and Tieran. "How did he know I wanted a vodka soda?" she muses.

I suspect I know why, but I'm not getting involved. I'm already *too* involved with the people on this team.

"Do you want another?" she asks, but I shake my head. I'm still nursing my first and have no intention of drinking more. Being here was already against my own rules; bringing more alcohol into it was not a wise move. "Let's go join the others."

She grabs my arm and starts dragging me toward a group of people in the far corner of the flat. When we sidle up next to Cavan, he stiffens slightly, nodding when Lottie thanks him for her drink. Myles stands behind Aanya, his arms wrapped around her stomach as he rests his head on the top of hers. And on the opposite end is Tieran, and a beautiful redhead hanging on his arm and standing *very* close, laughing at something he just said.

A pang of annoyance hits me square in the gut.

"I'm going to come with you to the next match," Aanya announces, drawing my attention away from the attractive couple. "It's time I come support my man as much as he's supported me."

"I'll be there too!" Lottie exclaims, pulling my friend into a hug as if they've known each other for years.

Aanya steps out of her hold, taking in her loud outfit and running a finger along the jewelry adorning her slim neck. "I *love* your necklace"

"Thank you! I made them, actually. This one is—"

The redhead laughs again, resting her palm against Tieran's chest. He smiles down at her, and it makes something inside me wither. He deserves someone he can be with out in the open, someone who can appreciate him fully, and that can't be me.

Another laugh scrapes against my skull like nails on a chalkboard.

I *shouldn't* be here. If Chapman got wind I attended a party at the home of a player, he'd find a way to use it against me. I'm sure of it.

Taking a cue from the Irish, I decide to slip out undetected. I briefly tell Aanya and Lottie I'm going to use the restroom. The lie rolls off my tongue easily, but I know if I tell them I'm going to leave, they'll try to get me to stay.

I can't have Tieran, but I don't want to watch someone else crack on with him either.

The night air is balmy as I slip out of the flat onto the street, heading toward my side of town. I've only made it halfway down the street when someone falls into step next to me.

"Nice night," Tieran observes.

"Go back to the party, Tieran."

"I think I'll walk. I could use the fresh air." He shoves his hands into his jacket pockets, walking alongside me.

"Is there anything I can say to get you to go back?" My attempts are futile. I know that once he's decided on something, he goes after it with singular focus. It's why he's such a force on the pitch.

"No can do, boss. It would be unwise of me to let you

walk home alone wearing that dress." I look over at him, and he makes no move to hide his obvious perusal. My stomach tightens, and I'm suddenly glad for my skimpy dress, enjoying the admiration from him.

We're both quiet; the only sound is my heels clicking against the pavement as we turn onto the high street littered with shops, bars, and people milling about.

"Did you have fun the other night?" Tieran asks, finally breaking the silence.

I glance over, hesitant to answer, afraid it might say too much. But I'm weak, and the words are coming out, unbidden. "I never want to do it again…" His face falls slightly. "But," a glimmer of hope straightens his shoulders, "yes, I had fun."

He holds his hand up to his head, cupping his ear. "What?" I say.

"I'm just waiting for you to say I was right," he gloats.

"You'll be waiting a long time, then."

"I'm a patient man." There's an insinuation to his words that makes me flush with heat.

I look over at him and his blue eyes are glowing under the lamppost lights. "Shouldn't you be getting back to your friend?"

"Who?"

"Red hair, leggy, sumptuous curves."

"I certainly could. She made it clear the invitation was open."

Jealousy ignites as we pass through a crosswalk. "What are you doing here then?"

"I guess I'm a martyr for wanting what I can't have." His brazen admission makes me stumble on my heels as he reaches out, steadying me with hands on my waist. "Careful, Hellfire. I'd love to hear your whinging if I had to carry you all the way home."

We're standing in the middle of the road, his hands on my waist, bright blue eyes suddenly serious as they peer into mine. The eye contact is intense—charged with a tension so palpable, I can feel it coursing under my skin.

A car horn blares, causing me to jump and step out of his grip as I scurry to get out of the road, Tieran hot on my heels.

"I'll be fine on my own." He needs to stop following me, stop texting me, stop doing things that make it really difficult to dislike him. Tieran Stone is poisoning my bloodstream, and I don't know how to rid myself of him. He is…everywhere—at work, on my phone, on my mind—his presence makes me feel electric whenever he's around.

I feel a sprinkle land on my skin, and I glance up at the clear evening sky. Must have been condensation from someone's air-con.

"I know you feel this too," he says.

I round on him, because dammit, he's right. I do feel it —this inconvenient, all-consuming attraction to him. He's peering down at me, skin paler under the moonlight, contrasting against his black shirt, dark hair falling into his hopeful face, a chain around his neck that I want to use to pull his face down to mine. "You're about to feel my foot up your ass."

I turn and start to quickly walk away, but he grabs my arm, spinning me around to face him. "Jade."

"Don't."

He takes a step towards me. I take a step back, and he follows.

Tieran is corralling me toward a shop window when Mother Nature decides to have my back and the skies open up, chucking down rain.

"Fuck," I exclaim.

Tieran grabs my hand, pulling me away from the wall. "Come on. We'll pop into the next bar and get a drink—wait out the rain."

I don't argue, because the slight rain has turned into a torrential downpour, already soaking my clothes and skin. As water fills the street, it becomes slick beneath me, causing me to slip in my heels. Tieran tightens his grip on my hand, and before I know it, he's guiding us into the first place we see called Stag & Vixen.

The bouncer at the door takes pity on us, waving us through to walk down a long hallway lined in burgundy velvet, floor to ceiling curtains. What kind of bar is this? The hairs on my neck lift and Tieran takes off his jacket, draping it over my shoulders to ward off the goosebumps that erupted across my skin.

Pulsing bass thumps through the walls, and when we make it to the threshold of the main room, I stop dead in my tracks.

We haven't come into a bar at all.

We walked right into the den of a sex club.

16

TIERAN

IT WASN'T TECHNICALLY a sex club. They couldn't call it that—but it was pretty damn close.

Every place my eyes settle is a feast of carnal pleasure. The room we're standing in is cavernous, easily reaching fifty feet in height with the same deep burgundy curtains lining the walls. At the centre of the room is a round stage, tables and booths placed around it, filled with patrons ready to drink to excess, waiting to watch dancers come out and perform. The space is dimly lit, with small, flickering candles set on tables, and only a few lights around the room casting a soft red glow on the suspended cages filled with *nearly* naked men and women as they dance languorously to the sensual baseline of the music.

Everything about Stag & Vixen feels seductive. From the lack of light around the room ensuring a lot of dark corners—little pockets of privacy where people can sneak off to engage in slightly more...illicit activities—to the right of the room, where a hallway with a neon sign above the archway reads, *'Where curiosity and desire meet to dance'.*

I would stake my precious car on that hallway leading to *private* rooms.

All I can think about is how uncomfortable Jade must feel right now. She can barely stand to be around me most days, and being trapped here, of all places, must be putting her on edge.

I glance over to find her standing stiff as a board, eyes darting around the expansive room with a flush climbing from her ample chest to her ears.

"Come on. We can find somewhere else to wait out the rain." I move to brush past her, but she stops me with a hand to my chest, and I flex a little under the touch, delighting in her warmth seeping through my shirt.

Her amber eyes trail from the scene all around us, down to where her palm rests on my chest, as if she doesn't know how it ended up there. Jade immediately removes her hand, eyes flicking up beneath inky lashes and locking with mine. So much simmers in that gaze as her eyes shift back and forth—weighing her options. I'd pay a year's salary to be inside her head right now, but instead, I wait on a knife's edge, unsure what she's making of all of this.

"We can stay and get a drink…just until the rain stops." The last part is barely a whisper. I was prepared for a sharp retort, a fight of some kind. I certainly didn't expect her to agree so quickly. Now I have to work overtime to keep from letting the happiness show or I'll spook her. I've been wanting to spend time with her for weeks while she's been working overtime to keep me at arm's length. I just never imagined it would happen quite like this. Yet, there's still a fool's hope in my chest that maybe she wants to stay here *with me*, not just to evade poor weather.

"Until the rain stops," I parrot, voice thick.

Risking life and limb, I place my hand on her lower back, bare from the dress that's been driving me out of my mind from the second she walked through the door tonight. I guide her from our spot by the entrance to the bar, where a mixologist is lighting a cocktail on fire, to the delight of the patron in front of him.

We quickly place our own order, and I scour the room looking for a place for us to sit while we wait for our drinks to be ready. It was busy when we came in, but the room has significantly filled up in the last few minutes, with tables mostly full and all the ones closest to the stage occupied. We stand there, close enough that I can feel the heat of her body wrapping around mine. After a few minutes, once we have our drinks in hand, a high top tucked into a secluded corner opens up when the couple heads toward the hallway of debauchery on the opposite side of the room.

"Follow me." I reach back and grab Jade's hand, pulling her toward the empty table before anyone else can steal it. Holding her hand is akin to holding a steel beam with how rigid it feels caged inside my grip, but I don't let go, dragging her deeper into the fray as we weave through the dimly lit room, curious eyes roving over her everywhere we go.

Performers mill about the room, seductively writhing to the lascivious music thrumming through the speakers. The dancers are in an array of hot pants, thongs, and jewel-crusted nipple covers that glow under the red lights as they tease the patrons with lustful glances and not-so-subtle touches. Greedy hands grapple to touch supple skin, and more than one dancer ends up in someone's lap.

When we finally make it to the table, I help Jade onto the barstool, hand still clasping hers as she sits, adjusting the skirt of her dress that shifted higher on her tanned thighs. Forcing my eyes away is a testament to my pure fucking will, but I know if I don't, it will conjure thoughts I shouldn't have in this environment, tempting as it may be.

Jade's honeyed eyes bounce around the cavern over the rim of her martini glass, taking everything in with a wide-eyed curiosity that surprises me. Is she enjoying this? At the very least, she's intrigued by it, and the thought of her getting excited by our surroundings has me sitting higher in my seat, unable to look away from her.

A hush descends upon the room, the lights nearly snuffing out as the ones surrounding the stage shift and alter to form a sultry haze of light in the centre of the platform. Two dancers slowly parade around the room, making a show of looking over the patrons getting caught in their enthralling snares. Never exchanging a word, they convey only with body language when they've found a couple to bring up onto the stage.

The male dancer slides up behind the woman sitting at the table they've stopped at, wrapping one hand around her waist and bringing the other hand up, slowly dragging his fingertips along her shoulder in a taunting caress. Her chest rises, falling faster and faster, before her breath fully hitches as the man brings his hand to her throat, squeezing until she looks up at him. He leans down, inching closer to her mouth, before he stops a hair's breadth away, veering off course and whispering something in her ear that has her nodding enthusiastically. When I look over at their counterparts, it's to find the female dancer in the lap of the woman's date, his hand clasping her bottom as she, too, whispers something in his ear.

The dancers share a brief glance, pulling the patrons out of their seats and bringing them onto the stage, where they each settle into a chair facing each other.

Apprehension churns in my gut as I flick a glance over at Jade, whose gaze never drifts from the scene. I break my one drink rule, tossing my tumbler of whisky back; if she can handle whatever's about to take place, then surely, so can I.

The male dancer settles in front of the woman, running his palms over her thighs before he grips her knees, ripping them open. She gasps, and he smirks, leaning forward to brush a kiss to the inside of her leg. From my peripheral, Jade shifts in her seat. The dancer reaches forward, building anticipation before reaching under the chair seat, pulling out a lead of rope and handing one of two bundles to his partner.

The female performer sensually parades around her subject, touching and teasing before she grabs his wrists, tying them in place behind the chair. She makes quick work of his ankles, securing them to the legs of his seat before she stands and straddles his lap, rolling her hips against his groin, forcing his head to drop back.

From three feet away, their counterparts stare at them with lust glazing their eyes. The male performer now stands behind his subject after tying her to the seat, running his hands down the front of her blouse, slipping beneath the chiffon and grasping her breast. Her mouth parts on a gasp as her spine bows slightly off the back of the chair.

The entire room is enraptured with the scene playing out on the stage, and from the corner of my eye, I can see Jade's chest heaving slowly, though her face remains impassive. It makes me a little perplexed and a lot curious that she hasn't gotten up and left.

I risk fully glancing her way, a compulsive need to look at her turning my head. The red lighting around the room casts a haze on the left side of her face, illuminating her otherworldly beauty, making the blue spot in her eye glow brighter with the contrast. The beading on her dress glows like fallen embers all over her body.

Hellfire incarnate.

She looks *sinful* in that tiny scrap of black silk being held up by gravity defying skinny straps, chest threatening to spill and her soft thigh peeking out from the slit crawling dangerously high up her leg. Jade's hands rest in her lap, where she fidgets with one of the delicate rings on her hand, the only sign she's even remotely affected—until she shifts slightly in her chair.

My body becomes hyper aware of that subtle movement. Surely, she's not—no, I'm reading too much into it. But then my eyes crawl further up her body, settling on her full mouth, where she's lightly biting the corner of her lip. She must sense me staring, because she looks over, sitting up straight and releasing her lip.

I can't help but grin before I bring my drink to my mouth, never letting go of her stare, hoping to rile her up. Only, she doesn't look away like I think she will. Instead, she uncrosses her legs, leaning closer to me as she reaches forward, and grabs her cocktail, downing the rest of her martini. My body tenses in anticipation when she holds eye contact, seductively curling her tongue around the speared olives before closing her mouth and slowly pulling the short skewer out from between her full lips.

Shite, now I'm hard.

"I—" I stumble on my words when a loud gasp from the stage pulls our attention, finally forcing us to break eye contact.

Based on the show, this is no longer a performance, and the dancers appear to be getting just as aroused as their subjects. All around us, patrons shift—hands slip under tables, lips find necks, and some couples get up to find somewhere more private.

On the stage, hands roam south, pinching and caressing as lips find skin. The man is very clearly turned on, indicated by the tenting in his pants as his dancer grinds against him, and his date looks like she's about to combust as the male dancer settles in front of her, inching his hand higher up her skirt. Their faces are screwed up in pleasure, begging for more—begging for the performers to take them to the brink. Gasps turn to outright moans as hands find their marks and—

Black silk curtains the length of a rugby pitch drop from the ceiling, carrying with them aerialists wearing nothing but leather body harnesses. The floor length fabric completely obstructs our view before we see too much— though that doesn't stop us from hearing it. Sex permeates the room around us, and that, in combination with the woman sitting next to me in the sexiest dress I've ever seen, makes my skin pull taut.

Soft murmurs devolve around the room as everyone is released from our trances, now watching the aerialists climbing the silks and putting on their own, less erotic show.

A moment later, a man in black dress pants and white button up approaches our table, offering his hand to Jade in invitation, angling his head toward the back hall. My hackles rise.

"Wanna go have some fun?" he asks, like I'm not sitting right fucking here.

I white knuckle my glass, pushing the whisky in my mouth through my teeth like a sieve before I swallow. "Remove your hand from her airspace before you leave here without one."

The man arches a brow at Jade, as if to ask, *does he own you,* before she shakes her head, and he walks away rejected.

The air around us grows taut with tension. "What the fuck was that?"

My jaw aches from clenching it so tightly, to keep myself from saying what's on the tip of my tongue.

"*Answer me.*" Her voice is firm, authoritative.

"You're not my boss here," I bite back.

Jade looks long at me before abruptly standing, striding away from the table.

Fuck.

I race after her through the cavernous room, weaving past servers, dancers, and at least two people wedged into a dark corner, bringing each other pleasure.

"Jade," I call after her. She's several feet in front of me, walking surprisingly fast for someone balancing on shoes with five inch toothpicks. "Jade," I say again.

Her only response is throwing up the middle finger right before she turns down *the hallway.* Surely, she doesn't realise what's down that tunnel, or she wouldn't have gone this way.

Like an obsessed puppy, I follow her.

"I don't think you want to go down here." I shove my hands in my pockets as I close in on her. There's only so far she can get down this hallway before she has to double back to exit.

She whips around, losing her balance in those deathtrap heels. I brace my hand on her waist helping to stabilize her, but she swats my hand away. "Why do you seem to think you're the authority on what I want, Stone?"

She's using my last name because she thinks it offers some sort of separation—all it does is make me hard.

My gaze darts down to her vicious lips; the words flying out of them are meant to cut me down to size, but something about being around her makes me feel ten feet tall.

"Stop staring at me like that," she bites, jaw clenched.

"But you're so lovely when you're yelling at me." The smirk curling the corner of my mouth makes her eye twitch.

"You're insufferable." Frustration is etched on her face. Because of me, or because of what she feels for me, I can't be sure.

"Yeah, well, so are you," I volley. "But you're also gorgeous. It's very conflicting for me." My shoulders lift and drop in a shrug.

Her eyes roll so hard, they're almost all white before she turns, going deeper down the dark hall lined with brocade wallpaper.

"Jade." She continues to ignore me. "Come on, the rain's probably stopped. I'll walk you home."

"Or, you can walk straight into the Thames," she volleys, never turning to look at me. "You can go. I'll get myself home when I'm ready."

"Like hell I'm leaving you here alone."

"I can handle myself. I've been doing it my whole life. I'm actually really good at it."

I sigh. "Fuck. I know that. I know you can. You're the most formidable person I've ever met, Jade. But I'm still not leaving you here or letting you walk home alone."

"I'm not giving you a choice, Tieran." Abruptly, she turns to an unmarked door, trying the handle. It opens under her touch; she tries to slip in and shut the door on me, but I wedge my foot in before it closes, following her into the dark.

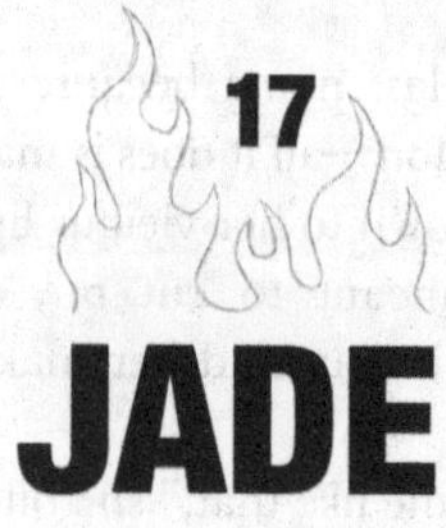

17
JADE

THE ROOM IS SMALL—DARK. It has low ceilings, walls lined with black curtains, low lit sconces, and one wall with a wide window looking into an empty room.

Tieran steps up behind me, gently grabbing my elbow. So gentle, and yet, it feels like a brand on my skin, searing in a way that makes me want to scream.

Stop touching me. Stop being so kind. Stop being so goddamn understanding. Stop being so perfect. Stop making me want to jump into your arms and never let go. I can't have you, I can't want you, and it's killing me. Stop. Stop. Stop.

I've been acting out, pushing him away with biting words and a piss poor attitude, and he just won't go—from here, from my heart.

"Jade." His voice is loud in the empty room.

I shake my head but don't turn. "You need to leave." It's a miracle my voice comes out as steady as it does.

"Turn around, look me in my eyes, and tell me that's what you really want. Because I don't think it is, Jade. You may be able to bluff a boardroom, but you can't fool me."

"You don't know me!" I throw up my hands in exasperation.

He tucks his hands in his pockets and shrugs. "I'd bet I know more about you than most people."

"Oh? Try me then." My arms cross over my chest, and

his gaze darts down and lingers, heating me from head to toe.

"You're fiercely loyal, even though no one in your life has deserved that of you." I start to say something, but he cuts me off. "I'm speaking right now, love. You can yell at me when I'm done." Well…ok then. "Your dad is your best friend because he's the only person you've ever felt safe with, and for good reason, Archie is the best and bizarrely good at online games." I can feel myself soften at the fondness in his voice when he talks about my dad. *Steel your resolve, Jade.* "You're brilliant and successful, but it's come at a price for you, one you shouldn't have to pay. Your favorite color is blue, though you never wear it—except on your toes, apparently. You hate bad martinis, but you'll take a bad one over a good beer. Despite your rigid routine, you have a sweet tooth that would surprise most. You have everything you could ever want, an exciting life, lots of opportunities, status—but deep down, I think you want something else, something softer." He takes a step closer toward me, forcing me to retreat.

The smile that lights up his face can only be described as feral. "How did I do?"

"All of that was google-able," I reason, shrugging my shoulders.

He huffs. "Bullshite."

He takes another step closer to me, but I move to the side, hedging closer to the window and out of his path. If he touches me, I might cave after that speech, because he unknowingly—

or knowingly, it would seem—hit the nail on the head. He even knows my favorite color is blue; how the fuck does he know that?

"Jade—" Whatever he was about to say is interrupted by a couple coming through the door on the opposite side of our window.

No, not a window—a two-way mirror, and we're about to get a private show.

They waste no time ripping each other's clothes off before the man has her on the bed with her legs spread. His head dives between her thighs, and she lets out a contented sigh of pleasure that has me shifting on my feet, very aware of the man behind me.

I turn my head slightly to look at Tieran, expecting him to be looking at the scene unfolding in front of us, but instead, his eyes are heavy on me.

I take one step backward.

He takes one step closer.

We're chest to back, but neither of us pulls away. It's foolish. I'm playing with fire, and I should leave, remove myself from this situation immediately. One time was an accident—a second time is a choice.

"Mmmm," Tieran hums close to my ear. "I want to trace the gorgeous flush crawling up your body with my tongue."

Everything in my body comes alive at his words, and the moans on the other side of the glass grow louder, more desperate. *I can relate.*

I take another hesitant step backward, colliding with Tieran's front. His hand immediately comes to my waist when I lose my footing, but he doesn't let go once I'm stable on my heels. We, or maybe just me, watches as the couple opposite us grunt into each other's skin, having switched positions so she's laying on top of him, sitting on his face while she focuses her attention on his cock, alternating between stroking and sucking.

Alarm bells ring in the back of my mind, telling me I need to leave. They turn into tornado sirens when Tieran starts softly rubbing my hip through the material of my dress. I can feel him against my ass, and it's making my thoughts scatter. It's making me stupid—reckless. I want to feel his hand on my bare skin, want to take what I want for once in my life. After years and years of doing what everyone else around me wants and expects, I want just one goddamn thing for myself.

And I *want* Tieran. I have from the moment I laid eyes on him in that godforsaken bar.

Subtly, I shift my hips, brushing against his hardened length. He pauses his soft stroking and squeezes my hip—hard. I bite back a moan at that strong grip, wanting more. I rock against him again, tilting my head up, raising my eyebrows, as if to say *"well?"*

His cornflower blue eyes flit back and forth between mine. "I don't want you to regret this in the morning," he whispers.

"Stop trying to reason with me and take what I'm offering." I push back into his groin again, and this time, his hips buck forward slightly, as if it was involuntary.

His head drops, and he groans into my neck, sending goosebumps up and down my body. "You're making this impossible for me. I've been spending weeks in *agony*, wanting to put my hands on you. Desperate to reach out and touch your soft skin, sink my teeth into your neck, and hear those sounds you make again."

My carefully curated control snaps.

"Then touch me. You can be agonized again tomorrow." I trail my hand up, grabbing his neck and bringing him down, licking at his mouth but not kissing him. Tieran's arms band around me, his hips bucking into my backside again, and I moan against his mouth.

"Promise me," he whispers against my lips.

"What?" I chase after him, desperate to feel his kiss obliterate me and put me together at the same time.

"Tell me you won't regret this tomorrow."

I pull back to see indecision warring across his handsome face. He wants to give me this, he wants this, but he's trying to do what he thinks is the right thing despite his body crying out for me.

It might be evil, but I give him a little nudge.

"If you don't want me, I can go find that other guy." My voice is a husky challenge, smiling an inch away from his lips, and his grip tightens to the point of bruising as he pulls me further back into his body.

"It's like you want me to end up on the news tonight, love." He licks a path up my neck before catching my ear between his teeth. "Is that what you want? For my name to be splashed over The Sun? Because that's what will happen if I see anyone else's hands on you." His words make me whimper when he places a wet kiss to the skin just below my ear.

"Please," I beg.

His right hand skirts down the plane of my stomach until he reaches the slit of my dress, slipping under the fabric. "This dress has been driving me out of my mind all night." He thumbs at the lace covering my center, humming when he comes in contact with the wet warmth coating the material before pushing it to the side and administering teasing strokes over my slit. He's touching me, but it's not nearly enough.

I cry out, head tilted back into the crook of his shoulder, undulating my hips, seeking more pressure, more friction. The couple across from us is forgotten when he cups my pussy, drawing two fingers through my wetness, teasing back and forth between my clit and opening.

Tieran circles around my entrance before spearing two long fingers deep inside me, forcing me up on the balls of my feet as I cry out at the intrusion. Bliss, unfettered bliss, blanks out my mind. His left hand trails up from my hip, teasing fingers brushing against my stomach, shifting upward to pinch my nipple before wrapping around the column of my neck while he simultaneously pumps his fingers in and out in perfect rhythm.

He tilts my head up and leans down, breath coasting over my lips. "There's no world in which I wouldn't make it out of here in handcuffs if someone else got to experience this."

"That's not your place," I gasp, defiant even now. His

resounding chuckles warms against my temple, as his hips thrust against my ass.

"I don't care if it's not my place. No one else is touching you." He uses his thumb to place steady pressure on my clit, working his fingers in and out as everything coils tight.

My breath hitches. Thinking right now feels impossible. "I'm no—I'm not yours. You don't get to make that decision."

"You feel like mine when your sweet cunt is clenching around my fingers." My walls pulse at his words, and he smiles wider down at me. "Do you think you would have gotten this wet for him?"

I pant out a whimpered breath squirming against his hard cock. He growls in my ear, "Answer me." A gruff echo of my earlier words lobbed back at me.

"Yes."

It's an obvious lie.

"Don't lie to me, love." He nips on my earlobe. "You can pretend all you want—tell yourself we don't work—but your body is betraying you. You want me more than you'll allow yourself to admit. Now, be a good girl and come for me."

He squeezes gently on my neck, and I unravel, body shaking as I come from the combination of his words and the mind-blowing pleasure he brings me with just his hands.

Slowly, he releases his grip around my body, rubbing my clit as the aftershocks of my orgasm heave through my body like a tidal wave. A sense of longing settles over me when he steps away, the warmth of his body dissipating. But when he slowly brings his fingers to his mouth, sucking them between his lips, Tieran hums out a contented sigh I can feel in my chest, and suddenly, I'm hot all over again.

I look down at his lap, noting the still raging hard on he's sporting. I step toward him hand extended, but he grabs my wrist, stepping further out of my reach. "When you admit you like me, I'll let you touch me again."

I raise a brow. "You're going to be waiting a while then."

"Keep telling yourself that, love."

The silence in the room is loud, but the implication is clear. I just made this...thing between us a lot harder to ignore.

When we remember where we are, I look over at the window and realize how easily the world around us faded when he touched me. Because the room on the other side of the glass is completely empty, and I never even noticed.

18

JADE

I DIDN'T LET him walk me home.

Instead, once my lust-addled brain cleared, I opted to run away and hail the first cab that came my way before Tieran could follow me. Maybe I'm a coward, but what the fuck was I thinking? I wasn't—that was the problem: I don't think around him. Everything becomes jumbled in my head, my good sense flies out the window, and all I see is him—his smile, those stupid dimples, his eager eyes.

A desperation came over me, one that felt inescapable in the moment. It was either give in to what's been burning through me for weeks, or leave. I didn't want to leave; I felt like I might die if I did. Every fiber of my being wanted to stay with him, to spar verbally with him…to have him touch me again. What harm would come from giving in *one* more time in a darkened room where no one would see us? Scratch the itch, and then I would forget it happened.

What an absolute idiot. Statues should be erected in my honor for the unfathomable levels of idiocy I so valiantly displayed.

Lying to myself and believing I could just pretend nothing happened was as effective as throwing grease on a fire, and now, everything is burning to the ground, my sanity first.

It was so much worse now, proven by the fact I've been

sitting in this meeting for thirty minutes, unable to focus, my mind dragging itself back to Tieran on a never-ending spin cycle.

When I'm around him, it feels like the one time I'm able to shut my brain off and just be. No expectations, no posturing. He provokes me at every turn, and it's as thrilling as it is infuriating. I can't even recall the last time I had this much fun with anyone, let alone with a man. My ex was convenient more than anything, and nothing about him made me feel alive, not like I do with Tieran.

Brendan was a hot shot studio manager in L.A., and when we met, things were easy and fun for a while— glamorous dates, yacht parties, dinners at Nobu with Hollywood's best. It was everyone's dream in Los Angeles, but the glitz of the city's social scene never excited me like it probably should have. Brendan reveled in every second of it, loved preening for the masses, especially when I was on his arm. It wasn't exactly a love connection, but I stayed out of some misguided sense of loyalty, too busy with work to even notice I was bored, of him, of our relationship. Then, I found him in bed with *my* assistant, Veronica. I mean, really, you couldn't be more original? But I guess originality was asking too much from a man who wore the same outfit every day—navy chinos, a dove grey button up, and his Rolex—because *every self-respecting studio manager has a Rolex*.

I should have left long before I had to hear Veronica's shrill gasps of pleasure, but there was a comfort in the predictable. I didn't have to work at it because there was nothing to it. My manager told me to forgive him, said affairs were normal in relationships like ours and that fans loved a power couple, but the problem was, *I* didn't want a relationship like ours anymore. Brendan didn't either, even though he was willing to stay for his image.

The decision to break up with him was freeing, like the weight of social expectation drifted away on the Santa Ana winds the moment I ended things. I wanted street tacos, and he wanted bite sized portions of toro carpaccio. He wanted a beautiful trophy, and I was starting to realize I didn't know what I wanted anymore. Our puzzle pieces didn't fit. They never did, and they never would.

Within weeks, and after *many* arguments with Maxine *and* financial advisors, I bought the Legends, moved across the world, and stumbled into a dimly lit pub, where I met a man with eyes like the sea. I kept getting pulled in, kept getting swept away. I was weathered stone lodged deeply into the shore, stubborn and obstinate, but his waves kept crashing against me until I slowly loosened and was pulled away into the current. Those eyes are what my memory keeps catching on today.

Electric blue staring back at me through the reflection of a watermarked mirror, faces flushed. Every time I covertly snuck glances of him at the party, his kind eyes crinkled in laughter at whatever his friends said. Later, the lamppost light reflected off them like a flash of lightning while he tried to get me to crack a smile.

I see that blue *everywhere*, even when I close my eyes to sleep. I can't escape them. He consumes my thoughts, even in my dreams.

I've made a mess—a delicious, complicated mess.

"Miss McKallen?" An annoyed voice jolts me out of my thoughts, and embarrassment makes my body flush with heat.

I sit up straighter. "Yes, Lawrence?"

Chapman scoffs. "Are you even paying attention? Shouldn't the *majority shareholder*, as you love to remind us, be more present in the meeting?"

The flat stare I give him would make most men wither. "Of course. Your earlier observation about our revenue stream just got my mind running. I've been brainstorming ways we can increase match attendance, as well as raise sales for team merchandise along with food and beverage. I have a connection with ties to some nationwide beer brands I'm going to reach out to for a meeting. I think we could partner with them to get a Knightsbridge-specific brew, something you can only get here during a match. It would have its own label, and we can look into branding for souvenir cups and mark up the price by an extra two pounds. Then there's a few food companies I've worked with that I want to speak to about elevating the food here. Sausage rolls are classic, but I think we can take it a step further, source from local farms to support our economy and garner good relations with hard working individuals as opposed to mega corporations. I'd like for us to appeal to everyone, no matter their socio-economic standing. A partnership with an established brand will help bring in new guests, but contributing to local business will build the community, and that keeps people coming back."

I survey the boardroom, and nearly every face looks impressed—all but one, and that one looks pissed.

"If you have any suggestions, I'm all ears. I'm not the only one on this board, and everyone's opinion is valuable," I add, leaning forward with my elbows on the table, resting my chin on the tops of my hands.

Ron looks like he wants to chime in, but Lawrence spears him with a look, and he slumps back in his chair, remaining quiet.

That's a problem. Chapman fancies himself a god here, and everyone fears speaking out against him. I need to figure out how to nip that in the ass if we are ever going to be a team that succeeds. We need to be a well-oiled machine for every aspect to run smoothly, to set an example for all the other sectors of the stadium. I also need the men who are afraid of Lawrence to speak up for themselves, because it's clear he's not going to listen to me. I'm not in the habit of babysitting grown men who like to throw temper tantrums every time they don't get their way.

"No one?" I urge, but the room remains quiet. "Alright, well, as a reminder, the Kingdom for Kids Gala is in a few weeks' time, and as donors, all of us should be in attendance. Please plan accordingly." I don't know much about our place in the organization or how we came to be benefactors, but I got an email from them this morning to confirm our contribution.

A loud bang reverberates around the room as Lawrence slaps his hands on the table, standing up from his chair. "Well, gents," he says, negating my presence. He slaps his stomach. "Time to get home to the missus, fill my belly, and empty my balls." The men around him chuckle, even as a few uneasy glances flit my way.

"I'm sure your wife looks forward to you coming home each night," I say sarcastically, standing from my chair at the head of the table and grabbing my bag to walk out of the room.

The stairs are looking like a great option, even in my stilettos, just so I can avoid being stuck in a tiny steel box with men and their over-inflated egos. I'm halfway down when the door pushes open and slams closed, loud footsteps sauntering down the stairs behind me.

"I'm curious," Lawrence starts. "Who do you think you are, speaking to me like that?"

I don't stop, continuing my descent. "I don't know, Lawrence. Who do you think you are being a blatant misogynist at every chance?"

"It's locker room chat with the lads. Lighten up."

"You aren't in a locker room, and they aren't your lads. You're a walking HR violation." Never mind the horrendous hypocrisy of that statement. I could hardly call him on violations when the captain of my team's been inside me on two occasions now.

"I'm above HR violations," he scoffs.

"The fact that you think that proves you shouldn't hold sole responsibility for the team." I finally stop and turn to face him. "The rules are in place to protect *everyone* under the Legends umbrella. No one is above them. You aren't God, Lawrence."

"And you think you are?"

"No. Just the *majority shareholder*, and if you won't give me the respect my position deserves, then I'll just *take* it." I spin on my heel and push out the door at the bottom of the steps.

"You'll trip up eventually, Miss McKallen," he shouts after me, "and when you do, I can't wait to see you break your ankle falling in those fuck me heels."

I don't stumble at his words. I don't tense. I don't let him see the apprehension coating my body like hoarfrost. Because there *is* something that could make me trip up if it were to get out.

Crystalline blue clouds my vision as I climb into the car I called to pick me up, ignoring the churning that's started low in my gut.

✦ ✧ ✦ ☆ ✦ ✧ ✦

"I got you a chippy from the shop, but they were all out of vinegar—a sin, I know. I hope you have some—" A crash comes from the kitchen, and my stomach drops as I rush into the other room to find my father on the floor.

Tossing the takeaway bag on the table, I drop down at his side. "Dad! Hold on, let me call for an ambulance." My usually organized bag is a labyrinth of crap in the way of me finding my phone. "Just hold on. I can't find my phone."

"Jade," Dad's gruff tone calls out, grunting with effort.

"I don't know why I let you convince me to only have Myrah on part-time, I'm asking her tomorrow if she can take on more hours. You shouldn't be alone."

"Jade."

I finally find my phone, ripping it out of my bag and starting to dial 999. "Just stay where you are, Dad. Don't try to get up, you might make it worse."

"I swear, you don't listen to me, just like your mother." That grabs my attention enough that I pause on hitting call, nearly breaking my neck to whip my head over and look at him in shock. Dad never talks about Mom anymore, not after the way their relationship ended. All the information I have is that they decided when I was young that it was better for them to be apart, and speak as little as possible. Dad stayed close by, and I split my time between the two houses until I was old enough to move to L.A. A week later, Dad packed up and left for England. Anytime I tried to bring it up, they both refused to talk about it. Mom moved on and remarried a couple more times, but to my knowledge, Dad has remained single. "I'm alright. I just tripped over my shoelace right as you came through the door."

I look down and see his shoe is, in fact, untied, and *maybe* I overreacted. Even still, I look him over head to toe to assess for any tremors or signs of distress, not fully believing he's okay. It was his way, after all. Ever since I was a kid, he would downplay everything to try and ease my mind. Fights with Mom, stressful situations at work—how much he missed England. Nothing was ever wrong when I asked him, but I knew it was a farce, and he was just trying to shield me from whatever reality he thought I couldn't handle. It made me want to double down and show him I *could* handle it. I wanted to help carry his burden, but he wouldn't let me.

So, I started doing the same thing he did—I held everything close to my chest. I became so good at doing everything alone, letting someone help me was a foreign concept. Even hiring my assistant was really just an attempt to appease my manager, who said I needed it. And we see how well that situation played out in the end.

After years of bad business deals, shady clout chasers, and cheating boyfriends, it only solidified that if you want something done right, you have to do it yourself. There isn't a problem I can't fix with my phone, a strong cup of coffee, and my favorite pair of stilettos. Getting other people involved only leads to more headaches in the form of errors *I* would have to fix. It was better to do it myself from the start, even if that meant sixteen hour days.

Dad pulls himself up off the floor, and I grasp his elbow to help him along.

"I got it. Don't fuss."

"Okay, sorry. Do you want some tea?" I ask, moving over to the kettle next to his sink.

"Does a bear shit in the woods?"

"Unless its name is Paddington. Barry's or PG's?" Most law-abiding citizens of the United Kingdom have a tea brand they're dead loyal to—so loyal, they will exclusively buy that brand for the rest of their lives and expect their entire bloodline to follow suit. Archie McKallen, though? He's a bit of a turncoat. One day, he's a Barry's loyalist, and then the next, he remembers it's an Irish brand, and furiously throws a PG Tips bag in his mug.

He definitely prefers the Barry's, but it all boils down to his mood.

"PG, please. Thanks, pumpkin." He shuffles into the sitting room, grabbing the bag of takeaway as he brushes past the table, walking a little stiffly.

With him out of the kitchen, I grab a bag of Barry's red and pop it in his favorite mug while the water starts to boil in the kettle. Once it's finished and I've prepared his cup, I bring it to him where he sits in his chair.

He takes a sip, eyeing the cup skeptically. "Did you use a Barry's?"

"No, of course not," I lie.

He takes another pull, swishing it around in his mouth. "Mmmm. Yes, right. Tastes English."

He and I both know that's Irish tea. He's just too proud to admit it.

I settle into a spot on the sofa opposite his beloved chair and cross my legs, wishing I had brought a spare change of clothes. Loud cheering blares out of the speakers on the tv in the corner of the room as Dad turns on the match that's set to start any minute.

"Why aren't you watching in person instead of on my uncomfortable couch?" he asks.

"I'll have you know I like metal springs digging into my coccyx, it keeps me alert."

Dad chortles as he pops a chip in his mouth. "Is it not mandatory to be there? You haven't missed a match since the season started."

"Technically, it's not, but I like to be there to show the team I'm invested in more ways than purely financial." He waves a chip filled hand for me to continue. "I had a few meetings I had to be on back in the States that required my undivided attention. Trying to take them from a car or train out to Bristol didn't seem feasible, and Maxine has been on me about being *present* for all my other commitments." Dad rolls his eyes at that.

As if it was even possible to forget the ten thousand things I've got going on at all times. I have always thrived on being busy, but at what point did staying busy become synonymous with being avoidant? My time in London has been illuminating in that department. I was still working constantly, but I was also being forced to do things purely for fun—for exploration. Everything felt just a little bit lighter. Responsibilities felt a fraction less dire. Aanya dragging me out, Lottie's effervescence, even Tieran's dogmatic insistence on me trying new things left a buzzing in my chest.

"Ah, that's a good lad." Dad's voice draws me out of my head.

When I look over, it's to see the Legends captain dominating the screen. He looks disturbingly good in his kit, the material clinging to his broad shoulders and sculpted body. I know that, in mere minutes, once the game is in full swing, sweat will heighten that view as a sheen coats his tanned skin, making his strong, tattooed thighs stand out under the stadium lights.

Tieran is currently chatting to our equipment manager, clapping him on the shoulder and shooting him a smile before he takes off toward the center of the pitch. Harry looks slightly in awe, and I can't help but empathize with him. Tieran leaves me feeling off kilter every time I talk to him too.

Across the screen, the men run back and forth, passing the ball, dodging in and out of opponents, and often getting tackled within seconds of our guys getting the ball. Our standing in the league hasn't improved much. The Legends aren't all the way at the bottom, but we're sitting squarely in the middle, a place no one wants to be. I can see from the set of Tieran's jaw that he's getting more and more frustrated by the minute.

"He's having a rough go of it this season, eh?"

"Hmm?" I ask, only half listening.

"My friend. He seems to be struggling."

"That's an awfully familiar endearment for someone who's only met him once," I chuckle. Ever since I bought the team, Dad's fancied himself an honorary player.

"Well, when you talk to someone *at least* once a week, you tend to think of them as such."

He says it so casually, I almost didn't catch it. What does he mean, he talks to him *at least* once a week? That can't be right…can it? Maybe Dad hit his head when he took his fall earlier.

"What do you mean?" I ask, stomach flipping over itself while I wait for him to stop grumbling at the television to clarify what the fuck he meant, praying he won't confirm what I think he means. I wouldn't survive it.

"The boy calls me every week, sometimes more."

Here lies Jade McKallen. Cause of death: being bashed over the head with a sickeningly sweet rugby player.

Why does he keep saying these things as if they aren't a big deal? I'm over here with a head that's about to explode, and he's acting like he just told me it's going to rain later.

"Why would he do that?" I whisper.

"Because we're friends. Keep up, pumpkin."

Dad is completely unaware of the mental gymnastics racing through my mind. Tieran calls my dad weekly? Why? Is it some ploy to get to me? No, that can't be right, because if that was the case, why hasn't he mentioned it?

"How did he get your number?"

Dad shouts at a bad call against the Legends happening on screen, and Tieran's angry, beautiful face fills the screen. His eyes are a blazing inferno of frustration as he shakes his head and spits onto the pitch before stalking away.

"He asked me for it when he came by that first day," he says around a mouth full of cod.

"What do you talk about?"

"Little of this, little of that."

My eye twitches, and I'm verging on a scream. Must men always be so vague?

Dad sees the mini meltdown I'm about to succumb to, and he sighs. "He always starts off by asking how I'm doing and if I've gone out for fresh air yet. Then, we usually chat about rugby, and we debrief on a show we're both watching that's new to the BBC."

I'm at a total loss for words. Tieran's asked me about my dad casually since that day he came over to check on him, but he never let on that they were in communication themselves.

"He usually asks about you at some point."

My head snaps up. "What?"

He harrumphs. "Silly stuff, like your favorite color, but every now and then, he'll ask something more specific, get curious about what you were like as a kid."

Well that explains why he knows my favorite color is blue.

My lungs are seizing, my mind is spinning, and the tips of my fingers are starting to tingle. Who is this man?

"He's a good one, Jadey. You should find someone like him. Please, for the love of Christ, don't stick yourself with another Thad."

Dad's attempt at humor eases the tension in my chest a little. "His name was Brendan."

"Potato, tomato. He was a twit."

He's not wrong, so I don't bother correcting him. Instead, I spend the next hour watching this enigma of a man fight for his life on the pitch, only to come up empty handed, disappointment written over the planes of his body, pasting on a smile I know isn't real.

I hate it. I hate that he can't see how utterly brilliant he is, how talented and kind and funny he is. He can't see how much everyone respects and trusts him—myself included—and it infuriates me. He should know, and that mask he puts on for the cameras and his team shouldn't be there. I want to kiss it off his face until he never has a reason to put it back on.

For weeks, I've been torturing myself, trying not to think of him, but in this moment, all I can think about is how I'm going to replace that artificial smile with a real one.

To: jademckallen@jaded.com
From: bjones@jonescapital.com
Subject: Status Update

Jade –
I'm concerned about the past several weeks' performance from the label. Ad revenue has dropped and marketing has reported a fifteen percent decrease in ad clicks from your socials. What is your plan to rectify this? Please have a report drawn up by the end of day.

19
TIERAN

MY CHEEKS ARE sore from the smile I've had plastered across my face for the last two hours, and my head throbs from the rowdiness of the team as we drive east back toward London. No one seems fazed by tonight's loss. There was general disappointment while walking off the pitch, but everyone seems to have let it go. So, I had to let it go too—or, at least, I pretended to.

Keep up morale. No one wants to see the captain moping over a lost game. I have to smile, strategize for improvement, and make sure they know we can do this. And I do believe *they* can; I just don't know if *I* can, and that's the problem.

All the feelings of inadequacy were only exacerbated when Coach Ballard pulled me aside after tonight's match.

"I gave you time, Stone. You told me you were doing better at the start of the season—that I had nothing to worry about. But the last few matches have left me with nothing but a clenched arsehole."

"I'm sorry, sir." My head drops in embarrassment.

"I don't want you to be sorry. I want to win a bloody match." Spit flies from his mouth. *"Do you still want a spot on the National Team?"*

"You know I do."

"Then get your shite together, Stone. I say this with as much fondness as I can muster for you—find a way to get over this...

meltdown you're having, or you can kiss your chance at the Olympics goodbye."

I've wanted to throw up since. Everyone around me is having a good time, planning which pub they're going to once we get back to the city. Davies is rambling about how many numbers he's going to get, how many *birds* he'll take home. The men are laughing—happy in the face of another loss—and I'm crawling out of my fucking skin.

Do they not care as much as I do? Do they not feel like all of London is waiting for them back at the city limits with pitchforks and lit torches? Or are they just not worried because they all know I'm the one fucking up, not them?

Mum sent an encouraging message to our family group chat in an effort to make me feel better. Lottie responded with a silly photo, and Dad didn't respond at all. The silence told me enough. He's disappointed. Why wouldn't he be?

I spend the next half hour with my hood up, watching highlight reels online of every wrong move I made. Maybe if I torture myself with my failings, it'll allow me to see how I can improve.

Every day, I get increasingly more frustrated that I haven't gotten out of my own fucking head. My mind constantly oscillates between our team's rank, my inability to play the game I was fucking born to play, letting my guys down, not qualifying for the National Team, and being terrified I'm going to disappoint my family if I can't get my shite together.

The only time my mind decides to rest on its ultra marathon around my brain is when Jade's around. I can't quite place what it is yet, but when she's near, I feel like I can breathe again. Which is confusing, because as the person who signs my paychecks, you would think she'd be who was scrutinizing me the most. From that first one-on-one meeting, it was clear she genuinely cares about each person on the team—not just for the sole purpose of how they will perform, but who we are, who we could become. She saw potential where others would see problems.

And hell if there isn't something refreshing about that.

A notification rolls over the sports recap video playing on my phone, and it's as if I've conjured her out of my fantasies.

HELLFIRE

How are you doing?

TIERAN

Was I so bad that you felt the need to check on me?

Just wanted to make sure I got an invite to the pity party you're probably throwing right now.

So you can leave it without saying goodbye again?

It's likely.

I'm wounded.

Seriously, where's your head at?

I'm fine.

Liar.

I debate it for a second, telling her the truth, but I don't want her to lose whatever misplaced faith she seems to have in me when it's the only thing keeping my head above water.

TIERAN

Do you text all your players to make sure they're okay?

Three dots crop up, wave, then pause before it repeats the motion and then stops all together.

It's dangerous to call her out on the obvious—we both

know she hasn't texted any other players, and this most definitely breaks whatever rules she's super imposed on our *relationship*. Seems ridiculous at this point, considering I've been inside her twice now, and I'm already desperate and waiting for a third chance to prove to her this...persistent ache isn't normal.

HELLFIRE

Just the ones with hero complexes who are probably being too hard on themselves.

TIERAN

I do have superhero level good looks, you're right.

I don't think that's what I said.

That's what I heard. Should I give you more reasons why I'd make the next great Marvel character?

You do love to listen to yourself talk.

I can think of a few ways you could shut me up.

So can I...

I'm grateful for the stiff fabric of my jeans holding my burgeoning erection at bay. It would be fucking embarrassing to be caught on a bus full of rugby players sporting a boner. Shifting slightly in my seat, I subtly adjust my pants, grateful no one is sitting next to me, because there's enough room to spread out. Only Cavan can see me from where he sits in the row next to mine but he pays me no mind, always more inclined to keep to himself post-match. Even still, I glance back, making sure whoever is behind me can't see what and who I'm texting. Thankfully, it's just our equipment manager, Harry, who smiles at me before looking back out at the road rolling by.

I grin at my phone, typing out a reply.

TIERAN

Oh yeah? Care to share?

HELLFIRE

Well, I don't think duct tape would hold up very well, so I'm thinking I'd have to cut out your tongue.

I don't think you want to do that, Hellfire. You haven't seen what my tongue can do yet.

Several minutes pass with no answer. I assume she's on her way to kick my ass in person for crossing the line. Either that, or I've ticked her off so royally, she's never going to speak to me again. But just as I'm about to put my phone away, a notification pops up, and I rush to open it—embarrassingly fast.

HELLFIRE

Stop trying to distract me.

TIERAN

Oh love, distracting you is becoming my favourite hobby.

Not needlepoint?

It's a close second, but you still win.

Lucky me.

Tell me.

Everyone in the world is fooled by my easy smiles, my nonchalant shrugs of indifference, the easy lies that fall off my lips anytime someone asks me anything related to the game or the breakup they're all hellbent on dredging up. But Jade McKallen's sharp, mesmerising stare sees it all. There is no hiding from her—I don't think I'd want to hide even if I could.

But a voice in my head holds me back, scared she'll see me differently. Call it residual ex trauma, but once I let myself feel relaxed around Olivia, things shifted. She started paying attention less, stopped listening when I spoke, and found reasons to bail on plans we made. She only stuck around as long as she did for the status—that is, until someone else was able to provide her with what I was also providing. I'm glad it fizzled out the way it did, but it still shook me. I no longer feel sure of myself, because I *didn't* see those signs until my face was slapped across the front of The Daily Mail with the headline: *'DROPPED LIKE A STONE: Girlfriend of England's favourite fly-half Tieran Stone leaves the rugby star for rival Oliver Hughes!'*

I had never felt the scrutiny from the public like I did after that. It was humiliating. Before, during, and after every single match, the same five questions were lobbed at me from every direction, and they all had to do with the scandal. My performance started decreasing after that, and a mask went up over my features anytime I was in public.

I secure it in place now as doubt wraps its hands around mine, guiding my next words.

TIERAN

It's all good, boss.

I don't wait to see if she texts back. I put my phone on silent, pull the hood of my sweatshirt over my head, and watch the motorway pass by out the window.

I'm not able to shake the sticky feeling of inadequacy for the rest of the ride home. I once read that meditation was a good tactic for keeping the rising panic at bay, but all it's done is make me more irritated and weirdly hungry.

After making it back to the stadium, I praised the lads for their hard work while giving a speech I didn't believe, wanting nothing more than to take a long bath to ease my aching muscles and slip under the water, never to resurface. Keeping a brave face was becoming harder by the day, and the stress of slipping up, of letting everyone down in a different way, was compounding my anxieties further.

As I pull up out front of my home, I spot a shadowed figure by the door shifting back and forth. Slowly, I get out of the car, the threat to call the police on the tip of my tongue before the person turns a little, stepping into the patch of light from the streetlamp, and the words shrivel up to nothing.

Jade McKallen is dressed head to toe in athletic gear, the black Lycra molding so perfectly to her toned thighs and round arse that my mind goes blissfully blank for the first time all night. The only thing I can think about is how slowly rolling the buttery material down her body would be the perfect way to unwind.

"What are you doing here?" I blurt out, snapping out of my indecent trance.

Jade halts her movements, her back turned to me. "Never mind. Forget I was here."

She takes a step, readying to flee and still refusing to look at me. My body reacts before my brain can catch up, and I reach out, gripping her arm before she can dart away. She's always running from me, always hiding, and I've reached my limit. "I'm gonna ask you one more time, Hellfire. Why did you come here?"

"I—" She stumbles over her words, looking everywhere but at me. "I was out for a run. Didn't realize this was your house."

"You're a better liar than that, love. Try again."

She finally glances up at me, indecision waring in her eyes as they flit back and forth, a beautiful frown marring her full mouth, brow furrowed. "I don't know. I shouldn't be."

Insecurity is a foreign look on her face, something that should never be there, but right now, it's written clear as day all over her features. Me and her, this connection that's been sparking between us since that night at The King's

Swan, it might be the one thing in her life Jade McKallen doesn't know how to control.

My gaze travels down her arm and settles on the bag in her hand. "What do you have?" I swipe my thumb along the inside of her wrist.

"Tesco meal deal." Her voice is barely a whisper.

A laugh bursts out of me. This woman has more money than anyone in this country, and she's standing before me with a *Tesco meal deal.* Fuck me, I said it that first night we met, and it remains true today: Jade McKallen is an enigma, a puzzle I want to spend hours trying to put together just so I can figure out what piece reveals her humour, which ones slot together to display her brilliance— her kindness, until all I can see is the entire picture of her— who she is.

"Don't tell me you're too good for it." A dark eyebrow raises high in challenge as an edge returns to her voice. A clear challenge.

"Give me that." I grab the bag out of her hand to see what's inside. Two sandwiches, a bag of prawn crisps, a side of sliced apples with peanut butter, and two drinks. "Approved. Come on, let's go eat."

"Oh, I don't think—"

"Jade," I interrupt.

"What?"

"Stop overthinking it. Just come inside and eat with me." Her eyes trail down to where I'm still holding her wrist and then travels up the length of me, holding a second too long on my mouth before she looks me in the eyes. Something within them shutters, and I know she's about to deny me, so I say the one thing I can think of to get her to stay, a last ditch effort to keep her around me. "I could use the company."

I think I *need* it.

She doesn't resist when I tug on her arm, pulling her toward my front door.

It's dark as I lead her inside. I toss my keys on the

entryway table and move to turn on the lights when a thirty-five pound ball of energy comes barrelling down the short hallway, launching herself into my arms.

I let out a grunt at having the wind briefly knocked out of me. "Hello, darling girl." I pepper kisses all over my Blue Staffy's perfectly round face as her tail wags furiously. "I know, I know, Daddy missed you too. I'm never going to leave you again." I nuzzle my face into her neck. "Who needs to work when I could be here all day with you?" Pebble pulls back so she can return the love with a hot lick up the side of my face, signaling me to set her down.

As soon as her paws touch the ground, she sprints over to Jade, taking her by surprise and knocking her over.

"Fuck, I'm sorry. She doesn't know how much she weighs," I say.

Jade waves me off, immediately wrapping her arms around the canine's chunky neck, hugging her tight.

Worst guard dog ever.

"I didn't peg you as an animal lover," I observe, surprised by the easy affection she's bestowing on my dog from her seat on the floor.

"Why? Because I'm cold and heartless?" Her eyes flare as she twists my words.

"You think you're cold?" Surprise is etched into my tone.

Jade avoids eye contact, opting to hold each side of Pebble's face, planting kisses on her cheeks and the sweet spot right between her eyes. She preens under the attention, face smiling, tail wagging, and I can't believe I'm jealous of my own fucking dog.

"That's what I've been told." She shrugs her shoulders, smiling softly down at Pebble, but the set of her shoulders is stiff.

"That's rubbish."

"Excuse me?" She finally turns to look at me.

"Whoever made you feel like you're either of those things is a pillock. Did they even try to understand you?"

"And you're the expert on all things me?" She scoffs.

"I've gleaned some things," I shrug.

Jade leans back on her palms, and Pebble rests her head in her lap. "Enlighten me then."

My voice drops, softens. "You're not cold, you're *focused*. You are successful and intentional with your time, and anyone who's called you heartless has clearly never bothered to see the real you. You uprooted your life so you could be near your father. Jade, you took the time to understand *every* player under your employ to make sure they felt heard. No one else had ever done that for us. Do you not realise how rare that is? How *valued* you made every man on the team feel? You quietly invest in small businesses." She raises her eyebrows at that. "Yes, I Googled you, and I don't care if that makes me pathetic. Which I am, by the way—pathetic for you." She blushes furiously, eyes skipping away from mine, so I take pity on her and move on. "You've shown up to gigs for Aanya despite not having time, and you're at every game even though it's not a requirement, and there's a million other things you could be doing. You *care* about people more than anyone else I've ever met. And, as if the rest wasn't enough to prove it to you, you're practically big spooning my dog on the floor." I step toward her, Pebble between us, now belly up, and I reach a hand out to Jade. She tentatively settles her palm into mine, and a zap of electricity shoots through my arm at the contact as I pull her up, tugging her further than necessary into my personal space. "So, no. You're not cold, Jade. You've just never felt safe enough to let someone stand in your warmth. They never deserved to."

Whoever they are, I want to kill them for ever making her think less of herself.

She searches my eyes with her own, and I track that spot of sky blue like my life depends on it, waiting to see what she'll say about my quasi confession. I shouldn't have noticed these things about her, but I did, and it's as much of an admission as tattooing on my forehead 'I like you' in big bold letters.

"Why have you been texting with my dad?" she whispers.

"Because I like him, and we're currently neck and neck on Words with Friends." That's a lie. I do like Archie, and I look forward to our daily text exchanges, but he is kicking my arse in the game.

"That's the *only* reason?" Implication saturates her tone, making it clear she doesn't fully believe me.

"It's the only reason I think you're willing to hear right now."

Tentatively, I reach out, grazing the tips of my fingers against the shell of her ear to brush a lock of hair that fell into her eyes when I pulled her off the floor. Her gaze flits down to my mouth, and my entire body tightens, begging to bridge that gap and finally kiss her again. It would be so easy to take another step, lean down, and take what I've been wanting for weeks. With anyone else, I would have, but with her, it means something—I *want* it to mean something. I want Jade to want it to mean something.

Even still, I can't help myself from cupping her jaw, fingers threading into her hair, thumb tilting her head up to look at me. The heat of her stare grounds me, settling something restless and weary within me. A moment of weakness before I pull away, grabbing the bag of food from her hand and leading her into the kitchen.

Jade breaks the silence. "Your place isn't what I expected."

"So you've been thinking about my home? What else have you been wondering about? The thread count on my sheets?" I smirk, pulling the contents of the bag out and setting them on the marble top kitchen island as she settles into the stool opposite me.

"I have wondered if your pillows are thick enough to effectively suffocate you." Reaching across the counter, she grabs her Diet Coke, unscrews the cap. and brings it to her rosebud pink lips.

"I can think of something else I'd rather you suffocate me with."

She chokes on her drink. "You have to stop doing that."

"Doing what?" I ask, eyes flicking up to hers as I toss a prawn crisp in my mouth.

"Saying things just to shock me."

"Oh, I promise you, they're all true, Hellfire. Seeing that gorgeous flush creep up your chest is just an added bonus." I toss her a wink just to irritate her further.

"Since you love to talk so much, how about you tell me where your head's at?" We're back to Business Professional Jade.

"I don't think you want to know where my head's at, *boss*." I round the corner of the island, settling onto a stool, scooting closer to her so I'm bracketing her thighs with mine.

She steamrolls over my innuendo. "Stop trying to distract me. Better yet, stop trying to distract yourself by flirting with me."

There she goes, seeing right through all my bluster again. I can't explain why I feel the need to deflect my emotions and steer her away from seeing too closely. Maybe it's pride; maybe it's because she's the last person I want to let down.

What would I even say? I have no explanation for what's been happening to me.

With that in mind, I rely on the one thing that's never failed me—my relentless and unwavering ability to chat my way out of any situation.

"But the colour your cheeks go when I flirt with you is so delicious, love."

Her stare is icy. "What are you doing?"

I fear I severely miscalculated. "What do you mean?"

"You keep putting on this mask—this false bravado. Why?"

Jade grabs the sandwich package sitting in front of her, peels back the film, and takes half out before swirling her hand around, pointing the sandwich at me accusingly. The sharp look in her eyes in combination with the furrow between her brows is disturbingly cute. She's got the heart of a lion and the face of a gazelle, and the dichotomy does weird things to my insides.

I contemplate lying, but it's clear she won't believe me or let it go. I breathe in steadily, but the exhale has a slight wobble to it. "When the mask is on, I can pretend to be who they all expect me to be, who they *want* me to be. They don't want to see what it's really like up here." I tap the centre of my head. "The fans don't want that. They want me to be untouchable—unobtainable. I'll lose my luster and become a real human to them, not this mythical athlete. You don't want that to happen, boss. It's not good for optics." Something flickers in her eyes, but it's gone in a flash. It would seem I'm not the only one wearing a mask.

I toss another crisp in my mouth and give her an easy smile. The mask, even after this admission, feels impossible to remove.

"What if I just want you to be you?" Sincerity rings through her tone, clear and strong.

It's a nice thought. A glorious thought, even, but the public's perception is everything when appealing to National scouts. They don't want a flight risk. They want stability—to know that who they're signing is worth the heavy price tag. I haven't been that player in a long time.

I turn away from her, reaching into my fridge to pull out a beer and popping the top off with the ring on my index finger. I take a long swig, but I keep my eyes leveled on Jade as her gaze rakes over me. "I'll show you mine if you show me yours, Hellfire."

She sits up straighter in her chair, placing the trash from her meal in the empty Tesco bag she brought it in.

Yeah, it's not as easy to strip yourself bare before a person, is it?

"It's getting late. I should get going."

Arguing would be pointless. We've both pushed each other enough tonight, and even though everything in me wants her to stay, to keep letting her poke and prod just to have her around, it's probably best for me to weather it alone. Try to maintain some semblance of dignity.

She walks to the door, me and Pebble hot on her heels. When we reach the front door, she twists and kneels, kissing my dog right between the eyes before standing once more.

For a moment we both stand there not knowing what to do or say. Should I hug her? I want to—fuck, do I want to. But we've been silent for too long, let the moment drag out, and now it's a little like saying goodbye to a new friend you're still getting to know, slightly awkward. Except I *do* know Jade, I think more than she wants to admit, and despite it being a rough day, month, *year*, her presence tonight did loosen some of the anxiety roiling through my chest. The persistent pressure was still there, but it felt lighter.

Taking a cautious step toward her, I lean forward. When she doesn't immediately retreat, I get closer until I hear her breath hitch a little. I'm an inch away from her rosebud lips when I skirt to the right, placing a kiss to her soft cheek right above a small, delicate beauty mark.

I breathe in her warm, slightly sweet scent before pulling away. "You're not heartless."

She looks up at me, mere inches away. "No?"

"No." My voice comes out rough. "Your heart is probably too big; it cares too much. You just don't let the world see that. So, thank you."

"For what?"

"For letting *me* see it."

20

JADE

"THE LATEST COLLECTION is under performing. The content from the influencers we've hired hasn't saturated as deeply as we would've hoped, and the *lack* of content coming from our founder isn't helping."

The not-so-subtle dig comes from the Chief Commercial Officer of Jaded. She's a veritable hard ass, but she's good at her job. It's why I hired her, but right now I resent it. The problem is, she's not wrong. My businesses rely on me and the content I put out to make sure we have consistent sell-through. It's not enough to design the piece, source the material, double check the research team did their due diligence on the ethics behind whatever company we buy from, triple check the manufacturing company we're using is up to code, have a hand in every step of the process, wear and test prototypes, provide feedback, test again, shoot ad campaigns, host events for launches, and probably ten other things I'm forgetting. I also have to film content for my socials that feels natural and organic, not like I'm selling them a product.

Which I am.

Lately, it makes me feel manipulative. I believe in my brand, and I love the creative process of conceptualizing something and watching it come to life, but I want it to be less about me, and more about the people I built it for. I want my designs to empower people and tell *their* stories. What makes me so special? Whenever I've attempted to broach the topic with Maxine or investors, they all balk at the idea of me stepping away from a front-facing role, suggesting I scale back on the design side, and going as far as to suggest ghost designers instead. The conversation that followed that suggestion was tense, and the only resolution we found that kept me in their graces was to continue on as I had been. Overworked, and at a stalemate.

It was no wonder I felt less and less enthused to plaster my face all over socials to talk about the new Jaded Double Breasted Tartan Blazer: only two hundred dollars, and you can look like me, dear foolish consumer! Maybe it was the overconsumption to compete with other brands that was burning me out on a thing I used to love—or maybe I've just outgrown it.

Maybe that's why I've jumped headfirst into things with the rugby team. It wasn't about me, it challenged me on every front, and every day, I felt alive because I never knew what was in store. Even still, guilt gnawed at me for not giving my all to my other businesses. Dropping the ball on them was not an option, or I'd find myself unable to pay everyone on the Legends payroll—or worse, I'd be at the mercy of Lawrence Chapman. I would rather saw my arm off with a rusty nail file than give that man the satisfaction.

"You're right," I say to the screen filled with tiny rectangles housing a dozen frustrated people who look to me to keep everything running. "I've been a little swamped, but that's no excuse. I'll call my photographer and schedule some time this week to get content done for this season's collection. I think it could work to our benefit to have London as the backdrop. People love an international angle, gives it more mystique."

Top of my to-do list now: find a photographer.

I jot down a note as we wrap up our meeting. My placations are likely only putting a bandage on the bullet wound that is their faith in me.

My dogmatic attempts to control everything are now coming back to bite me in the ass, but all I can do is deal with it and organize my time better from here on out. I've been getting distracted. Too many nights drinking wine with Aanya on my couch, too many nights out listening to live music, too many wandering thoughts about a six foot four rugby player with dimples framing a mischievous smile and sinful hands.

Hands I've seen take down two hundred pound men like it was nothing but were also so gentle as he tucked the hair behind my ear last night.

Stupid.

It was so fucking stupid to go to his house last night, even more idiotic to ask Aanya to ask Myles for his address. She didn't even hesitate, saying she loved that I was *"getting my tits out and being adventurous"* before making a lewd gesture with her hand. If Myles asked her why she was suddenly asking for his best friend's address, she didn't let on. It was a gross abuse of resources and friendship, one Tieran didn't even second guess before inviting me inside.

I've been trying to comb through my brain, figure out why, after all my protestations surrounding him, I somehow ended up on his doorstep. Why couldn't I stay away from him? There was too much at risk, and every day, I found myself walking a tightrope between what I should do and what I *want* to do. And last night, I wanted to see him— needed to.

His last text after the match had left me unnerved.

It wasn't premeditated… I certainly didn't *intend* to wind up on his doorstep, bag of food in hand, with the sole intention to make sure his night ended on a positive note.

I just…I could hear the disappointment in that final text, and it kept needling at me—how hard he was trying to act unaffected when he was carrying the weight of that loss on his shoulders. It turns out, he's been carrying more than that, too scared to let anyone see he's struggling.

Maybe we have more in common than I thought.

Nevertheless, I'm at an impasse. I need to stop seeking him out, need to stop letting him get under my skin, need to stop thinking about every touch—gentle or rough—but my control is a fraying thread waiting to snap.

Because Tieran Stone isn't just someone I'm lusting after—he's someone I *like*, and that is more dangerous than anything else.

My phone rings, blissfully distracting me out of my conflicting thoughts.

I answer without looking, balancing the phone between my shoulder and ear while I start to organize some of the ledgers and documents on the desk in front of me. "Hello?"

"You've been slacking on your responsibilities." Maxine's cool voice comes through the line. A sigh slips through my lips, and I pinch the bridge of my nose with my thumb and forefinger. "You think they're buying what you said during that meeting?"

"I handled it."

"You pat their head to make them feel better, but they won't forget. You need to stop messing around out there in London and come back home. Your *real* job is here."

My manager has never hidden her distaste for my abrupt decision to fly across the world and have a slight career shift. I'm less accessible here, a point I enjoy and she detests. If she had her way, I'd be on the first flight back to L.A., where she can continue to exploit my google calendar and line her own pockets. The more I dance for the world, the more money she makes.

"I got a little distracted. It's fine."

"You're unfocused and uncommitted. You assured me when you left that you would keep a tight ship, but from where I'm standing, it seems like everything is veering off course. I can't get a hold of you, you're zoning out in meetings, you're turning down brand deals—*easy* money. You're not staying on top of your content. CEOs don't get free time, Jade. Your fans are going to lose interest if you don't stay relevant. Brands will move on to the next hot thing if you under perform."

"I have more faith in the community I created than that." My attempt to fight back feels feeble, and I feel like a child being chastised for being curious.

"Don't be so naïve." The words are vitriolic. "You know how this world works—no one will care about you if you don't give them something to care about. They want to love you or hate you; it doesn't matter which one, as long as it's your name coming out of their mouths. Fading into the middle isn't an option."

The shrapnel of her words flies through the air and slices at my skin. A million invisible cuts pepper my body, and a sense of powerlessness oozes from the wounds. She's not wrong. I hate that she's forcing me to come to terms with the fact that I'm just a commodity to people, a dollar sign to corporations—even my own. It's a bitter pill to swallow.

Tieran's words from yesterday float through my mind. *I'll become a real human to them.*

"Come home. I've been following that team of yours, and they're not even winning. Don't throw everything away on a losing team, Jade." Maxine hangs up the phone, not allowing me a rebuttal.

Come home.

The thing is, Los Angeles never felt like home…but London is starting to.

* * *

"What the fuck was that?" Lottie stands on top of her stadium chair, shouting at the match referee for penalising Cavan for being offside. "Your eyes are offside for that shit call, Roland."

She drops down into her seat, a dramatic huff rolling off her glossy lips before she reaches down to grab her beer, taking a hearty swig. "Fuck me, that's good. This new?"

I nod my head. "I reached out to a London brewery a few weeks ago about making one of their in-house blends the official drink of the team. That's the Legends Lager. I pay them to supply the beverage, and they donate a portion of their profits to help bring rugby to underprivileged communities."

"Wicked." A smile lights up her face before she jumps up suddenly, her many layers of jewelry jangling. "Push it, go, go, go!"

We're playing one of the less impressive teams in the league, and the score is far too close for my comfort right now. This one should be in the bag, but the trajectory isn't looking good.

Tieran is in possession of the ball, running downfield, his muscular thighs flexing, making the dragon tattooed around his kneecap come alive, coiling and undulating with every step. I fixate a little too long on that dragon, inappropriately fantasizing about seeing it up close. I couldn't really be blamed, though, could I? Rugby shorts are pornographically short; it's not my fault my attention was diverted with all the naked flesh being served up on a turfed platter.

I momentarily lament the fact that I've been intimate with this god of a man on two occasions and have yet to actually see any of his body, since both times, he was behind me.

"Why are you pouting?" Aanya asks to my left.

I sit up, schooling my expression. "I'm not."

The crowd around us grows louder, and I focus on the match as Alfie, our team's scrum-half, latches onto the ball and kicks it past the opposition. Men scatter, running for the play as it soars over the twenty-two, bouncing off the pitch, and landing into touch. The fans get rowdy, cheering in excitement for the slight advantage that the lineout we're awarded offers.

Zaine steps over the outside line, as our forward players get into place. We're close to the try line, if the men can maintain their hold on the ball, and push against the opposition until they're over the line, we'll have this win secured. We need this win—*he* needs this win.

The stadium quiets, everyone focusing on what's happening on the pitch, my heart beating like the flap of a hummingbird's wings. Zaine's hands lift above his head, lobbing the ball with force past the other team's own attempt at a jump, soaring right into the arms of the Legends right lock, Connor Davies, as he's lifted into the air by his teammates. If he can score this try, I *might* forgive him for his piss-poor attempts at magic.

Davies drops down with a resounding thunk as our forwards close in around him for protection. Fists grapple around waists, twisting shirts and grasping shorts for grip as feet push into the grass for purchase. It's a lattice of men, and their grunts of exertion float through the air as the teams press against each other, the Legends attempting to get over the try line, and the other team trying to defend it.

"I am so turned on right now." Aanya's eyes are predatory, her stare laser focused on the men on the field.

Lottie and I exchange a look. "Uh, I know this is your first official match, but your man is further back on the field." She points a finger to where Myles shifts on his feet, waiting for a signal to assist if needed.

"Oh, I know exactly where he is. I wish he was in this sexy little waffle of men, though. Something about all that muscle packed together is just—" She bites her lip.

I hold back a snort. "So, are you and Myles doing alright?"

A commotion draws our attention just in time to see the opposition's lock tear the ball from Connor's hands, and the maul collapses as the ball is freed from the melee, exchanging hands quickly and without room for error. Cavan attempts to catch it when the opposition kicks the ball further downfield and away from their try line. The Legends shift, all of them now running toward their own line to defend, as Tierans hands fly through the air, shouting something I can't hear from where I'm seated.

"God, yeah. He's the most supportive person I've ever met, and I've been half in love with him since night one. Plus, he can do this thing with hips where he…" She starts to mimic the motion in her seat.

"Please stop. I shouldn't know these things about my players."

"I'd guess you know far more about Tieran." My head whips toward Lottie and back to Aanya, whose eyes widen in shock and then back.

"What—" My eyes fly around us to make sure no one heard. "What are you talking about? Did he—did he say something?"

"Please, my brother is many things, but he's not untrustworthy. He didn't say anything. I assumed." Uncertainty crosses her soft face. "Was I wrong?" She looks beyond me to Aanya, who's taken that moment to stuff her face with a sausage roll.

"Don't choke, Judas."

Lottie's voice is a cheerful melody as she continues. "There's no way I'm wrong. I could tell from that first meeting in the supermarket. Then, he brought you in for crochet, left Finn and Ekon's party soon after you did, and if all that's not enough to convince me, he's looked at you— like…three times tonight."

My cheeks flush scarlet, and I'm saved from having to respond when the crowd lets out a collective groan that shakes the stands. Tieran's face down on the turf, an opposing player on top of him while another steals the ball from his hands, takes off down the pitch, and scores another try.

What is happening? The first half of last season, he was an absolute beast. No one could get past him. Now, it's almost like he's handing them the ball. Did the whole ordeal with his ex fuck him up that badly? Is he still hung up on her, and that's why he's not been able to wade out of this ocean of self-doubt?

Something about the thought makes me nauseous.

When the game ends, it's raining, and the Legends walk off the pitch with their heads hung low.

"Alright, ladies, I've gotta go comfort my man with a pity blow job. I'll catch you later," Aanya says.

"And I've got a dinner to get to," Lottie starts to walk away, turning around quickly so her pleated mini swishes with the movement, "but you'll check on him?"

"What—no, I," but she's already skipped away.

I stick around anyway. Not because I want to check in on Tieran, but because I'm the owner, it's a part of the job description, and everyone else on the leadership side has left.

Most of the team is able to walk off the pitch unscathed, heading to the locker room to clean up before heading home or out for the evening, but Tieran's been roped into post-match interviews.

There's a smile on his face, but for once, it looks forced. No one else seems to notice it, but it's there, in the subtle pinch around his eyes. Something about this game in particular has really affected him, because the mask he's always so proud of is slipping. His shoulders are rigid, and he's picking at his skin, rubbing at the back of his neck, shifting back and forth as if he's about to sprint far and fast.

Question after question is lobbed at him, and the easy smile has fully left his handsome face, replaced with a frown. His chest is rising and falling in a more rapid succession, and the reporters are just getting started. They've doubled in size, surrounding him on all sides, caging him in.

From where I'm standing, I can barely make out the words, but I hear things like *losing streak, breakup, public humiliation, embarrassment,* and it's enough to make me want to rip out blades of grass on our perfectly manicured field.

Tieran stands there, weathering it all with no one to help him, no one to have his back, and I'm struck suddenly with how incredibly lonely he must feel. He's been carrying some misplaced sense of guilt for months, and I don't think anyone has been checking in on him.

Who's been making sure he's okay while he's been making sure everyone else is? Me included.

The media has gotten worse—cameras are being shoved in his face, the questions are increasing in hostility, and Tieran looks...scared. This strong, funny, kind man looks like the walls are closing in on him, and he doesn't know how to stop it.

That's all it takes for my composure to snap.

I march over to the crowd on five inch Pradas and elbow my way to the middle of the hyena frenzy.

I place my palm on Tieran's inked forearm, and I can feel a tremble vibrating through his body. Muscle rigid from the fist he's clenching eases a little under my touch, but I can see his harsh breathing from the corner of my eye.

"Gentleman, I'm so sorry to interrupt, but I need to steal him away. Ballard wants a word before everyone goes home." It's a lie; most everyone has left already. Still, I'll say anything to get him out of here.

Any additional questions they fling his way are ignored as I pull him away from the vultures and toward the player tunnel.

Tieran is heavy on his feet, looking but not seeing as I guide him from the media frenzy.

We're out of sight, but it's done nothing to help his state. He's still breathing too heavy, eyes clenched tightly, as if he can ward off whatever he's seeing behind his eyelids if he tries hard enough.

I think he's having a panic attack.

Up ahead on our left is a storage closet, and as we approach, I make a last minute decision to pull him inside. Maybe being enclosed in a small space will muffle the outside noise or make him forget where he is long enough to get him to calm down.

Thankfully, the door is unlocked, and once we're inside, I push him against the wall. It's like he doesn't even realize I'm here. His whole frame has locked up, he's deathly quiet, his eyes are flitting back and forth, and his breathing's rapid and shallow.

"Tieran." I step closer to him in the dark room and place a hand on his face.

He flinches. Why does that make me want to cry?

"Tieran." I stroke my thumb back and forth along his jaw. "I think your nervous system got overwhelmed out there, and you're having a panic attack. Can you tell me anything you see around you?"

A therapist I was going to once told me the best way to calm yourself during an episode is to try to name anything you can see, hear, or smell to try to reorient your surroundings.

He doesn't respond. "What about anything you can hear? Smell?"

Still, I'm met with silence and an alarmingly blank stare.

I hate this. I hate that he feels so out of body and I can't do anything to help. I miss his smile, his banter and his inappropriate flirting. I miss hearing his laugh, knowing it was aimed at me, making me feel warm. I miss the gleam of mischief in his eye every time he looked at me, and I miss him because he's not here right now. He's trapped in his mind, battling a demon I can't see or help him fight.

Wherever he's at right now, I can't reach him, but I can feel his hammering pulse against my fingertips, and medically, that can't be healthy.

My chest nearly brushes against him when I take another step forward. "Tieran. Come back to me." My voice is a whisper, and it cracks on the words. I brush his sweat-and-rain-soaked hair back from his face. "*Please.*"

My body seems to take over, because I'm suddenly flush

against him, raising the extra couple of inches he has on me, and placing a kiss on his cheek. "Come back." Another kiss to his other cheek. "Banter with me." A dangerous kiss to the corner of his mouth. "Make me laugh on the inside even when I won't show it on the outside." My words are a whisper against his lips.

"Please." I fully give in, kissing him squarely on the mouth.

Once. Twice. The third time, I linger, bringing my hands down to rest on his chest, letting my nails dig in, hoping it will give him something to anchor himself to.

At first, he remains still, but then his breathing starts to level out, his lips loosen, and his hands find their home on my waist, gripping me tight, as if he never wants to let me go.

When I start to pull away to check on him, his hold tightens, tugging me back in as he deepens our previously chaste kiss.

I should stop this, but I couldn't if I tried. I want to be selfish for him when he's always so selfless for everyone else. He needs me to tether him so he doesn't drift too far into his mind, into that black hole of self-doubt plaguing him daily.

Maybe it's cowardly, but in this dark closet, I can pretend our circumstances are different, and we're just two people who can't deny feelings as mountainous as Everest itself. Giving in to them wouldn't feel like a cataclysmic error in judgement, but rather, a relief as freeing as a dam bursting. So yeah, maybe in this shadowed broom closet I can admit without repercussion that I'm being selfish for me too, because I want this—him, more than I'm ready to admit..

Tieran's grip on my hip tightens. My hands shift from his chest and wind up around his neck. My pulse pounds in my ears, and he's sighing into my mouth, and in a singularly foolish moment of no turning back, I run my tongue against the seam of his lips.

The dam breaks.

Tieran turns us so my back is flush against the wall, knocking random objects we can't see onto the floor as he crowds my space and takes my mouth again. The ground beneath my feet wobbles, and the ground splits in half, ready to suck me into the Earth's core for giving in to this when I shouldn't.

I don't care.

It is *cataclysmic*, but it's not an error in judgement like previously presumed. Something that feels this right could never be an error.

His tongue sweeps in, knocking out all my good sense and making us both groan. He's everywhere, his hands skating down my back and skimming the top of my ass, the taste of him on my tongue, the smell of sweat and grass and *Tieran*—it all creates a cocktail that's getting me drunk.

This is why I should have avoided this, why I shouldn't have given in. I won't be able to give this up now that I really know how it feels to be held by him, kissed by him, with no convenient explanation.

One of his palms moves up to cup my face as he tips my head back to deepen the kiss, his tongue gliding deftly against mine. An embarrassing whimper escapes me, and I can feel him smile against my mouth. I tug on his hair, and the husky rumble of a laugh that bubbles up his throat is like music to my ears.

Worth it. Whatever comes of this moment will be worth it to hear that sound again.

His kisses slow into something more tender, something that makes me feel things I would rather ignore, and when he pulls away, my body inadvertently follows him.

He settles his forehead against mine and hums, a beautiful smile touching his mouth.

I've never been happier to see his dimples, and something in my chest loosens.

A suspicious gleam enters his cobalt eyes.

"What?" I ask, wary.

He shakes his head. "If I had known an anxiety attack was what would get you to kiss me again, I would've crashed out a long time ago."

I slap his chest and step away, but I don't get far before he's pulling me back, kissing me one more time.

21

JADE

A COUPLE DAYS after our kiss, I received a text from Tieran with an address and time. It would seem his eagerness to get me to experience new things isn't going away. The flutter that ran through my stomach upon seeing the invite was embarrassing, and the giddiness I feel days later is even worse. I'm loath to admit it but I like the attention, because his brand is different from the kind I'm used to—the kind that typically veers into scrutiny.

He thinks about *me*, what would challenge and excite me in equal measure. The nature of the activity itself doesn't matter; it's the fact that he assessed a need I refused to acknowledge, and he's following through. I feel seen for the first time.

Until I moved to London, no one cared whether I worked from seven in the morning until well after midnight. I had what everyone wanted—money, fame, success. I was living the dream, but I wasn't living, was I?

So, what have I been chasing? I have everything, working sixteen hour days to maintain a dream I'm not sure I ever really wanted, and I still feel unfulfilled. Life has been happening all around me with or without my participation. Is that really what I want for the rest of my life?

Tieran has been gently pushing me out of my comfort

zone since we met, and after every encounter, I've felt more alive. Irritated, but alive.

I want more.

That's how I find myself outside an unmarked, seemingly abandoned warehouse in Camden where I was sure to be murdered any minute now. I pull out my phone to double check the address, positive I got it wrong, when I see a text from Maxine.

MAXINE

I booked you a meet and greet at Selfridges on Oxford Street to align with the new collection hitting stores. They've already announced it on socials and are waiting for you to accept the collab to cross promote. Tickets are already selling out.

A pounding in my head starts up.

This isn't the first time she's promised my time without asking me first. I would just have to hope it didn't interfere with any prior engagements.

I open Instagram, find the tagged post that's already amassed thousands of likes in a few minutes, and accept the collaboration before tossing my phone back in my bag.

The entrance to the warehouse boasts a large, vibrant mural of Camden Town if it was on psychotropic drugs, with a neon sign in the center reading 'Le Freak'.

What am I walking into?

The invite link was vague, with details only saying to come limber, whatever that means, and in comfortable clothes. I'm equally concerned and intrigued, but one thing is always certain—where Tieran is involved, I'm sure to be entertained.

Begrudgingly, I have to admit, I kind of love it—the rush I get whenever he's around is unlike anything I've ever experienced. I shouldn't want it—him—but, against my better judgement, I do. He consumes my thoughts and it's an annoying, highly inconvenient thing to deal with. I've never been so unproductive in my life, getting distracted on zoom calls, zoning out, remembering dark rooms in illicit bars during board meetings, thinking about a soft kiss pressing into my cheek as the scent of him washed over me.

I didn't even hesitate this time when I received the link to whatever it is we're doing today. There was no momentary delay before refusing the invitation, no mental gymnastics around why I shouldn't be here, no trying to convince myself this isn't exactly where I want to be.

My resolve is sedimentary rock on a cliffside, slowly crumbling every moment I spend in his presence. I'm one wave away from eroding completely.

Even still, I take a step beyond the foyer into the main room of the warehouse, where I'm greeted by fifty foot silks, foam pads covering the floor, and hoops hanging from ropes.

Tieran booked us an aerial silk class?

Will he ever not shock me?

I scan the room of around fifteen people, looking for a familiar set of cerulean eyes and panty-melting dimples, but don't see him anywhere. Disappointment courses through me before I reason I just happened to get here first.

"Hey!" a person with fiery red hair, snow pale skin, and multiple facial piercings greets me while holding an iPad. "What's your name so I can get you checked in?"

"Oh, um, Jade." I pause as they scan through their list, a furrow lining their brow. "But it could be under Tieran," I hasten to add.

They recheck the list and then tap the touchpad. "There you are! Have you done aerial or silks before?"

I look around again, waiting for Tieran before I answer. "No, I mostly do Pilates."

"Not a problem!" Their reply is chipper. "This is a pretty novice session; nothing too advanced but still plenty of fun."

"Billie! Can you come help me get this knot untangled?"

"Be there in a second," Billie calls to their coworker

before looking back at me. "You can go ahead and set anything you brought with you against the wall over there, take off your shoes, and then join us in the center of the room."

I move over to where they indicated I drop my stuff and start to unlace my shoes, keeping my socks on when I notice everyone is still wearing theirs. I check my phone, hoping maybe there's a text from Tieran telling me where he is, but my screen only holds four notifications from Maxine, one from Aanya, another from Poppy confirming our one-on-one Pilates session this week, and about fifteen unread emails that have come in over the last hour.

Nothing from Tieran.

My stomach sinks. Is he not coming? He said before the crochet night that he wouldn't come if I didn't want him to. Was he giving me space now? Was I so unreadable that he couldn't tell space was becoming a non-issue lately? I mean, I showed up at his fucking door; what else does he need? For me to wear his jersey around town for everyone to see, or to actually tell him, "hey, I like you and wanna kiss you some more"?

God, that sounds horrific.

Why should his lack of presence bother me? He didn't say he would be here, and I can still have a good time on my own, even if I do have a mountain of work I blew off to come.

"Alright, everyone, let's get started," Billie's counterpart announces. "My name is Stasia, and we're going to start today's lesson by showing you a basic climb and foothold. Don't worry, we'll get to the fun stuff in a bit. Everyone grab a silk and watch me."

Stasia starts by demonstrating how she climbs up the panels, pinching the fabric between her feet, lifting with her arms, and pushing up with her legs, before she releases, sliding down effortlessly until she touches the floor.

"I'm going to walk around the room while everyone

tries, and I'll help as needed." She claps, and everyone hesitantly starts to attempt their climb.

Extending my arms into the silk, I grab hold, pulling myself up so I can wrap the fabric around my foot and use the tangled material as an anchor to slowly pull myself up. I've made it several feet in the air, and my arms are burning slightly from the ascent but I mostly feel stable from my foothold in the silk. I cast a glance around the room and everyone seems to be struggling at varying degrees, with one particularly burly man slipping time and again.

Beneath me, Stasia shouts, "Amazing job! You're a natural."

I smile to myself from fifteen feet in the air. See, I don't need Tieran to be here to enjoy myself, and I won't let him ghosting affect my experience.

"Christ alive, that's an incredible view," a deeply familiar voice rumbles from below me.

The sound shocks my system, surprising me enough that my grip loosens, making me forget I'm supposed to be holding on to something, and before I can course correct, I plummet to imminent death. I'm free-falling, arms pinwheeling through the air, body locked tight and bracing for impact, only moments from becoming a human pancake. But then strong arms catch me, caging me in their steady grip, just like I knew they would.

I hate how good it feels—how *right*. I hate how relieved I am that he's here, how it's making my heart patter like raindrops on a tin roof, erratic and loud. I hate that I feel lighter now, and not just because when he's touching me— holding me—I feel weightless, but because being around him eases something in my head while also settling something in my heart.

It's terrifying—thrilling.

There's a wicked gleam in his eyes when I look up at him. "Knew I'd get you to fall for me eventually." The cheeky fucker winks at me, making parts of me ache that have no business being sentient right now.

"I'd have rather hit the ground," I volley.

He leans in, lips grazing my ear, and my heart starts to thud so heavily, he has to hear it. "You're *so* pretty when you lie." Tieran's grip tightens on my waist and the space behind my knees, his thumb brushing a lazy stroke along my leg.

My breath hitches, and his smile widens, dimples popping.

"Put me down." I gently shove at his shoulder.

"Do I have to?" He sulks, even as humor coats his tongue.

The giggle that bubbles out of my mouth is girly and downright embarrassing. I want to stuff it back inside my mouth and throw myself in-front of a double decker bus, but Tieran's eyes soften as he gazes at me and murmurs *cute*. It's barely audible, but the open affection that's plastered across his handsome face tells me enough.

I'm about to ask him to let me go when Stasia rushes over. "Well, I didn't think it had to be said, but you're not supposed to let go of the silks. Are you daft?" Her tone reads moderately annoyed, and I'm about to apologize for my carelessness, but she steamrolls over me, directing her ire at Tieran now. "You're late, and I don't tolerate tardi—"

Before she can continue, Billie interrupts. "Stasia, stop. Don't you know who that is?" They nod in my direction, and my face flames. "That's Jade McKallen," they whisper. "She has millions of followers." My stomach sinks. Yet again, I've been relegated again to a statistic. I am a number of followers, not a person, and they only see me as a tool to make or break their business.

And Dad wonders why I don't get out.

"Oh, I'm—"

Tieran interrupts me before I can apologize, charm oozing from every pore. "I'm so sorry. I was having issues with my dog this morning, and it took me longer to get out of the house than usual.

Billie interjects this time, fearing Stasia will put her foot in her mouth again. "It's not a problem. Just go ahead and get into position." At that moment, one of the other students in the class calls out for assistance, and they let us know they'll be back to help us after getting them sorted.

Facing Tieran, I raise my brow. "Does your charm usually get you out of things?"

"So you admit I'm charming?" He grabs the silks dangling next to us, forearms flexing as he uses it as an anchor to lean forward into my personal space.

Meeting his challenge, I take a step forward, getting even closer, hovering my mouth an inch away from his. His smirk remains, but his breathing stops, his eyes flitting back and forth between mine. He's waiting on bated breath as his hold on the fabric becomes shaky.

What did he say to me that first night?

I like your brand of bold.

I don't stop. Instead, I bring my finger to the chain dangling off his neck, playing with the metal before I place the tip of my finger to his chest and trail it down his body, over the ridged muscle of his abdomen.

A low groan exits his mouth, and he squeezes his eyes shut, but doesn't pull away, doesn't ask me to stop.

The burning path of my finger halts just before the waistband of his athletic shorts, shorts that show off all his tattoos—tattoos I find far too sexy and can't stop staring at during matches, inked onto thighs I imagine fucking into me with powerful force as I come undone, finally getting what I've been aching for since that first night we met.

Focus. My thoughts always become jumbled around him, even when I have the upper hand. I want nothing more than to make him feel as off kilter as he's made me feel every day for months.

Leaning in, I whisper in his ear, "Like a snake charmer."

That snaps him out of the moment, and he rears back slightly as something that looks an awful lot like hurt flashes in his eyes.

I instantly regret my words, even though I don't know exactly what I said that was wrong. Still, I see the effect they had written across his face, and I want to slap myself for ruining what was supposed to be fun.

Before I can apologize, an easy grin settles on his face. A fake smile.

My insides squeeze and cramp to be on the receiving end of the expression he shows the world when he's not being authentic. I wither inside.

"Tieran—"

"Will you show me how to climb them?" He nods to the silks dangling from the ceiling. "Stasia was right, you're a natural."

It's obvious he wants to change the subject, and after what I did, I do too, even if it makes me a coward. Anxiety worms its way through my body, and all I can think about is the light dimming from his eyes because of my careless words.

"Sure," I say, voice a little wobbly.

I give him the basic rundown of how to lift himself, how to grasp the material between his thighs and loop his foot around to give the best purchase, even going as far as to show him visually by doing it myself. After several failed attempts and a sheen of perspiration along his brow, he looks visibly annoyed.

"How are you so good at this?" He takes a sip of the water he brought with him, and I watch a trickle of sweat glide down his neck and over the tattoo just below his ear.

I want to li—

He breaks my line of thought by reaching out and grasping my chin, wrenching my gaze away. "Eyes up here, Hellfire."

Humor shines in his eyes, and I internally breathe a sigh of relief to see it again.

"I do Pilates five times a week. You'd be surprised how strong you get from it."

"Are you insinuating I'm weak? I'm a rugby player, for fuck's sake."

"A rugby player who could benefit from Pilates, it would seem, if you can't pull yourself up a shiny rope." I pick invisible lint off his t-shirt before patting at his chest. "But that's okay, big guy. We all have our challenges."

The anxiety starts to ebb as we settle back into our easy banter.

Tieran levels me with a glare that promises retribution. "Right, well, that won't do."

Before I can stop him, he grabs hold of the silk and wraps it around his wrist. Soon enough, his arms start to shake from the exertion of lifting his massive body in the air, but he keeps going, pushing with his thighs and pulling with his arms. He's halfway in the air when the velocity from his speed, mixed with the jerky motions of his climb, start to make the silks twist around his body, cocooning him inside their warm embrace.

"Uh…Tieran?"

"Give me a minute." He starts to thrash around, but it only exacerbates the issue.

"I think you need he—"

"Don't say it."

"Big, strong rugby player, strung up in ropes."

"Jade," he warns.

"It's like a fantasy come to life," I tease.

"Yeah? You want to see me tied up?"

"Mmmm." I leave him in suspense for a minute. "Yeah, I think I do."

His eyes spear me from twenty feet in the air. "It's not very nice of you to say things like that when I'm not in a position to do anything about it."

"Thank goodness I'm not a very nice person then." I tug on the silks to emphasize my point, jostling him a bit.

"Stop doing that." His voice is stern. It's what I imagine he sounds like when he's leading the team. It's kind of hot, so I do it again. "Jade, if you don't stop, when I get down, there will be hell to pay."

"Sounds fun. Are you going to punish me, Captain?"

"Fuck, *stop*. You're making me hard when I'm hovering above a group of people. They'll think I'm a pervert." He makes a concerted effort to untangle himself, kicking his feet until he's able to get one free and use it as leverage to start untwisting himself.

Once released from the bonds of luxury, Tieran scales down the silk and drops heavily onto the mat next to me. When he rises to his full height, effectively towering over me, he subtly adjusts the slight bulge in his pants.

Unable to help myself, I snort a laugh.

"Do you think this is funny?" He arches a brow.

"Unfortunately for you, yes. It's hilarious."

"Wicked woman." The words have no bite to them, but he prowls closer to me, a wolf on the hunt, me it's willing prey. My blood hums through my body, waiting to see what punishment he might dole out.

I back up a step, ducking behind the fabric cascading from the ceiling. Tieran goes to grab the material to pull it out of his way and get to me, but I stop him. "Careful; I'd hate for you to get tangled again. Metamorphosis might set in this time, and you might transform into a big, masculine, rugby-playing butterfly."

He barks out a laugh so loud, it shocks the whole room into silence.

"Would you two please pay attention so we can demonstrate the new skill for everyone?" Stasia, who clearly doesn't care who I am and I love her for it, chides us.

"Sorry!" Tieran and I both say before we turn, smiling at one another.

The next hour passes in a flash of satin and laughter as Billie and Stasia take us through several introductory moves. It's easy to admit I had fun, but from the look in Stasia's eyes as we walk out the door, I don't think we're welcome back anytime soon.

We're standing on the street, watching a car pass by, neither of us saying anything. Where do we go from here? I don't really want this day to end, if I'm being honest with myself. If I was being really honest with myself, I'd admit I never want time spent with Tieran to end.

I built an empire by being smart—making logical choices, safe choices. But lately, I've been very, very stupid.

Fuck. I'm tired of playing it safe. Isn't that why I moved to London and bought the team in the first place? To do the bold thing—the risky thing. Am I really going to risk that on a man who makes my heart freefall in my chest every time he looks at me with those sapphire eyes? With every smile, text, random not-date, and cheeky remark, my good sense drifts away on the wind, leaving behind a sense of frenetic energy—a need my body recognizes but my head has yet to allow.

The Legends are a challenge my head wants, but Tieran is a challenge my *heart* needs.

And I've never backed down from a challenge.

"Do you want to get lunch?" The words are out of my mouth before I realize I've said them.

The smile Tieran throws me is soft, almost shy. "I thought you'd never ask."

♡ ◯ 48 ⇄ 117 ◁   🔖

Liked by **jademckallen** and **others**
selfridges **@jademckallen** will be at our Oxford Street location to show off the newest collection for Jaded! Stocked exclusively with us here in the UK 🏷️ Tickets for the meet and greet in bio!

hannahbronson I CAN'T WAIT!!!!
40 likes   Reply
tomsus93 who is she?
Reply
——— View replies (2)
lilipoultek **@selfridges** I'm having trouble with the link! Can someone help, i'll die if i don't get a ticket!
Reply
chessieburbank I can't wait to try on the two toned blazer 🖤
3 likes   Reply
aliciasworld does anyone else think her range is kinda 😵
137 likes   Reply
——— View replies (14)

"YOU'VE REALLY NEVER BEEN HERE?" I watch Jade as she takes in the enormity of Broadway Market, eyes bouncing around stall after stall. Aromas from every cuisine you can think of waft through the air around us, making my mouth water almost as much as Jade does in her tight workout clothes. We walked the length of Regent's Canal, talking the whole way, occasionally stopping to admire a houseboat bookstore or a particularly beautiful willow tree, until we wound up here.

"No, never." Her answer is punctuated with a loud rumble from her stomach.

"That's mad. In all the times you've visited for work or to see your dad, I can't believe you never came here." The market is popular amongst the locals, favoring this over the more touristy markets throughout the city. It's not the most convenient to get to, but it's worth the trip for the bao buns alone.

"Usually, when I come for work, I'm stuck going to Michelin-starred dinners with business associates, and when I visit Dad, we're usually getting takeaway from his favorite chip shop."

I whistle. "Michelin-starred restaurants. That must have been a hardship."

She smiles softly to herself before facing me. "Would it

surprise you if I said I'd much rather be somewhere like this." She nods to the market.

"A bit, yeah."

She looks a little sad, and it makes me want to push and pry to get her to tell me everything about herself she hasn't yet. I want her to show me how her brilliant mind works, tell me what she *does* love, find out what she wants out of life, because *I* want to give it to her.

I have this nagging need to take care of her, because I suspect she hasn't let anyone help her with anything in a long while.

Maybe not ever.

"It lost its luster a long time ago," she admits candidly. "Even fresh out of high school, when I first moved to L.A., all the lavishness seemed excessive. We grew up…not poor, because Dad always made sure we were okay, but certainly not well off. So, when I'd go to a restaurant on a brand invite, and I'd see how much was being spent on a meal that left me hungry…I don't know, it sat like a rock in my stomach. Five hundred dollars per person, and I would leave and find the nearest taco truck."

She starts walking away from where we had paused at the mouth of the market, and I'm helpless but to follow her.

"What was it like? Growing up in a small town and then moving to a place like Los Angeles?"

She thinks on it for a minute, biting the inside of her cheek, before answering. "I find that people are the same everywhere you go. Only the landscape changes." There's a bite of bitterness in the words as her eyes trace a sandwich stand.

"What do you mean?"

"In my world, I have rarely seen the beauty in people, they're always inherently selfish, oftentimes cruel. When I was twenty in L.A., it was someone cozying up to me, becoming my friend, only for me to hear them bashing me behind my back at a party, or a male business associate assuming I was the assistant, not the CEO. I've been cornered in a boardroom after everyone else left and felt up because they wanted me to *prove myself*. That happened more than once," she says wryly, and I want to fucking break something. "It doesn't matter how powerful I am, there will always be someone who wants to invalidate me, take something from me. My power, my body, my money. No one ever wanted to give me anything without receiving something in return."

"Do you find people in London the same as everywhere else?" *Do you find* me *the same as everyone else*, is what I'm really too scared to ask.

I study her face, trying to decipher an answer before she says anything, but her expression is unreadable. It's making my palms sweat as we weave in between stalls.

"Yes," she finally says, and my stomach drops. "But not everyone. Some people," she glances up at me before looking away, "are warm and kind. The type of person who made a lonely stranger in a pub feel a little less uncertain about life. Some people here have given me hope. I haven't felt that in a long time, maybe not ever."

"Hope for what?" I ask, waiting on the edge of a knife, begging for any morsel, any word out of her lush mouth.

She finally looks at me, a shy smile playing across her lips. "That there *is* more to life than what we see through a screen. I just had to leap across the ocean to find it."

I grab her hand, bringing her to a halt. Jade's breath hitches, and she glances down at where my fingers wrap around hers, where my thumb is now brushing lightly against the back of her hand.

"If I were to invite you over for dinner, what would you say?" It's a shot in the dark, and my heart is beating out of my chest. Every time we're together, I can see the reluctance ebbing away like smoke drifting from the tips of a flame.

"Ask me and find out," she challenges, a spark catching and flaring bright in the blue of her iris. God, that fire is addictive—it makes me feel like anything is possible.

"Jade, would you let me cook dinner for you tonight?"

She makes a big show of deciding, and it's driving me out of my mind to the point that I'm practically bouncing on the balls of my feet like I do pre-match. "I don't know…" She trails off, a smile starting to engulf her face, and the sight is so beautiful, my chest aches.

"Don't toy with me, Hellfire. You know you want to say yes." Her face scrunches a little. "Are you allergic to anything?"

"Cocky rugby players."

The smile she shoots at me in combination with the coquettish look in her eyes has me acting on impulse. Reaching out, I wrap my hand gently around her neck and pull her toward me, curving down and sealing her lips with mine.

For a brief second, she stiffens, but her surprise swiftly melts away, and she's sighing into my mouth. Her lips are soft and warm, and I feel dizzy, like London is experiencing a magnitude six earthquake, except it's just me—her, making everything about my world tilt and rearrange itself with seismic intensity.

How is everyone around us acting like the world isn't caving in and falling into place at the same time?

Jade coaxes my mouth open with her tongue, and the taste of her has me groaning, tightening my grip where it's still settled around her neck. She whimpers in response, left hand clutching my shirt as her other settles around my wrist, securing my hold. Sensation sparks through every fibre of my being, making the hairs on my body stand on end, and my flimsy athletic shorts tighten.

With monumental effort, I wrench myself away, resting my forehead against hers and moving my hand to thread through her dark hair. "If we don't stop, I'll be locked up for public indecency."

Her eyes are closed, her chest rising and falling as she concentrates on leveling her breathing. "It might be the only way to get us to stay away from each other at this point."

I huff a laugh. "Solid steel bars couldn't keep me away, love. Don't you know that by now?"

Her only response is a hum that vibrates through my whole body.

"Let's go shopping, gorgeous. We need groceries for this meal."

I don't give her a moment to hesitate or pull away, leaving no room for argument or refusal as I thread my fingers through hers once more and pull her around the market.

I push through the front door, both hands carrying heavy bags filled with the food shop because I refused to let Jade carry anything. We're barely through the door when Pebble barrels toward us, her tongue lolling out of her mouth and a big smile stretched across her wide face. Just as I'm about to set the bags down to give her the scratches she expects the second I get home, she veers off course, going to Jade instead.

"Hello, sweet girl." She crouches and wraps her arms around Pebble's thick neck, enveloping her in a hug, the sight making my chest squeeze.

Pebble was a shelter dog who had been found out in the countryside in pretty rough shape. They suspected she had been abused, with no clue how she was able to survive when they found her near the side of a motorway covered in blood and feces. I had recently signed up to be a foster for the shelter, figuring it would work better with my busy schedule to take care of her during the off season until she found a more permanent home, but one look into her soft grey eyes, and I knew my first foster dog was going to be an epic fail. She had endured hell and still trusted people, still wagged her tail, and didn't hesitate to hope for a better life.

Every day after she came home with me, she greeted me at the door, and every night, she curled up in bed and laid her heavy head on my chest before falling asleep. Within the week, I called the rescue and told them I wanted to adopt her.

Seeing her now, so open and comfortable with Jade, who is giving her such unfiltered affection, has a lump forming in my throat.

"I feel slightly betrayed. She's only met you once, and she ran to you first," I say.

Jade squeezes Pebble's cheeks, kissing her between the eyes, and says in the babying tone only reserved for cute animals, "Clearly, she has taste." She gives her another kiss before adjusting the crocheted bandana around her neck.

"No food scraps for you, traitor." My dog actually has the gall to look at me and then turn away, nuzzling further into Jade's chest.

I'm *not* jealous of my dog, goddamnit.

"I'm going to go start dinner," I mumble.

I expect Jade to stay a little longer, maybe put a little distance between us. She's already let me too close today, and the pullback should happen any minute now, but she surprises me when I hear the soft falls of her feet connecting with the hardwood as she follows me into the kitchen.

Wordlessly, we unload the bags together, setting the spices, sweet potatoes, peppers, chicken, and cheese onto the counter. As I start to pull out pans and the things I need to get started, I see Jade fidgeting with the spices, arranging them by height before changing her mind and alphabetising them instead.

"What are you doing?"

"Organising." I shoot her a look that conveys I'm not buying it. She sighs. "I—I'm nervous." Her admission comes with a look of accusation, like how dare I make her say it out loud.

"I make you nervous?"

She scoffs. "Don't flatter yourself."

I take a step closer. "Then why would you be nervous?"

"I'm not confident your food will be edible."

I raise an eyebrow and take another step closer, then another, until I'm directly in front of her, her back against the island counter. I reach out, caging her in on each side, leaning forward. "I can hear your heart racing."

"I must be experiencing a pulmonary em—"

I silence her with a kiss. It isn't urgent or filled with fire —it's calm, steady, like water easing along the banks of a river. *Natural.*

When I pull away, her body unconsciously follows mine, leaning forward, wanting more. I want to give her more, desperate to, but instead, I tuck a strand of her hair behind her ear. "You make me nervous too."

I place one final kiss against her cheek before handing her a pepper and instructing her to chop, intuiting that she needs something to keep her mind busy so she doesn't start overthinking.

"How's Archie?" I ask, slicing the sweet potatoes in half to place them on a baking tray.

"You're his best mate. You tell me."

I laugh. "I want to hear it from your perspective. How's he doing?"

"He's fine." Her chopping turns more aggressive. "Actually, no." She brandishes the knife, flailing it around to emphasise her point. "He's so aggravating. He acts like nothing has changed, as if he wasn't diagnosed with a neurodegenerative disorder. I keep asking him if he'll consider doing the deep brain stimulation treatments to manage his symptoms, but he's always been so anti-doctor, it's hard to get him to see reason."

"Is it getting worse?" Concern floods my body as I think about Archie. I've known him for a short amount of time, but it's become impossible to not adore the grumpy old man when he hands you your arse daily in online games. He's not humble about it either. Then, there's the complicated fact that I see so much of Jade when I talk to him, and that one afternoon with him left me unnerved, thinking about how handling his care is one extra thing Jade is trying to manage alone.

"He's the same for now, but it's only a matter of time. I want to get ahead of it before it escalates. His home health aide being there helps, but I basically had to force her on him."

"I don't think you had to do much forcing once Myrah started. From what I can tell, he fancies her quite a bit. He talks about her a lot in our chats."

Her mouth drops open before a wide smile takes over. "I *knew* it."

"Do you want me to try talking to him? Since he likes me more than you." I start chopping an onion to add to the skillet heating up on the hob.

She chuckles and considers it for a moment. "No, that's alright. He'll come around. I can be quite persistent."

"Do you ever let people help you?" I grab the chicken breast and begin to rinse it off, like I didn't just drop an emotionally charged atom bomb of a question on her. I need to know if she even realises she's bearing the burdens of ten people all by herself, or if she's just that superhuman.

"Not really, no. I don't find most people to be trustworthy, and it's always just been easier to do everything on my own."

Pulling out my chef's knife, I dice the poultry into cubes, season them thoroughly, and toss them in the pan with the onions. "Doesn't someone of your caliber at least need an assistant?"

"I could probably use one, but the last one fucked my boyfriend *while* on company time, so I quite literally *paid her* to betray me." Her tone is so casual, like that level of disloyalty is common for her.

"You don't sound upset," I hedge.

"It wasn't a surprise, and I honestly should have seen it coming. He wasn't happy, and she wanted my life—or, I guess, her version of it. I think I was more upset that I was shocked by it, than the fact that it happened. I've been surrounded by disingenuous people since my career started, social climbers, lecherous business associates, foes disguising themselves as friends... I should have known better. It's not like something like this is uncommon, but to not suspect what was right under my nose? In my own house? It was just further proof there was no one I could rely on, not even if I paid them. My manager only wants to line her pockets, my assistant's screwing my boyfriend behind my back, and people who said they were my friend only wanted to be around if I was providing them with something. I couldn't trust anyone, and I think it's skewed how I move through the world."

I walk to the fridge to grab her a drink, holding out a beer and a wine bottle for her to choose from. She chooses the wine, and I go grab glasses before pouring one for each of us, motioning for her to continue.

Taking the glass, she takes a long sip. "You know what's even more messed up? When my assistant found out I was moving here, she called me up and begged to come. She apologized for what she did and said would leave him if it meant she could come here with me. An ugly part of me preened at that," she takes another sip of her wine and smiles bitterly, "at how easily she was willing to drop him if I said the word. It hurt knowing I spent every day with her, and she was willing to betray me like that, and the only time she was sorry was when she realized the benefits she would lose once I was gone. In my life, in my line of work, relationships are transactional."

"Is that how you feel about me?" The candidness of the question sends the room into stark silence; the only noise breaking it up is Pebble going to drink from her water bowl as I move to the oven and remove the softened sweet potatoes. We both work to scoop the insides out, leaving a well in each centre. Neither of us speaks, and the prolonged silence makes me start to feel sick to my stomach.

"No." Anxiety releases from my chest like air out of a balloon. "I think that's why I haven't been able to stay away from you, despite every logical bone in my body screaming at me to keep my distance."

It's the first time she's admitted to it out loud, and the relief I feel that this isn't just a one sided thing is so palpable, I can taste it.

"Is it such a bad thing? I like you, and I think you like me too." Her silence permeates the room, making my stomach twist and turn. "The only thing I want from you right now is your time. Time to get to know you, nothing more."

Something akin to fear crosses her expression before she schools her features back to neutrality. "Enough about me. Let's talk about you."

I spoon the stuffing mixture into the now-hollowed out sweet potatoes, sprinkle some cheese on top, and set them in the oven to bake.

"What about me?" The bubble we've been in all afternoon is about to burst.

"Can I ask why what I said earlier bothered you so much?" I must look confused, because she adds, "When I said you were like a snake charmer."

Realisation dawns. "Ah, it's stupid…" I scratch the back of my neck, suddenly shy.

"Please tell me." When I look over, her honeyed eyes are so open, lined with a vulnerability that seems rare for her.

"Snake charmers are basically entertainment, luring someone in based on a lie. The comparison made me think maybe you see me the way the rest of the world does."

"I'm didn—Tieran, I'm sorry." She tentatively places her hand on my forearm, halting the assembling of our dinner. "I know who you are without the mask. I always have." *I always will*, echoes unspoken.

I laugh wryly. "Well, that mask is slowly crumbling

match after match, and everyone is about to see me for the fraud I am."

"Stop." Her voice is firm, filled with authority. "What is tripping you up? Is it the thing with your ex? That's when all the issues started, right? Are you…" She pauses, but it looks like she mentally berates herself before continuing. "Are you still hung up on her?"

"God, no. My confidence was shot initially, but some sort of disconnect was created after that. I couldn't get my head and my feet to work together anymore."

"We can fix that." She sounds so sure, and I think I could use a healthy dose of that confidence. "Stop throwing a pity party and get over yourself. Only you can control your mind and how you react to your circumstances."

"You think I haven't tried?" I snap, and the brow above her topaz and blue eye raises, so I soften my voice. "Jade, be pragmatic. I'm royally fucking it up out there, falling short match after match. Everyone knows it, and I wouldn't blame you if you wanted to drop me." Drop me as a captain, as a…whatever we are.

An inferno blazes in her eyes, her tone firm, and the Jade who runs multiple businesses and circles around men takes her place. "You're treating what you call shortcomings as a failure, and all it's doing is getting in your head and causing you to trip up on the field. You have to reframe it, turn your obstacles into opportunities. Because all you're doing is acting like your challenges and your fears are a mountain, unmovable no matter how hard you push, and it's killing you."

Her arm stretches out until the very tips of her fingers graze the tattoo on my right arm—a scape of the rugged terrain of the Highlands. The touch is featherlight, but I feel it *everywhere*. I take a step closer, and her hand shifts, palm settling in the centre of my chest, pressing down lightly. "But *you* are the mountain, Tieran. Stop trying to move it and learn how to *climb* it."

Who is this woman, and how does she have this

superhuman power to reach into my chest, grab my heart, and squeeze? "Do you really believe in me that much? I've done nothing to deserve it."

She doesn't hesitate or flinch when she answers. "Yes, you have. Do you know what every one of your teammates said to me during my one-on-one meetings?" I pause, not able to breathe. "They said you're the best leader they've ever had, that you inspire them to push themselves harder because they see how much you push yourself. Because you never fail to try and lift them up even when it's hard." Tears prick behind my eyes. "They see you fight day in and day out on the pitch, not getting the results you want, and then they see you smile and come back the next day, ready to try again. They believe in you just as much as I do, maybe more. It's easy to be a great player. It's a whole other feat to earn the admiration and respect of an entire team of men. You are a leader, Tieran. A damn good one too. The playing is secondary, but I've seen your talent on the pitch, and it's obvious why you've gotten where you are. You're just having a rough patch, but you'll find that spark again."

"I think you're my spark," I whisper into the space between us, moving another step closer.

Her cheeks tinge pink, and her chest starts rising and falling rapidly. "What are you doing?"

Another step. "Tell me to stop. If you want this to end here and now, you better say so." I'm within inches of her when I cup her neck, slowly leaning in. "Last chance to push me away, love."

Her only response is to grab the chain around my neck, pulling me toward her instead.

23

JADE

THE KISS SPEARS through my chest, lighting my body up like a wildfire.

Tieran wastes no time hoisting me onto the kitchen island and wrenching my thighs open to step in between them. The move was so effortless, so inherently sexy, it was almost like he had been mapping out the perfect path to get me in this position all night, like he was just waiting for me to say the word.

And now, he's kissing me like he's gone weeks in the desert without water, and I'm the oasis pond he's been scouring tirelessly for. Like now that he has me, he'll never be able to drink his fill.

Even with me sitting on the counter, he's towering over me, craning down so he can match me kiss for kiss as his left hand digs into my waist and his right hand holds my head in place to devour me. His tongue sweeps into my mouth, and the taste of him is such a drug, I can feel myself getting addicted with every brush, every nip, every soft moan that coalesces between us. I tug at his shirt, pulling away from his mouth only long enough to pull it up over his head.

Swaths of tan rippling muscle greets me, and my mouth dries up as I finally get to look at him up close with nothing keeping me from looking my fill. The whimper that escapes my mouth unbidden makes him grin like a fiend.

"Don't gloat." I try to sound stern, but my voice comes out too breathy.

Before me, Tieran sinks to his knees, face level with my core as he pulls my hips to the edge of the countertop. "Shut me up, then. Lift," he commands.

I do as he says, using my arms as leverage to lift my ass off the counter enough for him to grip the waistband of my leggings. He pauses, looking to me for permission, and I nod in confirmation. Hooking his fingers in, he starts to ease the leggings down before tossing them to the floor beside him.

Tieran sits back on his haunches, taking me in while I sit in front of him in just my practical black panties. Suddenly feeling self-conscious and wishing I had worn something sexier, I start to fidget. My legs shift of their own accord, beginning to close, and I pull my wrap sweater down to cover myself, anything to feel less exposed.

He swats my hands away and pulls my legs open again with his hands.

"Don't you fucking dare." His usually jovial voice is razor sharp. "God, just...fucking look at you. Lose the sweater." My nipples pebble under his order, excited he's taking charge.

Slowly, I untie the wrap at my waist, taking time with every movement and soaking in Tieran's heated gaze, his large hands stroking my thighs in a maddening motion. When I unwrap the sweater, shrugging the soft material off my shoulders and displaying my strappy, low cut sports bra, his eyes darken. The bright blue I've come to love so much is practically non-existent as he drinks me in.

Reaching a hand out, he pinches a nipple between his thumb and forefinger, and I writhe, head falling back from the pleasure coiling through my body with that one, infinitesimal touch.

"Perfect. The way your body responds to me makes me feel like a god, Hellfire." His hand on my thigh inches higher while the other toys with my nipples, alternating between the two. "If I touch your sweet cunt, will I find it wet for me?"

Feeling emboldened, I run my hand down the plane of my stomach, his gaze branding me everywhere I touch, until it slips under my panties. His grip on my nipple tightens, and I cry out from the bite of pain that ebbs into pleasure as my fingers ghost over my clit. Tieran watches on, enraptured, gently placing a chaste kiss to the inside of my knee. It makes my heart squeeze and thump and pop with tenderness in a moment that feels distinctly opposite.

I swipe my fingers through my center, dipping inside and pumping once, twice, before pulling them out. They glisten under the warm light of his kitchen, proving to him just how wet I am—how wet he's made me. Slowly, I bring my soaked fingers to his mouth, and when he realizes my intention, his eyes blow wide, engulfed in obsidian.

Tieran brings both of his hands low on my hips, gripping me so hard, it could bruise, pulling me even closer, all while I trace his lips in my arousal. "Is this wet enough for you?" I ask before plunging them into his mouth.

He greedily sucks, humming in satisfaction as his tongue swirls around the digits before releasing. He looks up at me through lowered lashes, and the sight of him kneeling before me makes anticipation course through my veins. His strong hands shift with intent, running south down my hips before grabbing the band of my underwear and ripping them clean off, baring me to him completely.

"It's a start," he says just before he puts his mouth on me and turns my world upside down.

Tieran licks a hot stripe up my center, groaning loudly and forcing an embarrassing wail out of my own mouth as he consumes me so thoroughly, my eyes cross.

"Fucking hell. I've been dreaming of your taste." Tieran's face is ravenous, and he reaches down to grab the impressive bulge in his athletic shorts, grunting as he strokes himself over his pants.

I lean forward so I can see him touch himself, but the way he's circling my clit with the tip of his tongue has every neuron in my body firing, until I give up and fall back to the counter. "And? How do I taste?" My question comes out breathy, uncontrolled. Everything about him makes me lose control.

Tieran pulls himself off my pussy only long enough to answer. "Like addiction. You taste…" He uses his fingers to spread me open, baring me further before he shoves his tongue inside me, using his other hand to rub my swollen clit. "You taste like I'll never be satiated."

He eats me like he's chasing the point where he'll be satisfied but can't get there. My back is bowing off the countertop, somewhere in the background, Pebble is trotting into another room, and I'm being absolutely wrecked.

It's never been like *this*. I don't think I would have ever gotten any work done if it was like this, because I never want Tieran's mouth on me to end. I would gladly spend days, months, years doing nothing but this.

I'm yanked out of my thoughts when Tieran abruptly stands, pulls me off the counter, and wraps me around his waist. The brisk pace he sets walking to what I assume will be his bedroom makes me giggle, but I promptly shut up when I feel the hard length trapped behind the material of his shorts bump against my naked center. We both groan, and I involuntarily roll my hips against him, making him squeeze me tighter.

"Careful," he growls.

I do it again, only this time, it's intentional. I tighten my hold around his neck, leaning in and licking up the tattoo just under his ear. "Or what?" I whisper.

He abruptly sets me down and spins me so my ass is against his front, his cock digging into my back. Calloused palms skate up my thighs and brush over my core in the lightest tease, scraping against the planes of my stomach before settling on my breasts overtop the sports bra I'm still wearing, the last line of defense before there's no going back.

One of his hands dives underneath the fabric as the other finds home on my clit once again, circling before he plunges his two middle fingers inside. I cry out, bracing my hands on his forearms and standing on tippy toes as his palm applies a steady, delicious pressure to the oversensitive bundle of nerves at the apex of my thighs.

"Tieran," I gasp out. "Fuck, oh my God."

"God can't help you here, love. Just me, and I'm going to make you come so hard, you're going to be upset you deprived yourself of this for months."

His reminder that there are reasons, good reasons, why I've been denying myself of him, of us, for so long comes to the forefront of my mind.

"Maybe we shouldn't do this. I'm—" He leans down and sucks on my neck, and my thoughts scurry in a million directions. "I'm in a position of power over you." It's a feeble attempt, my last ditch effort to get one of us to see reason, and it's failing miserably.

He pulls out, spinning me to face him suddenly, his gaze more intense than I've ever seen it.

"Not in here, you're not. Does this feel like you're the one with the upper hand?" He grips my throat roughly, pulling my face close. "In here, you do what *I* want—what *I* tell you to do. That's what you really want, isn't it? To not have to be responsible for something for once?" He uses his foot to kick open my legs before reaching down and stroking my soaked core. A pleasure laced sob crawls up my throat. "Let me be in control of this, let me be in control of your body. You can boss me around on the pitch all day, every day." He leans in and kisses me, tongue tangling with mine before retreating and leaving me whimpering. "*Fuck,* it makes me hard when you do, but in here, Jade? Here, you do what I want. Now, stop arguing, get on the fucking bed, and *beg for it.*"

"Excuse me?" My tone struggles for defiance, but as he prowls closer, I back up, easing onto the bed.

"You made me pretend for months that I didn't already know what it felt like to have your *perfect* body gripping mine." Slowly, he tugs on the waistband of his shorts as he eases them off his thick, inked thighs, until he's standing before me in just his briefs. They do absolutely fuck all at concealing the thick bulge straining against the soft fabric. "For months, I had to pretend I didn't know the drugging touch of your mouth or what you look like as you come." He grips his length, giving himself two rough strokes before he removes the material all together, and I finally see his cock—long, thick, *perfect*—as he eases onto the bed and hovers over me, his legs forcing mine wide. "So, if you want my cock, prove it. *Beg* me for it."

"Don't be a dick." My stubbornness rears its head, rising to fight back, but he rubs his thumb against my clit before pushing it into my channel. It's not enough—nothing else will ever be enough after him. I groan as he removes his finger and then gasp when I feel his shaft glide through my folds, coating himself in my arousal. "That's not fair." I try to reach out for him, desperate to touch him, feel the weight of him in my hands, but he pulls back enough that I can't.

"It's so easy, love. Tell me how badly you want my cock, how badly you want *me*. Admit that you *like me*, and I'll give you what you need."

His words come floating to the surface, and I'm trying to keep my grip on reality as he glides himself through my folds again, bumping his head against my clit in a torturous rhythm. *When you admit you like me, I'll let you touch me again.* The most unbelievable part is that he would do it. He would deny himself what he very obviously wants to get me to finally own up to my feelings.

Why the hell am I holding on to them so tightly? The line was crossed a long time ago, and all I'm doing now is putting us both through hell for no reason. Why shouldn't I choose something for myself for once? Is it so bad to want someone who wants me, someone who has forced me out of my comfort zone and shown me parts of myself I didn't know existed? My feelings for Tieran have been omnipresent since the moment I met him in that pub, and I haven't been able to shake them. It's why I keep finding myself around him, like we are two halves of a magnet, destined to find each other. A peace settles over me as I accept I want this, him. *Need it.*

I reach up, cupping his jaw as my eyes gaze into his. "I like you, Tieran. So much, it actually scares me. But if you don't fuck me soon, I don't care how much I like you—I'll kill you."

The smile that engulfs his face is so luminous, it almost blinds me. "There she is." The head of his cock nudges at my entrance but doesn't breach. I shift, trying to impale myself on his length, but he pulls back, and I groan in frustration.

Tieran leans into my ear, his dick lining up once more. "I like you too, boss, but I'm about to fuck you like I don't." Then, he thrusts inside in one rough motion, making my entire body shift up the bed as my vision goes spotty from the sheer pleasure of being full.

"Fuck!" I scream, lost to everything else except his perfect cock sinking in and out of me as he pins my hips down to the bed and pumps inside me over and over and over.

"See? Was that so hard?" He pulls all the way out and snaps his hips forward, plunging inside with a punishing thrust. "You're so—" he grunts out, trying to keep his grip on reality just like me. "Play with your perfect tits, Hellfire." I obey his command, reaching up and pinching my nipples as he pins me down and fucks into me relentlessly. "I've never felt anything more perfect than your cunt wrapped around my cock—so tight, so goddamn warm."

He pulls out suddenly, and I cry out at the sudden absence of him filling me. But he's suddenly down by my core, licking me, making me writhe and whimper as I plunge my hands into his hair for purchase and *pull*. He groans into my pussy, and the sound is so erotic, I flood his mouth, and he laps up every drop.

Tieran licks a final path from my entrance, all the way up my body, and kisses me so I can taste myself on his tongue. He doesn't stay long, determined to wring every drop of pleasure from my body when he pulls away and spreads my legs wide, slapping his hand on my clit and sending me headfirst into an orgasm that rips through my body.

Back bowing off the bed, crying out in pleasure, I get no time to recover before he's flipping me on my stomach and plunging back inside my tight heat.

"Ass in the air, baby." He helps me pick up my hips so my butt fits tightly against his hips in an angle that is impossibly deep. "Face in the mattress, love, but turn so I can see you. I want you to look in my eyes when I give you what you'll never deny yourself ever again." I comply, spine curving down to rest my head against the soft sheets of his bed.

"Where do you want my arms?" I ask, loving beyond reason that he's the one calling all the shots. There's a freedom in trusting him to take care of me—in knowing I won't have to tell him how to get me there because he's treating it like his life's honor to bring me pleasure.

"Behind your back." Immediately, I cross my arms against my spine, keeping my face twisted toward him on the mattress. "That's my good girl." Tieran palms my ass, spreading my cheeks right as I feel a glob of spit splash onto my crack. He pulls out slowly, gathering up the spit with his length, teasing in and out of my pussy with just the tip. "You're so bloody perfect, so fucking beautiful, stuffed with my cock. How badly do you want it?"

"Please," I whisper, aching to be full of him again.

"Louder." His voice rings with authority and makes me clench around nothing.

He reaches forward with his left hand, grabbing my crossed arms in one large hand, and it nudges him a little further inside. Not far enough. I wiggle my ass back, begging for more. "Please, I *need* you. I want you so badly, I can't think when you're around. *Please*, I need to feel you inside me."

His resistance snaps like a sling shot, and he uses my arms as leverage to pull my body back as he thrusts forward with his hips. It hits impossibly deep, and my eyes cross from the euphoria. Nothing could have prepared me for the feeling of rightness that settles as he pummels into me, relentless in his pursuit of our pleasure.

"Never in my life have I seen anything more beautiful than my cock sinking in and out of your perfect cunt." He punctuates his statement by bending over me and placing a soft kiss next to where he holds me in place against my spine. He groans as he straightens. "I can feel you fluttering around me. Do you want to come?"

I nod my head frantically, hair fanned around me like an onyx crown.

"Say it." He lands a smack against my ass, and his rhythmic thrusts turn frantic as his command makes me clench around him.

"Yes, please let me come." It's a plea—a prayer.

"Fuck. You're suffocating my cock," he grunts out, renewing his pursuit in destroying me. "I want to stay buried inside you forever, but I don't think I can hold off much longer, you feel too perfect."

Tieran reaches his free hand around my hip, applying pressure to my clit, and I could cry from the pressure of him stretching me wide, dragging in and out of my body.

When he swivels his hips and hits a spot deep inside me, I scream. It's raw and unfiltered, but I can't help myself as he wages war on my body, working to hit that sensitive spot over and over again until my body is shaking. If he wasn't holding me in place, I would have crumbled already.

"*Yes*, Tieran. Oh my—" Sensations burst through my

body until I come apart, climaxing so hard, all vocalization is strangled in my throat. My body shakes, and Tieran pounds into me, chasing his own pleasure as I ride out the wave of my orgasm.

"Fuck. Pulling out is going to kill me." Tieran snaps his hips, plunging into me as his grip holds firm on my waist.

I twist, settling my palm on his forearm. "Don't."

"Jade—" His face morphs into a tortured, desperate plea.

"I have an IUD," I reassure him. "Please. I want to feel it. I want to feel what I do to you."

Tieran leans forward, his cock pushing in further, making my eyes roll as he seals his lips over mine in a quick kiss. But it's over as quickly as it started before he pulls back and picks up pace again, pumping into me with renewed vigour.

His groans turn into murmurs that sound a lot like he's saying the same word on repeat: *mine.* Tieran snaps his hips a final time, pulling me back simultaneously so he's seated as far as he can possibly go, and spills inside of me.

He's curled over my back, heaving heavily when he releases his hold on my arms and I go boneless. The fall I'm expecting never arrives, though, because Tieran holds me steady until I'm able to push up on my arms. Stroking an affectionate palm down my spine, he slowly eases out of me, and the feeling of emptiness unsettles me.

That is, until I feel him prod at my entrance with his tip, smearing his release around my folds. "Fuck, you're a mess." He pushes his cum back inside me with his still-hard cock, and I'm sent into a series of aftershocks from the sensitivity. He pulls out again, falling beside me and dragging me into the canopy of his chest.

We lay in contented silence for several minutes before he speaks. "You don't…" He stops himself from continuing.

I shift up, pressing against his chest so I can peer down at him. "What?"

"Forget it." Something like insecurity flashes across his features before he schools his expression.

I lean down and press my lips to his, giving him something to ground himself to. "Please tell me."

"You don't regret it, do you? What we just did." His eyes search mine, desperate for an answer.

"No." Relief eases the tension in his shoulders. "I don't know where we go from here," I say honestly. "But I feel… happy around you. I haven't felt that in so long, I forgot what it was like. And selfishly, I don't want to lose it—I don't want to lose you."

Tieran pulls me down for a long gentle kiss. He doesn't try to turn it into something feverish, and neither do I, content to breathe each other in and keep the world outside our door separate from this happy bubble.

We only break apart when the smoke alarm chirps from down the hall. Jumping into action, Tieran sprints for his kitchen, smoke billowing out of the oven as a distressed Pebble watches from the entry. I rush to comfort her, covering her ears to muffle the shrill beeping.

Our dinner may resemble lumps of coal, but it was so worth it.

24

TIERAN

"WHAT'S THIS ONE MEAN?" Jade traces the two butterflies on my elbow taking flight up my arm.

She's standing at my side, looking like a freshly fucked angel, wearing nothing but my t-shirt as I wash the dishes from our dinner mishap and wait for takeaway to be delivered.

"It's a matching tattoo I have with Lottie. We got it a few years back. She's the smaller butterfly, and I'm the larger, obviously more manly one." I flex my arm under her touch as I scrub at very persistent food bits stuck to the tray.

"Why butterflies?" Concentrating is a feat of pure will when her hand hypnotically brushes back and forth along my arm. How am I supposed to get anything done when she's touching me like it's the most natural thing in the world?

"It's what Charlie wanted—something about metamorphosis or spreading your wings. I can't remember, but I clearly don't have an issue with getting random shite tattooed on my body, so I went along with it."

"No qualms with the whole '*my body is a temple*' thing?"

"Oh, my body is a temple. It's just more concerned with worshipping *you* than keeping my skin pure." I lean to the side and nip at her lip in a quick kiss.

Her cheeks flame with crimson, and she shifts behind

me, hand trailing down my arm and across my side to slide up my spine.

"What about this one?" Her fingertips glide over the hyper-realistic female form standing proudly between my shoulder blades, arms and head absent, wings splayed out in splendour. My favourite tattoo, even more so than the dragon that winds around my kneecap or the matching tattoo with my sister.

Jade's finger lightly traces over the detailed feathers. "Winged Victory of Samothrace," I state as I finally shuck through the last bit of char left on the pan. "A tour guide during a school trip to Paris said it represents power and resilience. Nike is the goddess of victory, and for years, philosophers have said the statue exemplifies a person's ability to overcome obstacles." Air puffs out through my nose as I realise how pointed that theme is for me right now when all I seem to deal with is obstacles. "It's something that's resonated with me my whole life, so when I was in New York a couple years back, I reached out to this artist named Jae, whose work I knew would be perfect, and he squeezed me in. It's been my favourite since."

My admission weighs heavy in the air. Suddenly, Jade's arms are wrapping around my waist, and she presses up on her tippy toes to place a soft kiss to the ink.

"It's my favorite too then," she whispers against my skin.

Her words burrow their way deep into my bloodstream, and all I feel is peace as I exhale a breath I feel like I've been holding for a year. Crazy to think that the person I should feel the most uncertain around is the one person who's never made me doubt myself.

I settle a wet hand against her forearm, rubbing my thumb back and forth before twisting my head in her direction. "Thoughts on dessert before dinner?"

Jade's smile stretches across my back, breath ghosting across my skin. "Brilliant idea."

"There's ice cream in there."

She disengages from me to walk over to the freezer, pulling the door open. Moments later, she's rounding on me, judgement in her eyes and a pint in each hand. "There's like…six different flavors in here."

I turn to face her, leaning against my sink and flipping the drying towel over my shoulder. "Lottie has a horrendous sweet tooth. I keep it stocked for her."

"Yes, I'm sure it's your sister who made you feel the need to have half a dozen flavor options at once," she deadpans.

"God forbid a man likes to have a little variety."

She rolls her eyes, and I suppress the desire to kiss her until her eyes roll back for another reason.

"Spoons?" I grab two from the drawer behind me, and she saunters over, chosen flavour in hand, and leans her hip against the counter next to where her phone rests atop it.

She eyes me warily. "What?" I ask, handing her the spoon.

She shovels a heaping amount of praline butter cake ice cream into her mouth, eyes narrowing slightly as she assesses me. "I'm just trying to reconcile who you are with me and who you are with the rest of the world."

Her phone lights up on the counter, an incoming call from someone called Maxine. Jade glances down, shoulders stiffening just before she declines the call.

"Well?"

I take a fortifying breath before laying all my cards on the table. "That first night we met, I went to The King's Swan because I was feeling sorry for myself. I had spent the whole season break in a self-induced pity party, drinking and moping and miserable. And I'm not sure why, but I decided to leave the house for a change of scenery that night. I was only one drink deep when you sauntered in, looking like you had the world eating out of your hand, every eye in the place tracking your movements, ready to kneel at your feet. One look at you, and my heart started galloping, pounding so hard against my chest, I thought it would burst. You were—*are* the most stunning person I've ever laid my eyes on. I wanted to approach you, but I kept thinking to myself, what chance did I have with you when I had nothing to offer but a mess? So, I stayed put. Then, you started laying into that drunk, and I could feel it for the first time in a long while."

When I pause too long, she softly asks, "What?"

"Happiness. Watching you absolutely eviscerate that bellend was the highlight of my entire break. I wanted nothing more than to know who you were, where you got your fire, and if it could burn me a little just so I'd feel something for once. But when he wouldn't leave you alone, this fierce protectiveness came over me, so I stepped in with the intention to get him to fuck off. I'd leave you to it, but then you asked me to stay. I knew it was a bad idea, knew I wouldn't be able to have you in any real way, but I couldn't help the pull I felt. So, I sat down, and instantly, I felt like myself around you. You didn't know who I was, and I didn't feel like I had to preen to get your attention." Jade levels me with a glare. "Alright, I preened a little, but only because, well, look at you."

Another call from Maxine pops up on her phone, but she silences it again, spoon idle in her pint of ice cream as she gives me her full attention, just like she always has. That sort of attention lately makes me feel like I'm drowning, but with her, it feels like the first breath of air after getting sucked under a riptide. It's *relief*.

"I thought about you for days after, kicked myself for not trying harder to get your number. I couldn't let you go, even after finding out who you were and what it would mean for us. I needed to know more, even if all I could have was that one night. I would cherish it because *you* chose *me*. The real me. I went home feeling hopeful for the first time in months, felt that same hope after our first official meeting in your office, and it became painfully clear to me. It didn't matter what I stood to lose if what I stood to gain was *you*."

Her eyes are lined in silver, and I step toward her, brushing an errant tear that falls against her petal soft cheek.

"It's a bad idea, this," she points between our bodies, "us."

"Bad ideas are usually the fun ones," I whisper, leaning in.

Her phone furiously vibrates again, and Jade's shoulders bunch, distress making its way onto her beautiful face. She lets the call go to voicemail, but only a second goes by before a series of text notifications appear.

"Do you want to take care of that?"

"No, it's just my manager calling me to tell me how deeply disappointing I am, that I'm failing my companies and staff." She aggressively digs into her dessert.

The statement shocks me still for a moment before I recover. "How could anyone think that? I've never met anyone more singularly dedicated to their work than you."

"Tell that to her." She points the spoon at the device lighting up again with more notifications. "She believes I've become distracted by my responsibilities here. She tried to convince me not to do this in the first place." She casts her eyes down. "The problem is, she's not wrong. My engagement on socials drops daily, I've been turning down easy brand deals, and my investors aren't happy with me. I just…I finally feel like I have purpose, but I don't want to let everyone else down. It seems like no matter what I do, it's not good enough."

"You aren't a machine. If she's determined to treat you like one, why don't you sack her? I'm sure there are plenty of other people who would gladly step in. You deserve more than someone who constantly harasses you." It comes out harsher than I mean for it to.

"It's not as simple as it sounds," she sighs deeply, casting her gaze downward.

Bringing my hand under her chin, I tilt her gaze up to meet mine. "Why not?"

"Because she's also my mom," she admits, and the shock must be written clearly across my face, because she laughs mirthlessly.

My mouth drops open, but nothing comes out as my brain starts processing everything she's ever mentioned about her manager—every selfish thing she's said, every callous thing she's done, every boundary she's crossed without a second though. All along, it was her *mum* who did those things to her, who caused her pain.

"Jade—" I start.

"Yeah, I know, pretty fucked up. It seemed like a good idea when I was eighteen for her to move with me to L.A. and help me start my career, but somewhere along the way, it changed her. It was helpful at first, but the work never ended. Every day, she had twenty more opportunities for me, and there was no time to relax or have fun. Even dating was a pre-determined, mutually beneficial arrangement. I couldn't do anything for myself." I settle my hand on her waist, trying to infuse comfort into the touch. She breathes in deeply, placing her own palm against my forearm, keeping me in place. "The ironic part is, it worked. All her pushing, all her overbearing managing…it's brought me here. So I can't be too mad, right? Where would I be without it?"

"You would have made it here without her. Everything you have is earned because *you* worked hard for it. Every company, every investor, every person on the internet has backed you because of who you are and the name you built for yourself. You would still have everything without your manager. The reason she's relentless is because she lives in fear of the day you realise she would have nothing without you."

Her gaze grips me as her eyes flit back and forth between mine. "We're not that different, are we?" Confusion must register on my face, because she continues, "You've fought to get to where you are; you *deserve* to be where you are. I want you to have more—everything."

I scoop her into a hug, arms wrapping around her waist, constricting in their grip but never wanting to let go. I can feel it course through me—love. The four letter word sits right on the tip of my tongue, begging to burst out.

The doorbell rings, breaking us out of the moment, lightening the heaviness in the air.

"That must be our food." I pull back slightly.

"Finish putting the dishes away, and I'll go get it."

Jade turns to head towards the door, her hips swaying hypnotically beneath the short hem of my shirt, and the thought of a Deliveroo driver seeing her in a state of undress has my brain short circuiting. It's the only logical explanation for the caveman reaction my body has when it acts of its own accord by chasing after her, hands wet, wrapping around her waist.

Jade squeals when I lift her off the floor, hauling her over my shoulder, spinning around and walking her back into the kitchen. "What is wrong with you?"

The chime of the bell sounds again.

"If you think I'm going to let someone else see you like this, you're sorely mistaken, love."

"Oh my God, don't be so territorial." The crack of my palm against her arse causes her to yelp and squirm in my grip. "Set me down you brute!"

I place her gently on her feet until she's stable.

"Ugh, now I'm all wet."

"Isn't that always the case when you're around me?" I wink and step out of her reach when she tries to swat at me.

"Go get the food before I have a good reason to plead insanity at the trial for your murder."

"You're cranky when you're hungry." Jade grabs the kitchen towel from the counter behind her and chucks it at me. I dodge, narrowly avoiding the assault, and call out over my shoulder as I walk away, "I love learning new things about you."

We're sitting on the couch in my living room, takeout from Send Noods, a Vietnamese pho shop nestled around the corner from my flat, scattered atop my coffee table while the tv plays softly in the background. Jade's long bare legs are crossed over my lap, shoulders slightly damp from where her dark hair is still drying from the quick shower we took before sitting down to eat.

Not even five minutes can pass without my gaze scoring over her body or finding some excuse to touch her, and my mind keeps unhelpfully shuffling through images of her naked body covered in iridescent bubbles that sluiced paths down the peaks of her breasts, all the way down to the valley of her thigh crease as she lathered up her skin, steam fogging up the glass surrounding my shower. It was indecent, and I desperately needed to get my head out of the gutter, but when I look over at Jade, her eyes are glazed, chopsticks halfway to her mouth, legs shifting like she's trying to relieve some tension. That look certainly isn't helping to keep my thoughts respectable.

"Stop that," I chide.

Jade snaps out of what I imagine is a very vivid, very dirty memory. "Stop what?" she says, feigning innocence.

"Stop thinking about what you're thinking about, or I'll slap your perfect arse raw." I squeeze her thigh tight with the hand not holding a takeout container.

"Is that supposed to be a deterrent?" she retaliates by seductively wrapping her tongue around the noodles dangling off her utensils, letting me imagine her mouth wrapping around something else instead.

I shake my head, smiling to myself. "I'm going to need to hydrate if I'm supposed to keep up with you."

"Would you like an electrolyte packet? I have one in my bag." Jade moves to get up off the couch, acting like she's going to get it for me, but I wrap my hand around her waist, tugging her back down to the couch. The takeout container of noodles she was holding tumbles to the floor, and Pebble wastes no time jumping on the scraps.

"Don't be a smartass." I lean forward and pick up the fallen to-go box, but Pebble nips at my hand, trying to steal it back from me, grumbling loudly when I hold it out of her reach.

Jade lets out an effervescent giggle, shifting forward to help me clean while also sneaking noodles to my dog and patting her on the head as they beam at each other from ear to ear. It makes something in my heart squeeze and then lift, seeing her so carefree and at ease here in my home —like she belongs here.

My body pulls towards her like a magnet until I'm kissing her, taking her by surprise before she melts into it, body softening into me. That is, until Pebble nudges her way between us, trying and failing to get to the noodles on the coffee table before trotting away. Jade laughs against my mouth, and the sound leaves me utterly defenceless.

"I love that sound," I say, breaking for air and peppering playful kisses up her neck before biting her earlobe.

Gooseflesh breaks out all over her soft skin, only exacerbated when my palms skate a path up her tanned thighs and under the hem of her shirt—*my shirt*. My hand settles on her hip as my thumb finds home in the crease of her thigh and digs in.

Jade groans in my ear at the soft pressure I place there.

I pull back slightly so I can stare into her eyes, letting that bright spot of blue sear into my soul like the hottest part of a flame. Defenceless. I am utterly defenceless when she looks at me like that.

"Your laugh, your voice, the greedy, husky little noises you make for me—I could get drunk on every single one." I tuck a lock of hair behind her ear, and she nuzzles into the touch.

Her eyes jump back and forth between mine, and then

she's pulling my face down to meet hers, kissing me with the understanding that this is so much more than either of us bargained for. She shifts, pushing me back so I'm sitting straight, giving her the opportunity to swing her leg over my waist and straddle me. Slowly, so slowly I might lose my goddamn mind, she eases down onto my growing erection. She's bare underneath my t-shirt, and I can feel the heat of her through the polyester blend sweatpants I'd currently like to set on fire.

Jade flips her hair over her shoulder, grinding down on me as she leans forward, licking up the side of my neck before latching on to my ear and making my dick twitch.

"Should I get you that electrolyte packet now?" she teases, pressing down.

I grunt at the pressure. "If you leave, I'll die." I dig my hands into her thighs, making it clear she's not going anywhere.

The light from the television dances across her features like light refracting off the seafloor. I feel like I'm dreaming, because there's no way she's real, no way she's on top of me, no way she's mine. But she's here, and she looks like a siren, ready to lull me to my demise, and I'm only too happy to follow her when she strokes a hand over the material covering my aching cock before she plunges her hand beneath the waistband and grips me firmly. My hips buck up involuntarily, and my mouth bites down on her t-shirt-covered nipple in delicious retaliation.

Her pressure doesn't let up, though, and she continues to jerk and twist me in her hand, resting her forehead against mine. "You could never die." She shakes her head vehemently, like the very idea disturbs her. "You're the most alive person I've ever met. Larger than life." She pulls me out of my pants and starts teasing me through her slick folds, breath hitching when the head of my cock hits her clit. "You make me feel alive too," she says and sinks down on my cock, the stretch making both of us groan as I fill her up, inch by blissful inch.

My head falls back on the couch, a deep sigh of pleasure falling out of my mouth as she envelopes me in her tight heat sinking down slowly until I bottom out entirely. Jade rocks once, twice, her walls loosening further to accommodate my size. I've never felt anything better in my life, and I don't think I ever will.

Being with Jade is not a feeling that can be replicated or chased after; nothing could ever compare to this—to her.

I cant my hips, testing a shallow stroke up into her, and she whimpers.

"*Fuck.* The way your slick cunt is gripping my cock makes me so insane, I want to trap you here and fuck you until you beg me to stop." I emphasize my point by slapping my hand down on her ass. *Hard.* "Now finish what you started and *ride.*" Her walls clench around my words, and it solidifies my gut instinct that this confident, powerful woman likes to be bossed around in the bedroom. *Needs it.*

Pure devilry crosses her angelic face. Balancing her hands on my chest for leverage, she pulls her feet under her thighs so her ankles rest on top of my quads. Then, she begins to wreck my world, lifting herself up and dropping back down my length, over and over and over, until I'm close to passing out from the sensation. My cock throbs, growing larger with every rise and fall of her perfect cunt.

"Doing okay there, Captain?"

"*Fuck,*" I grit out, shifting my hands from her thighs over to her waist, my fingertips leaving dents in the top of her arse. "I'm going to blow my load if you keep calling me that."

She wouldn't be my Jade if she didn't take that as a challenge. All-out war begins as she starts bouncing on my cock, and I'm of half a mind to send a very large gift basket to her Pilates studio for the feat of endurance she's displaying.

Jade's head falls to the side, her damp tresses falling into her face as the light from the hallway creates a halo of backlight around her in my dimmed living room.

She looks like a goddess.

She fucks like a demon.

I grasp the round globes of her arse and help lift her, the friction of my cock dragging in and out of her tight channel sending fireworks across the base of my spine. An involuntary groan crawls up my throat, and Jade's hands dive into my hair, pulling taut while she holds on for dear life as I begin to buck up into her.

The crack of my palm smacking against her arse reverberates throughout the room, and her walls contract around me, squeezing impossibly tight.

"Oh my God, Tieran. Oh my—yes, fuck me, just like that. You're doing so good, your cock feels so—*fuck*." Her words are slurred with pleasure, barely coherent as I pummel into her, balls slapping against her ass, drawing tight with the need for release.

"It's you, Jade. Only you make me this hard." I punctuate it with a harsh thrust. "Only you drive me this out of my goddamn mind with need." I slow my speed a fraction. "Look at me, baby," I command.

She doesn't hesitate to obey, eyes locking with mine.

"Yours. I am *yours*—" I thrust for emphasis— "and this pussy is mine. *You* are mine. No more depriving me, or yourself, of this. Do you understand?"

She mewls needily as she rocks against me, greedy for friction. "Yes. Yours. Mine." She whimpers in agreement, half out of her mind with pleasure. I'm not sure if she even realises what she's saying, but I pick up pace again.

"Need this—need you. Every day. As much as you'll give me." My tone is desperate and guttural, like her agreement, her admission that what we have can't be ignored, cured an affliction I've been suffering from for eternity.

Her walls grip me tight as her orgasm tears through her, and she shakes wildly on top of me, forcing my own movements to slow but sending me headfirst into my own climax, as I spill ropes of hot cum into her only moments after her own release.

Jade collapses onto my chest, our limbs tangling as I slowly move in and out, pushing the release that threatens to slide out back inside.

Wrapping one arm tightly around her, I place the other on the back of her head, lightly raking my fingers through her hair. "Hey." I tug on a strand until she looks up at me with a lazy, happy smile on her face. "I want to make sure you know that when I said you're mine, I mean all of you, not just this." I indicate to our partially naked bodies, still connected, and covered with sweat.

I can't describe the look on her face. Contentment, maybe? That's what I want it to be, at least—happy, settled, at home with me.

"You're mine too," she says before softly turning her head into my hand and kissing my palm.

My mind is quiet in a way it only ever is when she's around as we hold each other. When she looks up, the smile she gives me is brighter than the sun breaking over the dawn of a new day: beautiful, with the promise of more.

As I lean forward and kiss her brow, I think, if all it took was my world turning inside out, public humiliation and endless nights tossing and turning in a cyclone of self-doubt, I would do it all again, as long as it led me to her.

25

TIERAN

THE DAY IS GRIM, rain chucking it down all practice, but Ballard refuses to let up. The pitch is muck under my boots, and grime coats my entire body from running drills back and forth through sodden grass as my feet tear up the field, flinging mud onto my skin. It's miserable conditions, but matches aren't exempt from bad weather, and neither is practice.

Yet, despite the piss poor weather, I've felt lighter on my feet today than I have in months. My head is clear, and the constant noise and droning has eased to no more than a whisper. It's been bliss. The quiet, calm surety I feel after my weekend with Jade left me with a new perspective. If she can believe in me that much, why shouldn't I? I'm the one who's put in countless days becoming the best at my position. I've been here the whole time as I fought to earn my spot. It's about time I remember that and start acting accordingly.

The guys have been looking at me like I've sprouted another head with the obvious shift in my playing, but no one dares to speak of it and risk jinxing everything. Can't say I blame them either; I've been holding my breath all day waiting for a slip up, something, anything that takes me right back to the shite poor excuse of a player I've been for months.

It never comes.

We practice for hours, and with every drill, every practice play, I feel like I'm coming back to myself. For the first time all season, the calls I make are the right ones, and I'm anticipating how the offensive players are going to move correctly.

Liberation hums through me, but once practice is over, the doubt starts to creep back in. We have a home match in just a few days. What will happen when I step out under the stadium lights to the sounds of a raucous crowd? Will I fly or fall?

Stop trying to move the mountain and climb it.

Jade's words have drifted across my mind almost as much as she does since our night at my place. Every time her voice, raspy and melodic, floats in, it feels like a balm to my anxious mind. Her laugh, each biting remark, the soft sighs she makes—all of it feels like the answer to a question I've been asking myself for years, a final puzzle piece slotted into place.

A large hand claps my shoulder and nudges me forward as Cavan falls into step beside me on the walk back to the tunnels. "Good practice day."

Cavan Darcey has always been a man of few words, but the ones he chooses always hold weight. He measures them —their meanings—and speaks with intention. That can be either terrifying or comforting, depending on what he says. His quiet nature is a by-product of his childhood spent in the foster system, but despite his unstable upbringing, he's always been a solid rock at my side.

I nod in his direction, not feeling the need to fill the quiet with words. We walk together to the locker room, where Coach stands, hands on his hips, everyone around him clenching their arseholes tight with anticipation. The serious look on Ballard's face makes me want to hide instead of joining the fray like we are.

"I've heard rumours from other clubs that scouts have been seen at matches." A rumbling from half the team builds in the pregnant silence permeating the air. "Settle down," Coach chastises.

"Do you know if they're coming to any of ours?" Amari asks from the back of the huddle.

"No, they don't give out their schedules to avoid any attempts at any potential bribery or match fixing." He levels a glare at each of us, but it feels even heavier when it lands on me. "It goes without saying that you should be playing to the best of your ability at every match, but if you want to be considered for the National Team, there can be no mistakes in the coming events. Do whatever the fuck you need to do to stay focused, and don't embarrass me."

"It's like a warm hug," Myles whispers next to me, making me snort.

"I'm not taking the piss. Your futures are riding on impressing these scouts." He pointedly looks at me, face stoic, and I sober immediately. "Today was an improvement, but that needs to extend beyond the practice field. Keep your game sharp and your name out of the tabloids. The blokes watching are a conservative bunch, and they don't like their players being liabilities. No drama on or off the pitch, you hear?" He looks around at everyone nodding their agreement—all but Davies, who's rolling his eyes and scratching his balls until Cavan slaps him on the back of the head.

When Coach Ballard leaves, the rest of the players split off, some leaving to go home and some heading to the showers.

I take a seat on the bench in front of my cabinet, Cavan to my left and Myles settling in on the seat opposite.

I'm unlacing my boots, feet sore, when Cav speaks. "How's your mum, Myles?" His voice is soft, so at odds with his gruff exterior.

Our friend hangs his head low, the stress visibly weighing on his shoulders. "The tests we've done so far have been inconclusive, but," he pauses, and anxiety builds in my chest, "one doctor mentioned cancer."

"Fuck," I say, at a loss for words. "How is Candice handling that?"

"She's carrying on as if we didn't just have a two ton possibility dropped on our shoulders." He rubs at the back of his neck. "I know it's because she's trying not to worry the kids, but I can't be the only one freaking out."

"Just one mentioned it could be cancer? Did they say what kind?" Cavan asks.

"No, but she's due for more tests this week, and it should give us a better idea if it is or not."

"What can we do?" I feel helpless, thinking about how Myles must be feeling in comparison, knowing he's carrying the emotional and financial weight so his mum and siblings don't have to.

"Nothing. It's a waiting game, honestly. Aanya and I are going up to Manchester later this week to help."

My eyebrows raise into my hairline. "Oh? Already taking the missus to meet the family?"

The soft smile that lights up my friend's face is positively smitten. "She's already met them, actually," he admits.

"Really?" Cavan asks, also clearly surprised. We've both known Myles for a long time and have never known him to take a girl home to meet his family. "So it's serious?"

"I'm going to marry her." He says the statement with his whole chest, not an ounce of hesitation or trace of uncertainty. "I knew the second I laid eyes on her. Everything else melted away. She's it for me."

His words have amber eyes, one with a fire bright spot of blue, coming to the forefront of my mind. The way he's describing how he felt meeting Aanya is the way I felt when I first saw Jade, and a lump forms in my throat.

Fuck, I want to see her.

I miss her with a fierce, persistent ache in my chest. That ache makes me feel a little crazy, though. How can I miss someone so much when I only just saw her the day before? When we had only just sort of accepted what we are to each other? I never felt this way with Olivia, and I was with her for a year.

As if my longing conjured her, a text from Jade lights up my phone.

HELLFIRE

I booked us an activity this time.

It's for Sunday. Are you busy?

I had dinner with the family in the evening, but I would blow it off if it meant getting to spend time with her again, especially since this time, she's the one initiating the date. She's choosing this. She's choosing us.

TIERAN

I've got a couples massage with Mrs. Cline, but I think I can get her to agree to a throuple situation if you're up for it.

HELLFIRE

You know damn well she wouldn't let me through the door.

I'll butter her up.

She'll carve me up like a Thanksgiving turkey with the butterknife. She did not like me.

Only because she saw you as a threat.

A threat?

She could tell you wanted me.

Oh could she? Was that before or after I almost stabbed you with a crochet hook?

A crime of passion, to be sure.

Whatever you need to tell yourself.

"What are you smiling at?" Myles' question brings me back to the present.

"Nothing," I say, placing my phone face down on the bench.

"Oh? So it wasn't a certain brunette who asked my girlfriend for your address a few weeks ago?"

"Is that how she got it?" The question is an admission, and I realise I basically just confessed to two other players that there is something going on between me and our boss. I glance sidelong at Cavan to gauge his reaction, sure he'll be reasonable and tell me it's a bad idea.

Instead, he's smiling softly to himself. "Did you know too?" I ask.

"You look for her during matches, you know," he says plainly. "It's like knowing she's there grounds you."

Fuck. The fact that he noticed isn't good. It means someone else could too, and Jade definitely wants to keep this thing between us quiet. "Is it obvious? I mean, obviously, this isn't something we wan—" He cuts me off.

"Don't worry. It's just because I know you so well." Something else passes over my friend's face, something that looks suspiciously like longing, but I don't have the chance to ask him about it. Two seconds later, a harried Lottie is bursting through the door to the men's locker room.

Her eyes are red rimmed and puffy, mascara smeared down her face.

Cavan bursts up out of his seat, taking two steps toward her before he stops, growling low under his breath, "Give me a name."

I get up, placing a hand on his shoulder. "Settle down, Rambo." Moving past Cavan, I step toward my sister. "What happened, Charlie?"

One of our stadium security guards launches through the door. "Miss! You cannot come in here. I'm calling the police if you don't follow me off the premises."

"It's okay, Reginald. She's Tieran's sister; we'll handle it," Myles says. "Sorry for the trouble."

"Are you okay?" I ask my sister.

"Li—" A shuddering breath expels from her throat, and

my chest constricts with worry. "Liam broke up with me." Another tear falls down her cheek, and behind me, I hear Cavan shifting in place.

"Did he hurt you?" More sobs. "Charlie, please answer me."

"No, he didn't hurt me physically." Some of the tension leeches out of the room.

"Did he say something to you?" The growl of Cavan's voice asking the question sets my teeth on edge.

Lottie looks at him for a beat longer than necessary and nods in reply.

"He said—" she starts but breaks off when some of the guys come back from the showers, towels slung low on their hips.

Lottie looks around, eyes red and swollen as they widen in horror. "Oh my God. I can't believe I just barged in here like this and made an absolute arse of myself."

"You did not," I rush to console her.

"I did. This is what he was talking about. This is exactly why he broke up with me. I'm so—"

I'm about to ask her to elaborate when Connor walks into the room, face morphing from surprise to cocksure delight upon seeing my sister.

"Aye, if you wanted me naked, Tinkerbell, all you had to do was ask." Lottie rolls her eyes, not responding, but he doesn't let up. "I still have a few tricks up my towel I could show you."

Connor goes to swing his arm around Lottie's shoulders, but Cavan steps forward, grabbing hold of his wrist. "If you want to have a working wrist to play with, I suggest you keep your hands to yourself."

"Why don't you let her decide what she wants, old man?"

"Fuck off, Davies. No one on the team is dating my baby sister." It's my one effort to get him to bow out before I have to escalate the situation.

"Who said anything about dating?" the little shite says.

Both Cavan and I take a step forward before Lottie spins on Connor and lands a swift punch to his crotch. "Memorize that feeling, because that's the only time I'm touching your willy."

"You bi—"

"I suggest you don't finish that sentence," Myles advises before Connor hobbles off, bent over at the waist, writhing in pain.

"I'm sorry I caused a scene. I'm going to go now—nurse my wounded pride with an entire packet of Jaffa Cakes, and rewatch Gossip Girl."

"Do you want me to keep you company?"

"No, I think I need to be alone."

"But—"

"I'm sorry. I had a teeny tiny meltdown and came here cause I knew you'd be getting out of practice, and my friends are still in class. I'm fine… I'll be fine. Promise."

She puts on a brave smile I think is more to convince her that she's alright instead of me. A family trait, apparently. Even still, my stomach churns when she pops up on her toes to kiss my cheek before skipping away without another word.

Cavan's body leans toward her retreating form, a concerned furrow to his brow. I want to ask him about it, but Myles pipes in, voicing the thought on all our minds.

"We might need to pay a special visit to the university."

I snort out my agreement. If my game play or relationship with Jade isn't the thing to get me barred from consideration for the National Team, a smug professor might be if I ever find out what exactly he said to my younger sister.

26

JADE

HOME IS where the wine is.

Or, at least, it would be, if I hadn't arrived home to a note on my kitchen counter from Aanya saying she took my *last* bottle because she was running late to a party and didn't want to show up empty handed.

I had half a mind to employ medieval punishment practices for her thievery and have her hands removed on a butcher's block in front of the whole village. The only reason I'm not is because she needs those hands to play her angelic music, and I'm not in the habit of denying the world something that beautiful.

Undoubtedly, though, she will have her spare key privileges revoked, because what the fuck.

After the day I had, the only thing I was looking forward to was a *large* glass of cabernet, and now, that reality has been cruelly ripped away by my neighbors pilfering hands and inability to plan ahead.

On impulse, I pick up my phone and take a picture of me frowning with the note in my hand and shoot it off to Aanya. Then, on a last minute whim, I send it to Tieran too.

Aanya responds immediately with a million gifs all begging for mercy, and it's impossible to actually be mad at her. The woman is sunshine personified, and being angry

274

with her would be akin to holding a grudge against a bunny.

My head dips back into the fridge as I kick off my heels, groaning when my feet touch the wood floor and the aches start to level out.

Today has been non-stop, with hardly enough time to even eat. Sustaining oneself with an apple and a protein bar for the majority of the day is not conducive to keeping energy high. My stomach grumbles in protest as I shove things around, hunting for anything edible and substantial enough to curb the faint dizziness I'm starting to feel.

Giving up when I find nothing more than a cheese stick, ten different types of sauce, and a half-eaten stale sandwich from earlier in the week, I grab my phone, ready to rely on God's greatest gift to humankind—delivery.

However, the universe seems to be consorting with my manager—*mother*—in ruining my day, because as I go to put in an order, my phone rings with an incoming call from none other than Maxine herself.

"Can I call you back?" I ask, wedging the phone between my ear and shoulder so I can go through the takeaway menus that have been left on my doorstep by solicitors.

"I'd rather you didn't. Who knows if I'll actually get a call back." I can hear the ice in her coffee bash against the side of the BPA plastic cup she got from Alfred's. It's seven in the evening here, so it must only be eleven in LA, putting Maxine on her third coffee of the day.

I place the phone on speaker, pull up the website for an Indian restaurant around the corner, and put in a rush order before my stomach tries to eat its way out of my body like an evil baby Renesmee.

Maybe I'll watch Twilight tonight while I finish up some extra work.

She spends the next fifteen minutes droning on about a list of brands that have reached out for partnership deals, but I tuned her out halfway through because when would I even have the time?

"Hello?" She's mad, I can tell by her tone and the general distaste that always seems to be directed at me.

"I'm here."

"Did you shoot for the Autumn capsule today? You need to make sure you start teasing those products on your socials now."

"Yes. I told you I would, and I did." I had to drag myself out of bed at five in the morning after falling asleep only four hours prior, but I knew if I didn't do it, I would get a call from her to remind me of my responsibilities. As if I could ever forget them.

"Don't take that tone. I'm the one holding everything together. I'm the one stroking egos and reminding our many investors why you're still a good gamble while you have this quarter life crisis of yours."

A date with my toaster and bathtub is looking pretty romantic right about now.

My door buzzes, and I rush over to grab my food from the delivery driver, tipping him and saying a silent thank you as my mother continues her tirade of disappointment. I may have come to London for this new business venture, as well as for Dad—a thing she likes to ignore— but the distance was certainly a bonus.

I don't even bother plating up my food. I just grab a fork, head into my living room, and plop down on the floor, setting everything on the coffee table in front of me.

"Why do you sound so out of breath? Are you at home?"

Deep breath in, deep breath out. "Yes. Why?"

The bell rings again. *Did the restaurant forget something?*

My back and feet both bark out in pain as I stand and hobble to the door, body protesting every move.

When I open the door, I'm met not with the delivery driver, but with Maxine, and my fight or flight immediately kicks in. She's immaculately dressed in a boatneck Chanel dress, dark hair perfectly coiffed, and not a spot of makeup is smudged after a long travel day. Most unsettling though is the same unfeeling stare I've come to expect is in her dark eyes. I almost forgot about that. Is that what I used to look like to people?

My mouth hangs open in shock, my body going through the early stages of total shut down. "What are you doing here?"

"No hello for your mother?" She steps over the threshold, and my previously peaceful, modest flat—my safe haven—feels like a hand grenade was just tossed inside, and there's nowhere for me to duck for cover.

"Hello, Mom. What are you doing here?"

Maxine surveys the cozy flat with barely-restrained disapproval. "Your meet and greet is tomorrow. It's normal for the talent's manager to attend, is it not?"

My stomach grumbles. "Yes, I just didn't realize you would be there because you live five thousand miles away and didn't say you were coming."

"Well, here I am. I thought some face time would be good so we can talk about your..." she picks at the blanket draped over the back of my couch before dropping it as if catching some disease on contact, "priorities before I fly out after tomorrow's event."

"Lucky me."

"You could have chosen an apartment that was a little bigger, Jade. This place is the size of my closet. It's not very ideal to show off to your followers. You have to show them the life they want; you have to tell them what to desire."

"I like the size. It suits me." My career shift was something I was prepared to defend, but my home wasn't, and anger rises like a tide within me. I like that it's cozy, with charming details, and the fact that it doesn't feel too big—too empty. I like that I have neighbors I can hear, ones who make me feel less alone. Why can't I just have something the way I want it? Why does it have to be because I think others will approve of it? Does my opinion not matter?

"I'm sure Brendan would take you back—"

"Mom."

"—then you could move into the lovely Spanish Colonial he's renting out in Calabasas."

"Mom, stop."

"It has an infinity pool."

"You're not listening to me."

"You can get over your petty squabble. It was a minor indiscretion, and I'm sure he's sorry."

Not fucking likely. "Could you ever just take my side?"

"It's business, and he's good for your brand."

"Well, as long as it looks good on paper, who cares if I'm happy, right?"

"What does that have to do with anything? This is what I'm talking about. This place," she waves around with a sneer on her mouth, "has changed you. You never used to be so combative."

"Now, I don't believe that for a second. The Jade I know is always primed for a fight." Tieran's voice instantly soothes me, and when I look over, it's to see his towering form dwarfing the open doorway of my flat as he leans against the trim, hair damp from his post practice shower. In his hands are flowers and a bottle of my favorite wine, and the sight makes my throat tighten, my eyes filling with the threat of tears.

God, I missed him.

"Hi," I squeak out.

The corner of his mouth curls up as he holds my stare, and the warmth in his gaze feels like a blanket wrapping around me, comforting me. "Hey, Hellfire."

Tieran strides into the flat with the confidence of a king in his castle, not stopping until he's slinging his strong arm around my waist and pulling me in to place a soft kiss against my temple. My eyes close as I lean into the touch, taking solace in his steady presence.

"I'm Tieran. It's lovely to meet you." He extends a hand out in greeting.

"Maxine," she replies, eyeing up all his tattoos before hesitantly reaching out and giving him a half-assed handshake.

I'd love nothing more than to get him away from my mom so she can't find a way to dig her claws into him, but I also don't want to tip off that he's someone she could leverage to her advantage. She doesn't need to know he's one of my players or that he's successful in his own right. If she found that out, the wheels in her head would start to turn, and they wouldn't stop until he ran away.

"What is it that you do, Tieran?"

I interrupt before he can respond. "He works in finance."

Tieran lifts a brow but doesn't try to correct me, instead leaning into the fake job he gave me the night we met. "I love a good spreadsheet."

I think I love him a little bit in this moment—maybe a lot, if I'm being honest. It should scare me, the force of those feelings, but instead, I feel a peace settle into my bones, and strength like armor clicks into place as the warmth from his body curls around me. Nothing my mother says or does can touch me when he's by my side.

Mom's gaze bounces between us, jaw clenched, and I can see her mind turning, trying to find a way to manipulate the situation to fit her needs.

"Did you need something? We were about to eat dinner." I place my free hand on Tieran's stomach and feel him flex beneath my touch.

Show off.

"I just wanted to see where my daughter lives. Is that a crime?"

My hackles rise, and I'm close to snapping. It wouldn't be a crime if she was visiting because she cares about me, but the sad truth is, she doesn't want to see where I live to be supportive—she wants to snoop and find ways to manipulate me.

I didn't realize until I was out from under her thumb that's what she's been doing since I was a teenager. The betrayal stings, and Tieran must notice the hurt, because his grip on me tightens, and his thumb lazily strokes my side in a soothing motion.

I'm here. I'll always be here. It says.

"Well, I've had a long day crunching numbers, and Jade has been non-stop since five this morning. It's mad how hard she works." He nods his head in the direction of the dinner spread out on my coffee table.

It's as much of a *get the fuck out* as I've ever heard, and my heart swells even further for him. Yeah, it's definitely love I feel coursing through my bloodstream. I've never been more sure of anything in my life.

I risk a glance up at him to find him already looking down at me, a soft smile playing on his lips and mischief in his azure eyes when he winks.

I'm in deep, unending trouble where he's concerned.

Maxine hoists her shoulder bag a little higher, fitting it snuggly under her arm. A body language expert would say she's fidgeting from the tension floating through the air, but I know it's because she's attempting not to bash it against Tieran's head for dismissing her.

"Meet me at my hotel tomorrow, and we can arrive at Selfridges together. It's best to get there early, so we can make sure everything is to our standard." To *her* standard, she means.

My mother turns, strutting out of the still-open doorway, leaving me to follow behind her to close the door. When I do, I take a minute, staring at the back of the door with my hand still on the knob like I might run after her. Begging her to see me as more than a cash cow, plead with her to tell me she's proud of me, ask her if I didn't have all this wealth and fame if she would still love me. Does she really love me with it?

But I don't, because I know the answer already.

Deep breath in, deep breath out.

Strong arms band around my waist on the exhale, and Tieran's mouth drops to my shoulder kissing me softly over the fabric of my blouse.

"Come on, Hellfire, let's get some food in you and talk about what an absolute delight your mum is."

I snort out a laugh, happy to have the tension broken as he grabs my hand and leads me to sit down and eat. Tieran settles in behind me on the couch, strong legs bracketing me where I sit on the floor while I start to dig in.

Silently, I pass him a samosa, leaning lightly against the dragon tattooed around his knee, too exhausted to pretend I'm not rattled. His hands snake their way around my shoulders, digging in and kneading until the tension starts to slowly dissipate.

"Do you want to talk about it?" he asks, continuing his ministrations.

"No."

"Alright, we can jus—" he starts.

"It's just…" I turn slightly to face him. "Where does she get off?"

"It—"

"She shows up at my door, and I'm supposed to be happy about an unannounced visit? I need at least one business week to prepare myself to see her." Tieran digs his thumbs in deeper, working in concentric, hypnotizing circles that forces a grunt from the depths of my throat. "London was supposed to be my safe place, but even here, she's inescapable."

"But you don't want to sack her?"

I drop my biryani back into the container. "I do. But then I feel bad for even thinking it. She's done so much for my career, and it feels ungrateful to repay her by firing her."

"You paid her for all those things, though, so there's no need for repayment. She was doing a job."

"Yes, but—"

Tieran's fingers move from my shoulders up under my chin until he's twisting my face to look in his eyes. "When was the last time she was a mum to you, Jade?"

I search his eyes as I spend an embarrassingly long amount of time trying to find the answer to that question. The longer it takes for me to reply, the more devastation fills his eyes.

"When was the last time you let anyone take care of you?"

Tingles dance around my nose as tears threaten to build. "I don't know," I whisper.

His hand makes its way from under my chin and coasts up my jaw before coming to rest on the side of my neck, his fingers twining in my hair. Dazzling blue eyes search my face before resolve sets in them, and next thing I know, he's craning his neck down and placing a soft kiss on my lips.

It isn't rushed or dramatic, but it settles something within me while simultaneously making me feel cherished—*loved*.

And when he pulls away, I feel as if he's taking a piece of me with him, a piece I *want* him to have, because I know he'll safeguard it. I know he'll treat it as if it's the most precious thing in the world, the little piece of my heart that only beats for him.

"Eat up, gorgeous, because I'm taking care of you tonight," he says right before placing a sweet peck to the tip of my nose, hopping up from the couch and moving into my bathroom.

I don't think anything of it, continuing to inhale my food at an alarmingly rapid rate until I can't possibly take another bite.

After several minutes, Tieran still hasn't come back, and I'm getting mildly concerned about what could be taking him so long. When I go search, though, I find him checking the temperature of the bath he's just drawn me. The tiled room is softly illuminated by the candles I have spread about, one on the counter and one on the small corner table by the tub. Lemon and honeysuckle waft through the room, and when he looks back at me, tanned hand glistening with bubbles and water, my heart almost bursts.

"You—" I'm speechless, mouth gaping open like a fish, because I can't quite believe it. "You ran me a bath?" The words come out soft and nearly inaudible.

Tieran smiles, his dimple pops, and all I want to do is kiss it. "Don't get soft on me now, Hellfire." He steps over to where I'm frozen and grabs my hands, thumbs rubbing back and forth against my skin.

"Why?" My head drops against his chest, eyes casting down to where his strong, tattooed hands hold me so gently.

Tieran's voice reverberates through my whole body. "You've had a long day. A long few months, I'd imagine, carrying the weight of the world on your shoulders and never asking for a damn thing in return. Let me help you relax. Let me give you even a fraction of what you give me."

"What's that?"

"Peace."

I scoff. "I'm no man's peace."

"You're mine," he rumbles in my ear, his voice soft yet unyielding.

Tears threaten to spill for what feels like the thousandth time today. Does he know that his words are disassembling every brick I've built around myself like a fortress?

Tieran tugs on my hands, and I finally look up at him.

Adoration, pure and unfiltered adoration, shines in his eyes, and I don't know how to handle it. No one has ever looked at me that way. It is disarming and exhilarating in equal parts.

"Let's get you in the bath." He turns me, spanking my butt lightly to get me to move.

"Is this just your plan to get me naked?" I throw him a smile over my shoulder, stopping before the clawfoot tub.

"We both know I don't need a bath to accomplish that."

I whip around, smacking him on his chest, but he grabs my hand, brings it to his mouth, and places a kiss on my palm.

I can't deny the truth to his words, so instead, I glare, causing a laugh to rumble from his chest.

His fingers skim the hem of my shirt, pulling upward. "Lift."

I obey, raising my arms in the air as he pulls my blouse up over my head, dropping it to the tile. I'm about to complain about him dropping one hundred percent mulberry silk on the floor, but the look on his face stops me dead.

Unadulterated appreciation.

"Magnificent." He takes a step toward me until we're toe to toe, close enough that I can smell the scent of his bodywash. My heartbeat kicks up its pace at his proximity, never being able to anticipate his next move. Outside the bedroom, Tieran is easygoing, fun, and steady, but inside, he is unpredictable—rough. He is tailor-made to blindside me around every turn.

His hand strokes up my side, leaving a trail of goosebumps in his wake, and I shiver under the force of his unflinching stare. He runs the tip of his finger under the band, back and forth, before deftly unfastening the hooks. Slowly, the garment falls off my shoulders and drops to the floor, joining my blouse.

Tieran looks hypnotized, borderline catatonic, as he takes my peaked nipples in, reaching out and pinching a rosy bud between his thumb and forefinger as if it's compulsory. Like he can't help himself.

Suddenly, he's spinning me around, pulling me against his chest with his arm banded around my waist, placing a soft kiss to the space that connects my neck and shoulder, sneakily moving his hands until they're hooking into the band of my skirt, pulling it and my panties down together until I'm able to shuck them off the rest of the way.

His grip on my hips tightens, and I groan at the pressure, wanting his touch everywhere, all at once. I squirm in place, trying to relieve some of the tension collecting in my core.

Then, he's stepping away from me, his warmth gone. "Get in the bath before the water goes cold. I'll be right back."

Disappointment courses through my body that this isn't going where I hoped it was, but that dissolves the second my body hits the hot water and my muscles instantly start to loosen.

Within two minutes, Tieran is back, handing me a glass of wine before settling behind the tub. He pulls my hair to the side, accessing my shoulders and starting to knead until I'm groaning in pain and pleasure.

"You're really good at that." His hands move down my arms, squeezing and bracing me with his own in an almost hug. "I like these tattoos." I kiss the celestial pattern sitting atop a ridge of mountainous terrain that runs around his forearm. "Do they mean anything?"

He stops his movements but starts peppering my shoulder with small little pecks. "My mum used to make us go on camping trips to the Highlands when we were younger, something her parents did with her. I think it was her way of distracting us when Dad was gone on a longer drive for work, so we wouldn't feel his absence so much. We hated it at the time, especially Lottie, but every night, she would make us lay down and look up at the sky, count the constellations, and she would tell us fables until we fell asleep. I always felt so…small looking up at the stars." I tilt my head up, Tieran's voice soothing me as he lays his heart bare. "As I got older, the feeling of wonder remained, but the implications changed. Life was getting harder, things were changing, masking his absence was getting more and more difficult, until we eventually stopped going on those trips altogether. Things shifted and nothing felt permanent anymore. One day, Dad was home but not really there, and the next, he was gone again. One second, the press loved me, the next second, I was a pariah. At any moment, everything I've worked for could be taken away. Everything in life felt fleeting, here one second, gone the next. It started to shape the way I saw everything. But one day I looked up at the stars and realised they were the same ones in the sky on all of those trips, and it brought me comfort, because they were always there, even when they were hidden by the clouds. That at least would never change." He places another kiss on my shoulder. "The tattoo is the spot we used to go to as kids, so that when it's too hard to see the stars in the sky, I can still see them here."

My throat chokes with emotion. "That's really beautiful, actually."

"Don't sound so surprised," he chuckles in my ear, breath coasting over my skin.

"I'm not. I just never thought about it like that." He straightens a little in his position behind the tub.

"You have your own constellation." He connects the dots of the beauty marks scattered across my back—the places he previously had been kissing. "I think I'll use these stars as my reminder from now on."

He places a final kiss to my neck and stands, moving to the opposite side of the tub before reaching in and grabbing my right ankle. I place my arms on the edge of the basin to keep my balance, dropping my head back in ecstasy as he wages war on the arches of my feet.

"I love that your toes are blue."

"Foot fetish?" I tease, cracking an eye open. He's looking at me intently, so intently that I start to squirm under his gaze. "What?"

"Will you go to the gala with me? As my date." It's not what I was expecting him to say, and my heart takes flight at the same time as it nosedives.

"You know we can't go together."

"Maybe not, but you can still be my date. *We'll know*, even if no one else can."

Bitterness coats my tongue, because for the first time in my life, I want to be seen on someone's arm. I want everyone to know he's mine and I'm his, but I can't jeopardize his opportunity for a spot on the National Team. Thinking about the impermanence of our situation makes me want to throw up after what he just admitted, because for once in my life, I don't have a solution, and it's killing me.

But one look into his eager eyes so full of trust, kindness, and *love* has me speaking without thinking. "Yes."

The smile that stretches across his face is worth more money than I have to my name. It's worth everything—*he's* worth everything.

Out of nowhere, he's springing forward, scooping me out of the tub, and splashing water all over the floor. My legs wrap around his waist of their own accord, and my wet body soaks through his clothes instantly.

"Are you crazy?" I shout, devolving into a fit of giggles.

"For you? Most definitely."

I crush my lips against his, coaxing his mouth open and kissing him soundly, forgetting about all the work piling up in my inbox, about the threats to our relationship looming on the horizon, and, for once in my life, I do what I want instead.

27

JADE

TWO WEEKS HAVE PASSED since I fully gave in to the pull I feel towards Tieran.

It's been the best couple weeks of my life, and I wasn't sure if I should be moderately depressed over that fact or just let it be. Happiness like this has never come easy or felt this natural, and I feel like I'm waiting for the other rugby boot to drop.

Why was it this easy? Nothing ever was.

But with Tieran, everything feels effortless. Waking up to find him in the kitchen making me blueberry lemon pancakes, Pebble at his feet begging for scraps. It settled something deep within me, domesticity at its finest, and I never realized how much I could want that—an easy partnership with someone. Starting a family was never a thought because no one ever made me feel safe enough to even consider it. But now…now, my mind is imagining all sorts of futures, and every day, every time he makes me laugh, every time he kisses me like his life depends on it, I understand more and more that my life does depend on it —*him*.

It's a thought as scary as it is freeing, because I know in my bones he feels the same. I'm falling for him at a rapid rate—not because of who the world thinks he is, but because of who I know him to be.

Tieran would light up the deepest pit of Hell with his smile alone, and he makes me want to be better—bolder. I want to see the world through his lens; trust easier, laugh more, love harder. I want to give the world what he gives me in a cosmic sort of pay it forward. He's softened me in a way I didn't know would make me stronger.

But I have no idea how we're going to continue seeing each other when our circumstances tell us there is no future. I can't give up the team—he would never even let me consider it anyway—and there is no way I would jeopardize his chances of the National Team when his best shot of making it is through The Legends.

Problem solving is my thing, and I can't find a way around this other than to continue seeing each other in secret. An abhorrent thought. How cruel is the world that I finally want something for myself, and I can't even have it? Tieran deserves someone who can be proudly on his arm after what his ex put him through. He deserves the world. I want to give it to him, but I don't know how.

Maybe we just have to wait until after he secures his spot on the National Team before we go public. Would he be willing to wait that long?

All these thoughts crowd my mind as I walk into my office, but I halt upon seeing Lawrence Chapman hovering over the bookshelves covered in business books, personal achievement awards, and a few decorative objects. Uneasiness settles in my gut, just as it does every time I'm in his presence.

I steel my spine, because the last thing I'm willing to do is let this man see any form of intimidation. "Lawrence. What are you doing in my office without me here?"

He pops up from inspecting something on the middle shelf and holds up his hands in a supplicative gesture. "I've come to throw a white flag on the pitch."

Skepticism rings alarm bells as loud as bombs detonating. "I didn't realize we were at war," I lie.

"Didn't you?" When I remain quiet, he continues.

"Look, I see what you've done for the team, for the stadium, and I have to say, I was apprehensive at first—" I scoff, but he goes on, undeterred— "but you really are quite impressive."

Condescension sandwiched between compliments. What he means is he's surprised *someone like me* could effectively lead and improve a situation he never bothered to address.

I walk over to my desk, setting my leather handbag on the surface with a definitive plop, and sit down in my chair, crossing my arms. "Why the sudden change of heart? You've been leading the charge on seeing me out of this office."

"It's simple. Money. My return on investment has gone up since you started implementing your cute little changes."

Those *cute little changes* are responsible for a twenty three percent uptick in fan attendance, a ten percent raise in season pass purchases, and another thirty-four percent increase in food and beverage sales, but sure, cute and little.

"I'm glad you're finally coming around and seeing *my* efforts are what's best for the team. That's all I've ever wanted."

A muscle in his jaw ticks before he schools his features back into neutrality.

Years of working with egotistical men has taught me to never trust their words, but rather, the merit of their actions. While I want to believe he's here because he wants what is best for our team, I'll wait to see if his movements reflect his flowery speech.

I'm not going to hold my breath.

"Yes, exactly. Me as well, of course." His hands are locked behind his hips, and he rocks back and forth on loafer-clad heels while a stiff smile resides on his face.

A pregnant silence fills the room. "Was there anything else I could help you with, Lawrence? I have a meeting in a few minutes."

My meeting isn't for another half hour, but something

about him being here and the way he's suddenly flipped a switch is unnerving.

"No, no. I just wanted to come in, apologize, and let you know you've got my support."

"You haven't, though."

"Sorry?"

"You haven't actually apologized." He looks decidedly uncomfortable as he stares at me. I raise a single eyebrow and wave my hand through the air. "At your leisure."

Chapman's eyes flicker with a restrained annoyance that makes me want to laugh because of how clearly painful this is for him.

"I apologize, Miss McKallen. I underestimated you—"

"And belittled," I add, because I can't help myself.

"Yes, that too. I apologize for my maltreatment. We are colleagues, and I hope it can all be water under the bridge from here on out."

Smiling politely, I say, "It's buried under the Millennium."

He wastes no time scampering out of my office, probably off to terrorize whoever he's cheating on his wife with this week.

I spend the precious few minutes I have before my meeting reviewing new designs for the spring collection, drafting an email to Jaded's developers on sample changes and call outs in quality control, before opening Instagram so I can schedule my post for upload later in the day.

When I open the app, I'm assaulted by the engagement announcement of my ex-boyfriend and my former assistant. He holds her around her waist, pressing a kiss to her cheek that still somehow keeps his own face forward in the image as she holds her hand out, showing off her ring. It's beautiful, maybe the one he would have bought for me one day.

I feel nothing but a deep, bone shuddering relief that it's not me in the photo.

Instead, I have something that feels bigger than the cosmos—someone I *love*, who I'm pretty sure loves me back.

I'm nervous. Why am I nervous?

Checking myself over in the mirror in the adjoining bathroom of my office, I scan the outfit I had delivered at the last minute for tonight's match. The rich burgundy of the two piece suit makes my complexion look warmer, my amber eyes glow brighter, and, quite honestly, it makes me feel like a badass. I love it.

Quickly touching up my makeup and finger combing through my hair, I don my favorite pair of nude pumps and head out towards the VIP section of the stadium for tonight's match.

The stands are filling as we near the start of the game. Fans are decked out in mock team jerseys and the new Legends-specific graphic tees I designed a few weeks ago, all sporting a pint of the nation's finest brew, Legends Lager. My spirits lift immensely, seeing the camaraderie of the fans getting excited to come out and watch the boys play.

This is what Tieran needs to see. They're here to watch them, even if it doesn't pan out exactly how he wants. Just like I am. It'll take a lot more than one rough season to get loyal rugby fans to turn their back on the team.

I pull out my phone, taking a video of what I'm seeing so I can show him, and I quickly forward it along with a text he probably won't see until after the match.

JADE

[Video attachment]

They're almost as excited to see you as I am.

Tieran starts typing immediately, and my heart begins to gallop in response.

CAPTAIN

If I were you, I'd be more excited to see me
after the match.

JADE

Oh? Why's that?

You're wearing our colours, and it's making
my dick hard.

I whip my head up to see the players have made it out onto the field, standing at the sidelines, getting warmed up. Tieran shoots me a wink and nods down at my phone, forgotten in my hand the second I saw him.

CAPTAIN

I'm really hungry, love.

My cheeks flame as I scan around to make sure no one is behind me to see.

JADE

Ok, enough of that. How are you feeling?

CAPTAIN

Nervous.

JADE

Climb the mountain, baby. I'll be cheering
you on from over here.

CAPTAIN

Baby?

It was a slip of the tongue, but it feels right to be so free with my affection.

JADE

Do you have a problem?

CAPTAIN

Yes, because now all I want now is to hear
you call me that while you're in a lot less
clothing.

Can I keep the heels on?

Who's being bad now?

Have fun out there. Remember why you love it.

Three dots appear, then disappear, then appear again.

CAPTAIN

You got it, boss.

I'm smiling down at my phone like an idiot and nearly jump out of my skin when someone comes behind me on the stairs.

"Your ass looks incredible in those trousers." I turn to see Aanya leaning against a railing, looking like a Legend herself. She's wearing Myles' shirt replica, six sizes too big and belted at the waist. It stops mid-thigh, and she's paired it with a mesh top underneath, heeled combat boots, and a host of bangles crawling up each arm. Her winged liner is severe, so sharp, it could cut.

"You can't even see my ass. The jacket covers it." I laugh.

"I'm using my imagination."

"Well, thank you. That wasn't the goal, but it's noted."

"You-know-who will love it. You look expensive, like you run this place."

I swat at her arm, looking around yet again to see if anyone's heard, but there's luckily no one close enough. "I *do* run this place, and will you keep it down? Someone could hear you."

"I know. It's so hot."

"Will you stop hitting on me?"

"Not until you agree to one night."

I snort, knowing she's not actually serious. "I don't think you-know-who is open to sharing."

"That's fair. To be honest, I don't think I could stomach

being with anyone but Myles at this point." Her stare is wistful as she looks out to find him on the pitch.

The thought behind her words felt familiar, like they've been something floating around in my own head for longer than I was willing to admit.

"Excuse me, can I get through please?" Lottie pushes her way through the aisle, heading in our direction. If not for the slightly limp pink hair, I'm not sure I would have recognized her. She's wearing dark grey sweatpants and a matching hoodie, completely devoid of the color I've come to expect her to wear. She lacks any of her usual cheeriness and is only wearing two necklaces when her base minimum is four. Aanya shoots me a concerned look before reaching over and crushing Lottie in a hug.

"Hey babe, you alright?" Aanya asks.

"Yeah, of course." Her voice is leeched of life, and the words do the opposite to comfort me. Everything about her right now feels wrong.

Her skin is slightly splotchy, as if she's been crying. "Are you sure?"

She won't look either of us in the eye, but it has to be a good sign she's here right?

"Yes, just a rough couple of weeks, but the match will make me feel better. They always do." She sits down, wrapping her arms around her waist, almost curling in on herself like she's trying to shrink away from the attention.

Aanya and I take our seats, instinctively bracketing her as the players take to the pitch. Tieran walks out toward the center line so he can do the coin toss, and I feel like there's a determined set to his shoulders that wasn't there in previous games.

The coin soars through the air, flipping end over end until the referee catches it and indicates toward Tieran in favor of our team. The stands erupt as our fans cheer at the advantage. He keeps his composure and gets in position just behind the halfway line so he can deliver the first kick of the match.

Tieran places the ball on the field and stands, shoulders back but head bowed. Then, his head turns slightly in our direction, and his eyes find mine from three hundred feet away. The world stops under the weight of that stare. To everyone else, it looks like he's taking a moment to center himself, but I know he's looking for me to steady his nerves —to see the one person who will always believe in him. My chin dips in the most infinitesimal motion, and I hope it's enough to convey to him everything I know to be true.

You can do this. You *are the mountain.* You *are the indomitable force. Nothing in this world is strong enough to hold you down. I believe in you enough for the both of us.*

Tieran cracks his neck, bouncing on the balls of his feet while mapping out a course in his mind for the trajectory he wants with this kick. The crowd goes eerily silent, waiting on the edge of their seats, as if they too can feel the shift in the air.

I can see him take a steadying breath from where I'm sitting—can already see the sweat start to glisten on his skin, despite the cool breeze curling around us. Then, I see the tension slide off his shoulders, see his lips curving upward, and the divot I love so much pops in his cheek right before he takes two powerful steps back and charges forward, strong thighs flexing with every push against the grass. Tieran's foot connects with the ball, and I swear, I can feel the thud reverberate throughout my whole body, or maybe that's just the beat of my heart about to burst out of my chest.

This is different.

His eyes ignite with a blazing inferno as the ball soars through the air, and all the men on the field scatter. All I can see is number ten—the joy on his face as he runs across the field, dodging player after player, shouting to his teammates. I couldn't tear my gaze away if I tried, and all I feel is an overwhelming sense of pride.

Ekon is the current carrier of the ball when one of the

opposition's players takes him out at the calves, men from both teams piling on to try and get the ball from him.

Brighton's center grabs hold of the ball and makes a run for it, only to be quickly intercepted and flanked by two of the Legends. It's airborne a moment later in an attempt to get it to a teammate when Tieran materializes out of nowhere, grabbing it out of the air, clutching it to his chest and running in the opposite direction like he's being chased by a hoard of zombies.

I'm off my feet, Lottie next to me grabbing ahold of my hand, more full of life than she's been since arriving, and we're screaming *go, go, GO!*

Men are grabbing for him from every direction, but it's almost like he's levitating, completely untouchable. He's twenty feet from the try line, and my heart is in my throat, wanting him to have this win more than I've wanted anything in my life—aside from him.

Number nine from the opposition dives for Tieran when he's three feet from the line, and I think I might throw up if he takes my man down when he's this close to proving to himself that he's still got it. But the contents of my stomach stay inside my body when he anticipates the move and jumps out of his grasp at the last second, diving for the try line, touching the ball to the ground, and scoring the first try of the match.

Tieran skids across the field, letting out a roar of exuberance as he jumps up, grass and dirt coating his shins, and kisses a camera that was filming the whole thing.

I'm going to need to find that video later and save it to my phone for…personal reasons.

The noise from the stadium drowns out to nothing when Tieran turns back toward the field and finds me, even though we're hundreds of feet away. He's pointing down at something, and it takes me a minute to realize he's pointing at the mountain inked on his forearm before pointing back at himself.

I'm the mountain, he says without words, and I nod back at him, beaming with incandescent pride.

The rest of the game follows the same pulse-pounding rhythm, and before I know it, the clock runs down, and the Legends have won their first game of the season.

Aanya and Lottie are balls of frenetic energy, each grabbing one of my arms and yanking me toward the team on the pitch. Aanya is immediately launching into Myles' arms, and he's spinning her around until they fall to the ground in a heap of laughter. Harry, the team's equipment manager, is chasing after players with bottles of water. Lottie has a mad case of the zoomies, the win having pulled her out of her funk temporarily as she hops around the players, giving them all high fives. She even trips over her own feet, and Cavan has to help her up, a soft, exasperated smile touching his lips. And Tieran—Tieran's walking toward me, looking like an absolute god wrapped in a sweat-soaked rugby uniform straight out of my dirtiest dreams.

He stops a foot away from me, and it's too far. "Hey, boss." His voice is low enough that with the sounds of exuberance, it's easy to get lost, and no one but me hears it.

"Hey, Captain." I'm fighting a smile.

"You know you're going to have to wear our colours every match now."

"Why's that?" I ask, playing along.

"I've finally got my good luck charm."

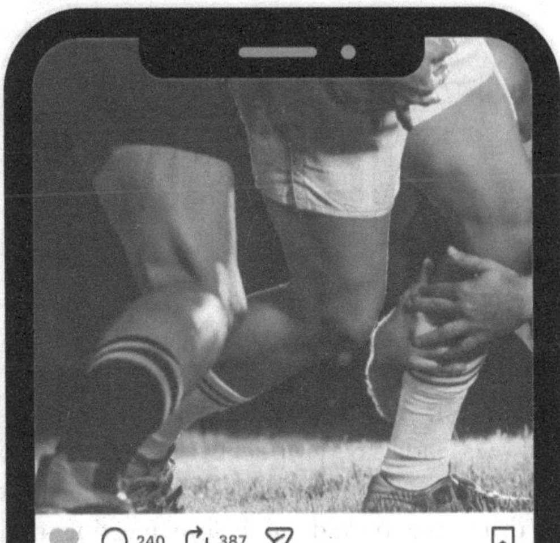

♡   ⬡ 240   ⇄ 387   ◁   ⬚

Liked by **tieranstone** and **others**

bbcsports someone lit a match under Legends captain 🔥

rugby_world did anyone else feel the shift when he stepped up to the ball?!
458 likes   Reply

officialstonefanpage HE'S BAAAAAACK!!!
6 likes   Reply
—— View replies (9)

col.waddingt0n393 total fluke. He's been playing like trash for months, there's no way he's had a complete 180 overnight. He'll trip up again.
27 likes   Reply

   tieranstone @col_waddingt0n393 fuck, I hope not.
   53 likes

   petebaker @tieranstone 👀👀
   —— View 13 more replies

londonlegends thats our captain 🗿
109 likes   Reply

rugbyrich I just hope he keeps it up
3 likes   Reply

28

TIERAN

"WHERE ARE YOU TAKING ME?"

"You'll see," Jade says cryptically, a slight tilt playing on her full mouth. A drop of coffee gathers on her bottom lip from the drink she picked up before meeting me at my house, demanding I let her drive my vintage cherry red Porsche. I took one look in her determined eyes and decided to hedge my bets. Her eyes softened upon seeing the row of green and pink crochet knots tied onto my keyring, before ripping the keys out of my grasp and hopping in the drivers side. Turns out, she's a better driver than me, albeit not afraid to go fast.

"Is this the end of my life? Should I be calling my family to say final goodbyes?" I tease, staring at her profile as she handles my car with expert care, shifting gears like she's bloody LeClerc himself. There's absolutely nothing this woman can't do.

"I guess that depends on how good your hand-eye coordination is."

I scoff. "You know how good it is."

"Exactly. So you should be fine…I think."

I was officially curious. When I asked Jade after the match what our date would be, she kept it vague, only telling me she'd meet me at mine because we needed to take my car. I had no idea what to expect, and, in classic Jade style, she kept me guessing.

That's all I've done since I met her. It's a singularly humbling experience being with someone like Jade. She makes me braver, stronger, more vulnerable—she makes me want to be better at everything, and it is an honor to be with her, because I know she doesn't *need* me. No, she *wants* me. She's choosing me, every day, regardless of the risks.

I'll choose her every day in spite of them, because nothing matters now without her. I never want to win another game or accomplish any goal if she's not by my side to celebrate with me.

I reach over to grab the hand she's resting on top of the gear shift, bringing it to my mouth and kissing that one finger that means more than the rest before placing it back down and settling my palm against her upper thigh.

She drives us through winding country roads, and the sun shines through the window, illuminating her in a soft glow, making her eyes blaze like hellfire. Sometimes, I'm scared to blink, afraid when I open my eyes, she'll disappear, and I've imagined this whole thing. How could someone utterly flawless, someone so horrendously perfect *for me*, exist in this world?

After a half hour of driving while serenading Jade with every song the radio was able to pick up on these narrow back streets, we finally pull down a road paved in cracked stone. I try not to wince at every unavoidable pothole as my car dips and scrapes the ground. Four minutes feels like four hours until we pull up to a nondescript brick building with a bright red door. Jade whips the car into a spot between two others, and I grab her hand as we walk inside. When she squeezes back in response, I swear, the swelling in my chest would have lifted me onto the moon if she wasn't holding on.

Inside is pretty nondescript, boasting a small gathering area where a few people stand and several solid oak hutches run along the back wall. There's a check-in counter to the left, with a sign reading *Shoot Your Shot* and a stout man with a wiry ginger beard flipping through a clipboard.

As we approach, he looks up from his work and quickly does a double take. "Tieran Stone?"

I nervously glance at Jade, who subtly steps a little behind me so she's out of view in case he recognizes her too. "Yes, sir. Lovely to meet you…" I trail off, waiting for him to introduce himself.

"Barnaby." I'm barely able to hold back my wince as he crushes my hand in his grip. "I 'ave to say, Stone, that last match was electric. It was so good to see you on fire again; I knew it would 'appen eventually. Told me mates you was just 'avin a rough patch, but e'll be back, I said. And nows, look at ya! Bloody country worshiping at your boots again."

I wasn't quite sure whether to be charmed or offended, but in a fit of self-preservation, I decided to settle for charmed. "I appreciate that, Barnaby. I'll keep making you proud."

"Is that Miss McKallen 'iding behind your shoulders?"

His frank question takes me by surprise, and my brain shuts off for a second before Jade steps out from behind my back. "Hi, Barnaby." Jade gives him a megawatt smile that strikes me dumb momentarily.

Barnaby's eyes dance between us, alight with the kind of glee one gets only when they're in on a secret. "Saw your name on the bookins list but thought it must've been a different Jade McKallen until I looked up and saw 'im. Figured it couldn't 'ave been a coincidence at that point."

"Sherlock should fear for his job." Barnaby goes quiet before bursting into laughter. "Look, I'd appreciate it if you didn't mention seeing us here. I wouldn't want anyone to get the wrong idea."

A blank stare crosses his face before a giant, mustache-covered smile replaces it. "I 'aven't the foggiest what you mean. I've never met neither of yous."

"Good man." I make a mental note to send him some tickets in the post when I get back to the stadium.

Barnaby corrals us all together to make his introductions. "Alright, lads and ladies, who here has done archery before?"

I whip my head to Jade, who has a big smile on her face that makes me decidedly not want to be anywhere people are around. "This is what you picked for our date?"

"Is it a date? I don't think that was ever established." Coy sarcasm drips from her smart mouth.

She yelps lightly when I pinch her side in retaliation, and everyone turns toward us, looking mildly annoyed. I mouth *sorry* before leaning over to whisper, "You know it is."

"I tried to choose something a man would like to do. Did I do okay?" There's a brief flash of insecurity on her face, but it's gone in a second.

I shift my body to stand behind her, wrapping my arms around her waist and resting my chin on her shoulder. "You could have dragged me to the market for the weekly food shop, and I would have had the best time. I enjoy everything I do when I'm with you."

"I hate that I love how cheesy that sounded." I place a peck against her neck, and she squirms in my grip.

"Behave and pay attention before you get us in trouble," I reprimand, smiling down at her.

Someone to our right in the group coughs loudly to get our attention, and we both jump, refocusing on Barnaby while he goes through all the safety precautions of handling a bow and arrow before instructing us to sign the liability waiver and grab equipment from the cabinets.

They lead us outside, and everyone in the group lines up in front of their assigned targets, awaiting instructions from Barnaby on what comes next. An overeager gentleman from down the line steps forward to grab an arrow out of the quiver a few paces in front of him, but Barnaby blows a whistle that's materialized out of nowhere so loudly, the fellow drops the arrow and clutches his ears.

"No touching the arrows 'til I say so, understand?"

Gone is the jovial man who looks like he belongs with the Fellowship, and in his place stands a drill sergeant.

We all murmur our understanding before he goes over all the safety precautions one more time, passing out three-finger gloves and forearm guards to each person.

He suits himself up next, showing us how to secure the garments, and goes straight into demonstrating how to hold the bow, making us all pull on the centre of the string so we can feel the resistance.

After thirty minutes of instruction, getting used to the weight in our hands, and faux nocking that leads to letting us fire arrows off at the dirt, Barnaby has finally decided to let us take aim.

Jade steps up first, looking like a modern day Artemis—confident, strong, and so absolutely beautiful, I feel like an arrow is flying through my chest every time I see her. Today, she's clad in soft denim and a plain white long sleeve t-shirt that hugs her body, and sneakers. It's the most casual outfit I've ever seen her in, and this comfortable, carefree version of Jade is so cute it makes me want to throw myself in front of the target just to put me out of my misery. I would gladly stand at the tip of her arrow if she's the last thing I get to see.

I pull myself out of my borderline pathetic thoughts. "Bad time to mention I had a huge crush on Katniss Everdeen growing up?"

She pulls the loose hair off her neck, lifting it into a ponytail that showcases the long column of her neck. "What was it that got your gears going? The archery skills, or the pretty face?"

"It was her smart mouth, actually. I guess I've always had a type," I say pointedly, looking up to find the sun gilding her face in gold. She's rolling her eyes at my words but a smile lights up her face, and I feel like the luckiest bastard in the world that I put it there.

"Careful; my aim's just as good as hers."

"I don't doubt it, Hellfire. If anyone's going to be a natural, it's you. Unless it's crochet, at least."

Her eyes narrow. "Low blow." She grabs an arrow from the stationary quiver in front of us.

Jade gets in position, widening her legs and raising the bow in her left hand while nocking an arrow into the centre string.

I step up behind her, so close that I hear her breath hitch, and the warmth of her back heats me through my clothes, warding off the chill in the air. "I know you just wanted me to touch you."

"Careful, Captain, or this arrow might go a little off course." She pulls the string back with ease until her elbow jams into my sternum, as if the string isn't so taut, it takes all your strength to hold it in place. She flicks her gaze back, smirks at me with mischief, and with a soft release of her fingers, fires.

The arrow spirals through the air and pierces just on the edge of the centre target, effectively making mine and everyone else's jaws drop.

She turns to me with a pout lining her mouth. "Not quite as good as Katniss, I suppose."

A stray lock of hair has fallen out of her ponytail, and I reach out to brush it out of her eyes. "Better."

A gorgeous flush tints the top of her cheeks. "Your turn," she whispers.

I brush a quick kiss to her temple before I step past to grab an arrow and take position.

As I pull back, I feel the telltale sign of nerves creep up. Even here, even after finally winning a match, the anxiety of under performing takes root. I take a deep breath, trying to let it go, and release, but the arrow flies wide, landing in the grass to the right of the target.

"Try again," she says, gentle and encouraging.

I grab another arrow, and when I lift my arms, I feel Jade step up behind me. Her soft hands run up my side, and my pulse starts to gallop.

She reaches up, hand wrapping around my elbow, and my gaze snags on her petal pink nails, so soft on the fiercest person I've ever known.

"Pull your elbow back—good." She moves to clutch my hand. "Soften your hand for me, my love." I almost release my hold completely just so I can kiss her, but she moves out of my reach, coming to stand at my back. "Straighten your spine, but make sure your knees aren't locked—good. Now, the bow should kiss your mouth—"

"I'd rather you kiss my mouth."

"Be a good boy, and we'll talk."

I chuckle, feeling the anxiety ease out of my body just from the proximity of hers. Taking a deep breath in, I go to shoot, but as I release, I feel her hands slip around my waist, fingertips skimming beneath my sweater and brushing against my bare skin.

She's playing games with me now. I can feel her smile against my back.

Focus, Tieran.

At the same time, I pull back and let the arrow fly, her fingers dip lower, and she taunts, "Maybe you just wanted *me* to touch *you*."

My body jerks from the firmer touch, and the arrow soars off course on a wayward trajectory until—

"FUCKIN' JESUS MARY AND JOSEPH!"

"Oh, fuck," I say at the same time Jade says, "Holy shit."

We both follow the direction the arrow went and discover it's found a home in Barnaby's thigh. Twenty minutes later, the ambulance has arrived, medics tending to his thankfully shallow wound while he looks like he wishes he could put an arrow in me.

Maybe season tickets would be better.

"I think maybe we should go," Jade suggests.

"Good idea." As we're walking towards my car, I shout over my shoulder, "Send me the bill, mate! I'll get it sorted."

He flips me off in retaliation, but there's a small quirk under his bushy mustache that makes me think he can't be too mad.

"I'm curious," Jade starts. "Does maiming people work up an appetite? Cause I'm famished."

The laugh that bursts out of me is loud and slightly manic. "It does, actually, and I know just the place."

"You brought me to your parents' house?" Jade whisper-yells at me as I tug on her arm, trying to drag her toward the yellow front door of their home.

"It's Sunday. Mum's got the roast going. Come on." She digs her heels in, looking like an adorably angry cat, hissing at me.

"Tieran. I am not dressed to meet your parents. Look at me." She furiously indicates down at her body, as if I should see anything other than absolute perfection.

I surprise her by leaning forward and placing a kiss to her lips that has her melting into me. I pull back slightly and cup her face. "You're bloody perfect, my love. Dad won't even notice you, and Mum's going to adore you so much, she'll probably try to trade me for you. Stop worrying."

Jade's mouth is still set into a frown, but she acquiesces a step, then another, until I'm pulling her through the front door. Shouts can be heard from the foyer as they ping pong throughout the house. Mum's in a one-sided heated debate about which *Big Brother* character should win in a season that aired four years ago, and Lottie is standing just outside the sitting room, on the phone with someone.

"No, I can't get out of dinner," she says. "Because it's a weekly thing, you know that." She pauses, and I can vaguely hear a masculine voice on the other end as we step into the doorway. "I'm sorry, you know I didn't want to miss it. I'm going to come by after dinner, I'll just be a little late." Her eyes start to glisten. "I *do* support you." A tear falls. "Please don't be like this. I haven't seen Dad in weeks; I didn't want to miss him." Lottie looks up at that moment and sees us standing in the doorway. "I've got to go. I'll see you soon. I lo—" She stands and turns away from us to furiously wipe at her face.

I step toward my sister. "Charles? What happened?"

"It's nothing. Liam's just upset I can't go to this party with him tonight."

Liam? I thought her and that bellend broke up. "Liam?" The question is clear in my tone.

"We got back together, but I'm pretty sure he just broke up with me again."

Fury drenches over me in a tidal wave. "I'll end him."

Jade puts her hand on my forearm, rubbing affectionately in an attempt to calm me down. "I've got this," she says to me. "Lottie, I'm going to say this as delicately as I can, but that man is a fuckwit."

Lottie sputters out a laugh, and I have to hold myself back from shouting *I love you* at the woman who has ingrained herself into my life so thoroughly, I will never be able to extricate her.

"I'm sorry—actually, I'm not. He's a twat who wouldn't know his ass from his elbow even if it hit him in his stupid face. You," she points aggressively at my sister, "are absolutely perfect. You are creative, kind, hilarious, and so damn beautiful. I want to know why that stuffy loser thinks he deserves you."

"It's complicated." Lottie says, sounding dejected.

Jade looks over at me and then reaches to interlace our fingers together. I swear, I breathe easier with the feeling of her hand in mine. "It doesn't have to be." For the second time in five minutes, the instinct to blurt out that I love her is on the tip of my tongue, begging to burst free.

"Sweetheart, who are you talk—oh, Tieran, you're here. Who is this?" Mum steps into the room, drying her hands on a tea towel covered in daisies.

"Mum, this is Jade, my…" My mind blanks, not knowing how I should introduce her. Friend? Boss? Lover?

"His girlfriend," Jade finishes, and I snap my neck down to look at her, only to find she's already looking up at me with a soft, slightly challenging look. "It's nice to meet you, Mrs. Stone."

Mum rips her right out of my arms and envelopes her in a hug. "Call me Harriet, sweet girl. I'm so happy to meet you." Jade stiffens momentarily, but then she slowly brings her arms up and hugs her back, closing her eyes and inhaling softly. It makes me wonder about the last time she received a mother's hug.

Mum pulls back slightly, but only to yell out for Dad. "Charles! Come meet Tieran's girlfriend!"

Charles Stone comes ambling into the room, looking down at his phone with glasses balanced on the tip of his nose. When he looks up, skepticism lines his eyes. "Do I know you?"

Mum smacks him on the arm, voice raising several octaves. "This is Tieran's girlfriend, Charles." Dad's looks over at Mum, his eyes softening a fraction in a way they only ever have for her.

"Right. Nice to meet you." It's a lukewarm greeting at best as they shake hands, and a weird silence fills the cramped hallway.

"I'm going to show Jade around before dinner. We'll be back." I push at her lower back to lead her out of the sitting room and up the stairs until we're standing in the bedroom I lived in for the greater part of my adolescence.

She slowly walks around my room, noting the blue plaid bedding, old school textbooks, a rugby ball signed by the National Team from when I was seven, and framed photos lined up on my wardrobe. Her eyes catalogue every bit of this room, seeing what she can put together about what she doesn't already know about me, filling in the blanks from my childhood.

"Girlfriend?" I prowl closer to her, resenting the distance between us.

A sheepish look fills her eyes. "Was that okay? I know we haven't talked about it, and maybe we should have before I said anything, but—"

I bring my hand up to and cup her neck. "Jade."

"—it just felt right and—"

"Jade." I lean my forehead against hers, pushing her back against the wardrobe.

"But if you're not ready, we can just pret—"

"I love you." The second the words are out of my mouth, I feel a relief so acute, my knees threaten to buckle.

"You—what?"

My thumb lazily grazes her jaw. "I love you. I have for a long time, and I figured, since you're my girlfriend now," she lightly slaps my chest, "I should tell you how I feel— have been feeling. You don't have to say it back. I just wanted you to kn—"

"I love you too." The words rush out of her mouth like an avalanche, and I feel crushed by the magnitude of happiness hearing those words come from her mouth. "And not because you said it, but because you are the best person I've ever known, and not loving you was never going to be an option for me—"

I crush my lips to hers, and the world spins and tilts until all I know is Jade—her mouth on mine, coaxing open my lips until the taste of her kiss dances along my tongue, her perfume, warm and sweet, invading my nostrils, the feel of her soft hair sifting through my fingers.

She is *everywhere*, woven into my soul in a way so fundamental, I'm not sure how I endured before I had her quiet strength to anchor me.

Her lips are soft as flower petals, but they're firm against mine as she kisses me with a fevered sort of reverence. This is so much more than a kiss. This is the beginning of the rest of our lives, because there's no way in hell I could ever let her go now. No universe in which I could give this up with her.

She is mine, and I am hers, and no force on this Earth could tear us apart.

For the first time in a long time, the anxiety that's been looming over me like a spectral monster, waiting to feast on my fear, is nowhere to be found.

In its place is love and trust and connection.

Deepening the kiss, Jade whimpers into my mouth, and I bend down to grab under her thighs, wrapping her legs around me. My hands find their way to her arse, squeezing and digging in as her hands rake through my hair, tugging the strands as the bite of pain makes my cock twitch beneath my jeans.

I band one of my arms around her waist, needing to hold her tighter, desperate to have her as close to my body as possible while my lips find the answer to questions I've been seeking my whole life.

Jade. Jade. Jade.

She rolls her hips against my thickening cock, making us both groan in pleasure. I spin around, holding her firmly in my grasp, and set her down atop the chest of drawers I have against the wall. Breaking away from her mouth, I trail kisses down her throat, and she mewls into my ear, needy and wanting. When she slips her hands under my shirt and scrapes her nails down my stomach, I have to stifle my groan, biting her neck.

"Quiet, or your family will hear," Jade whispers on a husky laugh into my ear.

I lick and suck, soothing the spot I just wounded before kissing my way back to her mouth.

"I can't help it. Whenever you touch me, I go out of my bloody mind." I nip at her bottom lip, and she smiles against my mouth.

I dive in for more, coaxing her lips open with my tongue. Running my hands up her thighs, I settle my palms against her waist, gripping her tightly and getting lost in the euphoria being this close to her induces.

"Yes, I'll let them know the roast is ready," Lottie shouts, accompanied by overly aggressive stomping up the stairs.

I pull away from Jade, groaning as I rest my head on her shoulder, slowly coming to terms with the fact that we have to stop.

The laugh that trickles out of her mouth is soft—effervescent.

A light knock on the door alerts us of my sister's presence. "Ummm…if you guys could stop doing whatever you're doing, that would be great."

"We'll be right down," I call out before we hear her footfalls walking away.

Jade hops off the furniture and checks her lipstick in one of the frames atop it.

"You look perfect," I say, openly admiring her.

"I look like I was about to get fucked," she panics.

"Like I said, perfect." Smug satisfaction rings through my tone, clear as the crystal blue waters of the Mediterranean. "Let's go. You've not lived until you've had my mum's duck fat potatoes."

We only make it to the top of the stairs before I stop to scoop her up in one more kiss that sets my world right.

29

TIERAN

WE'VE WON another two matches since the last, and the papers are now saying we're experiencing a comeback.

It feels like a gross understatement.

The way I feel now compared to the way I felt a few months ago is like I was body snatched and put into a completely different person. Transformation is what has been coursing through my veins in the few weeks since Jade's pep talk. I no longer feel dread when I step through the double doors of the personnel entrance to the stadium. Instead, I feel invigorated—like a dam burst, releasing all the shite muddling my brain.

In its place is peace and focus.

In its place is a woman who loves me and believed in me even when I was at my worst and couldn't believe in myself.

I refuse to do anything but prove her right.

The tunnel leading to the locker room has all manner of crew roaming around. A couple other teammates are ahead of me, janitorial staff pops in and out, and just as I'm about to walk into the locker room, Ballard stops me with a hand to my chest.

"McKallen wants to see you in her office."

I try not to let the excitement show on my face at the prospect of seeing my girl. Never mind the fact that I *saw* her this morning in my bed…several times, and then once more in the kitchen over breakfast.

It will never be enough—being with her, listening to her tell me about her day, having her ask me about mine, cooking dinner together, waking up with her spooning Pebble and me spooning her. I want it every day for the rest of time, and then I want to be greedy and demand to have her in whatever comes after death.

"Sure thing, Coach. I'll be back soon." He nods, clapping me on the arm. He looks as if he wants to say something but decides to withhold whatever it is.

Jade's office is only a short walk down the corridor, and before I know it, I'm standing at her door about to knock as Harry, our equipment manager, walks by.

"Hey, Harry. You alright, mate?" He looks a little skittish as I address him, but he's always been a little socially awkward.

"All good, sir."

"We're friends, no need for formalities. Is everyone being good to you?" Namely Connor, who has a penchant for bullying the poor lad.

"Yes, sir—" I raise my eyebrow and smile slightly. "Yes, Tieran, everything's good."

I knock on Jade's door and hear her call out, "Come in."

"Good. Let me know if you need anything." There's a weird look in his eyes as I open Jade's office door, and he looks beyond at Jade sitting at her desk, then back to me, nodding before he scampers away.

Odd.

I push the interaction out of my mind and step into Jade's sun-drenched office. She's sitting at her desk, worrying a pen in between her lips as she bites on the end, looking sexy as sin. A billion fantasies rush to the forefront of my mind, the first being me bending her over her desk, pushing up her skirt, and making her writhe atop all her paperwork.

"Stop looking at me like that, Mr. Stone."

"If you want me to stop looking at you like this, then you shouldn't look like *that*." She rolls her eyes, but there's no heat behind it, a tiny smile curving the corners of her mouth.

The small smiles are my second favourite. It's the one she typically reserves for when she's trying to act unaffected by my charm, but it cracks through anyway. My favourite smile is the one I know is specifically reserved for me, the uncontainable one that lights up her face and makes her eyes glow like a flame. The smile I've never seen on her face around anyone but me. It was unguarded and real, and it never fails to strike me speechless. I feel like the luckiest bastard in the world to be on the receiving end of that level of magnificence—feel unworthy of it, but I'm too selfish to not beg for more.

"How are you feeling?" Jade's question forces me out of my daydreaming about…well, her.

I take a seat opposite to her desk, leaning forward and resting my forearms on top of my thighs. "Good. Great, actually. I'm excited more than anything."

"Maybe the match will help you shake off some of that incessant energy you always have," she snipes playfully.

"I can think of a much more enjoyable way for that, love." I sit back, legs spreading wide as I spear her with the heat of my gaze. "It involves you on your bed with your nails raking down my back."

Her eyes go molten before solidifying in challenge. "Win the match, and you can have me any way you want."

My dick hardens in my soft knit joggers. "Careful with your promises. You don't know what you're asking for."

"Is that supposed to scare me?" The fire in her eyes ignites as she scans me head to toe, her gaze searing over every inch of my body.

"Nah, baby. I just want you to be thinking about it when I score the try that's going to win this match. That way, you'll remember what's coming for you after."

Jade stares me down like a lioness stalking its prey, and I have the distinct feeling that even though I'm the one making the bold claims, she's the one calling the shots. "Get on the pitch and put your money where your mouth is, Captain."

I smile a devil's grin, making her sit up straighter in her chair. "Yes, boss."

The energy from the crowd combined with the players on the pitch is nothing short of frantic. Up until this point, the match has been evenly tied from team to team. The second we score a try, Birmingham scores the next. Back and forth, the ball is transferred, men are tackled, rucks are formed, and all I feel is a pulse-pounding surety that this match is ours for the taking. Even with Birmingham being in one of the top spots for the Premiership, and the whole rugby fandom believing they would be the ones to win, I just know it's ours.

The score is tied, and the opposition has possession of the ball, heading downfield toward the try line that could win them the game, only minutes ticking down on the clock. Then, the stands erupt into a steady bass drum, a familiar chant ringing out over the crowd; *Legends, tales of old, men with feet of gold.* On and on, the song rings out as sweat pours down my back despite the chill in the autumn air.

"Ekon! Grab their centre!" I shout, and he nods, running in the direction of the player holding the ball. He doesn't see Ekon approach from behind and falls like a tree when he takes him out at the knees. "Cav!"

"Got it," Cavan's voice is a whisper on the wind, but I hear him all the same. He joins the fray, wrestling the ball away from Birmingham's centre. Myles knows without me saying anything to get in there and slip the ball from his centre pair, but before he can, a forward on the other team steals it out of his hand and runs far faster than he looks able to.

We're close—too close—to another win to let it go in the final minute. I can taste the victory on my tongue when I hear Jade's voice in my head: *you can have me any way you want.* And it's that dark incentive that fuels the superhuman pump of my legs as I run faster than I ever have. Cavan and Myles are ganging up on the other player, and he's about to pass the ball to his teammate, but I get there first and latch on to the ball, pausing only for a second to turn and dodge the player that it was meant for. Then, I'm running like I have Hermes winged sandals attached to my feet.

The volume around the crowd is explosive, and my heart thumps out of my chest, but I can't stop with the players closing in on me. I'm ten metres from the line, and I remember another time I was in this position, so close but still falling short of the mark. Not today. I'm different now, better than I was before.

Seven metres.

I pass where Jade, my sister, and all the other VIPs sit on the sidelines, and I can hear Jade yelling the same cry as the crowd. Her voice rings out over the din of thousands and reaches my ears even from forty feet away. Her voice, her cheers, are for me. Always for me.

I incline my head a little in her direction, smiling wide enough that the dimple I know she loves, the one she's taken to kissing in recent weeks, pops in my cheek. This is for me, that smile says, but it's also for you. Always for you. I swear, I can hear her screaming louder in response to that smile.

Two metres.

I feel the fly-half from Birmingham grab my jersey, and I stumble a step, falling out of his hold and pumping my legs even harder, begging them to run, move, to get us across that line.

One metre.

I take a leap and dive over the line, landing on my stomach, sliding over the chalked demarcation, and touch the ball to the grass, scoring the winning try of the game we were predicted to lose. All around me, the stands full of fans lose their minds, and a single chant begins to build in surround sound.

STONE. STONE. STONE.

My teammates rush to me, clapping me on the shoulders before lifting me in the air to revel in the sounds of the game I love more than *almost* anything.

I find her in the stands wearing all burgundy, her arms slung around my sister's shoulders, Aanya to her right, hugging a stranger. She's crying out my name with the crowd, the brightest smile I've ever seen lighting up her magnificent face, and I levitate out of my body, thanking the universe for all the hardships I faced over the last year because it brought me her.

After an hour, many press interviews, and a shower later, I'm finally packing up to leave for the evening, aching to get home to my girl and all the promises that were made prior to the match.

"Stone!" I jump at the sound of Ballard calling my name in a gruff, authoritative tone.

"Yes, sir?"

"Good job tonight. That was a hell of a winning play and a great one for the scouts to see in person." He says it so casually, I almost don't catch it.

"I'm sorry—scouts?"

He huffs. "I would've thought McKallen told you during your meeting. National scouts were at tonight's match." Buzzing fills my ears, drowning out everything around me as my thoughts swirl in a whirlpool. They were here, they saw me play. Maybe my dreams aren't dead after all. Why wouldn't Jade tell me? "I spoke with them briefly, and it was hard to get a read on them, but there's no way they weren't impressed by tonight. Just keep doing what you're doing, stay out of trouble, and I think you've got a shot."

Stay out of trouble. Does doing unspeakable things to the person who signs my paychecks constitute trouble?

Probably.

"Understood, sir."

"Good man." He claps me on the shoulder. "Get some rest. I'll see you at training."

After he leaves, I head over to my locker to grab my bag, noticing my phone lighting up with a notification.

HELLFIRE

Meet me in my office.

Despite Ballard's warning from two minutes ago, I grab my bag and head towards definite trouble.

I don't bother to knock when I make it to Jade's office for the second time today, striding in and closing the door behind me.

"Why didn't you tell me there were scouts here tonight?"

She rises out of her chair to stand in front of her desk, leaning back slightly. "I didn't want you to worry. I wanted you to have fun and not get in your head about it."

"Don't you think I should have made that decision?"

"No, I don't. I manage this team and my players, which means I make hard decisions I think are to the benefit of them." She crosses her arms over her chest, and it pushes her tits together in a way I find *ridiculously* distracting. "I won't apologize for it. You played phenomenally, and they would be fucking idiots to not want you."

I prowl toward her, crowding her in against the edge of her desk, towering a foot over her. A rumble reverberates through my chest as I stare down at her, arms crossed and face defiant.

I place a hand on either side of her hips, leaning down to whisper in her ear. "Were you thinking about it?" I place a kiss just below her left ear, and her breath hitches. "Were you imagining all the things I could do to you when I slid into the in-goal and won us this match? Because I was."

Jade's chest begins to rise and fall more rapidly as I kiss a path down her neck. I pull back, bringing a hand up to her chin to force her to look at me. Once I have her gaze, I glide my hand down between the valley of her breasts, over the plane of her stomach, until I reach the band of her pants. I tease my fingers over the top of the material, flicking the button open in one deft movement and dipping my finger inside ever so slightly. Back and forth I trace lazy patterns over her soft skin until she's squirming.

"I thought I could start by tasting your sweet cunt." My hand dives beneath the material and cups her over her lace panties, feeling a damp warmth there. The whimpers she makes when I start to tease back and forth go straight to my cock, and I have to hold back a groan at seeing her like this. "Fuck, you're so sexy when you're at my mercy." I dip a single digit into her underwear, teasing at her entrance, feeling the wetness gathered there already. "So wet for me, so hot and tight." I pump my single finger inside her channel, and she cries when I immediately withdraw. "But then I decided on something else I wanted more."

She looks up at me, eyes needy and desperate. "Oh?"

"Get on your knees, boss."

Her eyes liquify at my command, flick to the shut door, and then she slowly sinks to her knees until her arse rests against the heels of her feet.

"So subservient," I tut.

"Careful. I've been known to bite."

I grip her chin roughly, staring down at her in awe. "What?"

"I'm just thinking about all the idiots who ever told you you're cold." I shake my head. "They were wrong—you burn hotter than anyone I've ever met. I can't imagine you being anyone else other than you. I love your fire, Jade. Don't ever douse it for anyone, least of all me. Burn me for all I care, I want all of it, all of *you*."

My thumb rubs softly against her cheek, and she leans into the gentle caress. "Now, be a good girl and take me out of my trousers. I've been aching for your mouth all day."

"Yes, Captain."

Fuck me, every time she calls me that, it makes me feel like I'm on top of the world, and I guess I am, considering the hottest woman on the fucking planet is currently running her long nailed hands up my thighs and grabbing hold of my belt. Smoothly, she undoes the buckle before popping the button of my pants and reaching in, grabbing me firmly in her grip.

Cool air caresses my hot shaft when she pulls me out of my briefs, and her hungry stare locked on my proud cock has me close to spilling my load before she's even gotten her pretty mouth close.

"Now it's your turn to put your money where your mouth is, Hellfire." A mischievous glint passes over her face before she gives me one rough tug. "Tongue out."

She complies easily, pink tongue coming out to moisten her lips before she leaves it hanging in the air between us. I grab hold of my shaft and tap the tip on the flat of her tongue, leaving it to rest there.

"Such a pretty sight." I push in an inch, until just my tip is inside, pulling back before she can close her mouth around me. I tap again, precum beading at the head, leaking out onto her tongue. "Such a good girl, doing what I say." I press in, retreat again. My hand finds its way to her jaw, the tips of my fingers breeching her hair. I stroke her cheek with my thumb, gazing down into her amber bright eyes. "You know I love you, right?"

She nods, shifting on her heels, trying to relieve the tension building in her core.

"Good." I shove my cock deep into her throat, and she sputters at the invasion, grabbing my legs to keep her balance. I groan at the feeling of wet heat encasing me and the sight of her mouth stretched wide around me. "Are you okay?" I ask.

She answers by taking me in another inch until I've bottomed out, tears pooling at the corners of her eyes. "Fuck!" My hips start to move, bucking into her waiting mouth like this is where I was always meant to be. "Look at you, spit leaking down your throat because you can barely fit me inside your perfect little mouth." Jade bobs her head in time with my thrusts, and my head falls back at the sheer ecstasy of her mouth gliding over me.

Hair falls into her face like waves of obsidian from the work she's putting in. I reach forward to gather it up, but the movement only serves to push me impossibly further into her mouth. I nearly come on the spot as her throat contracts around me.

Dark strands wrap around my fist, and I grip the thick mass tightly. "I want to see my cock sinking in and out of you. I want to see the look on your face when I spill down your hot throat."

She whimpers, and I lose all control, fucking my cock into her mouth over and over again, hitting the back of her throat until all she can do is gag around me and hold on for dear life. Belated gratitude floods through me that she's bracketed between me and her desk, keeping her in place so she's not at risk of falling over.

Jade is a mess of smeared lipstick, swollen lips, and watery eyes as she takes me. No rush on the planet is better than this, not even being on the pitch with thousands of people chanting my name. Nothing compares to this feeling —nothing compares to *her*.

Jade shifts again on her heels, a mewl sneaking past her lips.

"Does sucking the soul out of my body turn you on, Hellfire?" She nods her head in assent, not daring to take me out of her mouth long enough to respond. "Do you want me to fuck you, baby? Ease the ache building between your soft thighs?" She shakes her head no, tapping my thigh as if to say, *this is about you*, and fuck, if that doesn't make me love her more. Always selfless, my Jade. "Touch yourself then. I don't come without you."

She wastes no time slipping her hand into her pants to start rubbing her clit, and I nearly combust at the sight. "That's it, baby. Make yourself feel good now, and later, I'll fuck you like you deserve."

She moans around my length, and I thrust, feeling the telltale signs of my impending release as sparks dance up my spine and I grow impossibly stiffer.

Jade's sucks turn erratic, her focus going haywire as her moans turn louder, vibrating around my cock, sending me jerking forward. I spill inside her mouth just as she crests the final wave of her own pleasure.

I fall forward a little, catching myself on her desk before standing upright and easing out of her mouth. I quickly tuck myself back into my pants and kneel until we're eye to eye.

"Are you okay?"

She nods, bringing her fingers up and pushing them into my mouth. "You said you wanted a taste." Her voice is a raspy midnight caress as I lick the sweetened musk of her release from her skin.

The sound of her stomach grumbling breaks the heated tension in the room, and both of us break out in laughter.

"Let's go get you some food. You're going to need to keep your energy up for the rest of the night I have planned for you."

She takes the hand I extend for her to stand, and we sneak out of Knightsbridge Stadium, stealing away into the night.

30

JADE

THE RED SILK of my gown shines under the lamplight as I walk up the steps into the hotel, careful to hold up the full skirt of my dress so I don't trip. The bodice is tight, with a strapless, low sweeping neckline and a dangerously high slit going up the thigh on the voluminous skirt.

Aanya kept saying I was going to send everyone into cardiac arrest with the way my tits looked, Lottie vehemently nodding her agreement as we all got ready at my flat earlier. I never had real friends and was quickly learning that with the right ones, it was easy to get attached.

The gala tonight is one all Rugby Union teams are invited to, rivalries aside. Tieran told me it's the one night a year each club puts their grievances on hold to come out and support because it benefits Kingdoms for Kids, a charity with an emphasis on placing kids in loving foster homes. The money made tonight will help fund the organization for the next year, providing meals and allowances for the children and their foster families.

Long story short, everyone behaves for the sake of the kids.

The hotel boasts an old world sort of charm, with warm lighting, chestnut wall paneling and floors, large, filigreed silk rugs, and ornate chandeliers hanging in every room. The extravagance is multiplied tenfold as I waltz into the grand ballroom behind a group of men dressed in tuxedos, beautiful women draped on their arms. It's hard to keep my jaw from dropping when the crowd clears and I take in the whole room. The rustic wood has been replaced with marble columns, gilded accents everywhere, and renaissance murals displayed on the ceilings. Crystal chandeliers line the vast room, hanging upwards of fifty feet high. Music trills through the air, winding around couples swaying on the expansive dance floor while others amble around, sipping champagne.

I'm struck speechless, taking in the grandeur of the room, when someone sidles up next to me. "Evening, Miss McKallen."

Cavan Darcey stands tall next to me, as handsome as he is severe.

When I asked him during our one on one meeting what his goals were, his answer was painfully simple: to win. We haven't spoken much since that day, but I know he knows about me and his best friend.

"Thank you," I feel the need to say. "For your... discretion," I add on, not sure if he heard me.

"We all have our secrets, Miss McKallen." I follow his dark eyes across the room to where they're settled on a beautiful woman with pastel pink hair wearing a dress that looks like liquid silver is pouring down her body. The expression on his face is one of tortured awe as he admires my friend. He closes his eyes and takes a deep breath, almost as if he's trying to will the image of Lottie away, before he slowly turns his gaze to me. "Plus, you make him happy—happier than I've ever seen him. That's all I care about."

A lump the size of a boulder lodges itself in my throat. "I feel the same about him."

Cavan's lips curl at the corners ever so slightly, barely noticeable. "If you'll excuse me, I have some things to check on. Enjoy your evening."

No sooner has he gone than I feel a pair of eyes heating

me from head to toe. I find him within seconds, a crowd of people around him, talking and laughing, trying to get his attention but failing, because all his focus is on me.

His gaze rakes down my body like a phantom caress, and I suppress a shiver at the intensity of his stare. I step further inside the ballroom, my heels clicking against the floor as he tracks every move, hands tucked into the pockets of his dress pants.

He looks devastatingly handsome in his tux. The white of his button up is a stark contrast to his midnight black jacket and tanned skin. The only tattoo on display is the one inked on his neck.

Ephemeral, it reads.

I asked him about it one lazy morning as we lay in bed, Pebble between us at the foot of the mattress.

"It's not important," his voice is husky, still groggy from misuse, as he strokes my bare hip softly.

"Mmmm," I hum lazily, still tired from sleep. "Why?"

"I don't think it's true for me anymore."

"What do you mean?" I ask, eyes closed, foot grazing the dog shaped hippo at my ankles.

"Ephemeral means lasting for a very short time." He leans forward, pressing a kiss to my forehead. "But you feel everlasting," he whispers against my skin.

Tears prick the backs of my eyes even now, and I feel a stab of pain that I can't just walk up to him and kiss him how I'm aching to. He must see my face shift, because he takes an involuntary step toward me. *Are you okay?* he mouths.

Before I can answer, Finn is at my side, sweeping me onto the dance floor, shocking a bark of laughter out of me.

For the next twenty minutes, I'm passed around on a rotation of handsome rugby players, all fighting for a turn to spin me around. I can't say I'm mad at the development; if anything, it drums up a warm buzzing in my chest.

I'm rolling my eyes at something Connor just said when

a deep rumble sounds from behind me. "I'll take it from here, Davies."

I don't know what look is on Tieran's face behind me, but for once, Connor doesn't argue. He just nods and bows out, mumbling something about wanting to hit the free bar.

Tieran comes to stand in front of me, and I'm almost knocked on my ass at the intense look on his handsome face. His blue eyes blaze bright as he takes me in up close for the first time all night.

"Torture," he whispers.

"What?"

"Absolute bloody torture to be this close to you when you look like everything I've ever wanted, and I can't hold you properly." He extends his hand to me. "But I'll settle for a dance."

I hesitate for a second, wondering if it's wise, but then I decide I don't care so much in this moment. Hopefully, the fact that I've danced with pretty much the entire team at this point will work in our favor and not draw attention.

When my palm settles into his, warm and calloused, it feels like I've come home. Something restless settles within me after running in circles in the desert. I've been coasting on auto pilot for so long, it never registered that I was burnt out and so lonely, using self-isolation as a defense mechanism. I learned to handle everything on my own because no one was going to come rescue me. They didn't have to, not when I learned to shoulder every burden on my own. But Tieran barreled into my life, blindsiding me completely, and forced me to slow down—and for the first time, in my life I felt safe. He gave me a soft place to land after running never-ending marathons with no support, no one to cheer me on or tell me things will be okay when they're hard. That feeling of security is almost terrifying in its reality.

He sweeps me into a slow dance, one hand holding mine and the other settled on my waist, pulling me into him. The band softly plays an instrumental version of Sweet Nothings as we sway, bodies close but not touching.

"I missed you today," he says, low enough that no one but me can hear.

I smile up at him coquettishly. "Why are you so obsessed with me?"

I mean it as a joke, but his expression morphs, serious as a statue. "I am—"

"I was joking," I laugh him off.

"I'm not. Jade, I—" He takes a second to gather himself, his head shaking a little. "I stopped *breathing* when you walked in. You're—fuck, you're breathtaking."

My heart stops cold in my chest at the declaration, and for the first time, I feel everything he says I am. Powerful. Beautiful. Strong.

"Might have to have that checked out, it could affect your playing."

His head falls back on a laugh that's far too loud for the gentle song floating around the room. We dance until the final chord progression, reluctant to let go of each other at the end but knowing we have to. "Let's get a drink," Tieran says.

He ushers me toward the back wall, where the open bar is set up. We're waiting at the back of the queue when the couple at the front turns around, and my heart drops.

Standing before me is Oliver Hughes and Tieran's ex-girlfriend, Olivia. She's insanely beautiful in a fitted blue dress, with a plunging neckline showing off her ample bosom.

"Oh my God!" Her voice is like nails on chalk boards, but I don't know if that's because I hate her by default or because her voice naturally sounds like cats being dragged in cheesecloth down a cobbled alley. "Babe, look who it is!" Oliver grunts an acknowledgment, smug arrogance written all over his face.

Tieran's face is unreadable, but he acknowledges her with a curt, "Olivia."

"Isn't this funny," her voice chimes. She hasn't even acknowledged that I'm here. "Last time I was at this gala was with you, T, and now I'm here with Ollie."

Rage courses through my body as she talks about the choices she made as if we're talking about the weather patterns for the next week. I want to pop her pretty, platinum blonde head right off her neck.

"Praise the lord for small mercies," Tieran says sardonically, forcing a very unattractive chortle from my throat.

Olivia's eyes pinch a little, and then she finally looks over at me, and her eyes go round as saucers. "Oh my God!" she parrots again. "You're Jade McKallen! Holy fuck, I've been following you for years. This is insane. God, you're even more gorgeous in person. Can I get a selfie? My girlfriends will never believe me if I don't."

"Can we go?" Oliver complains. Olivia ignores him, waiting for me to respond as she holds her phone out expectantly.

"Sorry, no. Tonight's about the kids. I'd prefer to fly under the radar."

"Christ, that's cool. Isn't she cool, babe?" Oliver's gaze lands hard on me, heating as he takes in my dress, sweeping down over my bare thigh.

A growl slips out of Tieran's mouth, possessive and predatory as he steps slightly in front of me. Oliver's already walking away, clearly bored with the whole conversation, and Olivia hardly notices, her attention back on Tieran.

"You look good, T." Her eyes trail down his body, and I have to remind myself the night is about the children, or I would be hauled out of here by security. "Really good. We should *catch up* soon."

Her implication is more than clear, and I'm about to take a step forward, but then Tieran is pushing at the small of my back. "Our turn. Have a good night," he dismisses her, ushering me forward in the queue.

"Are you alright?" I ask once she leaves, unbothered by his dismissal and with a gleam in her eye.

"Hmmm? Oh yes, I'm fine. I'm going to go use the bathroom quickly. I'll come find you later." He pauses like he wants to give me a kiss before departing but then realizes he can't and strides toward the exit.

I watch him go the whole way before the disgruntled bartender grabs my attention and I order a champagne.

I'm standing at one of the back walls, feeling uneasy after the encounter with Tieran, his ex, and the sudden shift in his mood when a voice pops my peaceful bubble.

"Don't you look ravishing," Lawrence exclaims with absolutely zero sincerity.

"Lawrence." My voice is clipped. "Where's the missus?"

"Left her at home with the kids. Gotta see what's on offer here, and I couldn't well do that with her attached to my hip."

I down the rest of my drink, desperately wishing another could magically appear in my hand. "Do you have any respect for women?"

"The ones who do what they're told."

My face doesn't hide how I feel toward him. "You're disgusting."

"Careful, Ms. McKallen. That mouth of yours will get you in trouble one day, maybe even soon." There's a weird look to his eyes I can't decipher. It's knowing and smug and so damn cocksure, it makes my hackles rise.

"What is that supposed to mean?"

He taps his glass against my empty one. "Have a good night." And then, he strides away.

The whole conversation leaves me feeling rattled, and I decide I'm going to go find Tieran, needing his presence to ground me.

I head out of the ballroom in search of the bathrooms when I hear voices around a small alcove. I slow, straining my ears to listen when I hear Tieran's voice, then Olivia's.

My heart starts pounding so loud, I have a hard time hearing what's being said until I inch closer.

"Come on, T. No one has to know," Olivia says, and my mind conjures images of her running her hands down his chest. I feel physically ill at the thought.

"Stop, Olivia." His firm voice does little to ease my anxiety.

"You remember, don't you? How good it used to be with us." I'm going to throw up. "You could have me right now, in this alcove." Her voice is soft and seductive, the total opposite of my raspy resonance.

"I don't want you. Olivia, so stop touching me and let me pass."

"You're playing hard to get. That's cute."

"Stop it." His voice is edging on panicked, and the sound breaks my heart, pulling me out of my trance as I step around the corner to see her roaming her hands all over *my* man.

"I think you should take your hands off him." I don't even recognize my own voice. It's cold—lethal and filled with the promise of violence if she doesn't stop touching him.

Olivia's head whips to me. "Oh, it's not what it looks like." She honest to God winks at me. "We have history. I'm sure you get it."

"I don't, actually. From where I'm standing, it looks like a desperate girl who finally realized what she fumbled and is now looking really pathetic trying to force herself on him. I would suggest you go find your sad excuse for a date and stop touching my bo—" I catch myself on the word boyfriend at the last second— "player before you embarrass yourself further."

Her face goes beet red, and she swallows hard, at a loss for words.

"I always thought you were putting on this *too cool for everyone else* persona, but you're just a heartless bitch, aren't you?" I flinch at her words as they strike home, reminding me of all the other times other people said something similar.

"Fucking leave, Olivia," Tieran bites out.

She pouts, finally relenting as she walks away with a sway to her hips, as if she's walking a fucking runway.

"Are you okay?" Tieran asks, placing his hand on the side of my neck, pulling me closer to him.

I breathe in the scent of his cologne, crisp and clean, with a soft undercurrent of sandalwood.

"Yes, but—"

"But what, baby?"

"Can we go?"

His smile lights up the dark turret we're standing in. "Let's drop off a fat check at the donation site and sneak out of here."

"Did that upset you?" I ask, unable to hold back the question that's been running through my mind since we left and started walking along the banks of the Thames.

Tieran's thumb traces a lazy path along the back of my hand while our fingers are interlocked. It's nice, holding his hand out in the open. "Hmm?"

"You left when we were waiting for drinks. Were you upset about Olivia? Does it still hurt seeing her?" My heart beats out of my chest, nervous to hear his answer but happy the river's current can sweep me away if it confirms my worst fear—that even though he says he loves me, maybe I was just a bandage over his wounded heart.

Tieran stops dead in his tracks, but I don't register it until I'm being yanked back by his hand now clutching mine even harder than it was before.

"What? No! Fuck—no, baby. I'm sorry. I didn't think about how that would look to you." He steps closer to me and releases my hand, only to cup each side of my face. "When I saw her, I felt so stupid. I couldn't believe I never realized how wrong she and I were, and I only know that because how I feel about you is—" He pauses, trying to find the words. "You're like the wind, Jade. Everywhere, all around me, lifting me up and breathing life into the world —into me. When I walked away, it was because I was seconds away from showing everyone exactly what you are to me. I needed a second to get myself under control before I did something that put you at risk. When I came out of the bathroom, she was waiting and cornered me before I could get away. You know the rest."

Insecurity claws at me, making me feel foolish. "I was worried that—I started to feel like maybe it would be easier for you...if you were still with her. She's beautiful and uncomplicated. You deserve th—"

Tieran leans forward and kisses me, effectively stealing my breath and making me lightheaded. I clutch the lapels of his tuxedo for balance as he scrambles my brain with a kiss so tender, I can feel it stitching pieces of me back together I didn't know needed healing.

"Being with you is the furthest thing from complicated for me," he whispers against my lips. "Whenever you look at me, it feels like a thousand tiny lightning bolts striking every inch of my skin. I know you think you're hard to love, but it's the easiest, most unavoidable thing I've ever done." His eyes bore into mine, pleading with me to understand. "Nothing could have stopped me from falling so horrifically in love with you. You are fierce *and* kind. Bold *and* soft. Terrifyingly smart *and* maddening." He smiles, and I let out a soft laugh. "I have never met anyone like you, and I *know* you're too good for me, but I'm too much of a selfish prick to care. *Everything* feels possible with you by my side. All I want is to give you what you give me, and I'm terrified I won't be able to measure up to all *you deserve*. There is not, and never will be, a limit to what I'm willing to do to show you just how magnificent you are."

Even now, after all we've been through, he doesn't see what I see.

Beside us, the river sparkles under the light of the moon, reflecting like little diamonds dancing on the water. "I've never felt like I belonged anywhere, Tieran. I didn't have friends growing up, had even fewer when I entered adulthood. You've seen what my mother is like… The only time I ever felt safe growing up was when I would watch rugby on weekend mornings with my dad. But being isolated for so many years…I think it messed me up."

"You're not—"

"I'm not finished. From the moment I met you, I felt like I was home, even when the very thought of you terrified me… Some days, it still does, but talking to you at the pub that first night was the most fun I had ever had in my whole life, and every day with you since has been the same. You are funny and infuriating and selfless. I—I think you might be the best friend I ever had," I admit begrudgingly, if only because I know his head will grow two sizes from the truth.

"Try not to sound too put out about it," he laughs.

"It's an upsetting revelation." Tieran pinches my side in retaliation.

"Aanya is going to be fuming when I tell her," he teases, grabbing my hand once more and pulling me along the sidewalk.

"I'll deny it. I'll scheme an elaborate tale about you being a compulsive liar."

"My love, we both know the only person you're able to lie to is me."

My cheeks blush, thinking about all the times I did lie when I was denying all the feelings I had for him. "I'm reformed."

"Is that so?"

"Yes. I've been the picture of virtue." He raises a single brow at me, as if to say, *oh really, with the things we've done?*

My blush magnifies, and I face forward, gazing toward the city's skyline. The Elizabeth Tower, illuminated in golden light and housing Big Ben, stands proud, the stunning spires of Westminster just beyond, and in front of us on the left is the giant Ferris wheel that spins tourists around at a leisurely pace while they observe the sight of London sprawled out before them.

"Do you want to go for a ride?"

Tieran's low voice breaks me out of my daze. "What?" He nods toward The Eye, and I get his meaning. "Oh, no. That's a gimmick meant for tourists."

"It could be fun."

"Someone might see us. We're already being reckless, walking around and touching each other the way we are." I may not be as recognizable here as I am back in the States, but it has happened a few times, and I wasn't with a six-foot-four, absurdly hot rugby player who is fairly famous in this country then.

His expression turns severe. "I don't want to hide what you are to me."

"And what's that?"

"Everything, Jade. You're everything."

My heart stalls in my chest. The way he's looking at me as if his world stops and starts because I'm alive is not something I'm used to, and I'm starting to get drunk on the feeling of his open adoration. He's so free with his feelings, so uninhibited, with no expectations of me.

I must be silent for too long, because he jumps in before I can respond and tugs me forward. "C'mon, Hellfire. It's late, and I'll bribe the uni student running the line to give us our own car. Let's go do something we'll never forget."

Maybe I should be worried about the mischievous glint in his eye, but I've come to realize I don't care what happens, so long as he's by my side for it all.

31

JADE

AS IT TURNS OUT, there was no need to worry, because the carriage attendant at the massive Ferris wheel didn't even look up at us as we approached, and hardly any people were in line due to the late hour. Even still, Tieran smoothly slid a hundred quid into the young man's hand, who didn't bat an eye as he counted the money and motioned for us to get on the carriage that was slowly approaching.

The egg-shaped bubble has a single bench in the center surrounded by windows, allowing panoramic views of the skyline, and it's moving so slowly, you can barely feel it at all. I walk around the whole space, the skirt of my dress swishing along the floor as I come to stop along a pane of glass facing out. Parliament is sprawled out on the right, the Tower of London on the left, with Tower Bridge spanning the gap between the two. God, this city is beautiful.

I absently wonder what my life would have been like if I had grown up here instead of back in Maine. Even if my dad had chosen to move home after the divorce and I just spent summers and holidays here, who could I have become?

Tieran settles in behind me, close enough that I can smell his cologne, fresh, with a bite of sandalwood and cedar. "Stop thinking so hard." His arms wrap around my waist, and his lips find their home, placing a soft kiss on the exposed side of my neck. My eyes close at the contact, and I settle into him further, placing my hands over his on my waist.

"It's hard to turn it off sometimes," I admit.

"So tell me about it then." His chin settles on my shoulder while his arms tighten around me.

"I don't think I know what I'm doing anymore." The admission comes out as a whisper, but it feels like an explosion dropped into the middle of the room, sending debris throughout my carefully curated world. It's almost like finally speaking the things I've been feeling out loud releases this toxic gas of truth that slips through my grip when I try to gather it up and shove it back inside.

"Keep going." Tieran nudges me with a nuzzle to my neck, sending shivers snaking up my vertebrae and raising all the tiny hairs on my body.

"Until I came here, I didn't realize how backwards my priorities have been—how alone I've felt my entire life." In the distance, London sparkles under the light of the moon, bathing everything in its cool glow. "I've been living my life on auto-pilot for so long, I never second guessed if I was on the right path—if what I was doing was truly what *I* wanted. Everything I did was for other people. What do they want to see? Will they like this outfit? How will they react to the breakup? Should I go to this event because it will help my image? It was exhausting." I take a deep, fortifying breath. "But when you live your life through someone else's lens, you're really not living, are you?"

"No," he breathes against my temple. His exhale almost feels like relief, and I know he must be thinking about the dad he loves who always worked too much and wasn't present when he was home.

A hollow ache settles in my chest, forcing me to be honest with myself. I never understood how loud the loneliness was until he came into my life, and everything went blissfully quiet.

"I almost missed all this."

"What?" he asks.

"Life. *Friends*." The word huffs out of my mouth, the taste of it foreign on my tongue. I guess it was before I moved here. I think of Aanya and Lottie, unable to imagine my life without random wine nights or having them screaming profanities that make the men around us blush during a match. I think of Myles and Cavan, who have displayed superhero levels of loyalty to the people they love. And then, I think of Tieran, an unexpected wrench thrown into my metaphorical machine, clanging around my hollow insides and disrupting everything about the way I view the world until I was forced to see the potential in what it could truly offer me—not what I could offer it. Tears threaten to spring to my eyes because, despite my resistance, he never wavered in his quest to show me I am worth loving.

This is what it's all about.

Not the business deals or the zeros in my bank account. Not the accolades from people who don't know me. Individually, all those things are great accomplishments, but without people to share them with, they don't have meaning.

Tieran places a kiss on the crown of my head. "What does the woman who has everything want out of life, Jade? You want the moon? I'll lasso it down from where you hung it. You want a quiet life? I'll get us a house out in the country where Pebble can run around in the garden out back and nap on the wildflowers. Whatever it is, say the word, and I'll give it to you."

I twist my neck and capture his lips with mine. "This," I whisper against his mouth. "You. Us. This place. Our friends." I search his electric blue eyes and find nothing but love. "I just want you."

I spin in his grip, my hands grabbing hold of his torso, and crush my lips against his.

My pulse gallops to a run as his hands dive into my hair, expertly using them to tilt my head up and devour me. My grip tightens as I meet his tongue stroke for stroke, a fire starting to burn low in my core.

His scent curls around me, warm and inviting, when a wicked idea ignites. It's foolish, stupid, risky, but with Tieran, I've never been able to think straight enough to see reason. Why start now?

My fingers trail lightly down his sides, coming to rest on the top of his belt before shifting inward. Tieran's lips move to my neck, nipping and biting on my pulse point, driving me mad with want. It will never end; for the rest of my life, I will want him. Beside me, inside me—everywhere all the time.

My hand shifts down further, grabbing him over his pants and already finding him half hard. He jumps from the contact, clearly not anticipating me being quite this brazen.

"What are you doing, Hellfire?" His head tilts in question, but his eyes burn as they stare down at me.

"I'm not denying myself what I want." I pull on his belt buckle. "You told me I wasn't allowed to do that anymore, remember?" I see the moment it clicks in his brain, the night he said those exact words to me as takeaway containers of noodles littered the table behind us and the television bathed us in its glow.

He groans. "We can't. Not here." I can see his desire to be rational fading. He and I are the same, insatiable in our need for the other, but his head is telling him to be cautious despite the appeal.

I, on the other hand, have no such compunction. I already accepted I was something of an exhibitionist now, because with Tieran, I've never cared where we are. I just know I need him.

He abruptly steps back and out of my reach before I undo his belt entirely. Tieran turns his back to me, walking the length of the glass pod, now halfway through its rotation, before he comes to stop at the other end.

He shoots a smirk over his shoulder before slowly

pulling his loosened bowtie from around his neck. Impeccably muscled arms lift over his head, making his white button down pull tight across his back and diverting my attention momentarily from what he's doing.

What is he—it registers two seconds later. He's using his bowtie to wrap around the security camera in the far part of the room.

He gives me no time to ruminate on the fact that I didn't even think to check for cameras, because he's stalking towards me, gaze darker than I've ever seen it. I take a step back but bump into the rail screwed into the glass paneling.

Tieran grabs my waist when he reaches me, spinning me around to face the city views. A laugh bubbles out of me at his dominance. That is, until his fingers find the slit of my dress and dance up the exposed skin of my thigh. "Is this what you wanted?" My amusement quickly turns into a moan as he dips his hand into the skirts of my dress and makes contact with my center, finding me already damp with arousal.

"Mmmm," he grumbles in my ear. "Wicked woman.' I gasp when a single finger dives beneath my underwear, stroking a lazy path through my slickening folds. "You like the thought of someone seeing you being fucked so hard, you see stars?" I nod until my head falls back on his shoulder. He focuses on my clit, rubbing in small lazy circles as I clutch his sleeve. "You know what I like?" I stutter out an unrecognizable word in response. "I like that I'm the only one who gets to see you like this, that I'm the only one who has ever made you feel mindless when you're always so focused, so worried about everyone else around you, wound tighter than a seaman's knot." He catches my earlobe between his teeth. "Let me *unravel* you."

Slowly, Tieran pulls my panties down, reminiscent of the night we first met. I kick out of them, the heel of my stiletto getting caught before he bends slightly and pulls them off completely.

Then, the infuriatingly genius man reaches up again

and uses them to cover the camera resting slightly above our heads.

I can feel him growing hard behind me, his impressive erection pressing against my ass even through the voluminous layers of red silk. He brings his hand back to my center, cupping me possessively, and I grab his arms. I love the feeling of him owning me like this, in a way I would only allow with him, because of who he is to me.

"Can I, baby?" he asks as he starts to tease me with his fingers again. A nod and a mangled cry is all I'm able to get out before he's growling out a husky *thank fuck* in my ear.

Tieran doubles down on his efforts, and if it wasn't for him holding me up, I would have crumpled to the floor in a heap of pleasure.

He alternates between dipping into my opening and gathering up my wetness, to rubbing soft but firm circles around my swollen clit. The teasing is driving me mad; I'm begging to be filled, but the second I think he will finally put me out of my blissful misery, he goes back to working me up, making me delirious with frustration and lust.

"Tieran." His name comes out garbled.

He sucks hard on the spot just below my ear, marking me, but I don't have it in me to care that I'll have to use industrial strength concealer to cover it up tomorrow. It'll be worth it.

"Tieran, I—" My voice catches and releases a cry as he finally spears his fingers into me, my walls clenching around him. He pumps his hand in and out, careful to make sure his palm bumps against my clit in tandem.

"Is this what you wanted?"

I nod, wiggling my hips to help his movements, desperate for more friction, more heat, more *him*.

"Use your words, Hellfire. I love when they bite." He nips my ear and thrusts his hips into my backside.

"Stop talking," I manage to get out with absolutely zero force behind the words.

"I think you like it when I talk." He presses another

finger inside, stretching me further and causing me to cry out. "I'm gonna give you a third because I want to make sure you're ready for my cock when I bury it inside your pretty cunt."

My first orgasm tears through me at his words, and he chuckles in my ear. "Coming from my words? Yeah, I'd wager you actually love it when I talk."

"You're insufferable," I pant.

"You didn't seem to be suffering when you were coming on my fingers."

"You know what I do love?"

"What's that?"

"When you shut the fuck up and *fuck me*."

I feel his foot slip between mine, kicking at my right one, forcing me to spread my legs open before he taps the left, splaying me wide for him. "Do you want me to fill you, Jade?" His voice is a low, whispered seduction in my ear, and I suppress a shiver.

There's hardly any use denying it. He's already gotten me wet and worked up, and I'm far too turned on not to see this all the way through. "Yes."

He lets out an inaudible grunt as he slowly starts to pull up the layers of my skirt. "I wish I could take this dress off, lay you down, and fuck you hard into floor, but with the chance that someone could see us…" I look up at the pod above us but can't see anyone. Relief and disappointment courses through me in equal parts. "They don't get to see you like that. That's for my eyes only."

"So territorial." I twist back and capture his lips with my own, and he wastes no time coaxing my lips open and laying siege to my mouth.

He pulls away as quickly as it started. "I *am* territorial of you, Jade. You're mine. Mine to love, mine to protect, mine to fuck." I can hear as he unbuckles his belt with one hand, using his other to continue pulling up my dress. "Call me a brute, I don't quite care, just as long as you also call me yours."

My heels put me at the perfect height for the tip of his cock to line up at my entrance, and I jolt at the feeling of him pushing through my lips. Slowly, he rubs the swollen head back and forth through my folds, and I liquefy against him, anticipation building through my body. I press back, encouraging him to take it one step further, but he pulls back slightly, tearing a frustrated sigh out of me.

"Say it." His shaft runs back and forth again as he rocks, soaking his length with my arousal before notching his head at my entrance.

"You're mine." My voice is a soft growl, drunk on love and lust when he snaps his hips forward and sinks in all the way to the hilt.

Both of us groan as Tieran falls forward slightly, hand landing hard on the glass of the car, his chest resting against my back. He takes a moment—whether to give me a chance to adjust to his size or because he needs it himself, I don't know.

"Yes, I am. So hopelessly and unequivocally yours."

I clench around him, and his free hand grips my hip roughly.

I do it again and feel him twitch inside me.

He tests a shallow thrust, and my eyes roll back in my head at the feeling of him dragging through my channel, stretching me wide to accommodate his size. My head drops, taking in the sensation of being so perfectly full. Never in my life have I ever felt like this during sex. I always thought I had a fairly good time in bed with partners, but it was nothing in comparison to what I know now. With Tieran, every time felt new and exhilarating—I would never get enough.

"Fuck, you take me so well."

The praise fills me up like helium, and if he wasn't holding on to me, I might float away.

Tieran pulls the skirts of my dress until I feel cool air caress my skin. "God, look at you, stretching around me." Another shallow thrust, and my head drops lower. Tieran's right hand snakes into my hair, wrapping around his fist, and I'm taken back to the first night we met. His hand in my hair, and we're in a very similar position, only this time, we have more clothes and more room. Pulling my head back, he says, "You take in your view," he nods to the city skyline, "while I take in mine."

He pulls out to the tip before thrusting back in and setting a punishing pace that has a sheen of sweat forming all over my body. In the distance I see buildings illuminated like lights on Regents Street at Christmastime, cars driving across the bridge and people walking along the bank of the river. I can't process any of it, though, as Tieran drags in and out of me, and I lose myself to the pleasure.

"Fuck," I cry out when he hits that spot deep inside my body that has sensation lighting up across my skin. "You're so thick, so deep—how do I feel?" I clench around his thick shaft as it drags in and out of me.

"*Fuck*, Jade. I want to live and die inside your perfect cunt." He groans loudly, and it echoes off the glass walls around us, ratcheting my pleasure higher hearing how I make him feel.

"Make me feel it for days after," I pant out, breath fogging up the glass. "I want the reminder of you with every step I take."

He goes from thrusting to pounding into me, heeding my wish and rocking me forward with every punishing push of his body. Pleasure dances across my spine, and I clamp my hand down on his thigh, needing to hold on to him.

There's nothing soft about the way he's fucking me, and we're both far from quiet as we race toward that final pinnacle, the Ferris wheel now settled at the very top as London unfurls before us in a wave of beauty.

My walls start to flutter around him, signaling my impending release, and he growls loudly in my ear, "God-fucking-damnit. You feel like a fever dream, too perfect to be real." He snaps his hips and it pushes me forward, forcing me to brace my hand against the window so I don't smash my head on the glass. "Get used to the word forever, Jade because that's what this is."

The scream that leaves my mouth on his next plunge is guttural, sending me headlong into an orgasm so intense, it has me convulsing around his length, squeezing him in a vice grip.

"Can I come inside you, baby?"

The question nearly makes me come again, but my body only grips him tighter as his thrusts grow stilted from how tightly I'm still suctioned to him. "Yes, please," I mewl, wanting, *needing* to feel him inside me.

He grunts and continues pounding into me, the friction sending aftershocks coursing throughout my body like I'm a high voltage wire powering this whole damn wheel. Seconds later, he grunts out his release, jerking into me as I feel warmth fill me, the lubrication adding an additional slip that allows him to move leisurely as we come down from our high.

He places a soft trail of kisses along my shoulder, slowly working in and out of me as he spreads his release. making a mess of me.

"Fuck, that's pretty." When I look back at him, he's staring at where we're joined.

"Pervert," I laugh.

"Absolutely depraved when it comes to you, love." Slowly, agonizingly, he pulls out of me and helps me get my clothes settled before fixing himself.

"I'm sure that's what the tourist board had in mind when creating this ride." The laugh that bursts out of him is so loud, and his smile is so wide, the dimples I love are on full display. I smile up at him, not quite believing we just did that, and we spend the rest of the ride holding on to one another. There's no music playing, just the distant sounds of street traffic, but he leads us in a gentle sway, almost as if we're dancing. When the ride is over, and we've reached the bottom and exit the carriage, he slings his jacket back around my shoulders, grabs my hand, and leads me home.

32

JADE

THE MONDAY FOLLOWING THE GALA, I step into my office and immediately come to a halt. "Why do you keep showing up to my office uninvited?"

Lawrence Chapman is sitting with his feet crossed at the ankle, propped on top of my desk like he owns the place, not me.

"Can a bloke not come by to say hello to his colleague?" There's an arrogance to his voice that makes my gut churn, and I have the distinct feeling this is not going to be a pleasant encounter.

"They can, but you don't. So again, I'll ask: what are you doing in my office uninvited for a second time?" I don't make a move to sit in the chair opposite, instead sitting on the couch at the front of the room.

I place my bag and coffee down on the marble table and cross my legs, infusing my entire body with a nonchalance I certainly don't feel.

He knows something; he must if he's here right now, looking so at ease and smug as fuck.

"I told you one day, that cocky, better than everyone else attitude would come back to bite you in your nice arse." He leers at me from head to toe, and a thousand ants skitter over my skin in response. "I told you you'd slip up, and I'd be there to watch you fall."

Okay, this might not be as bad as I think it is. He could be bluffing in an effort to get me to admit to something that could incriminate me.

"I'm curious, Lawrence. What is it that you think I've done?"

He slowly untangles his legs and stands from my desk, sauntering his way over toward the bookshelves lining the left wall.

"It took longer than I thought it would. You're smart, I'll give you that. I underestimated you at first, but then you started to get careless." He runs his hand along the shelf, as if searching for dust—like that would be some kind of proof to my inadequacy—but it comes away spotless. "But my patience paid off. You did so much grunt work getting this place sorted, and now, I'll reap the benefits of your hard work."

"*My* patience is wearing thin, Lawrence. Get to the point."

"You're going to sign your shares over to me."

I pinch my brows between my thumb and forefinger, feeling the edges of a headache starting to creep in. "Why the hell would I do that?"

He claps his hands so loudly, I jump a little in my seat. "I'm so glad you asked." He starts walking around the room, a jumpiness to his step that's putting me on edge. His eyes border on manic as he reaches for the shelf two paces in front of him, pulling out a tiny device tucked behind a small planter. "See this?" He holds up the device. "This is a microphone, state of the art technology. It picks up sound bites, isolating all background noise, and then uploads the file directly to the computer it's linked to."

My heart starts to beat erratically out of my chest. This is so much worse than I thought.

"It's funny, because for a while, I thought I wouldn't find anything. It was just day after day of you droning on in constant meetings for hours on end. I started to wonder if you ever did anything else. I had *almost* given up, but then, the blissful day arrived." He's pacing in a tight circle, hands gesticulating wildly like a madman. "See, I was listening to the latest sound byte, thinking all hope was lost, when the unmistakable sound of illicit activity came through the line. You're a naughty girl, from the sound of it."

The yogurt parfait I had for breakfast threatens to come back up.

He turns slightly, reaching behind him and grabbing something wedged between two decorative objects on the shelves, small enough that I wouldn't be likely to notice.

"So I pulled up the video feed." Yup, the granola is going to surface. "Imagine my delight when I saw you on your knees for none other than the team's captain. *Your* employee." He tsks. "Very naughty indeed. Though it certainly looked like a good time for Stone. I knew your mouth was a nasty, foul thing."

My stomach twists violently. "Why would you do this?"

"You took what was owed to me, and I needed proof if I had any shot in getting you out. Lucky for me, I had a credible source who alerted me to your…inappropriate relationship. But their word wasn't enough. This, though," he holds up the small surveillance camera, "this is more than enough."

Credible source? I thought we had been careful, but maybe someone saw something in the way we look at each other. It was probably clear as day to anyone who saw us.

It suddenly clicks. "That's why I found you in my office that day."

"A little slow to the draw." His eyes rake down my body, pausing on my breasts for longer than comfortable. "At least you're pretty."

The comment rankles, but I compartmentalize it like I have every other time some bastard in a suit said something similar. "What do you want?"

His smile is predatory. "You'll sign your shares over to me and get the hell out of my stadium."

The desire to push back rears. "And if I don't?"

"Then this video will find its way to my contact at The Daily Mail."

"You're running the risk of ruining your star player's career." It could mean a swift death to The Legends; surely, Chapman cared about that?

"I'll find another fly-half, and we'll bounce back. You, however…" He shrugs, totally unaffected.

My mind starts racing a thousand miles a minute. Tieran's done nothing but dream of making the National Team, and with the way he's been playing, he has a good shot. If this video goes live, it threatens to upset the conservative list of selectors who want a squeaky clean team. Could I really let that happen? Could I really be the reason he might not make it to the Olympics? He would resent me forever for being the thing that kept him from his dream, and that, more than anything else, would kill me.

He sucks a breath through his teeth, continuing his ranting while my mind whirs a thousand miles a minute. "I mean, who's to say you didn't leak it yourself in an attempt to sell clothes, or lipstick, or—" he swats his hand through the air, "whatever the hell you hock to the airheads that follow you. No matter how you spin it, it looks bad, and the public famously loves controversy. Scouts and business investors, though? Not so much."

Would the stakeholders attached to Jaded pull out after this hit the press? After the way I've been handling things since moving here it's possible. Especially if the loyal fanbase I've built over the last decade leaves me behind because I'm no longer this shiny perfect picture they've idolized.

"Well!" Lawrence's boisterous voice cuts through the battle taking place in my head. "I can see you're having a lot of thoughts, and because I'm so benevolent, I'll allow you some time to think about your decision." He tosses both devices in the air, catching them in his waiting palms and pocketing them. "I'll be taking these. Wouldn't want you thinking you have anything you can use against me."

The hate that fills my body when he laughs at the look on my face nearly makes me launch off the couch to strangle him.

He walks to the door with the swagger of a king, stopping at the threshold and looking at me still sitting on my couch. "You've got till tonight to make a decision. If I don't hear from you by nine, the world will know what you look like when you're gagging on it by morning."

I've ignored Tieran's texts all day while I try to figure out if there's any way out of this without losing everything we've worked for—without losing each other.

A migraine pulses at the edges of my temples as thoughts form as quickly as they fizzle away. I can't think of a single thing to fix this mess that would leave us unscathed, and I'm slipping perilously close to a meltdown. I *never* had meltdowns. No matter how harrowing the situation, I pride myself on staying composed and professional.

That was before my heart was involved, though.

Now, I'm floundering around like a fish on dry land, because I can't think of a way out of this without the total evisceration of my heart.

My first instinct is to go to the authorities, because what he did has to be illegal. But with the proof in his pocket, what would they do? It was all hearsay. I'm in a room, and the walls are closing in rapidly, backing me deeper and deeper into the corner.

Focusing on work after Chapman left my office was impossible. All I could think about was everything he had seen on that camera, every look on Tieran's face, every moan that fell from my mouth.

But I don't feel embarrassed by what was on the video. I feel *violated*.

He took a moment between two people who love each other and turned it into blackmail. And the worst part is, it's going to work, because, as smart as I am, I can't puzzle my way out of this.

My phone pings with a notification as I get out of the taxi dropping me off outside of my dad's house on the outskirts of London.

♥

I miss you.

My heart squeezes painfully in my chest, and holding back the urge to shatter into tears is next to impossible as I walk through the gate to the modest, two-story home.

I don't bother knocking and walk through the front door to find him on the sofa in his sitting room, BBC Sports playing reruns of the last Legends match on the tv in the corner. My soul feels like ashes on the wind as I see the familiar figures running around on the screen.

Dad turns toward me, brows lifting into his salt and pepper hair. "I didn't know you were coming by." His tone is surprised.

"Hi, Dad." I paste on my best fake smile. The last thing I need is for him to worry about me, it wouldn't be good for his condition. "What are you doing?"

His shaky hand waves through the air, clutching the remote. "Watching the lads play. That Stone boy is something else. You better make sure you keep hold of him."

He may as well have plunged a rusty butter knife into my chest and twisted it. "What?"

"Tieran. You can't let another team snatch him up. He's too good, especially now that he's back to his old self."

Right, the team. Because he doesn't know Tieran and I are involved romantically. Not until tomorrow morning, when he finds out alongside the rest of the world in the worst way possible.

"He's just such a raw talent. Look at him, anticipating

the defenses moves here." Dad stands and moves close to the tv, pointing at a tiny image of Tieran running across the pitch. "And then, he literally dances around them like he's toying with them. It's brilliant."

It was. I remember watching that moment live and feeling like I was going to burst out of my skin from the electricity pulsing through the stadium. Everyone around me buzzed with excitement, cheering and latching on to one another, and all I could do was stare at the number ten running across the grass with pure light beaming out of his eyes.

"There's no way the National Team haven't got their eyes on him. They'd be fools to let his potential pass them by."

The knife twists further, slicing through arteries and soft tissue until I'm bleeding out on the floor, ending me where I stand, because I know what I have to do, and I've never felt more broken in my life.

I stand up abruptly, needing to put distance between me and the pixelated version of everything I'm about to give up.

"You alright, lovey?" Dad asks, concern etched across his lined face.

I smooth the wrinkles out of my dress and paste on another smile. "Of course. I'm just gonna go get some dinner started."

I don't linger to hear what else he might have to say, rushing to the sink in the small, outdated kitchen to splash my neck with cold water in an attempt to calm the full body shaking starting to take over.

My lunch threatens to rise in my throat when I reach for my phone and shoot off a text that effectively crushes my spirit.

JADE

Fine, you win.

LAWRENCE CHAPMAN

I knew you were a smart girl.

My feet are heavy, the stilettos of my heels getting scuffed with every drag against the pavement as I walk up to the Victorian-style building of my apartment.

I don't see him sitting on the front steps at first because my head hangs; I'm too tired to keep it upright any longer.

"Jade." Tieran reaches out for me, but I step out of his hold, unable to stomach the feeling of him touching me and knowing it'll be the last time. "Jade?" The confusion in his voice sends a dagger clean through me.

"You shouldn't be here." I try to move past him, still refusing to look into his eyes, but he stops me by grabbing my hand.

"Baby, what's going on? Archie texted me and said you didn't seem yourself. Did something happen?"

"Go home, Tieran."

"I am home, Hellfire. You're my home." Tears flood my eyes, and my knees threaten to buckle. He's my home too, and I'm holding a match in one hand and kerosene in the other. "You're scaring me, Jade. Please talk to me. Whatever it is, we can figure it out." The pleading in his voice nearly makes me turn around, throw my hands around his neck, and beg for forgiveness, but I'm doing this for him, for his dreams. There's nothing I wouldn't do to give him the life he's worked so hard for, and that includes flaying myself open to protect him.

I don't know how I'm going to do this, how I'm going to make this believable enough for him to let me go without a fight. My mind races a million miles a minute, trying to come up with an excuse.

What comes out of my mouth is, "I have to move back to Los Angeles."

"What?"

"My investors are getting too restless with me being gone and are threatening to pull out of Jaded. I have to go back as a sign of good faith."

"Alright, you can go now, and I'll join you when the season ends. We can make it w—"

"No."

"Jade." It's a plea—a prayer.

"This was a wakeup call, Tieran. I've been too distracted, letting every area of my life slip. Investors are losing money, and I'm losing their trust. When I go back, it needs to be alone."

"Look at me." He tugs on my hand, begging me to turn and face him. I steel my spine and will away the moisture starting to pool in my eyes, letting the light drain, back to the old me. When I turn around, his brows furrow at what he finds on my face. "Haven't you been happy here? With me?"

"That's irrelevant."

"I don't think it is."

"I don't get to be happy, Tieran! I get to work and build an empire, and I don't have time for this anymore. I have to get back to the real world now, my real life, where million dollar corporations are relying on me to make them successful. It was fun while it lasted, but that's all it was: fun."

"That's fucking bollocks, and you know it."

"Don't make this harder than it has to be."

"You love me. You said it—I *felt* it, Jade." He steps forward, one hand cupping my neck and placing the other over my heart. "I know you felt it too."

I try to pull out of his hold, but he stands firm, not letting me go. "I got caught up in a moment. I let my guard down when I came here, and now, I'm facing the consequences." My voice has never sounded so lifeless. "I have to go back before I lose everything. I won't risk all I've worked the last decade for." I take a deep breath before delivering my final blow. "It's not worth it."

He jerks back, finally letting go of me, and I immediately feel frozen all over. "*I'm* not worth it, you mean." A statement, not a question, and I want to die at the devastated look in his eyes that makes them dim to a darker blue. I don't rush to disagree, knowing I'm bringing his biggest insecurity to the forefront after he's worked so hard to battle those demons away. I lock down every emotion, every urge to stuff my words back into my mouth, to tell him I love him and that will never change. But I don't say any of that. I just look off into the distance with lifeless eyes and let him come to his own horrific conclusion—let his insecurities poison his mind and do the work for me, like the coward I am.

He pushes his tongue into his cheek, smiling ironically, and tilts his head up to the starless sky, looking for the one thing he always thought was a constant and coming up empty. I can see his eyes lining with silver, and I almost cave then, almost get on my knees and beg for forgiveness and tell him everything. But I don't.

"Maybe they were right."

I can feel the hammer about to drop, but I ask anyway. "Who?"

He rubs at the side of his neck, right over the scripted *ephemeral*, and I know he's thinking I proved his point from all those weeks ago. *Nothing ever lasts.*

"Everyone. I never believed it for a second, but now? This is the first time I've ever felt that you were cold—cruel." Something within me withers and dies, and he searches my face, looking for any sign of life or fight from the Jade he knows me to be. I remain resolute, and he scoffs. "Have a nice life, Ms. McKallen." He shakes his head, turns around, and walks away, taking my heart along with him.

When he's out of sight, I finally crumble, and the

eruption of sobs I worked the last few minutes to hold back comes bursting out of me in a torrent of pain.

It's for the best. He'll make the team, go to the Olympics in a couple years, and become everything he ever wanted to be. I'll be a blip in his life on his way to greatness, and eventually, he'll forget all about our time together.

And me—well, I'll be alone, loving him from afar, because for me, what we had *is* everlasting.

We just don't get to have it.

33

TIERAN

IN MY LIFE, I've read countless slander articles about myself, been cheated on and humiliated in front of the world, had broken bones that took months to heal, but none of that hurt as badly as Jade shattering my heart into a million pieces.

For two days, all I've been doing is picking up my phone to plead with her to tell me what changed, but my feeble pride stopped me. Instead, I threw the device to the other side of the room—not before taking one long look at the photo of her I had saved as my background, though. I still couldn't bring myself to change the image of her in that red dress the night of the gala, no matter how much it tortured me. She had been on the opposite end of the ballroom, the chandelier crystals reflecting light against the planes of her cheekbones like starlight dancing across her face.

How could she stop loving me so easily when there was no force on Earth capable of getting me to stop? Two nights now, sleep has evaded me, because every time I close my eyes, I'm haunted by the look of nothingness in hers. The scent of her skin, sweet vanilla and bourbon, still clings to my pillows.

It's a sick sort of torture—wanting to bury my head and

breathe her in despite it making me feel like I'm being split in two.

The only thing I want to do today is wallow in self-pity and cuddle with Pebble, but duty has me walking through the staff doors at Knightsbridge, sunglasses still perched on my nose to hide my red-rimmed eyes. Playing a match right now isn't ideal, and I would be lying if I said I'm not worried about being capable of it right now.

Will Jade even be here, or is she already in a first-class seat, flying five thousand miles away from me with my heart in her hands? What will happen to the team when she leaves?

It's not your problem.

The mental reminder is a slap in the face that wakes me up enough to hear the frantic whispers coming from around the corner. I slow my movements, straining my ear to listen in.

"You said you weren't going to do that," the voice hisses.

No one replies until the same voice speaks again, and I deduce that whoever is speaking is on the phone.

"You're *lying.* It's all over the news."

I chance a look around the corner and spot a panicked Harry pacing back and forth, face red, his free hand pulling at his hair.

"What you made me do was wrong." His face is verging on purple now. "They're good people. They don't deserve this."

Harry does figure eights throughout the open hallway. "I'll have to live with my part in this, but you took it too far, Mr. Chapman."

I rear back. I don't think I've ever so much as seen Lawrence say a single word to Harry. Why would they be on the phone right now?

Whatever is said on the other end of the line exacerbates Harry's anxiety before he pulls his mobile away from his ear and pockets the phone, conversation clearly over.

"Harry?" I say, stepping out from my hiding spot so I can check on my friend.

He leaps out of his skin and pales to a ghastly shade of white when he sees me. "Mr. Sto-one" he stutters, clearly on edge.

"You alright, mate?" Harry's always been a skittish lad, but right now, his eyes are wild, resembling a cornered animal looking for a way to escape. "You seem upset."

"I—" He looks around me before deflating and finally meeting my eyes. "I'm sorry, Mr. Stone."

"Tieran. We're friends, Harry. You should call me by my first name."

He looks like he wants to discard the invitation to reject formalities. "I haven't been a friend to you." When I give him a puzzled look, he continues, "I'm so sorry, I shouldn't have done it. I shouldn't have believed the promises he made."

"What are you talking about, Harry?" Something toxic sinks low in my gut and starts to fester.

"I've been watching you…and Ms. McKallen." My heart constricts so painfully at the sound of her surname, I almost don't register his meaning.

"What do you mean, you've been watching us?" I have to be sure, have to know exactly what he's talking about and if it could possibly tie back to Jade's untimely breakup two nights ago.

"Mr. Chapman has had me watching Ms. McKallen in the hopes he could find something on her to get her sacked. I—" He pauses.

"Keep going." My voice fills with a strange sense of calm as I urge him to continue.

"I thought I sensed something between the two of you, at that first match when she called you into her office, and I told Chapman." My heart is in my throat. "He promised me a promotion if I watched her and found something he could use against her. Every time I've seen you together, he's known about it." My fist clenches around my bag, and the movement doesn't go unnoticed as Harry blanches further. "I'm so sorry. I know it was wrong. He promised me no one was going to get hurt, but—" He breaks off his sentence, looking everywhere but at me.

"But what, Harry?" My thoughts scatter, voice going frantic, because if he's implying what I think, then someone did get hurt. If it wasn't me, then it must be Jade, and the thought of her in pain makes me ready to fight. "*But what?*" I shout, causing him to jump in place.

At that moment, Myles rushes into the hall, eyes worried and hair standing on end, as if he'd been running his hands through it. "T—"

"What?"

He holds up his phone, and a news article flashes across the screen, but he's too far for me to read it. "There's a story running about you…and Jade. It's—they're saying some pretty heinous things."

I rush over to him, the team's equipment manager forgotten, and snatch the phone out of his hand.

Wanks for Wins: Legends owner Jade McKallen giving out sexual favours to players?

My stomach roils in disgust at the vile words filling the screen, and I scroll to the next one.

Who's Really the Boss? Multi-Millionaire influencer turned Legends Owner won't bow down in a boardroom but will in her office.

I read countless articles, all about Jade, my name barely even mentioned despite being half as responsible. I'm used to the heat from trash rags, but the fact that none of these are condemning me, instead easily pitting Jade as this perverse monster, makes me see red. They're defiling everything we are, taking this beautiful thing we had and staining it in an ugly wash of colour when she was the very thing that kept me tethered to this world.

I torture myself by looking at one last article.

Ruck or Fuck! It looks like the owner of The Legends got too comfortable in her office.

That one goes on to say there are blurry camera snapshots of me and Jade in a compromising position in her office. How the fuck do they even know that? How could they *possibly* know that?

It dawns on me that Harry might know. I whirl around, and he's still standing ten paces away, looking like he wants to curl up and die. "How does the press know about this?" I hold the phone out so he can see the article.

"Chapman hid cameras in her office," he says, ashamed.

"Fuck," Myles hisses.

Violence coats my body. "I'm going to fucking kill him." I start to storm off to fulfill my promise when Myles' arm shoots out, stopping me.

"Let me go," I seethe. All I can think of is getting my hands around that measly little fucker's neck and snapping it.

"You can hate me all you want, but I'm not letting you do anything to harm yourself. Jade wouldn't want you to hurt your career more than it's already been affected."

My stomach lurches at her name, and I reach for my phone, dialing the one person whose voice I need to hear more than anything, but it goes straight to her voicemail. Even the sound of her monotone voice ringing out over the speaker soothes a small part of me.

I try calling her another five times, getting the same result, so I send a text, not knowing if she'll receive or ignore it.

"Fuck!" Frustration and devastation war with each other for top spot.

Our sudden break up made a lot more sense now, and if I know my girl, I bet Chapman used this to blackmail us. Jade being Jade, felt she needed to bear the burden by herself. My beautiful, brilliant, bold woman still doesn't get it. She isn't doing this alone anymore, and she never will, not as long as I draw air.

Coach Ballard comes striding down the corridor. "Do you two plan on joining us? We have a match in an hour, and everyone's waiting on you guys to have our pregame."

There's nothing I want to do less. I *should* be running to Jade's front door, not up and down on a pitch, but she won't even answer my calls. Fuck, she may have already skipped town back to L.A.

"Stone." Ballard grabs my attention. "The press wants to do pregame interviews with you for, uh," he scratches the back of his neck, "obvious reasons. I can tell them to suck my ball sack if you prefer."

I'm about to agree with him when a thought occurs to me: Jade might not answer my calls because she thinks she's saving me, but if I know her, I bet she'll still tune into the game.

"Actually, Coach, I would like to talk to them, but I need to talk to the team first. I need their help with something."

I look to Harry, who's been cowering in the corner this whole time. "Do you want to make it right?" Ballard looks between us with confusion, and Harry nods vigorously. "Good. There's something I need you to do, but you'll have to be quick and go unnoticed."

"Going unnoticed is my forte, sir."

That will work in my favor for what I'm about to ask him to do.

RUCK OR FUCK!

It looks like the owner of The Legends got too comfortable in her office.

HOLY HR!!! The tea couldn't be hotter even if it was served up by one of the royal staffers on a twenty-four carat tray.

Arguably, one of the world's most successful women, Jade McKallen, influencer turned business mogul turned owner of London's own Premier Rugby Club, the Legends, has been caught having an inappropriate relationship with one of her players!

Who's the player you ask? None other than Tieran Stone!

Just when we thought he was done being splashed over the front page, he surprises us with the scandal of the year. AGAIN.

34

JADE

I AM A CERTIFIED MASOCHIST.

It's the only explanation for why I pull the remote out of the sofa cushions after a lousy attempt at hiding it so I wouldn't turn on the sports channel just to get a glimpse of Tieran.

Not talking to him for two days has been excruciating. I shut my phone off after I ended things, not able to bear looking at my background and the picture he took it upon himself to save as my wallpaper. It made my chest ache to see him smiling wide as he pressed his face into my neck.

It was a particularly cold morning that day, and I kept harping on how I needed to get out of bed to get ready, but Tieran banded his arms around my waist, holding me in place. A second later, his leg had joined his arms in locking me down, and he started peppering my face and neck with soft bites and gentle kisses.

An errant tear slips down my cheek. I would give up everything to my name for one more minute of lying in bed, wrapped in his arms.

I wipe it away, set the remote firmly on top of the coffee table, and go back to the files strewn in front of me. Don't look; it will only make things worse. Just do what you always do and throw yourself into work. Ignore that there's a gaping hole in your chest, and maybe, eventually, things will be okay.

Diving back into my job full force was jarring, and catching up on the things I let slip over the past couple months is already overwhelming, proven by the mountains of paperwork and no less than thirteen tabs open on the laptop in front of me.

I'm reviewing the latest line sheets for an upcoming Jaded collection, comparing the fabric composition of a belted wool trenchcoat to a version we had last year, making sure the improvements I requested were implemented, but my mind strays to the remote acting as a paperweight.

I reach out but snatch my hand back. *No, it won't help anything.*

I move on to study last week's performance for e-commerce as well as the wholesale division, shifting back and forth between documents in front of me and ledgers on my laptop, trying to make sense of the small shift in revenue. I blindly reach for another page, but my hand grabs the remote instead.

Just a look—I just need to see him for a minute, and then I'll let him go.

I start scrolling through the channels, hugging the large bowl of ice cream I've been having for lunch and passing over countless programs in search of the game. I nearly miss it, but my heart would recognize that flash of blue anywhere.

I backtrack, and there he is, standing proudly in front of the team's gryphon logo printed on a banner—a replay of a pregame interview that must have happened no more than a half hour ago.

Cameras are shoved in Tieran's face, flashes illuminating his tanned skin as reporters talk at the same time, peppering him with so many questions, it's impossible to decipher one from the next.

He is so beautiful, it's hard to breathe looking at him

now, and just like that, every thought of business and responsibility is gone.

Tieran smiles, the charming fly-half of The Legends taking over, no dimples in sight, telling me the real version I broke two nights ago lurks just below the surface. But for now, his mask is securely in place. "Settle down, you lot. I can't answer any questions if I can't hear them."

He indicates to a woman in the back raising her hand. "You."

"Sharon Purcell with SkySports, Mr. Stone."

"Hello, Sharon. What's on your mind?" To anyone who doesn't really know him, he seems confident and collected, but I can see the bags under his eyes from sleepless nights, the tightening of his shoulders indicating he's not feeling as at ease as he seems.

"You've caused quite a stir, Mr. Stone." Tieran nods his head as they speak. "The National Team has been scouting if rumors are to be believed. Some say they've been watching you and are none too pleased about the tabloids as of late. Are you worried your dalliance with Ms. McKallen will hinder your chances at clinching a spot on the roster?"

Tieran leans forward into the microphone. "No."

Sharon looks a little taken aback, as does the rest of the room, as murmurs break out amongst the crowd. I'm a little confused too, honestly, because what the fuck does he mean?

"Would you care to elaborate?"

"It's as simple as this—if they want me for my ability on the pitch, then it shouldn't matter who I love." My heart is a hummingbird in my chest.

The room explodes into a cacophony of noise and camera flashes as every reporter falls over themselves to ask the next question.

Finally, one breaks out over the din, louder than all the rest. "You must admit, in today's climate, the situation around this…relationship is a bit uncouth."

As if he expected this question, Tieran fires back, unperturbed, "She and I met before we even knew who the other was. We were just two people in a pub. We didn't exchange names or jobs, content to be ourselves without the weight of expectations pushing in around us. I can't begin to describe to you how freeing that felt," he murmurs. "Needless to say, we were both blindsided when she walked into the conference room to introduce herself as the new owner of the team." He stares down every one of the cameras in his face. "But let me be perfectly fucking clear: *I* pursued *her*, and every vile article disparaging her character and praising me as some sort of god is wrong. She has done more for this team than any previous management, and despite the connection we had, she tried to stay away from me. She was willing to deny herself happiness to do what she believed the world expected, that's all she's ever done her entire bloody life. I was in a bad place when she found me. She didn't care who I was or what I had to offer, but she met me where I was and coaxed me back from the dark. Why in the world would I care if the entire universe thought that was wrong?"

A tear escapes, and then another joins, dripping off my chin onto the paperwork in front of me.

"So it's love then? Not just a fling?" I don't know who asked it—I don't care much, because all I can focus on are Tieran's eyes, his mouth, the determined set of his jaw, the way he defends me after what I did to him—said to him.

He looks down the eye of the camera, as if the next part he's saying to me and only me, like he *knows* I'm watching. "This game has given me so much—friends who are like brothers, community, opportunities—but *she* has given me more. Love, security, strength—her heart. She will *always* be more important, and I will not lie to my country, or to the people who have loved this game and supported me for years by giving her less than she deserves: the truth. Jade McKallen is the force that drives my body to win; she's the most intensely caring person I've ever met and the steady voice I've needed when I was feeling unworthy of this position—of her. There is nothing in this world, no title or trophy, that could get me to give her up. *Nothing.*" His vehemence sends chills skittering all over my body.

Blood rushes to my ears, drowning out any follow up questions he's being asked, and tears form anew at his confession. It isn't fair, none of this is fair, and I'm furious at the world for giving me this perfect person, only to rip him away.

"I've got it from a good source saying McKallen is selling her shares to Lawrence Chapman."

Tieran's whole body locks up as he tries to school his surprise into neutrality. "I don't know anything about that."

"Your girlfriend hasn't told you?" another shouts, but he ignores it, jaw clenching.

"Stone! Do you know how your relationship got leaked?"

"I have my theories, and I'd like for that person to know one thing." Tieran stares down the camera, a lock of dark hair falling into his face as his upper lip curls into a snarl. "You made a mistake when you fucked with my girl, and I'm coming for you with everything I've got."

I'm almost turned on as much as I'm terrified, because if Tieran decides to play hero, he could officially screw up his chances to get called up to the National Team, and I can't let that happen.

Without knocking, Aanya bursts through my front door, looking harried and on edge. "Holy shit, you look awful."

"I'll be sure to come to you anytime I need a confidence boost," I deadpan.

"Shit, sorry, babe, it's just... I've never seen you in sweats, or with your hair in a messy bun and...have you been crying? Your face is all splotchy..." She looks down at my coffee table of work, tears, and half-melted ice cream. "Are you seriously working right now?"

"Is there something you need, Aanya, or can I go back

to wallowing?" I shovel a spoonful of raspberry ripple in my mouth.

"You have to see this." She comes around the couch, digging the remote out from under my thigh and plopping down beside me. Changing the channel takes two seconds before she finds the one she wants and is turning up the volume.

My eyes scan over the screen in confusion before it registers what the broadcasters are saying.

"It's completely unprecedented. Never in the history of the Union has a team refused to play."

Refused to play? What the hell are they talking about?

"It's absolute insanity, but the whole Legends team is standing in solidarity with Stone. They won't play unless McKallen gets reinstated as owner."

I jump up off the couch. "*What*?" I whip my head to look at my best friend. "This must be a prank."

"Afraid not." Aanya nods toward the television, where the team stands along the stadium seats, talking to the reporters, each player telling them how the club has improved since I took it on.

This is—this is too much. They should be stretching, warming up, getting their heads on straight to play this match, but instead, they're singing the praises of a woman who already resigned.

Confusion morphs into sadness that's now morphing into anger.

I start moving about my flat, throwing my ice cream bowl into the sink hard enough that it probably cracks before I storm into my room.

Aanya follows me inside, looking warily at me as I tear my closet apart looking for the one pair of casual shoes I own. "What are you going to do?"

"I'm going down there," I say, finally finding my sneakers and slipping them on. "There's only about thirty minutes left before they risk the game being forfeited in favor of the opposing team, and I'll be damned if they throw away everything they've worked for."

They can't afford to forfeit this game, and all their little stunt would accomplish is to significantly hurt their ranking. They've been playing well the past few weeks, but it hasn't pulled them out of the hole completely, and they could run the risk of relegation. But if they keep playing the way they have been, there's still time for them to make it to the Premiership.

I don't bother making the rest of myself look presentable, and I try not to think about the photographs that will be splashed all over the media of me looking my worst as I grab my keys from the dish at my front door.

I turn to find Aanya standing in the middle of my living area, looking conflicted on what to do. "Well? Are you coming?"

She snaps out of her stasis and smiles. "Fuck yeah. I wouldn't miss the chance to watch you put a team of grown men in their place."

* ⋄ * ⋄ ☆ ⋄ * ⋄ *

We make it to the stadium with barely five minutes to spare, and I'm running down the stairs leading to the field, people moving out of my way and whispering about me at the same time.

She's here!

Stone's risking his chance at the Olympics for her?

Did you see the photos too?

I block out all the noise, even as something inside me starts to wither.

The men are still hanging around the line of reporters when I make it to the bottom. "What the hell do you all think you're doing?"

Every pair of eyes snap over to me, a pair of cobalt cutting through me like a laser, but I ignore him. I have to in order to make it through this.

Shouts go up from the team and then the stands around them, making my heart race and dread pool in my gut.

"Jade." I hear Tieran's voice, but I ignore it.

"You have not worked as hard as you have to give it all up now. You have too much riding on every single game at this point. Get your asses on the pitch and start warming up."

"We've only gotten this far because of you," Cavan says, and I meet his deep eyes filled with quiet sincerity.

"That's not true. I just gave you the tools you needed. You all did the rest."

"Jade." Another attempt to grab my attention goes ignored.

"You believed in us. From day one, you did more for us than anyone else ever did," Finn chimes in.

"Then repay me by getting on the pitch and winning this match." They all look towards Tieran, who won't take his eyes off me. "Please," I urge, voice cracking slightly.

"Alright, you heard the boss," Tieran says. "Let's go win a match!" A rally cry goes up from all the men as they start bouncing on the balls of their feet, heading toward the field.

All but one.

Tieran comes toward me, and I cast my eyes down. "Baby, please." His voice is soft as feathers. I shake my head, unable to look at him, feeling so unworthy of his adoration and knowing that none of this changes anything. I still have to walk away. I still have to give this all up for him to have his best shot. "Look at me, Jade. You look so beautiful, and I'll do anything if you'd just look at me. Let me see those eyes."

I take a page from his playbook and put on a mask, cosplaying a version of me that isn't a heartbroken mess, because it's what he needs to have the motivation to get out there and play his heart out.

I take a deep breath and lift my eyes to his, letting mine rage with a fire I know he craves. "You'll do anything?" I ask, and I see a shiver creep up his back before he breathes a sigh of relief and nods. "Then get on the pitch and *win.*"

He smiles devilishly and winks. "Yes, boss."

The second he turns to jog out and join his teammates, I attempt to flee, but every Legends fan cages me in, keeping me from escaping.

"Come on, let's sit down. They're not going to let you go anywhere until the match is over." We take our usual seats, and I shrink into mine, feeling like everyone in this entire stadium is staring at me.

I hazard a glance up and, yup, they actually are staring at me. They're likely thinking about the violating article that posted blurry, barely-censored images of me on my knees and—oh God, I'm going to be sick.

"Fuck off, you shrimp dicked buffoons." Lottie comes striding through the seats before taking her own and placing a hand on my leg. "You look a mess. You alright?"

"You two should start a podcast on how to be uplifting members of society," I mumble.

You look so beautiful, and I'll do anything if you'd just look at me. Let me see those eyes.

Tieran's agonized voice floats to the forefront of my mind, soothing like a balm.

"It's actually kind of nice seeing you like this," she comments, and all I can do is stare at her, mouth gaping. "No! Sorry, that came out wrong. You're just always so put together. I was starting to think you were superhuman."

I huff, feeling far from untouchable at the moment.

Halfway through the game, several phones ping with alerts, and a whisper rumbles through the crowd.

A rock sinks to the bottom of my gut as I feel eyes shift my way again. Maybe I'm imagining it, but it's almost as if I can taste their anger, hear their vitriolic thoughts. *You did this. You put him in this position. You're the reason he's throwing away a shot at his dream.*

"Fuck," Aanya says as she tries to hold the phone away from my view. Even though my stomach heaves with impending doom, I rip it out of her hands to see a headline splashed across the top in bold lettering that threatens to make the excessive amount of ice cream I had earlier resurface.

SOURCES CLOSE TO THE NATIONAL TEAM'S BOARD OF DIRECTORS CONFIRM RECENT EVENTS ARE MAKING THEM RECONSIDER THEIR LINEUP.

My heart is running around on the pitch, totally oblivious to the fact that his career is imploding in real time, and I can't fix it. The truth has been pulled out of the glass bottle, and there's no shoving it back in.

Just then, my own phone chirps, but not with a news alert like everyone else.

> MAXINE
>
> Who knew sleeping with a finance guy would
> cause such a scandal.

I bristle at her calling out my lie from the day she ambushed me in my flat and Tieran showed up.

> MAXINE
>
> I've already had the board reach out to me
> saying you've been unresponsive in
> addressing their concerns. This doesn't look
> good for optics, and you need to do damage
> control, or you'll end up with nothing.
>
> It's time to end the fantasy and come home,
> Jade. Having it all is a lie women tell to make
> themselves feel better. Your level of success
> will always come with sacrifices.

I look out to the field and spot him immediately, just as he looks over at me and smiles, those damn dimples finally popping again. My heart falters, my nose tingles, my eyes *burn*.

My life *had* always come with sacrifices, and I was content with that. But I never anticipated having to sacrifice my heart, never thought I would care for anyone enough that letting them go would feel like severing a limb. The phantom pains are already lighting up my body from the loss.

I send a quick email to the board, ignore my mom's texts, and pocket my phone. Shrinking down in my seat, I attempt to ride out the rest of the match without drawing attention to myself, but not a second goes by when I can't hear the whispers or feel their eyes boring into the back of my head.

The buzzer for half-time finally rings, and the players start to trickle off the pitch. Now is when I need to attempt to escape, while fans are distracted grabbing more beer and going to the bathroom.

I stand, telling the girls I need to make a few phone calls before the second half starts, and they thankfully don't question me.

I'm only halfway up the stairs when I hear him. "Jade!" The deep resonance of his voice stops me in my tracks, and I glance over my shoulder to see him vaulting over the barricade and taking the steps two at a time to reach me.

He's sweaty and out of breath from the exertion of the last forty minutes of non-stop play, but his eyes are alight with joy. That is, until he sees the look on my own face.

"Are you okay? I didn't get to ask earlier, and—fuck, love. Are you alright?"

Looking at him is too hard, like trying to stare at the eclipse because it's this great, wondrous phenomenon even though doing so threatens to blind you.

"I have to go," I whisper nearly inaudibly. "I only came to make sure you didn't throw away your future."

His face falls slightly, but he doesn't try to mask it anymore, the pain he used to harbor inside so no one would know it was there. It's now sitting proudly on his sleeve. "We can figure this out," he says, but I'm already shaking my head.

"The news is….it's not a good outcome, Tieran. I can't be the reason you give up your dream. I won't wake up one morning to see resentment filling your eyes. It would kill me."

"More than this is already killing you?" he asks boldly, challenging me.

"Yes."

He stays quiet, eyes jumping back and forth over my face like I'm some quantum physics equation he can't figure out yet. I cast my eyes down, the eclipse causing my eyes to blur.

"Do you remember what I told you?" I can't look at him while he speaks—can't bear to see the love in his eyes as I sacrifice my heart for him. He forces my chin up as tears stream down my cheeks, and he wipes them away before settling both palms on my face, holding me in place. "I told you I was going to take care of you, just like you've been taking care of me. Trust me, baby, I'm going to fix this." He crushes his lips to mine, and a cracked sob flows from my mouth to his as the tears fall in front of the whole world. "I love you, Jade."

He runs off without knowing the extent of what the headlines are saying, without knowing the true severity of it all.

He leaves without knowing there is no fixing this.

There is only forgetting.

35

TIERAN

THE TEAM'S energy is exhilarating as we walk through the tunnels, riding the high of our victory. Yet, all I can think about is getting to Jade, kissing her until she forgets about the past forty-eight hours, and then never letting her go.

It would seem the universe has other plans, though, because as I walk into the locker room, I end up bumping into Amari, who's come to a standstill behind the crowd of other players.

"What's going—" Suddenly, Cavan is standing in front of me, blocking my view.

"You need to keep a level head right now." In the worst of times, Cav is always the steady voice of reason. He's slow to anger, to emotion in general, but right now, he looks concerned and pissed at the same time.

That's when I hear his voice, and everything in my body goes tight with barely restrained anger. Lawrence Chapman is at ease in the middle of the room, his ruddy face set in a self-satisfied smirk, and I'm one second away from killing the pompous fuck standing in front of *Jade's* team, acting like he owns it.

My knuckles go white from clenching my fists at my sides, and I take one step forward, my foot falling like an anvil of doom, before Myles grabs my arm to hold me back.

"Ah, there's the man everyone's been talking about." My jaw clenches hard enough that I could crack a molar. Seventeen different, inventive ways to hurt him without anyone finding out run through my mind. "Gather 'round, lads. We've got some housekeeping to go over."

I move over to my locker, careful not to get too close to Chapman in case my thinly veiled restraint snaps and I decide to lay him out like he deserves.

Grabbing my phone out of my bag, I shoot off a quick text to Harry.

TIERAN

Is everything sorted?

Three dots pop up immediately before his reply comes through.

HARRY

On our way.

TIERAN

Hurry.

"Lawyers are going over the paperwork, but I think it's safe to say that as of tomorrow morning, there will be changes within upper management. Ms. McKallen is gone, and everything will go back to rights." The room is quiet enough to hear a pin drop, but several eyes shift throughout the room.

Ekon is the first to break the silence. "What do you mean, Ms. McKallen is gone? Is it official?"

"Due to her gross misconduct," I snarl at his words, and the bastard smirks, "she's decided the best course of action would be to move on to…new opportunities."

"Like hell she decided that," I growl, rage coursing through every fissure of my body.

"She felt it was better for the club as a whole to not

tarnish our image further by continuing to flaunt around like a sl—"

"Finish that sentence, and it'll be the last thing you ever say." The words are on the tip of my tongue, but it's Cavan who says them before I can.

I look to my friend, who's vibrating with barely-leashed fury. The same man who's slow to anger, who is always composed and unflappable, is seething with rage for my girl. I wish she could see it. As I look around at my brothers, I see Cavan's outrage mirrored in their faces, and I wish she could see the impact she's had on this team in such a short amount of time. The woman who never had any true friends to look after her has a whole team of them here.

"Nevertheless, the little stunt you all pulled today won't happen again. Let this meeting serve as a warning to fall in line, or you'll find yourself working at your local Nando's come next season."

"Why don't you tell them the truth, Chapman?" I cross my arms and lean back against the shelves holding our things, trying to stall long enough for Harry to get here.

"And what would that be, Stone? That you've been boinking the boss?" He sneers derisively. "Is that why your game got good suddenly? Because you had someone to show off for? Or was her cunt just so magical, it gave you super powers?"

Myles adjusts his stance to position himself in front of me, reading my body language and deducing that the threads of my patience are fraying at a rapid rate.

Hold out, Tieran. It'll be worth it when we wipe the arrogance off his mug.

I loosen my limbs, easing back onto the wall again to adopt a careless stance. "I was referring to the fact that you've been harassing Jade for months because you feel entitled to her job. A job you don't deserve and would fail spectacularly at." His face darkens. "See, the thing is, Lawrence, Jade has earned everything she has, unlike you. She's smart, savvy, and works harder than anyone I've ever met. But you're a raging arsehole, so you sit around and wait for people to hand you things because you're a lazy sack of cow shite."

"You would say those things, considering how hard she *worked* you."

"And when you couldn't find a fault with her work ethic and everything she was doing to make this club better, you decided to invade her privacy." He splutters, looking around at the guys who are all standing straighter at my revelation. "You violated her by having her watched, followed—*filmed*, and then you blackmailed her into handing her shares over to you."

"And it worked," he snaps. "Daft girl didn't even care how it would affect her. All she was worried about was what this scandal would do to *you*."

I rear back as if he slapped me. "What did you say?"

"I used her love—" he spits the word out as if it's poison — "for you against her. When I showed her the evidence stacked against her, the only time she tried to change my mind was on your behalf."

My heart thumps painfully inside my chest. It was so perfectly Jade, to be thinking of someone else as she was backed into a corner with no way out. God, I love her.

"Either way, she agreed to my proposal within hours. Seems she was hellbent on protecting you."

"So then why the fuck did you renege on your deal?" I shout. "Why, when she gave you everything you wanted, would you still need to shove a knife in her gut?" I'm off the wall now, chest heaving as my breath comes in harsh gasps.

Jade. My Jade. Taking on the world alone because she didn't want to burden anyone else. When we make it through the other end of this, I'm going to love her so hard, she doesn't even remember the word *alone*.

But not before spanking her arse raw for not coming to me for help. It would be a sweet sort of punishment, one we would both enjoy.

"I d—" Chapman starts but is interrupted when the door bursts open, and a stream of cops comes through.

"Lawrence Chapman?" one asks him.

"What is the meaning of this? We're in the middle of a private meeting."

"We're detaining you for violating the Protection from Harassment Act. Please cooperate and place your hands behind your back." The officers move in on him, but he steps out of their reach.

"You must be joking. You have no proof!"

Harry steps forward then, with Reginald in tow holding the large ring of keys that give him access to every office in the building. "Actually, they do." He pulls a laptop out of his bag—Lawrence's laptop. "And if the laptop containing the images and video footage you used to extort Ms. McKallen isn't proof enough, I'll be providing them with the transcripts of our messaging."

"You spineless son of a bitch." Chapman manages to rip out of the authorities' holds, lunging for Harry—for the computer in his hands.

The soft-spoken equipment manager flinches, locking up and waiting for the blow to land, but then I'm there, stepping in front of Harry and throwing my entire body into a rear hook across his face.

Bone crunches against my knuckles, and the satisfaction I feel cancels out any pain when Lawrence hits the floor, the thud reverberating around the room.

My chest heaves as I crouch within inches of where his cheek is pressed to the linoleum floor, blood leaking from his nose. I whisper only loud enough for him to hear, "You fucked with the wrong person when you went after Jade. Something you may not know about me, Lawrence: I *will* throw it all away for someone I love. There is no purpose in my life greater than taking care of her. So, you better pray to whatever god you believe in that the evidence we find on that laptop holds up in court, because if it doesn't," I pause leaning in further, "I'm going to make the pain you're in right now feel like a holiday in Ibiza."

I signal to the police, and they hurry over, stretching his arms behind his back, cuffing his wrists, and pulling him upright. He jerks against their hold, wincing from the pain of being jostled around as they yank him toward the open door and out of sight.

I watch as he goes, feeling one small weight float off my shoulders as another, much heavier boulder comes to rest atop them.

"What now, Cap?" The question comes from Connor, of all people, and I finally turn to face my team—my brothers, the men who have stuck by my side and whose loyalty never wavered. Pride shines through every set of eyes I meet, and a sudden realisation hits me like a high speed train: even when I was at my worst, they never saw me the way I saw myself. They were just waiting for me to catch up.

Looking at every last one of them, I say, "I'm going to go get our boss back."

The confidence I felt when I left the stadium quickly starts to wane the closer I get to Jade's flat. In its place is anticipation mixed with apprehension.

I'm almost positive she broke up with me only because of the stunt Chapman pulled, but a small demon in the back of my mind pokes at my insecurities until they're red and tender. She said I was a distraction, and maybe that's what she needed for a time, but she was ready to put it behind her now and go back to L.A., back to her life there and everything it came with.

It would annihilate me, but I would weather the heartbreak because it meant for a small time, I meant something to her, even if she meant everything to me.

But there was another part of me screaming she belongs here in London—with me.

I pull my car up to the curb outside Jade's home, barely coming to a full stop before I'm throwing myself out the door and ringing the bell to her flat.

Minutes stretch on with no answer, and I start to panic. Did she leave already? Night's fallen, and I count the hours that have passed since I saw her last, but…no, between the second half of the match, post-game interviews, and the whole ordeal with Chapman, it's only been a few hours. Four, tops, and she wouldn't have left without saying goodbye to her dad first.

Her dad.

A light flares bright in my mind as I race back to my car, slide inside, and throw it into drive. Within a half hour, I'm knocking on his door, feeling hopeful and a little out of breath.

My fist pounds against the door over and over until a very agitated Archie yanks it open. It's funny how I can see little bits of Jade in his irate glare. The *"are you insane?"* look on his face makes me miss her even more. It's equal parts disturbing and comforting to find her in this person she loves so much.

"Have you lost your bloody m—" I step further into the glow of the hallway light spilling out onto the front step. "Oh, Tieran, my boy!" Archie's wizened face brightens when he sees it's me. "Did you see my last Word with Friends?" He leans against the doorframe as his lips lift in a smile. "Give it up, lad. There's no way you can top quaalude."

A chuckle escapes my mouth despite the stress coursing through my body. "I'll best you one day, Arch."

As Archie ushers me in with a trembling hand to my shoulder, I strain my ears for any sign of Jade, but I can't hear anything outside of this week's presenters on Gogglebox playing on the tv. No rustling around in the kitchen, no doors upstairs being open or closed; it's as if her dad is the only one here. But…she wouldn't just leave, would she?

"What brings you by, son?" My stomach flips at the endearment, making me picture a future in which he calls me that because I'm family.

"I'm looking for Jade." I look around again, hoping the sound of my voice will make her magically appear and start laying into me with her sarcastic tongue.

His face turns grim, and my stomach sinks down to my feet.

"I would have thought she'd tell you…"

"Where is she, Archie?" My voice is pleading, edged with intense desperation.

"She left to go back to L.A. I told her not to go," he hastily adds on, but I'm unable to focus on what he's saying as my body threatens to crumble. She wouldn't give up on us. I couldn't fathom it—couldn't even entertain it, because the Jade I know has never given up on anything in her life. That is, until she relented to Chapman's whims in order to save me. "I told her she needed to stay and stick it out. I knew something was happening with you two long before the news came out. I've never seen my Jade so carefree—so *happy*." He just launched a javelin clean through my chest. "She's never had that before, a balance to her life. Work was the only thing she ever focused on. No matter how much I tried to encourage her to do other things, she always brushed it off, always had her mom in her ear to dissuade her. But you," he pats my face affectionately, "you got her to slow down, to do something for herself for the first time in years—you brought her balance."

"She brought me peace," I admit, wanting him to know any effect I had on her, she had on me tenfold.

"You love my daughter, Tieran." A statement, not a question.

I feel the need to answer anyway. "More than every star in the sky."

He weighs my words, his expression inscrutable before

he walks over to the small table under the window of his sitting room. He pulls out a pad and pen, scribbling something down before tearing it off and handing it to me, his hands steady for the first time since I've known him.

"Go bring her home then."

Hope swells within my chest when I glance down at the slip of parchment to find an address in black ink staring back at me.

Jade made a mistake thinking I would let her leave, that I would be the same as everyone else who had put themselves before her. She would always come first; there was no other alternative' when she engraved herself so deeply into my soul.

So, I hug Archie, pocket the piece of paper, call Lottie to ask her to take care of Pebble, and drive straight to Heathrow.

Jade might think distance will be enough to make her forget about me, but I won't go down without a fight.

36

JADE

MY SOUL FEELS like it's slowly dying sitting at the head of the boardroom table in Jaded's downtown L.A. office. Outside the window, the sun shines as a bird flies by, carried by a warm breeze beneath shimmering wings, and all I can think about is how I'm longing for the damp grey skies of England, for a warm bed in a cozy flat that actually feels like me, tucked into the arms of the person I love with our dog at our feet.

My stomach has been in knots since I left my dad's house, promising to check in as soon as possible.

Whoever said it was better to have loved and lost than never love at all was a raving lunatic, because I feel like someone reached into my chest cavity and ripped out my heart. I haven't been able to eat, sleep—*function*—since I left. Not that I've had the chance. The second my plane touched down, a car was waiting for me at the airport, ready to whisk me straight to the office. I didn't even get to go to my house to drop off my bags. Maxine made it clear I had *more important* things to do, and the basic luxury of an after-flight shower was not one of them.

Now, I'm listening to the head of marketing drone on about actionable engagement, launch events and key performance indicators, wondering when the job so many people dream of started to become a nightmare to me. I used to love this—I thrived on the rush at one point in my life, and now, I felt like it was eating me alive, sucking the life force out of my body to sustain itself.

Did I feel this strongly before I moved to England? Or was it because now that I've had a taste of a different reality, this one seemed like flavorless dust on my tongue? I've only been back for a few hours, and already, it was hard to stomach.

I don't know how to get back to loving this part of my life—if I even can. In hindsight, I don't think I realized how much it drained me until Tieran showed me what life could be, back before I spent my free time fantasizing about going on vacation during the off season with him, or the simple act of coming home and being greeted with Pebble at the door and Tieran uncorking a fresh bottle in the kitchen, his lips on my temple as we snuggled on the sofa to watch a movie, not a single phone in sight. I'm consumed by a tortured maelstrom of thoughts. Around and around, scenes play out; me in maroon, cheering Tieran on at every game. Sunday night roasts with his family, weekends out with Lottie and Aanya, Saturday morning classes at Flex Appeal, a coffee from Flick the Bean before we stroll the farmer's market for that week's groceries—hell, I'd even take another crochet class if I could just *go back*.

Back to London, back to walks with my dad, back to Tieran and his stupid dimples—back *home*.

Except it isn't my home anymore, Los Angeles is, and I have to accept that. I did what I had to do to make sure Tieran gets what he deserves, and I won't be the thing to hold him back now that he's playing well again.

"Jade?"

I snap out of my reverie, feeling cold and a little bitter. "Yes?"

"I asked if you thought the deliverables were attainable for you to complete within the next couple of days? It's imperative to get the photoshoot booked and underway so we can get all the imaging to design for them to complete the marketing assets for the Spring line."

I look around to a room full of people, all staring at me, the weight of their gazes pressing down on my shoulders in a way that has me shifting to sit up higher in my chair. Usually, I'm the one in control, and it's my scrutiny that makes people nervous, but with their eyes on me, it feels like they're passing judgement. I suddenly feel like I'm the size of a thimble.

"I'd like to use more models instead of myself as the central ad campaign," bursts out of my mouth unbidden, and the only sound in the room is the central a/c running through the vents.

It was the natural idea for me to be the face of my own company. I never thought it needed to be any different. It's my company, my name, my face attached to the label, and the best way to have control over how it's perceived by the public is to have my hands on every facet. But distance has a funny way of giving perspective, and I'm finding that, for the first time in my life, I wanted to…delegate.

A thought so absurd, everyone in this room is looking at me like I've sprouted a tail.

As I sit in this boardroom, in my starched, all-beige business suit, as I listen to everyone talk about the same shit we talk about every week, I come to a realization—this isn't what I want anymore.

I want color as vibrant as a sea off the coast of Mallorca. I want the sounds of my closest friend playing her guitar humming through the door when I come home. I want the smell of petrichor and grass floating through the air on a rugby pitch after it rains. I want the taste of homemade blueberry lemon pancakes on a Saturday morning. I want the feeling of warm, tattooed arms banded around my waist as a soft, dimpled smile brushes against my neck.

I want a life.

And I'm allowed to want those things—I *deserve* them.

Years of never considering what I truly want because asking for more was selfish when I already had so much, and all it took was a few months in London to understand I never had anything at all. Nothing that really mattered, at least. And like an idiot, I let it all go.

"You want to use models?" the head of our production line asks.

"Yes." I sit up abruptly, the people around me startling. "And I think… I'm sorry, I need to go," I say, standing and grabbing my bag, frantically shoving my laptop inside.

"Jade, are you okay?" Our head of marketing's voice is confused, edged with a tinge of panic.

"Yeah, it's just…" I look out the window, close my eyes, and take a deep breath. "It's really beautiful out. I think I'm going to go for a walk."

"But…we're in the middle of a meeting."

"I think you guys can handle it without me." I don't stay to listen to what they have to say and walk out of the office, a weight lifting off my shoulders the second I step outside.

Like most days in L.A., it's beautiful out, and even though I'm longing for the rain, I can still be grateful for the sunshine.

I don't stop walking until I end up standing outside my house two hours later.

It feels different now as I stare at the sleek lines of the modern home in front of me. It's emotionless and far too big. I'm not sure how I ever lived here, because this place is not me at all—I don't think it ever was. I just wasn't ready to admit it to myself yet.

Maybe I could sell this house and move into something cozier. I don't need all this space; all it would do is serve to remind me I'm the only one filling it.

Shoving my morose thoughts aside, I trudge up the front steps, through the front door and into the vast foyer.

The walls are grey, the Italian concrete tiles on the floor cool underneath my feet as I kick off my shoes by the door. Everything about this place is stale—suffocating.

I move further into the house, about to take the stairs up to the second floor so I can finally take a shower, when I hear a voice. I tip toe closer, something in my gut telling me to be quiet.

"I know, it was a brilliant move." Maxine. Leave it to her to show up uninvited and further ruin my day. I'm about to tip toe upstairs when, "No, of course Jade doesn't know." I stop dead in my tracks, craning my neck so I can hear her better without alerting her to my presence.

What don't I know?

I stand behind a tall oak cabinet, blocking my body from view as she sits in the living room.

"The buffoon thought he could blackmail me." She pauses, listening to whoever she's talking to, and my heart starts to race. "All he did was arm me with everything I needed to get her back to L.A."

My heart stops and starts and stops again.

"No, he didn't even question who I was before sending me an email with snapshots from the video. When I hopped on a call with him, he said he would leak the video if I didn't get my client out of his way."

My stomach threatens to heave as I continue listening to a conversation that reeks of impending heartbreak. My mom has been in communication with Chapman, and she never said a word to me about it. This whole time, she knew he had information on me that could ruin my and Tieran's reputations, and she didn't warn me.

"I told him he could take his video and shove it up his ass," Maxine laughs haughtily. I take a gamble and peek around the corner to where she's lounging on the couch, drinking a glass of wine. "Men are always so short sighted, but I suppose he got what he wanted, and so did I. Jade will never know I'm the one who sent those photos into the press, and she'll assume he did it. Now, I have her back here, ready to work again. No more fooling around." She lifts the glass to her lips, taking a long pull of her drink as she listens to the other end of the line. Leaning forward she sets the glass down on the lucite coffee table. "Of course, I already have her next month booked solid."

Lifeless walls close in around me as my vision goes spotty, forcing me to place a hand on the wall for balance. The room spins, blood rushes to my ears, and my body goes numb at the admission spoken so baldly—so *proudly*–as it reverberates around the room.

My legs act of their own accord, moving into her view, and then my mouth is speaking, but I barely hear the words —can hardly recognize my own voice. "What the fuck did you just say?"

Maxine's typically unflappable face pales when she sees me in front of her, but then she stands, straightens the front of her tweed dress, and smiles. "Darling! I didn't hear you come in." The recovery from fear stricken to completely unaffected should be studied in a psychology masterclass on narcissists.

"*What did you just say?*" I've never heard my voice sound so virulent as the question pushes through my teeth on a hiss.

Her right eye's subtle twitch is the only signal she's nervous. "Oh, nothing. I was just telling Joyce I have a few events coming up, including a meeting with a big five publisher. They want you to write a book!"

"I don't want to write a book."

"Just think about the possibilities. You could write a self-help tell-all inspiring young girls who want to be like you. It would make you look fantastic, and the sales would be through the roof. You could do an entire book tour!"

"Answer the question."

"Then there are a few brands that want you to speak at their creator events. It's great exposure and would go a long way toward fixing your image after…well, you know." She gasps and snaps her fingers. "That would be a great place to start talking about your book."

"Did you leak those photos to the press?" She must see something on my face, because she finally relents.

My mother rolls her eyes before looking at me in mine. "I did it for your own good."

The crack reverberates through the room before I even realize I lifted my hand and slapped her.

"I'm so—" She slaps me back, and tears immediately well in my eyes.

"You ungrateful little bitch."

Devastation is replaced by rage in an instant. "I'm the ungrateful one? You've been whoring me out to the world for the greater part of a decade for a payout!"

A sneer pulls at her mouth. "Oh, get off your high horse. You benefited greatly from everything I did for you. Look around." She motions to the house around us. "Look at what you have—what I made possible for you."

"You didn't do shit! *I* did. *I* got me here. I didn't see you sitting next to me at the midnight business classes I took or receive your help with the hours and hours of editing well into the night. It wasn't you who fostered relationships, or your name and experience that made the deals. The only thing you succeeded at was guilting me into bringing you to L.A. so you could leech off me. And I let you. Why should I expect even a semblance of loyalty from you? It's not like you're my mother. Just someone under my employ, right?"

She tries to speak, but I cut her off. "Never once did I ask for the endless brand deals you forced on me when I was overworked and burnt out. All I wanted was to create Jaded and focus on the one thing I enjoyed out of all of this, but you wouldn't let me. You had to infect that with your poison too, trying to control everything. And now this? How could you do this?"

"You have responsibilities here, Jade, and being over there...being with him, it made you lazy. It got you home. Now, everything can go back to normal."

"I wasn't lazy, I was happy! For once in my life, I was happy, and you ruined it. It will never go back to normal. I will never be the same. You—" I choke on my words. "You made me hurt the person I love most in this world. I walked away to protect him from this, and it broke something in me. There is no normal now." My chest is heaving with pain and heartbreak and rage, and she doesn't even look remorseful.

Tieran's voice, strong and steady, comes to me like a guardian angel, always looking out for me, even now. *She lives in fear of the day you realize she'll have nothing without you.*

That's exactly what I need to do, what I should have done years ago. "From this moment on, you're no longer my mother, and you're no longer my manager. You're fired."

"You can't fire me. Who will manage your career better than me?"

"It's funny how you don't need a manager when you don't have a career to be managed, and you saw to that the second you sold those photos to The Daily Mail." I turn on my heel and stalk back toward my front door. Hand on the knob, I stop and give her one last look over my shoulder. "I hope you got a good price, because that's what you'll be living off from here on out."

I wrench the door open, not knowing where I'm going to go or what I'm going to do, just that I need to get as far away from this house as possible.

But I don't get far, because as I step out, a car pulls up to the curb, stopping me short as an impossibly tall figure with dark hair and shoulders I would recognize in the dark exits the car.

I blink once, then twice, not quite believing what I'm seeing before me.

Tieran pulls his bag out of the car and turns, coming to a halt when he sees me outside the front door.

From where I'm standing, it almost looks like he breathes a sigh of relief. His shoulders loosen, his face softens, and a small smile curves the corner of his full mouth, making the dimple on his right cheek just barely indent.

My heart beats a million miles a minute as I look upon the face that, from that first night in a dingy pub, made me feel safe and understood for what felt like the first time ever.

"What are you doing here?" I ask, close to convincing myself I'm hallucinating, as if he's a mirage in the desert.

He shrugs, the muscles in his shoulders flexing under his shirt. "Someone once told me L.A. has really good taco trucks. I thought I'd come see for myself."

Nothing can keep the smile off my face as I realize he's recounting the night I told him I preferred the taco trucks to a ten-course meal. Tieran has never not listened to me, never failed to make me feel heard, cherished—loved. I was a prickly person before him but he never cowed away from my thorns, and that understanding—that protection, made me feel safe enough to be soft like petals. It's a wondrous thing to be with someone whose only expectation of you is love.

And love is the easiest thing to give when it's stitched into every fiber in my bones.

"Come here, Hellfire. With you smiling like that, I'll die if I don't have you in my arms right this second."

I waste no more time. I'm off like a light, running across the shallow yard and down the driveway, launching myself into his arms. My legs wrap around his waist, my own arms squeezing around his neck so tightly, he might have to tap out soon for his own safety. Tieran nuzzles his face into my neck, breathing me in and letting out a contented groan.

Here. Mine. *Everlasting.*

"I'm sorry," I breathe into his neck. "I'm so sorry. I hated the things I said to you that night. I just wanted to protect you. I didn't want to drag you down to hell with me."

"Where you go, I go."

I pull back to look into his lapis-tinted eyes. "Just like that?"

"It's so simple. *Uncomplicated.* You are the love of my life. I've learned what it's like to be without you, and I have no interest in that life. I will follow you to the ends of the Earth, Jade. Wherever life takes you, I want it to take me too."

I release a breath. "God, I love you." I clutch at my chest with one hand as it expands to near bursting. "You remind me that life can be this wondrous, beautiful thing, and when I look at you, all I see is possibilities. I look at you, and I see the world laid out before us."

He tightens his arms around my waist, resting his forehead against mine. "When did you get so sappy?"

I pull back enough to swat at his chest, my fist meeting a wall of solid muscle. "Shut u—"

His mouth is suddenly on mine, effectively shutting me up with lips, teeth, and tongue. At first, it's fervent, conveying the need coursing through our bodies after what we've been through, but it swiftly settles into something sweet and tender. His lips connect softly with mine as everything that's felt wrong over the past few days suddenly shifts into place, the final piece of the puzzle I've been putting together my entire life.

Months ago, I flew five thousand miles away from everything I knew, and landed in the safest hands I could have ever imagined.

Tieran pulls back, his hand cupping my jaw as his thumb presses into the underside of my chin, tilting my head up to look at him. "So, where do you want to go, Hellfire?"

"I want to go *home*."

TIERAN

TWO YEARS LATER

NEW ZEALAND HAS PUT up one hell of a fight from the second we stepped onto the pitch to the deafening roar of the crowd's welcome. The second we score a try, they score the next, and on and on. It's both frustrating and exhilarating, because I know we're giving the world a good show. A record breaking, memory making match that will be talked about for years to come.

The fact that I'm even here after everything is a testament to perseverance. In the weeks following me bringing Jade back to London, the scouts had called up a few different players but not me. Ballard ended up reaching out to his inside informant. They weren't going to call me up…not yet. It was a punch to the gut but not wholly a surprise. Half the season, I played like shite, and while I had been playing well during the second half, it had only just begun. Admittedly, the team's admin was right to be worried about my performance streak. Their job was to build a team that would win them medals and glory, and the first half of my season gave them no indication I would be a safe bet.

Even that news couldn't bring me down in the wake of having Jade back home, back in my arms, back in my bed. The pity blow job helped too.

On the flight back to the UK, I told her what happened

with Lawrence. We knew him being out of the picture wouldn't solve all our problems, and we weren't sure if the case against him would hold up in court since finding out Maxine was involved, but it at least took care of the question of if her career with The Legends was in immediate danger. Though, the impending doom of a human resources meeting was certainly on the horizon. We spent the rest of the plane ride holding hands, making a plan, and maybe joining the mile high club.

When we showed up to the stadium the following Monday, we were ready to fight and defend our relationship. Imagine the surprise we felt when HR informed us that because of the unprecedented nature of Jade being the only female to ever own a rugby club, there was no rule in place saying she couldn't date a player. In everyone's interest, and to make sure the club was protected, we filled out waivers stating that our relationship was consensual and that nothing was untoward. Jade, being the boss she is, also put clauses in place that any decisions made on my behalf would be split equally between all the shareholders. She would not hold any final authority over my career and therefore couldn't interfere if things were to go south between us.

I kept telling her it wasn't necessary, that I trusted her implicitly with all that I am and ever would be, but she wouldn't budge. Leave it to my girl to be stubborn about protecting the people she loves. I wouldn't let her have the last word, though, and I punished her thoroughly later that night for even entertaining a reality in which we weren't endgame. She was moaning and writhing as I edged her for hours, whispering one word over and over into her skin: *forever, forever, forever.*

Our love was everlasting. It's the one thing I knew would survive eons and travel across time and space, more permanent than any star in every galaxy.

She grounded me in every way; I wouldn't be here, minutes from wrapping up the most important match of my career, if not for her, because a year later, I *did* get called up.

But the clock is running down. New Zealand holds possession of the ball, and I need to figure out a way to get it back.

Back and forth, the ball switches hands between New Zealand's players while we fight tooth and nail to get to each man who makes a run for the try line. Everyone from both sides is playing as if their lives depend on it. The second one player has a ball, we're taking them to the grass, but then the ball changes hands and is off again. My legs push hard against the ground as I fight to keep up, the clock ticking closer and closer to that final whistle.

The stands are going wild, yelling out at every catch and release in time with the thudding of my heart. My breath saws in and out in ragged pants, sweat soaking my clothes as dirt and grime coat every inch of my body.

I just need one opening.

I'm a few feet behind New Zealand's left winger, almost parallel, as my outside centre comes up behind him. Before my guy can take him down, the left winger drops the ball with the intention to kick, and I push my legs even harder to bridge those final few feet. The ball connects with his foot, soaring through the air, and before it can make it to its intended target, I leap up, stealing it to my chest.

The crowd explodes in a riot of excitement when I land on my feet, doubling back and running in the opposite direction. Seconds remain on the clock, and I swear, I can hear Jade over the cacophony of voices screaming at me to go.

Her voice in my head is the motivation I need to go harder. After all the support she's given me over the past two years, this win is as much for her as it is for me.

I'm twenty feet away from the line, two opposing players closing in but not nearly close enough to stop me as I push the final few metres and dive for the posts. I flip over the line and touch the ball to the grass seconds before the final whistle rings out over the crowd.

The stadium explodes, and my teammates scatter, running around the pitch in excitement while jumping on each other's shoulders. They reach out for me, but I dodge them, weaving in between celebrators like I'm still running an active play on the pitch in search of the only person I want to celebrate with. I spot her with ease, dark hair whipping in the wind, cheering with the fans around her dressed in my jersey, looking more radiant than the sun that beats down on my neck.

My legs pick up their pace, running toward my home—my future.

Shock slows my pace when Jade starts scaling the barricades in an attempt to get on the field. More than one security guard attempts to stop her, but the way she evades their grasp rivals the playing done on the pitch today.

She's close enough that I can see her beaming smile, pride seeping through every pore, and then her lips are moving, calling out to me. "You did it! You're an Olympian!"

She launches herself into my arms, forcing me to rock back on my heels. I lose my balance until I fall on my ass, Jade landing on top of me and huffing out a giggle.

Her hair falls all around me in a halo of dark silk. I instinctively reach out and brush a strand from her face.

"How does it feel?"

She's so beautiful, I'm having a hard time concentrating. "Hmm?"

"Do you feel any different now?" She starts poking at my temple with her index finger. "Your head's still the same size. That's a good sign."

I toss my head back into the grass and laugh. "I just became an Olympian, and you're already busting my balls."

"Someone has to keep you humble."

Her topaz eyes are filled with so much love and

unfiltered joy, it makes my chest ache. This woman who, when I first met her, was so closed off to connection, so lost in her work, she didn't know what it was like to live, now craved those things. She's the one planning our next holiday before I can even get to it. She was brave enough to leave behind a life that no longer suited her, reshaping her entire career so she could focus on the parts she loved and leave behind the others. She was still the CEO and head designer of Jaded, but all the other tasks she loathed but felt obligated to do were delegated to other people. She was still active online, but only when she wanted to be. She took control of her life instead of letting others choose for her. I was in constant awe, and I still can't believe I get to call her mine. "I won long before today, Hellfire."

Her gaze softens. "I think becoming an Olympian has made you soft." She jolts forward, kissing the tattoo now inked to the other side of my neck. *Everlasting*, it reads.

"You know what I think?"

"Hmmm?"

"When the business slows down for you a little, I'm going to make you my wife."

"Is that so?"

I brush the tip of my nose against hers before softly pressing my lips to her mouth.

"Mhmm," I hum in pure contentment. "I think I'd like you bossing me around forever."

Sports • 3 min read

STONE SCORES WINNING TRY OF THE 2028 MEN'S OLYMPIC FINALS!

No stone left unturned as England's fly-half clinches the win in the closest match ever to grace the Olympic pitch.

ACKNOWLEDGMENTS

I'm going to sound like a broken record but I can't believe we're here. Writing Blindsided was such a different experience from writing my debut. I was more sure of myself, had more confidence in my writing, was less critical, and it's only because of the lessons writing Silver & Hendrix's story taught me. I relied less on the affirmation of others and found that strength within myself. But I would be remiss if I didn't get to love on the juicy support system that has been by my side throughout the process of writing another book.

To all the readers, bookstagrammers, and TikTokers who took a chance on a bookstore in NYC, and who have been by my side championing a rugby team in London. Your support is sometimes the reason I push extra hard on days when it all feels impossible. Thank you for every post, story, DM, and your unwavering enthusiasm for my books. I'm humbled by your kindness every day. And a hearty amount of extra love to Jessie, Hannah, Tiegan, Janalee, and Korina who never falter in their support.

To Nicole M Rubino, my critique partner and one of my very best friends. Thank you for your endless voice memos (always equipped with yelling children), infinite support and your constant readiness to listen to and or help me work through writing blocks. Thank you for being not only a great support in my writing but for also being a person I can always rely on. I treasure our friendship more than you know. (and for all the thirst traps you send—keep those coming.)

Jen, Carla & Natalya—thank you for always letting me

ramble about my dreams and for being crazy enough to believe in them too. To Jen—you were the first person to hear this crazy idea. Thank you for texting me that day over two years ago about the Olympics, therefore prompting me to tell you the most vague idea about a rugby book I wanted to write. Blindsided is here because of that one message you sent. To Carla—my sensitive little monster. The world's ultimate fangirl. Thank you for always fangirling over my characters and for loving them so fiercely. The world needs more people who love as hard as you. To Natalya—you never fail to bring up my books in any room you're in. You are dogmatic in your championing of my work and I swear on every Nerds Cluster in the world, when I make it big, I'm hiring you as my manager. I love you guys so much.

To Lauren—I'll never not be thanking you. Your belief in me carried me through years of struggle while writing my debut and it's insane to already be talking about a second book. You are the blueprint on what a girl's girl is and I'm lucky to call you a best friend. To many more years of friendship, lunch/work dates, and books written. Oh, and thank you for letting me steal one of your favorite boy names for Tieran!

To Katie—thank you for keeping me endlessly entertained and tethered to reality. You've been encouraging me from the beginning and never fail to call me silly when I struggle to believe in myself. Shoutout to Princess Leia, who deserves to have her name splashed in a book (and because I know this will be your favorite part of your acknowledgement. Hi stinky!)

To Abbey—thank you for your dedication to reading this chapter by chapter, offering up encouragement and feedback. And for foolishly giving me your phone number and thus a direct line to you. That was silly of you but you can't take it back now. I love you, thank you for going on this ride with me. And I'm sorry for the vinegar packet thing.

To Natalie—thank you for all the countless times you've listened to me ramble about literally anything. From Silver Linings to Blindsided to mundane shit happening in my life, you've heard it all. Thank you for all the graphics you've made for me and my books and for constantly reminding me that my books are good.

To Laura, one of my absolute best friends in the world who is one of the only people on this list to have known me when I still had brown hair—thank you for helping me go violet all those years ago, and for sending me care packages when I'd move to make sure I was taking care of it. And for being an absolute legend and taking my author photos.

To Sam, for being constant and steadfast in my life. Thank you for being persistent in your 8:30am phone calls, and for always being a voice that brings me comfort. I have so many fond memories with you by my side and having you in my life is such a gift.

To all the fellow authors in my life who inspire me daily: Scarlett St. Clair—I'm so blessed to have you in my corner. It's a special thing to have you tell me you're proud of me, impressed by me. I know you measure your words carefully and to have you say those things is priceless. I can't wait for your next visit so we can finish BDB. Lana Ferguson— thank you for always being so willing to pause your own commitments to help me when I need it. I'll be forever grateful you slid into my DMs all those years ago. Love you, son. To Kate Golden, who is a human ball of sunshine always ready to offer advice or to cheerlead, you are a joy to know. To Sophie Morgan who came up with the title of this book and listened to many rambling voice memos on IG when this book was just a kernel of an idea. And to the many authors I've met since publishing my first book, I am in awe of the love and support we show each other.

To my family for always rolling with my crazy ideas and supporting me no matter what. I love you all and miss you with a fierceness only a long distance daughter could. I promise I'll come home soon.

To Rhiannon, my rugby loving Welsh savior. Thank you so much for answering my crazy DM for help. I truly believe our meeting was a cosmic gift from the universe. One I've never been more grateful for. Thank you for being willing to help me make sure I was being faithful to this great sport and for being so so kind. I already wanted to visit Wales, but now I want to simply so I can thank you in person.

To my editor Alexa of The Fiction Fix—thank you for being someone who not only polished this book until it was gleaming, but for also being a person of high moral fiber, using your voice and brilliant brain to help and advocate for authors. You'll always have a client in me as long as I continue to misplace commas. So forever.

To my cover designer and interior formatter, Alex of Novel & Navy, who has the patience of a saint and who took on every challenge I dished out. I appreciate your dedication to making this cover perfect and for switching out pictures for me seven million times. You're the real MVP.

To every single artist I've hired along this journey who have brought my characters to life in a way I never could have imagined. Your talent boggles my mind.

Always save the best for last. To my sweet baby pup, Miley. We've officially written two books together Moo Moo and I've never been more grateful to have this way to measure time with you. Thank you for all the grumbles that forced me to slow down and pay attention. You've been bossing me around for over fifteen years now and it's safe to say you're the best boss I've ever had. I love you infinitely.

COMING SOON

Book two in the Legends of London series is expected early 2027. To stay up to date, subscribe to Violet's newsletter below.

https://violet-page.myflodesk.com/dsdkk5wyre

ABOUT THE AUTHOR

Violet spends her days indulging the voices in her head by writing swoony love stories filled with humor, heart and heat. She lives in New York City and when she's not writing or dreaming up how to make her imaginary friends fall in love, she's rewatching a comfort show for the twentieth time, taking a coffee fueled walk around the city or fantasizing about a faraway land where she'll be swept off her feet by an absurdly tall morally grey villain.